WHERE THE WIND BLOWS
The Call

BOOK 2 OF WHERE THE WIND BLOWS SERIES

by Dorothy Gable

The wind blows where it wishes, and you hear its sound,
but you do not know where it comes from or where it goes.
So it is with everyone who is born of the Spirit.

– John 3:8
English Standard Version

DEDICATION

THIS SERIES IS dedicated to faithful believers; may we continue, resting in the power of God.

Precious in the sight of the LORD is the death of his saints.
– Psalm 116:15

CHAPTER 1

THE DOOR LOCKED behind him. Hearing the servo slide the bolts into place, a shiver ran down Tom's spine. This time, though, he was only a visitor at county lockup—not a district detention center. No razor wire topped a high fence, no steel runways led to gray walls.

Tannish-brown buildings occupied a quiet street south of town. All the same, this was a prison, and he was here to visit Cindy. After emptying his pockets, a brief pat-down, and listening to a recitation of the rules, Tom stepped through the door and walked to an empty small round table.

Even though he knew the drill, his heart skipped a beat when he watched Cindy emerge from the lockup side and scan the tables with a hopeful, frightened, questioning gaze. He returned her brilliant smile, nodding when she focused on him. Her face was bereft of makeup, her long, blonde hair straight. She still looked beautiful in a bright orange jumpsuit.

"It's good to see you," he greeted, clasping his hands together before him on the table. He longed to hold her hands and hug her, but he dared not threaten their visit with his expulsion.

They drank in the sight of the other for countless moments. Cindy broke first. "Thank you for teaching us and trying to make us ready."

Tom shook his head. "What happened?"

Cindy sat back, recalling the day—the day of the first baptism of six new converts, the day they discovered some of them were infiltrators—the day their lives changed. "You were at work?"

Tom nodded. "Caleb too. He transported Mrs. Hathaway."

"Did she make it?"

"She'll never walk again. I suspect they moved her to a secure medical complex for detainees." He licked his lips. "Pastor Hathaway, Dr. Wilcox," he turned his head. "What happened?"

"Well, Pastor had them give their testimonies on the shore. Then he said Christ was the only way to heaven, and the woods behind us exploded with full-on SWAT. The kids were terrified. I froze. They shot Pastor and Dr. Wilcox when they moved to protect the children."

"Did they say what the charges were? Did anyone have illegal Bibles in their possession?"

Cindy shook her head. "Mr. Ohr said he'd heard more HCL laws had been passed but couldn't get the specifics. Telling someone Christ is the only way to heaven is now hate speech. And more phrases are considered illegal." She noticed a shock run through her youth pastor.

"Don't be sorry. Instead, rejoice for us who have been privileged by God to pay the price for our witness. As Jesus said in Matthew, '*Blessed are you when others revile you and persecute you and utter all kinds of evil against you falsely on my account. Rejoice and be glad, for your reward is great in heaven, for so they persecuted the prophets who were before you.*'[1] You taught us that; you lived it. No regrets." She smiled.

Tom worked to hold back his tears. Truly, seeing ones he cared about suffer was hard to handle. "Going to trial?"

"Why? According to the law I'm guilty and proud of it."

"No more hiding," he said quietly.

"What's next? You pled guilty." Her eyes scanned Tom's face, waiting for an answer.

"Sentencing—I assume they'll send you to a federal prison camp. They pulled strings to have me sent to a maximum security penitentiary. The type of prison depends upon your security level. How can I help you?"

"Just pray." She smiled. "The agents were looking for you. You and

Caleb not being there—that was surely of the Lord. Thank you for discipling us."

They talked of little things—the food, how hot the cell blocks were. Cindy laughed about the rough jumpsuit and joked about being dressed in orange—a real fashion statement.

She stepped through the door leading to the cell blocks. The guards buzzed him through, and he emerged in the bright sunlight. Tom breathed in the hot, heavy air. He was free. She was not. He'd be there for her—visits, put money on her commissary account, write letters. That mattered, he knew.

Tom found himself at Caleb and Alice's apartment and knocked on the door. Caleb answered.

Tom sat at the round kitchen table. "How're you doing? Your mom?"

Caleb shook his head. "Still numb, I guess. You see Cindy? I heard she's still in town."

"You were right. They didn't move her to district court. What city is that in anyway?" He laughed when Caleb shrugged his shoulders. "I hope you never have to find out. She's doing well."

Caleb nodded. "Mom's mad—mad at the Hathaways, mad at Dad, mad at the world. And I'm…" He looked away and squeezed his eyes to hold back the flood. "Alice and I are sitting pretty just as if it didn't happen. I'm an EMT. She's a dental hygienist…" He looked at Tom. "…with a baby on the way."

Tom nodded through the tears. "New life. God gives new life." He leaned forward and said, "Never forget; you follow God wherever He leads you. While Jezebel pursued Elijah, 7,000 Israelites remained faithful to God, going about their lives and holding God in their hearts. You be there for your mom, live for Christ at the EMS, serve Him in your church. We each have a different calling."

"Yeah, yeah, the eyes, the ears, the feet." He grasped Tom's hand. "You're welcome in our church anytime."

"I know." Tom shared what Cindy had told him.

"They're still gunning for you. Time to move on?"

Tom shook his head. "Have nothing on me, so I guess that means I stay here for the meantime." He stared out the window. *Somehow, I'll find out the date of her hearing and be there for her.* She'd listed the others who had been arrested. *I'll keep track of all of them.*

CHAPTER 2

THE NEXT DAY, Tom walked to the Lincolns' house and took a seat at their kitchen table. He knew Ginger and Bibi would be home from school soon, but he had come for something else—a listening ear, a sounding board. The ache he felt in his soul stole away physical hunger.

Betts nodded at the coffee pot, and he helped himself to a cup. Normally, he would have jumped up to dry and put away the dishes in the drying rack. Instead, he stared.

Noting the expression on his face, Betts said, "I'll get Pastor."

Stafford emerged from his tiny study and sat. "Visit lockup?"

Tom nodded.

"Any of your teens there?"

"Cindy. Don't know where the two others are." Tom pulled out an envelope and passed it over. "My offering."

Stafford peeked at the pile of bills. "What you doing? You can't keep giving like this."

"Pastor, when they arrest me, and they will, they'll take it all. I'd rather you get it. Put it toward clothes for the girls, decent meals for your family."

"You live like a hermit."

"What am I doing? Pastor, what am I doing for Christ? I work 50 or more hours a week, sometimes days in a row answering the phone, handing out forms to be signed."

"We've seen you in action, young man, and your calm presence in the midst of a family's worst day is doing God's work. The question isn't is the job important, but is this your call?"

"I thought I knew." Tom sat back. "It's like I've been walking in my sleep—going through the motions, knowing how to stay legal." He shared what Cindy had said. "In that case, we are not ashamed to be criminals for Christ." He met his gaze. "It's been in the back of my mind for a while. I'm not satisfied serving God with my time off. I want to walk the streets of Wichita and tell everyone about the free gift of salvation. But how?" He shook his head.

"Tom, if we had the funding, I'd bring you on staff in a heartbeat. What about Caleb's church?"

"Not the best fit."

They paused, hearing the front door slam followed by the pitter-patter of running feet. He turned in his chair to catch Bibi running toward him. Ginger followed behind, a cool teenager in her last year of middle school.

"Tom!" Bibi squealed in delight and hugged him. Ginger nodded with her sweet smile.

Tom winked at her. Stafford retreated to his study. "What's up? Need help with homework?" His eyes narrowed when she shook her head.

"Ms. Betts, can I go over to Rany's house to study?" Ginger asked.

Betts set her hand on her hip. "Your turn to help with supper and the dishes, Ginger. Now get to your homework. Tom's here if you need help."

The teen nodded in acquiescence and stepped to the front room. Bibi piled her workbooks on the table, and Tom started with the Bible memory verses. "Now, Miss Bibi, you want to win that Bible quiz time or not?"

She laughed and rattled off the verses.

After Tom patiently answered her many questions, Bibi trotted to the front room to join the other children. Betts joined him at the table.

"What's up with Ginger?" he asked quietly.

"She's growing up."

Tom looked out the window. In a different time, with a good wife, he would have adopted the girls himself. "You're doing a good work taking them in."

CHAPTER 3

T OM SLIPPED INTO the courtroom. Spying empty rows near the front, he resisted the urge to hide and walked confidently to the third row and took a seat. Two agents sat directly behind the district attorneys. A friend who worked at the sheriff's office had told him they called it "expedited enforcement"—multiple cases processed quickly in local courts.

Cindy entered from the left and stood in front of him. He smiled when she looked back at him, winked and flashed a mischievous grin.

The judge read the charges.

"Guilty," her voice clear and strong.

"Do you wish to make a statement?"

"I do. 'I am not ashamed of the gospel of Christ for it is the power of God for salvation to everyone who believes.'[2] Jesus said, '*I am the way, and the truth, and the life. No one comes to the Father except through me.*'[3] Before He returned to heaven, He commanded us to share this message of love, of redemption, of rescue from the grip of sin. We share this not to hurt but to warn."

The *tick-tack-tick* of the court recorder captured every word. Tom held his breath.

She continued, "I do not regret sharing this message of God's love to the world without compulsion or threats. This country was founded on religious freedom, and witnessing is a central part of our faith. We will continue to follow God as He leads us. I throw myself on the mercy of the court, reminding your honor, that such statements are not spoken in hate, but are sincere expressions of God's love."

The judge studied her thoughtfully, stared at the charges on the paper before him and cleared his throat. After a brief statement of regret for this law, he said, "Upon your sworn guilty plea, by the laws of the United States of America, this court sentences you to twenty-one months in prison. You will be remanded to the county sheriff for the length of your sentence."

The judge rapped his gavel, glowering at the agents. Their protestations muted, they stood, shook their heads and walked out. A few glared directly at Tom.

Tom nodded at Cindy. "A gift," he said quietly. And it was—a short sentence to be served at the county lockup with no parole or probationary restrictions. She nodded in return, her brows drawn together despite her brave words. He understood.

CHAPTER 4

A week passed quickly. Tom drove to the Ohrs' lakeside cabin. Randy opened the garage, and Tom parked the car. They entered the house through a windowed walkway. The quiet real-estate attorney led him to the sitting room. Tom stood, gazing at the placid lake, bounded by lilies and graceful willows.

"Help yourself to coffee."

Tom poured a cup and sat in an armchair, looking out through the large picture windows at the lake, as still as a mirror. "It's going to be a lovely spring."

"Evie's already prepared another flower bed."

Tom nodded, remembering Evelyn's lovely arrangements. "What did the membership decide?"

Randy traced the edge of the handle of his mug. "Most are looking elsewhere."

Tom nodded. "Not very popular, are we?" His hollow laugh fell flat. "According to what Cindy told me, I can no longer keep their law and follow God."

The lawyer slid a folder along a coffee table. "These are the current statutes and regulations. I know we've been avoiding this for some time—choosing between God and country." He shook his head.

Tom nodded, letting out his breath. "I've been thinking of joining Pastor Lincoln's church."

"We've been to White Steeple, Caleb's church. It's a good, solid work. I didn't want to tell you. I know you'd make a great pastor."

"Maybe 20 years ago. I've come to terms with never being a traditional pastor. What the Lincolns are doing in this city, that's where He's calling me."

Randy smiled. "God knows what he's doing. My only regret is Pastor didn't give you more chances to preach. You did have an impact on the teens."

It didn't feel like it.

"Son, a wise elder once told me that every ministry has its beginning and end, but what doesn't end is the service we do for the Lord each day. Follow God. Remain faithful. Remember, we usually don't see the full effect of our ministries here on earth."

"I keep reminding myself." The ache to give up all but preaching the gospel pounded in his chest.

Randy rose; they hugged briefly. "We won't forget you in our prayers."

CHAPTER 5

Tom worked six shifts in three days. He rolled from bed late the next morning and rubbed his eyes, relieved he didn't have to report to the ED for 72 hours. He stepped through his morning routine of a quick breakfast, prayer, Bible memory and a shortened workout. Leaving his car at the apartment complex, he ran to the Lincolns' neighborhood. If he wasn't into running three miles, he could always hop on a bus; the contacts often yielded good opportunities. His drive to evangelize increased with every stride. He prayed again—"Lord, if it's Your will."

The girls would still be at school, but the usual toddlers and preschoolers romped in the nearby park. Tom stopped and called out their names. Many ran to him to hear another story. Tom picked one from the adventures of David.

After saying his goodbyes, he headed for the Lincolns' house and let himself in through the back door. The kitchen was quiet. Betts' footsteps sounded through the floorboards along with muted strains of her singing gospel hymns. Tom removed the chaos of breakfast and put away the clean dishes. Stafford's typing in the back study sounded through the walls.

Tom was reading a Bible and sipping his coffee when Betts entered with an armload of towels. "Laundry day?"

"Every day is laundry day around here, young man. Don't you go Cheshire cat on me. I see what you done—clean my kitchen, so…" She placed the towels on the table and sat. "What you want?"

"What? I can't be a blessing?" he joked back. "Anyway, Pastor busy?"

"Always busy, but he's interruptible." She poured a fresh cup of coffee.

"What's up?"

Betts sat still, her shoulders slumping slightly. "They upping the rent again."

"On your storefront?" He added, "We found the perfect house. Over on North Ash."

"Isn't that across the interstate in Power District?"

"Just the other side of the highway. Plenty of abandoned homes up for auction."

She nodded. "Well, tell the man, but...he's not one for change."

"Understood." He grabbed Stafford's coffee along with his and walked back to the office.

"Getting hot," he said. "Got a moment?"

"Nice to see you, Tom. Working today?"

"Finally have a few days off." He slid over an envelope.

Stafford smiled. "I think we have to stop meeting like this." He counted the cash. "This will help."

"Betts told me about the rent." He leaned in. "Jazz found a good prospect that could be converted into a nice church—a sanctuary, classrooms, maybe even a shelter."

The pastor smiled, sat back and wiped his brow.

"How can you stand the heat with the door closed?"

"Quiet." He pointed to a small fan under his desk.

Tom released a breath. "The hit essentially destroyed Hathaway's fellowship."

"Sorry to hear."

"That clears me to hop on your wagon—if you'll have me."

"Like I said...if we had the funding."

"I get that," he interrupted and then sat back. "Then pray with me for God's direction in my life. I'll do what I can with my time off. Anyway, the old caddy from Grandma Katie needs a good deal of work. Any of the high schools around here taking in projects for their mechanic classes?"

Stafford pulled out a card, wrote a name and phone number. "This is the man to talk to. You ready to give up your car?"

"Now that I don't need to get out to the suburbs, I can walk or take transit." He smiled. "Opportunity." Tom glanced at the clock. *The girls won't be home for a few hours.*

"Listen, I have some calls to make. You're welcome to hang here. You good?"

Tom nodded. He checked his phone when it buzzed. He read a text from Caleb inviting him over for supper. "Thanks, going to Caleb's for supper—after I spend some time with the girls."

Stafford gathered his visiting Bible and satchel. "Oh, Tom, going to St. Louis next week for a regional pastor's conference. The senior pastor is a friend of mine. Jordan's an associate there. Come with me. They might know of an opening."

"I'll see if I can get the time off." He swiveled back to survey the wall-to-ceiling bookshelves. A commentary on Jeremiah caught his attention. He fumbled in his pocket and pulled out a tattered photocopy of his handwritten notes from North Platte. Glancing at the pastor's computer, he realized he could have been updating his doctrine sheets and messages. *I need my own laptop.*

Ginger was in a good mood. They walked to the local ice cream parlor, and she began to share. He winked at Bibi when they returned to the house and announced he couldn't stay for supper.

The walk to Caleb's was long, but Tom was not about to ask Betts for a ride. He approached the building the same time Alice, Caleb's wife, joined him. "Hi, Alice. Caleb said I could come."

"Of course, he did. I told him to." She smiled, entered the code in the keypad and swung the door open. "It's been a while. How are things?"

Tom filled her in while they climbed the two sets of stairs. "How are you going to manage with the baby?"

Alice smiled. "One step at a time."

The table was set and aromas of meatloaf and buttered green beans drifted from the kitchen. "Didn't know you were so domestic," Tom commented when Caleb emerged with a dish towel in his hand.

"Hi, Honey," he greeted, kissed her cheek and winked at Tom. "Part of the transformation. You should try it."

Tom shook his head and laughed.

"Anyway, we have another guest coming."

Alice walked into the kitchen. "All right, gentlemen, I'm here, so grab a soda and scoot while I finish this up."

"She mixed up the meatloaf last night and left detailed instructions for the beans." He smiled and led Tom to the sofa. "Well?"

Tom relayed Randy's assessment.

Caleb nodded. "Now I don't feel so bad. Most of your teens have joined our program. We're growing. I can set up a meeting with our pastor."

He shook his head. "I'm working with Pastor Lincoln."

"You don't have to explain."

Nothing was official, but he didn't need a program to tell him what to do. Any day he could walk the streets of Wichita to share the Lord. The ringing doorbell broke his train of thought.

Caleb jumped up from the couch. "Hi, Mom," he said as he buzzed her into the building.

"Your mom's here?" Tom rose.

"Relax, Tom. This was Mom's idea."

They waited by the door.

"Tom, it's so good to see you." Mrs. Wilcox stepped forward and shook his hand before handing him a black leather case. "I'm sorry our last meeting was rough."

Tom nodded. Before he could say anything, a brilliant smile lit her face.

"I'm moving forward. Some say it's too sudden, but I know it's time." She pointed to the case. "I think my husband would have wanted you to have this."

Seeing her nod of encouragement, he accepted the case and pulled back the zipper to see a lightweight laptop with all the accessories. Stunned with the magnitude of the gift, he said, "I just started praying today for a laptop."

"He delights to meet our needs before we ask." She spoke calmly.

"Thank you."

CHAPTER 6

Letting go of dark shadows and reaching for the days ahead, he cleared his schedule and rode with Stafford to St. Louis, Missouri. He always looked forward to an excuse to visit Ryan and Patty. Trying to forget the Task Force, Tom stared at the wide, open fields with scattered clumps of trees and houses.

The suburbs of St. Louis seemed to go on for miles. It was past rush hour, but traffic was still heavy. They grew quiet when Stafford navigated the city streets, following the GPS turn by turn until they stopped in front of a large brick building.

"That place is huge."

"Well, they have some local benefactors who believe in investing in the community." He pulled up the narrow drive to park behind the building.

"I thought Jordan's church was a storefront like yours."

"This church hired him shortly after his release. They needed an associate pastor with street smarts. Being the youth pastor is a big job with this ministry."

Tom didn't bother to ask how they managed to escape the Task Force. He reminded himself to be thankful not every fellowship had been shut down.

A young woman with a staff badge handed Stafford a room key, a conference packet and a list of local restaurants. "Glad you could make it. Enjoy your stay."

They followed the map, found the east stairs and headed up to the third floor. "Betts packed food for tomorrow." The small two-room suite had a functional kitchen in a small living area, with a double bed in the next room. "Are we meeting with Jordan?"

"No. You can use the car to visit Doc Ryan and Patty."

Thankful for Stafford's generosity, he headed out to visit his friends.

Settling into a comfy couch, he smiled at Ryan. "You still working the ED here?"

"That's the plan. I love the variety in emergency medicine."

Patty asked for an update on their old church. Tom gave the sanitized version.

"The Lord is still working, Tom," Patty assured him as she held his hand. "I'm glad you're okay."

Tom shared his hopes and dreams for a full-time, inner-city street ministry.

Patty and Ryan nodded in understanding.

Tom read the four-color brochure titled "Standing in the Gap: Proclaiming the Good News Today." He looked forward to hearing their solutions to the latest HCL regulations.

Jordan met them at the coffee bar, donut in hand. He surveyed the room. "Let's get you acquainted."

Stafford seemed ill at ease. He shook hands with the group of men, saying little. They moved on, stood by the door and watched the crowd mingle. "You know these guys?"

"Not really. The senior pastor and I go way back. You?"

"Just Jordan.

Tom cornered Jordan during the break for lunch. "Hey man, do they think they can keep the latest laws and remain faithful to the Great Commission?"

Jordan pulled him aside. "Listen, they're doing good work. Know how to navigate this. Don't you think we need to wake up? It's not Mayberry anymore."

"Well, some of my teens were just arrested for sharing Christ is the only way to heaven. How do they get around that?"

"Come on, Tom. You know the drill. There aren't enough agents on this planet to take out every faithful Christian. Most arrests happen for other reasons. Why do you think they hit your church?" He thumped Tom's chest. "Didn't you hear? We can't be visible without a presence in the community. We can't have facilities or programs or outreaches without funding, and that doesn't come from sitting in prison."

Tom noticed Stafford in the distance talking to the senior pastor. "You joining us for lunch?"

Jordan shook his head. "Invited a guest."

"Fine, see you around." He followed Jordan to the fellowship dining room and watched him walk up to a tall, slim figure.

He watched the man turned around, embrace Jordan and then head straight for him. "Tom!" he greeted with delight. "Jordan, why didn't you tell me Preacher would be here?"

Tom found himself embraced in a bear hug. "Riser, what you up to?" He shot a glance at Jordan, now making his way to join them. "Our mutual friend's keeping us both in the dark."

"Coaching a local team. My preacher here helps me stay on the straight and narrow. Bring your pastor and drop by at three tomorrow." He wagged his finger at Jordan.

Tom introduced Riser to Stafford, and they found a table. Pastor Lincoln quickly had Riser sharing his life story and salvation testimony. Jordan stayed halfway through before he excused himself to help set up for the afternoon tour.

Tom glanced at Riser. "How's your family?"

Riser lifted his brow.

"Sorry, man, didn't mean to step on your toes. In Hannibal we rarely had time to just hang. How did your wife take the changes in you?"

"Well, she left, then she came back, she left again, and maybe she's back. Two of the three kids decided to stay with me the last time she left. When she's not happy, she lets me know she came for the kids." He shook his head. "If I hadn't seen you walk through the fires and keep your faith, I think I would have lost mine. Jordan's spent too much time on me."

Stafford said, "Son, every person is worth our time. Never forget that. You're bearing the fruits of the past, but working through it. In time, God will redeem the whole. That timing we have to give Him and, in the waiting, He's doing a work in us that will reap future rewards. Never forget to look up when life knocks us down."

Riser nodded. "That's why you have to come tomorrow afternoon— both of you. Tell them the Bible speaks truth we can live by." He laughed. "Didn't know how hard coaching was until I tried it. Now, as a Christian, I have to live the faith and be a good testimony. Can you come?"

"It would be an honor."

"How'd a nice guy like you end up in Wichita?"

"Had just graduated as a mechanical engineer when Betts and I found the Lord. One thing led to another, and God made it clear He wanted us full-time. So, we went back to school. She completed the Bible certificate, and I finished another bachelor's degree in Bible. The Lord led us to Wichita, and we're still there. Couldn't imagine doing anything else."

"Respect that." He sat back. It looked like he had more questions, but Jordan returned to introduce Riser to other visiting pastors.

Tom and Stafford followed the group. They worked their way through the fellowship hall and classrooms. The worship center was the size of an auditorium with a grand piano beside the praise band instruments. The group settled into padded seats. An audiovisual presentation highlighted their satellite campuses, soup kitchens, second-hand shop and medical clinic. On their way out, Tom spied a closed door with red lettering, *Recycling Center,* near the espresso coffee bar. He asked a nearby assistant pastor.

"We participate in the Bible reclamation project," he said and surged forward.

Stafford whispered, "Pastor's got quite the enterprise here." He proposed heading back the next afternoon after meeting with Riser's team.

Tom agreed. "I've seen enough."

The next day they slipped out to the parking lot on their way to the stadium. Stafford opened the car door to let some of the excess heat escape. "You ask that question?"

"No need. Wichita's where I'm supposed to be."

The pastor's eyes wrinkled with a warm smile. "Great to hear."

Tom added, "Jordan knows me well—very well. He called me a loose cannon."

Stafford glanced over. "We don't cause waves just to stir the pot, but if we're working so hard to get along maybe we need to rethink our priorities." He sighed. "He sent them out two by two. Let's challenge others to go out with you."

"When?"

"Prayer meeting. We'll present the opportunity to the congregation and see what God does."

"God gave me a laptop last week. I can work on my papers. Maybe you could fix them—seeing you have the degree."

Stafford laughed. "Paper and practice. That's all it boils down to. You're an empty suit, without the practice. We all have to stay teachable."

Tom let Stafford speak to the group first. He stood next to Riser.

"The man's good."

"Yeah, and he takes in orphans, helps the community—really walks the talk."

Riser stepped forward and introduced Tom when Stafford was done.

"Quite some testimonial from my friend—I don't quite walk on water." Light laughter ran through the team. "Seriously, Riser helped our groups get together starting with playing ball in the yard. Made lots of guy nervous, but he forged the way. In Christ, we can reach out to those not like us. Christ did it many times, and His crowd didn't like it either." Tom shared the charge to love others, especially with the most important message of all—the good news.

CHAPTER 7

THEY MADE IT back to Wichita in time to catch the last half of prayer meeting.

Elder called Pastor to the front. "Our pastor survived the wilds of St. Louie and has returned. Give it up, Pastor."

"Thank you, Elder. I'm glad we made it here before you all broke up for prayer. Seriously," his tone settled out, "God calls us to work while it is day."

"Preach it, Pastor," a voice called out.

"While we draw breath." He glanced at Tom. "If you know Christ, you have experienced the wonderful gift of salvation. God didn't call us to sit on the porch, hide out, or cover our light. Every person we meet is a soul who needs the Savior—if he hasn't already accepted Christ. Some are like us. Some are different, but we can still share the good news."

He scanned the room. "Christ sent them out two by two. I have a young man here—some of you know him—who feels burdened to share the gospel in Wichita." He nodded at Tom.

"I want each of you to consider. Will you share this precious faith? Will you care enough for that person next to you to reach out and connect? Tom wants to do that. He has been doing it, but I'd like to see others go with him. Two by two." He walked briskly across the long narrow space in front of his congregation. "I'd like you all to pray whether the Lord is calling you."

Tom expected Stafford to share a few verses and give the charge before separating for prayer, but he didn't. He looked at Tom. "Share your vision."

Tom walked around the side rows and along the end cramped with an old piano, mic stand and battered guitar. He wet his lips; his mind temporarily blank.

Stafford wrapped him in a hug. "Just say what God lays on your heart and release them to prayer."

He looked at the sea of faces—from dark black to chocolate brown and pearl olive. Before him sat the nations—God's work. "Thank you, Pastor Lincoln." He gave a brief description of his journey with Christ, then said, "Jesus can save anyone—even those who seem unredeemable. We can't tell by looking at people if they're ready. We can't even tell by how they respond to the message. A few months ago, a man named Wallace visited your fellowship. You remember him? Did he tell you his story?"

When most nodded, he added, "I saw Wallace when I was in Hannibal in the basement of Building Four—that was the DU or disciplinary unit. He was in Unit L—24/7 lockdown every day for the worst of the worst. After my cellmate became a Christian and started helping with the DU visits, he began to talk to me about going into Unit L. Everyone thought he was crazy. The guards laughed in his face. But one Christian officer stood up and secured permission for us to go in two times a week. Wallie talked to them about God's love and how He loved them. I went in with him to pray while he preached. Week after week the officers and other inmates laughed at us. Some days we'd leave Unit L covered in spit, garbage and feces, but he didn't give up. Later, I learned from Wallace that ten men walked out of there. When I met him here in Wichita, he thanked me for going in. Wallace has been set free in Christ. God arranged his release, and many of you had a chance to talk with him.

"The time is short. Someday every one of us will go to heaven. Christ will ask us to account for our service to Him. We don't have to know the whole Bible or be able to answer every question. If you know Christ, you can share your story, your hope and what He has done for you.

"I will be praying that some of you will go out with me to share this story. I like to tell stories to the children. The little ones need to hear. The businesspeople, the cashiers, the waitresses and the ones who live in the streets all need to hear. When I'm not working at the hospital, I want to be out with another believer, looking for God's lost ones. The verses we share are seeds for future harvests. Jesus saves. He rescues. He gives us the privilege to have a part in the miracle of salvation."

Later that night Tom looked at the small group assembled at the Lincoln's kitchen table, talking through logistics and details. He walked back to his apartment, seeing the possibilities more than the dimly lit walk or dusty stairs.

He pushed open the door to his apartment and switched on the light by the front closet, casting shadows on the open laptop on his second-hand kitchen table. He saw the way—keyboarding his lessons on the laptop at the Lincolns, meeting up with whomever God would send that day and going out, two by two. The vision melted away, and a deep tiredness seeped into his soul along with a joy—he had his purpose again.

CHAPTER 8

TOM TOOK THE bus to Caleb's house a few weeks later. He had asked to get together, and Alice had offered to feed him. Tom sat with Caleb in the living room while she cleaned up.

"Jordan's church is fully cooperating—even have a recycling center in their worship hall to take Bibles. How does your church handle it?"

"We keep the laws, but that doesn't include collecting Bibles or information. Pastor has an inside source who keeps us up to date on the changes. Heard rumors they will be turning the Bible into a storybook. Goes way beyond just removing some verses."

"Not surprised. They reporting their supporters?"

"Most give cash anonymously. It's a hard balance, but so far I think they're doing the right thing."

Tom nodded. "Glad you have a good place."

"Wants me to sign up for online Bible college courses."

"Decent colleges still exist?"

"He has some picked out for me to look over. You want to check a few out?"

"Sure."

In answer to prayer, he had no overtime requests for two months. May and June were a blur of walking, talking, and listening. Women, young and old, accompanied him to the city's parks to tell stories to the children and talk to their mothers or fathers. Ginger often went with hm after her chores were done, and they began to develop a deep bond. He began to drop by coffee shops and strike up conversations especially with those sitting alone.

Tom looked at the clock at the ED on a Friday night late in June. The day had been hard, and he had to stay an additional four hours to cover the load. Twelve minutes remained in the shift, but it was 11 p.m. and too late to try to hook up with a witnessing partner. He could go home, eat and sleep in preparation for his next shift in ten hours, or he could strike out on his own.

As he turned aside to check the treatment board, Ches, the head nurse, approached. "Listen, I know you're on tomorrow. Head home. I think we can handle it."

"You taking a break?" It had been a while since he had had a chance to talk with Ches, but the man shook his head. "Front desk might have it under control, but the patients you sent us still need a lot of tending along with this crew."

"Your class is still in session," Tom quipped. They said their good-byes, he logged out of the system and headed to the locker room.

Tom walked over to the Power District, blocks away from a busy boulevard. He sauntered along a quiet street with small worn-down homes. Some yards were well kept, others straggly with more bare ground than grass.

On a corner, lights from an open liquor store illuminated a small collection of shops and storefronts. A tall man smoked a cigarette just under an awning that extended along the building's front and wrapped around the side. He would not have been visible to most walking along the main street, but his silhouette was easy to spot from Tom's vantage point.

Feeling the assurance, Tom approached. "Hot day," he said casually.

The man glanced his way and blew his smoke away from Tom. He said, "Yeah, heat coming in early this year," but his eyes clearly said, "Get lost."

Tom probed, trying to find the point of connection and an opening comment to introduce the gospel. Ignoring his jittery nerves, he pressed on despite the man's refusal to be drawn into a conversation, knowing he had to share something.

"Well, have a good night. Heading home after finishing a shift at the emergency department. I've seen how quickly things happen that can change your life. It's good to be ready." He had created his own wedge to the gospel. Tom gave the shortened version, ending with Jesus as the only way to heaven.

He had voiced outlawed phrases so many times they usually didn't jab him—but his nerves jumped, especially when the man surveyed him with a cold, hard gaze.

"Scram, now, before you get an opportunity to meet your Maker you're so proud of." Their eyes locked.

"What I said is true—all of it. The worst thing that can happen is to die in your sins." Tom headed down the dark side street.

The man tapped his Bluetooth connection. "Did I miss the target? Did that guy scare him off?"

"Doesn't look like it. Our target's not showing up on any of the street cameras. Must be a no-show."

"Great, what a waste."

"Maybe, but you just hooked your next collar."

"What, Joe Bible thumper?"

"He's on that Task Force's most wanted list. Slipped their nets during last spring's raid, remember?"

"How could I forget?" The officer looked down the street. "He's long gone."

"We know where he works and where he lives. Process the recordings, run it by our Task Force liaison, file the charges and pick him up. He's local, not going anywhere. Good for your stats."

"Pick another location." He memorized the directions playing in his earbud and headed to the next setup.

Two days later Tom started his shift. It was a quiet, midweek day in the midmorning doldrums. The heat intensified, and he heard some of the techs quip it was too hot to be outside.

He arranged his desk, surveyed the active list board when his eye spotted two men in suits approaching. The waiting room was virtually empty, and the few in the treatment rooms didn't seem the type to warrant law enforcement visits.

Their eyes were locked on him. His mouth went dry. "Can I help you?" he inquired.

He finally recognized the man to whom he had talked in front of the liquor store. Thanks to God rose up that he'd been alone.

"Tom Hutton?"

"Yes. I'm Tom Hutton."

"Step away from the desk."

Before he could finish his statement, Tom lifted a finger, "Just a minute, officers." He turned back to the nurses' central hub. "Nurse Asters, could you come over, right now?" He tried to say it quietly but heard the edge in his voice. His mind ran through another praise that they were arresting him here and not at the Lincolns'. He explained calmly, "These officers are here to arrest me. You'll need to find a replacement."

"For tonight? How long?"

"I'm not coming back." Tom met the man's gaze, knowing he didn't dare hug him or even move. "It's been an honor and a pleasure to work with you."

Within an hour he was standing before the judge and hearing the charge—one count of hate crime speech. He pleaded guilty and requested sentencing. The judge glanced down at the charge summaries, folded his hands together over the papers, looked up, and sentenced him to one year in county lockup. No protests were heard from the prosecutor's table—the Task Force agents were long gone.

Tom tried to hold back his relief and joy. His witness would continue in Wichita; he could see the girls and people he knew. He had survived worse prisons. *This should be just fine,* Tom continued to tell himself despite his stomach flip-flops when the door slammed shut behind him with the sounds of keys and chains echoing in the distance.

CHAPTER 9

CHRISTINE WORDEN ENTERED the small coffee shop near the elevator in her building. Her management position at the Secret Service fell into predictable routines. Every day she grew more determined to leave the public sector as she contemplated her last set of classes for her law degree. Chris ordered a latte, and as she headed to the condiments counter, she glimpsed a familiar figure who nodded in greeting. "Joe Lyle? What are you doing here?"

He nodded. "Hello, Chris. I see you remember me."

"Of course, but..." She nodded, deciding to go another direction. "Here for an interview?" Christine stood across from him at the raised table, waiting to see if he wanted to talk.

He looked past her. "I already accepted a position in investigations—cyber division. Have a minute?"

Chris sat down. "I'm listening."

"Do you have any contacts for Masters?"

"Yes." It had been a while since they had connected.

"Did he tell you he now holds the Regional Director position for the Northeastern District?"

"No, thought he was Assistant Executive Director."

"That was phased out with the latest re-org. Kincaid created four districts, four directors." Lyle sat back. "You were never really on board, were you?"

She narrowed her eyes, gauging his reaction. "And your loyalty to the Task Force?"

He swirled his cup and looked up. "Had a chance to work in intelligence, outreach, besides other divisions." He nodded to her, "Your projects were well-run, orderly." He leaned forward. "I can't say the same for many of the other divisions. Lately, the ones getting promotions are the true believers."

"Like Cooper or Otis?"

Lyle nodded. "Did you hear about their prisons?"

"Yes. Will showed me his plans for Rosemont."

"How did it seem to you?"

"He had an ambitious plan to turn an old Boy Scout camp into a Level One facility modeled after the Bureau of Prisons. The architectural drawings made it look like a resort."

"It never happened." He lowered his voice. "They have seven prisons—four function similar to minimum security facilities, but they're really re-education camps. The length of sentence is not considered for placement. Arrival units are spartan warehouses with limited movement. They are required to sit through hours of indoctrination. To qualify for general population, they must agree to fully comply with all the regulations."

"How do they get around the fact many of those statements are in legal Bibles?"

"The solution is already in the works. An editor in the Literature Division showed me what the legal Bibles are going to look like—a collection of ancient myths with Christ and the significance of His resurrection presented as superstition and legend."

"Lyle, did you become a Christian?"

"What do you think?"

Chris nodded, "I know the pressure." She surveyed the quiet coffee shop. "Did you hear they killed Asa Shirring?" Seeing his nod, she shared her time with Fran and her transformation in Christ.

"You're not the only one. The way they handled arrests and their forgiveness in the midst of persecution demonstrated the Bible's veracity and God's love." He wet his lips. "I managed to stay under Kincaid's radar. Didn't have a case file on me." Seeing her puzzled look, he continued, "Kincaid forced out all the talented female agents like you. But I'd wager Masters couldn't walk unless he wanted to enter Leavenworth as an inmate. The Task Force has an investigative division that develops trumped-up charges on top agents, judges who don't give long enough sentences and prosecutors who haven't yet seen the light." Noting her confused look, he added, "Have almost air-tight security and exchange commission cases on many. They're pulling 98-percent conviction rates. Anyone who steps out of line gets a visit from Barrie or Otis—Kincaid's lap dogs. Suddenly, they're cooperating."

Chris' face paled.

"Maybe he knows, maybe he's onboard, or maybe he's in the dark. Masters is one of a small number of high-profile agents Kincaid uses to paint a respectable image on the Hill. How does he justify Rosemont?"

"Wait, isn't Rosemont the model?"

"For their *death camps*." Seeing her grim face, he continued, "Those who don't sign on to the new initiatives are transferred to a prison where they are not expected to survive their sentences." He relayed the details in general terms, trying to tamp down the images of what he had seen before he left the Task Force.

"Thank you for the warning. I'll try to find out whether or not Will condones what is happening."

Lyle nodded. "It's the least I could do for him." Lyle drained his cup and threw it in the trash on his way out.

Chris studied the back wall, forcing herself to breathe, remembering the sorrows of Asa's death. She shook herself back to reality and sent a text to Will. "It's been a long time. Let's catch up. The usual place? What's open for you?"

CHAPTER 10

OUNTY LOCKUP WAS considerably different from federal prisons. It only took a week to transition to general population, be assigned to laundry duty, and find his place in the large dorm area. Tom surveyed his list of approved visitors, added Caleb's name, and turned in the form. He had money in his commissary account and had already received phone calls. The Lincolns made it clear they would visit. A glance at the clock told him evening chapel would begin soon. He made it back to the reception area to line up.

Caleb, flanked by a teen and an older gentleman, greeted them warmly. Tom slid into Caleb's embrace when he drew near. "Not breaking the rules? How'd you manage this?"

"On the rotation. You can get your name on the list. Check with your officer."

"Sure, why not? It's great to see you."

"Gather round, pull up a chair, grab a Bible." He handed out the study booklets and scanned the room. "Butch not here tonight?"

"Paroled out."

"Good to know. I'll follow up on that. For the new guys, here are your books."

Caleb was well prepared—answered their questions, making sometimes confusing doctrines understandable, and applied them to everyday life.

"Good job," he said when they filed out.

The next day his case officer called him to a small interview room and pushed a form across the table. "You're new here. Family visit coming up. Put their names down. Need to get them added to the list right now."

"Sure." He wrote down Stafford, Betts and the girls. Having family helped.

Tom could hardly wait the two weeks. He saved his clean uniform for visiting day. When he saw them lined up on a bench along the far wall, it took effort to walk and not break into a run. Stafford and Betts hugged him; Bibi clung to his hand. He reached out to Ginger and patted the bench beside him. "It's great to see you."

Bibi chatted, Betts corrected some of her stories, and Stafford shared encouragement from his favorite Psalms. Ginger said little.

"Hey, Ginger, you okay?"

She looked past him. "Yeah, just fine."

He could see she worked at keeping her lip from trembling. Her eyes seeped out the agony of their separation.

"Even when we are apart, we are together in the Lord." He longed to share more, speak of looking past the sorrows of this life, but a commotion on the other side drew their attention—an unsteady toddler fell hard on his bottom, sending red, sugary liquid up over the top of his sippy cup and onto the chairs and those sitting nearby. The laughter stopped his wails, and he began to giggle. Everyone giggled in return.

"It's good here. I'm so glad you could come." He said as they neared the end.

"Keep the faith, Son," Stafford said.

A week later the day officer approached. "Journalist is asking for you. Will you see him?"

"Sure." Tom followed him to a small room off the admin area. A young man appeared with a pad and a small voice recorder.

"Cecil Rhodes, *Wichita Press*, so glad you could see me."

"You get at least one free pass," Tom quipped. "What are you working on?"

"You and your hate-crime charges. Seems to be an interesting story and the bosses are always looking for something new. So," he set up the recorder, settled down with a pad of questions and dug in. They were thorough, starting when Tom first heard about the laws.

They ran out of time, and the officer tapped on the window. "Do I get a second bite?"

"Yes. Can you mail a copy of your article?"

"Of course." He looked at his watch. "This is a feature, so we have time for another good session. Next week?"

"Look forward to it." Tom rose with him. "Thank you for listening to my story, and…" he added, "Be careful."

Cecil cocked his head slightly. "Right, like this is such a dangerous profession."

He had shared about his uncle and memories of Pastor Hathaway. He wanted to relay the fears but didn't want to sound paranoid. "Not usually."

CHAPTER 11

I T TOOK A month for Regional Director Will Masters to meet with Chris. The air was still warm, and the courtyard tables gleamed in the glow of a setting sun. Chris arrived on time at 8:30. Will texted his apologies for his arriving at 9.

Chris nodded when the waiter escorted him to their table. "Do you need to see the menu?" Noting Will's tired eyes and shake of his head, she ordered for both of them. Dark circles rimmed his lower lids, Will's face was drawn, the worry lines along his brow evident.

"My, you're stressed. I heard you're Regional Director for the whole Northeast. What does that position entail?"

"Maine to Minnesota, Missouri to Virginia. It's a daunting job." He settled in his seat and drank in the sight. "You look amazing—as always. The service doing good by you?"

"No complaints. We have a good management team. The directors are reasonable, experience the usual turnover of agents. The training programs are as good as they've always been. We have the occasional disciplinary issues to monitor and chase down, but overall, it's a good fit for now. And you?"

Will looked away. A slight breeze fluttered the napkin under his lemonade. His eyes scanned the nearly empty courtyard and ended gazing into Chris' brown eyes. "Cell phone in the car?" Seeing her nod, he smiled for the first time and sat back a little, running his finger down the sides of his drink. "So much to do, so quickly. Just when you think you've done the job, Kincaid changes things or adds something else. I'm still up for many of the Hill appearances. You can't believe the persistent questions, the backroom drama, the hours and hours of posturing, trying to remember the question in the midst of the lecture." He looked at Chris.

"Many unexpected accusations?"

"Some want to know about the education outreach, others question why we haven't handled their pet issue fast enough…" His eyes hardened. "Then there are the ones who think nothing of ambushing us on the underground trolley or at the cafeteria. You wouldn't believe what they're saying."

"How's Rosemont doing? Is it the model facility you envisioned?"

Will ate another cheese stick and met her gaze. "I set the process in motion, but my transfer to Regional Director took me out of the day-to-day oversight of the prison projects. The renovations were handled by the warden and his staff."

"Do they report to you?"

"I sign off on the final reports, but no, I've not had a chance to do any on-site visits to Rosemont. Barrie tells me Kincaid is directly supervising that facility. The two other camps in my district seem to be going well."

"Do they know when you're scheduled to visit?"

"I assume so. My aide arranges it. Everything looked fine."

"I heard from a reliable source that Rosemont has been turned into a death camp, and it's not the only one. Have you heard this?"

Will dropped his gaze. "How could this be true?" They grew silent when the waiter brought their food and served the entrees.

"Thank you," Chris beamed and smiled. Once he was out of range, she said, "My source personally visited Rosemont."

"Is he still with the Task Force?"

She lifted her head. "Are you still on board?"

Will set his knife down. "Not like last year." He shook his head. "Kincaid has ten agents supervising the registered churches, pursuing the smallest of infractions. Did your source say anything about trumped-up charges?"

Chris was glad to hear Will's perceptions were changing and relayed what Lyle had said. "I think the test will be seeing if Rosemont is what they say it is. You deserve to know."

"Appreciate that." He reached for her hand. "Enough about my work. How are the professors treating you?"

Chris smiled. "Some don't seem to like any of us and call us ignoramuses unfit for the courts. I have my advocates and know the ones who require special handling. Classes are stimulating and draining at the same time. I'm almost done. Professor Tompkins wants me to apply for a clerk position with the Supreme Court."

"You did very well if you caught Tompkins' eye. Why not go for it? It's been five years already? We have to do this more often." Will reached for her hand.

"I'm interested in criminal law."

"You'll be great. I prefer investigating, but…" He cocked his head. "You're different, in a great way—blossoming into full beauty."

Chris smiled through tears welling up. "It feels good to hear that." Sensing assurance from the Lord, she shared about her time with the Shirrings and Fran's testimony. "I believe in Jesus Christ, and He gets me through every day." She wiped her eyes with a tissue. "Even helps me with the law studies, if you can believe it."

"At this point, with what I've seen, I would."

CHAPTER 12

A MONTH PASSED, and Tom realized he had not heard from the reporter. A wordless prayer rose up for a phone call or visit. The next Saturday Tom's face brightened when Stafford visited.

"Just the man I need to see."

They began with the usual queries. Ginger was struggling but still on track. "I don't think anyone's walk with Christ is easy." He shifted. The room was sparsely packed. "Could you contact a reporter for me? He interviewed me last month and said he'd be back, but I haven't heard from him."

Stafford paused, deep in thought. "What is his name?"

"Cecil Rhodes," Tom began.

"With the *Press*?" Stafford interrupted. Seeing Tom's nod, he rubbed his hands together as he said, "Died in a car accident two weeks ago."

"Did *they* say it was an accident?"

"Yes, want me to follow up?"

"No, he was going to do a feature on my story and the HCL laws. It's…just…" He almost swore, kicking himself that he'd not been forceful enough with his warning or shared the gospel directly.

"God's in control. Your story will get out." He placed a gentle hand on Tom's arm.

Tom nodded, a sliver of fear rising up. *They haven't forgotten me.*

A few days before the next family visit, two officers took him from laundry to his bunk. "Pack," they ordered without explanation.

He loaded his worldly goods in the trash bag. At the supply counter they gave him an orange jumpsuit. "Where am I going?"

"Change. Five minutes."

A van with darkened windows waited in a chilly causeway between two buildings. The back doors opened up to reveal two low benches with others already inside. They swapped out his hardware for a full set brought around from the front. His items were shoved in a lower side compartment hanging between the wheels. Tom scrambled in as best he could with shackles and belly chain in place. He shivered with the cold wind.

Three sat on the left. The guards chained him on the right next to two others. Tom stole a glance at them, but no one said a word while they completed securing him, signed off on the paperwork and shut the back doors. Only bare slivers of light seeped past the covered windows.

The one next to him glanced over. "You done this before?"

"What? Get transferred?"

"Been in prison before?"

"Yes." He didn't know who he was with. "You?"

"No, it goes like this?"

"They never let you know ahead of time."

"What you in for?"

Tom looked at the middle-aged man's face inches from his own, recognizing the fear etched along his brow. He stared at the others and realized he had not heard one curse word, not even when the van came to abrupt stops almost slamming the forward passengers into the metal wall of their compartment. *Why am I afraid? I survived Hannibal.*

"Twelve months for sharing the good news with an undercover narcotics officer." Tom laughed, thinking about it. "I'd been witnessing for months, and they only charged me with one count—12 months in county lockup. Where are we headed?"

"We're all being transferred to the Task Force prison at Mt. Vernon, Illinois."

"They have their own prisons?" When he saw the nods, the bile rose in his throat. "I take it you're all HCL terrorists?" He followed with a short laugh. "My first five years were in federal prisons. So, they found a way to shut us up."

The middle guy on the other side nodded. "Got that right. Our witness in the prisons was strong, if you could keep it together."

He listened to their stories, and added his own, welcoming the distraction. Tom prayed the prison guards would not be as cruel as the agents.

———⊗———

They arrived at Mt. Vernon the next day. Tom surveyed the large open garage area with chainlink fence enclosures—his new home. They were fed rice in the morning and soup in the evening with three bottles of water a day. He wrapped the thin blanket around him, perched on a thin pad and prayed.

Five days a week they sat in a room, listening to lectures trying to convince them to sign on to the new initiatives. He clung to God to withstand the temptation of better quarters and three meals a day.

After three weeks only six were led to a van to be sent to Rosemont. He heard the rumors that it was worse, but he couldn't imagine how that could be.

CHAPTER 13

THE DRIVE TO Rosemont, just north of Minneapolis, took eleven hours. They stumbled out of the van in the dark and were led to a white building near a paved parking lot.

The guards removed the hardware, had them shower and handed them gray-striped pants with a matching long-sleeved shirt. Guards took fingerprints, snapped mugshots, noted some entries on their paperwork and dropped them in an already full in-basket on a side desk.

Tom put on the socks and slid his feet into the slippers they handed him. He carried his water bottle, towel, blanket, pad, along with a metal cup, bowl, and spoon he had just received.

"Only get one set. Don't lose them."

The guards led him outside. Tom breathed in the brisk air. Illuminated by floodlights, he saw stands of dense evergreen trees ringing a grassy area with some lingering patches of snow bounded by high chainlink fencing without razor wire. Guard towers covered the perimeter of the property.

"$100 bonus for every lookout who shoots an escapee."

The detainees were led to a long, low building that hadn't seen paint in decades. Bars blocked every window. The front entrance hosted carts with large water jugs.

He had never experienced intake like this. The guards collected the barest of information. Didn't seem to care about the length of their sentences, security level, educational status, or any emergency contact information.

Past unsecured double doors he saw six doors with numbers on them. The guards reached for the clipboard hanging from a nail by Door One.

"Can't go by that." The lead guard slid back a cover over a small, chin-high window. "Not too full. Put in two."

The other guard pushed Tom and Steve through the door, the bolt falling into place.

Twenty pairs of eyes stared at them—men of all ages wrapped in blankets, who were sitting huddled together for warmth. A white-haired man rose from a group on his right—tall and rail-thin, flecks of gray streaked his short beard. "I'm Mitch, welcome to Rosemont."

Tom shook his hand. "Tom Hutton."

"Steve," Tom's companion said, his eyes wide.

Tom glanced about the room. "Are you all HCL?"

"HCL? Meaning are we here because of our faith in Christ? Yes. Came through the camp in South Carolina." He smiled through cracked lips. "Pastor from Arkansas."

"It's a pleasure."

One by one they rose, introduced themselves, and shook hands.

Tom's breath caught when a frail elderly gentleman rose with the help of two beside him. He went to meet him. "Dr. Mitchell? From Mt. Zion Bible College? I took your Greek classes."

"Pete, call me Pete. We're all the same, now. Sorry, I can't place you, Son." He narrowed his eyes. "Hutton?"

"Tom Hutton. Would have graduated the year after the college closed. Never had a chance to finish."

His friends helped him sit, introduced themselves and gestured for the newcomers to join them.

Tom tried to settle, letting the feel of the room sink in.

"This will be your life now, Tom," Mitch said. "We get a cup of rice in the mornings followed by a visit to the bathrooms. Late afternoon is a cup of soup followed by our last visit to the bathrooms."

"No programs, exercise yard?"

"No. We have our own schedule. Things will go better if you don't try to interfere."

"Of course. Carry on. Any of the guards receptive?"

"A few, but you don't get many chances. They pull us for kitchen or cleaning duty. Did you see the guard towers?"

Tom and Steve both nodded.

"It's like they're giving us a chance to run so they can shoot us."

Another said, "A few of the guards are kind—bring some extra food." He would have continued, but his neighbor jabbed him.

They asked for their stories. Steve's was short, his voice trembling. Those closest to him reached out in empathy and kindness.

Tom shared his journey until he mentioned memorizing the Bible.

"Memorized the Bible? Really?" some called out.

Tom nodded. "As much of it as I could. Have to review constantly."

Tom did the best he could with the passages they requested. A small argument flared up over different versions. Tom let the conversation swirl around him until it died of itself. "I laid up the Word in my heart that I might not sin against God. In the depths of despair in the hole or locked in with others, God used His Word to sustain me."

"Is that it? What else did you do in there?" someone called out.

He smiled. "God gave me a ministry." As he looked about the room, he saw steady eyes shining past the sallow skin, slumped, rail-thin shoulders and scruffy hair. A tear rolled down his cheek. He recited from Hebrews 11 of those who had been tortured for their faith. *Of whom the world was not worthy—wandering about in deserts and mountains, and in dens and caves of the earth.*[4]

"The great cloud of witnesses," Dr. Mitchell's deep voice rose up. "These times should not take us by surprise. Years without persecution have dulled us to the cost of following Christ that is a reality in many countries. But we look for the city on a hill—the city of God. 'But as it is, they desire a better country, that is a heavenly one. *There-*

fore, God is not ashamed to be called their God, for he has prepared for them a city."[5]

Tom nodded. "Abraham's walk of faith. He saw beyond this fallen world to the eternal rest of God. Despite the hardships God gave me many opportunities." He told the stories of those who had become dear to him. "I had to be thankful and grateful. The agents who arrested me, the guards who kept me, I needed to pray for them as well as the inmates. We need to pray for all because God can do a work in them."

Many nodded. Some shared their bitter struggles. One man broke down in tears, describing the pain of losing his family and a friend's betrayal. Those nearest to him reached out. A tall man rose and worked his way to those huddled about the weeping man. "Samuel, it's okay to cry. You're not alone."

A tall man with black eyes and dark brown curly hair worked his way to him. He said softly, "I'm Aster. Samuel's a new arrival. It can take time to adjust to this place." Aster called on the one whose turn it was to lead the devotional time. The steady voice, though low at times, reminded them of God's constant love and care. Others added stories or their favorite verses. One started a chorus, the next a hymn and their voices rose to heaven.

Room One had a schedule of sorts with some exercise times—walking around the room, calisthenics, or simple games. The younger ones participated more than the older ones.

By late afternoon the door swung open, and Aster rose.

A younger man with sandy hair and hazel eyes moved closer to Tom and whispered in his ear. "That's why no one sits near the door. They open it without warning."

"What's happening?"

"They're selecting the day's workers. Get to cook the soup and rice, clean up and…"

Tom didn't get a chance to ask what the other duties were. He was already sick of being in one room. Before he could gather his legs under him to volunteer, a hand pressed him down. The man on his right shook his head.

"You can call me Winston and thank me later. You don't need to work for them."

Others nodded. "Listen to him. Heed his warning."

His newest neighbor patted Tom's knee. "I'm Dale. I know it's hard to remember all the names on the first day. They don't let me go either. Aster and Winston keep track. The guards often put the workers back in different rooms."

"When's stand-up count?"

"What's that?" Dale said.

"This your first time in prison?" Tom looked around. "Any who have been in federal prisons?" Less than half raised their hands. "They don't keep track of where we are? They don't care how long we're supposed to be here?"

They nodded. "No letters, phone calls, visitors, or commissary."

"No basic supplies?" Tom worked to keep his voice from cracking.

"We shower once a week. Everything's piled together, and we get a kit later but can't guarantee it was the one you had before. You have to keep track in here." The man tapped his head.

With the sounds of food carts, everyone stood, formed a line, holding their bowl and water bottle.

Tom followed Dale. An inmate filled the water bottle, and another filled the bowl. They separated into small circles. Tom drank the warmth of the soup, too hungry to care about the flat taste and spongy vegetables with stringy meat.

Dale leaned toward Tom. "It's Dr. Mitchell's turn. He's always interesting."

Tom nodded. "You go to college?"

"Finished my masters. Love Hebrew. You interested?"

Tom nodded but didn't get a chance to answer. The groups rotated to face the professor. His voice sounded clear and certain.

They sang for the rest of the evening and closed in prayer. Some curled up to sleep; others talked quietly amongst themselves. Tom rolled to stare out the window. Sadness threatened to overtake him. No hope rose up to comfort his soul. Casting down the thoughts, trying to stop the slide to despair, he resumed his place in Psalms and worked through them one by one until sleep stole him away.

CHAPTER 14

WILL MASTERS STOOD in his walk-in closet, eyeing his two $1,000 suits. The Lexus was sold, but he couldn't part with the suits. He vacillated between the black shiny double-breasted or more traditional navy. Lately, if called to the Hill on short notice, he wore his weekly suit, but this meeting smelled different.

Sean, his executive assistant, had been ordered to clear his schedule to attend a closed session. His aide only knew the assignment came directly from Kincaid.

Will slid the shiny black jacket from the wooden hangar and held it against his ties—the bright red one would work.

Will arrived at his office on the third floor more than an hour before office hours and settled into his chair. His computer booted up quickly and he scanned his emails, placing them in inboxes for later action.

His hand paused with the last entry from accounting and opened the attachment. Studying the monthly and year-to-date spending for the departments under him, he worked through the columns of numbers. The second document compared spending to budget. Wages were higher at Rosemont, while the other prison camps seemed to follow budget projections. Rosemont's numbers were also skewed in supplies, food, prisoner goods and telephone charges; some accounts were greatly under-expensed, including utilities. Will drilled down to specific reports.

Based on his research with the Bureau of Prisons, two prison camps followed expected percentages; however, Rosemont's numbers were off in most categories.

Will closed the link when Otis entered his office with a steaming cup of coffee.

"Abstaining today?"

"Just checking the day's damage. You never know if there's a fire to put out." He matched Otis' ever-present smile. "So, a private meeting? Who's attending?"

"It's at the Dirksen Building."

"Senator Roxston?" Otis nodded, and he pasted on another smile.

"You see what's in the pipeline from Literature Division?"

"Not my jurisdiction." He waited. It was Barrie's baby, supposedly, but he knew Kincaid was the driving force behind it.

Otis leaned forward after glancing down the hall. Kincaid would be coming in any minute. "Word leaked, and we need to handle this quickly."

"Does *he* know? And what exactly got out?"

"Of course, he knows why Roxston set up this meeting. Latest Bible edition was posted on the network three weeks ago for internal eyes only. You're on the short list for access." He sat back as Will navigated to the link, observing the man's drawn brows, frozen face and restrained breathing. "You know this was inevitable. Only logical—can't have text of outlawed speech in approved Bibles, can we?"

"Of course," Will agreed, closing the document before meeting Otis' gaze. He worked at setting a neutral face. "So, tell me about the opposition."

Otis provided the details, along with suggestions on how to counter their objections.

"Why not send Barrie? It's his baby."

Otis shook his head. "You know why. We're a team, and we, especially Barrie, don't do the Hill as well as you. Besides, they're still leery of him after the Easter problem."

Will nodded. He remembered how Barrie had burned his bridges on the Hill when he tried to get Senator Wrash arrested for an innocuous Easter message to staff and supporters.

"They need to see a unified effort; show them we are all on board and bring them into the fold."

This was different. "You sure about this? It's not a Bible anymore. You'd be directly outlawing their religion."

Otis laughed. "We need to expose and eliminate the last of the resistance."

Will hesitated. The top leadership and many of the agents spent too much time in the DC bubble. "Patience is a virtue." He leaned forward, looking for an indication of how flexible he could be. "Perhaps in a few years. Give us time to point out the inconsistencies." Another idea occurred to him, but he rejected it outright. *Otis is right—it is inevitable.* However, he felt in his bones this move would embolden the opposition and strengthen their resolve, but he hadn't survived on third floor by voicing his opinions.

Otis rose. "You square?"

Will nodded. "I'll check out the lay of the land, see what Roxston's take is, smooth ruffled feathers, but I suspect it will take time." He lifted his brow, gauging Otis' reaction.

"New edition's set to be released in January with advanced copies sent to our larger religious affiliates in time for the Christmas season." Otis tapped the doorframe on his way out. "They're sending a limo for you."

Will nodded, wishing he could hand off Hill appearances to another capable, up-and-coming executive assistant.

Sean buzzed the intercom and told him the limo was waiting. Will glanced at the clock—more than thirty minutes before his usual departure time. He scrambled to finish last-minute adjustments on a global email to employees about the upcoming holidays and grabbed his slim briefcase. Sean met him at the door.

Will wondered where Sean stood with their mandate. His assistant either was willing to sacrifice his convictions for ambition or he was another true believer in the mold of Otis and Barrie. Will remembered he had once seen advancement as his ultimate goal. Now he felt trapped and unable to pull free.

Senator Roxston's aide met him at the reception desk. Will followed him to a lower-level room converted for conferences. The man extended his hand for Will's cell phones.

"Secure meeting?"

The aide nodded. "At their request. The senators don't want to read their statements in tomorrow's news feeds."

The room was devoid of Internet or phone connections. Senator Roxston and his side-kick senator from Nebraska, with their aides sitting behind them, were already at the center of the table. The aide positioned Will across from them in the middle of the long table. Pads and pens were laid out. Roxston's aide placed a slim book at Will's chair and exited the room. The heavy wood paneled door closed behind him.

"Is this the new Bible?" Will forced out the words.

"A beautiful, elegant edition that comes closest to the spirit of the Task Force, wouldn't you say?" He didn't wait for an answer. "Senator Wrash and his group agreed to meet." The senator leaned forward and passed a draft of their amendment to the HCL laws.

Will quickly scanned the short document. It would exempt this Bible from any hate crime laws. "Would it pass?"

"It might—if they can get enough people to flood the phones. We walk a tightrope. So far, Congress has approved the initiative, but we risk a backlash if we go too far too quickly. Kincaid's a friend. This is as much a courtesy for him as for them."

Will smiled. "Greatly appreciated." He returned the draft and flipped through the slim book. "The Bible is central to Christians. Releasing this edition might drive more groups underground where they are not as easily monitored."

"A fine balance between competing groups."

A knock sounded on the door. At the senator's call, his aide let them in. The senators entered with their staff. Smiling, shaking hands, they jostled for seats closest to the center. Roxston opened the meeting, asking each senator to introduce himself. Will jotted shorthand notes, including descriptions of the aides.

The senator introduced Will. He felt their egoistic smiles bore the warmth of tiger sharks circling wounded prey.

Will nodded, assumed a pleasant demeanor and thanked them for the opportunity to represent the Task Force. Some spoke extensively, seeming to forget they were unrecorded behind closed doors. Will listened, answering questions when he had direct knowledge.

"Gentlemen, you are aware of the laws. The mandate for the Task Force allows us to codify hate-crime speech and literature. Bringing the older literature regulations up to current speech statutes only make sense."

"The Bible is God's Word," Senator Matson stated forcibly, "but that does not mean we condone hate speech. We've accepted the approved version, but this..." He waved a poorly printed copy of the proposed edition. "...is not acceptable under any terms."

"If I may restate, Senator Matson, are you saying having an approved Bible containing statements that are illegal to be said in public is acceptable? Are you proposing allowing it for private faith, in the spirit of the First Amendment?"

The senator nodded. Many of the others agreed.

Will pulled out his Bible from his briefcase. "How do you reconcile this with the statements in Matthew 28 and Acts 1 commanding Christians to share the gospel, which includes Jesus Christ's statements that He is the only way to heaven?"

Matson said, "They are already abiding by current regulations." He pulled out several tracts and slid them over. "They share their faith by speaking in general terms and provide materials to read at home and not in the public square. We can't put every Christian in prison. In an individual's home with his family, the freedom of religion dictates the right to a Bible. This concoction of stories is no Bible."

Will could see that Senator Roxston was holding himself in check. "What would it take to delay adding your amendment to the next funding bill?"

"Rescind this monstrosity. Stick with the approved text. It has passed muster with the clergy. The majority feel it is adequate for the Christian community while not offending other groups."

Senator Roxston closed the session and thanked them for their time. Will rose to shake their hands as they filed out.

"Close the door, Will." Senator Roxston stepped closer and lowered his voice. "Let Kincaid know. We table the updated version. I predict in a few years it will be accepted without objection. Don't let him forget Task Force regulations need our support."

"Of course, Senator. I will relay your message." People did not argue with Senator Roxston. Will knew in his soul they'd have a civil war if they pushed this now.

Right before Roxston exited the room, he added, "And good work at Rosemont. It's the wave of the future."

A chill ran up Will's back as he replied, "Thank you."

CHAPTER 15

WINTER HAD ARRIVED at Rosemont by mid-November. The night guard passed out thermals, but Tom was still cold.

When the guards came for a volunteer, Tom tried to work his way to the door, but the longer-term residents volunteered first. Tom organized room cleaning and participated in group exercise, but he longed for a chance to get out of Room One.

Rich, a large-boned man with a gray-streaked beard, sat next to him after returning from his duties. "Tom, seniority, get it? You've been here only a month."

Tom cradled his hands. "Almost Christmas."

Rich lowered his voice, trying not to let some of the other newer residents hear. "It's more than cooking and washing pots. There's the trash duty. It's rough." Rich wet his lips. "We're trying to protect you. You're short, right? Just six months left?"

"Seven, but who's counting?" Tom tried to joke.

"Get that. I was here a year before I stepped forward, so wait a while."

"You're short too, right?"

Rich nodded. "Word's gotten out that you can recite Scripture. In a little while, we'll try to get you with the other groups. Be patient."

Tom nodded. He found himself in a back corner near Dale. They were friends already. It had taken one day for him to learn the Hebrew alphabet. They spent a week going through Psalm 119 in Hebrew and English. Tom quietly said the first section in Hebrew still stumbling in the usual places. Once the day's volunteer left, Tom asked, "How many days do you have left, Dale?"

"About the same as you."

"We can go out together. I'd like that."

"Can't tell just anyone." He nodded toward the door. "Marcus, the night guard who brings us oranges and apples, asks how we are doing and really means it. That's the one we tell."

They both looked over when the group in the right corner raised their voices. "Arguing again." Dale shook his head.

"It's hard in here. Hard when we're kept from helping others, can't talk to family. Too much time to think. This has been the hardest prison I've been in."

Dale looked aside. "I wonder how my Annie's doing. Who's helping her raise the boys? Are they okay? Did she get arrested?" He stared at Tom. "Mom and Dad don't get it. They accused me of being a deadbeat dad and gave me the same lecture they gave my brother for growing weed in his bathroom. Somehow I have to hold on through June."

"Keeping our minds busy with Bible memory and learning Hebrew helps. You remember another Psalm?"

"Yeah, Psalm 2. You know it?" The lines crinkled around his eyes. "Of course, you do." He began in Hebrew. Tom followed in English.

The long months of winter wrapped Rosemont in snow. Marcus brought boots, hats and mittens and organized a crew to pile snow around the cell-block building. At first Tom and Dale tried to see who could pile the fastest and create the taller piles. Their energy level waned quickly, and they worked together to finish their two walls. Marcus had them follow the other guard to a small yellow building.

Dale commented, "This must be the sick house where Pastor Rick is staying."

"Where Dr. Mitchell went a few weeks ago? I hope he gets the help he needs. Sounded like pneumonia."

"Tom, it's hospice—not an infirmary. They'll make him as comfortable as possible."

He stopped and let the shovel fall. "But they can't, it's…" his eyes darting about.

"Tom, most of these guys will die here. They know this. We have a chance. At least they're going to a better place."

"I know, but it's still hard on the ones left behind."

Once done with the snow shoveling, the guard walked them back to the cell block. Tom's stomach twisted, and an overwhelming desire to run threatened to overtake him.

Marcus said, "Thanks for the effort. Tom, Room Three is asking for you again. Collect your stuff."

"See you in a few," Dale said.

Tom grunted and wondered how long he'd be stuck in Three. He swallowed his groan when Donnie pointed out a spot next to him along the center right wall.

"Tom, just the man. Working outside?"

"Insulating the building by throwing snow up against the walls. It should help."

"They certainly have enough snow around here." Donnie waxed long about his Alabama home.

Tom settled in and scanned the room, looking for the three elderly pastors who kept the arguments from escalating.

Cecil said, "The last one left a few days ago."

Donnie launched his next diatribe. He went on for a while before four in the back and six near the front entered the fray with their points of doctrine and interpretations. Tom recited requested verses and tried not to get caught in the middle.

Each room had its flavor—One was solid, with a program schedule of sorts that marked the times of the day; Two was laid back, but could be fun bursting into song or story telling; Four seemed to congregate the Bible scholars; Five was quiet, almost morose; he had never been to Six; but Three could be a hornet's nest.

He gritted his teeth when Earl and Donnie added personal jibes about their ministries and love of the faith. Earl asked Tom to recite a verse to make his point. Still tired from shoveling, amazed at how it had drained his energy, he uncurled his legs, using the leverage from his left knee, rose and leaned against the wall. Without the elder pastors, the discussion was spinning out of control.

"That's enough. You're both right and both wrong. We can't just look at these verses while ignoring their context. But the larger problem is the lack of love for one another. Christ calls us to shower upon our brothers in the Lord the love He extends to us."

Donnie tried to interrupt but Tom continued, "Raise your hand if you believe Jesus is the only way to Heaven." His eyes noted every hand raised. He listed off several key doctrines. "We are here at Rosemont because this is important to us, but these side issues," he said as he leveled his gaze at Donnie and Earl, "we can agree to disagree on. No one here has all the answers, understands every mystery, but we all claim Christ as Savior and believe we must share the good news with others." With a lowered voice, he said, "Christ commanded us to love one another as He loved us. He gave His life for us. He said that by this love the world would know that we were His disciples. Does the world today know we love Christ by the way we treat each other?"

Tom saw many heads nod; he hoped a few would rise and support his points, but no one stood.

"So, you want to shut us down?" Donnie glared at him.

"Not at all. We can discuss, but no personal attacks. Share your point, citing relevant verses respecting the context, and leave it." His eyes scanned the room. "I will pray."

Tom knelt and reached out to those sitting nearby. "Lord, may the words of our mouths and the meditations of our hearts be acceptable in your sight, O Lord. You are our rock and redeemer.[6] May our fellowship be sweet as we rejoice in the Lord our Savior and be glad."

He sat back, still holding hands as others joined in, praying for the agents who had arrested them, their families and churches left behind. He nodded at Sam in the far corner who started a simple praise chorus.

The voices blended, sifting through the door and out into the hall.

Marcus pulled the door open. Silence descended. "Don't stop. Please don't stop." He joined them in "Holy, Holy, Holy" while lifting his phone to film the prisoners singing praises to God. After several songs, Marcus put away his phone. "Thank you. Many are praying for you. We are trying to get the word out about your suffering. We pray every day this prison will be shut down, and the law revoked. You are not forgotten." Marcus' voice caught, and he shut the door.

The echo of the bolt sliding into place sounded through Tom's soul. He asked Donnie, "Why does he stay?"

"We asked him to. After working here for a week, he apologized and said he had to resign. Pastor Rick let him know how much he was helping and how much harder it would be if the good guards left. He agreed to stay and talked another into staying as well. They work the night shift where they have more liberty to help. We have to be very careful not to talk about what they do."

Tom nodded and prayed to be returned to Room One—which took three days. Tom found a spot near Dale, and they resumed their Hebrew.

CHAPTER 16

DEEP INTO WINTER, Tom listened to Ron arguing with Rich in a whisper. He knew the man was short, but could he be past his release date? *Wouldn't the guards know?*

Dale met his gaze. "Getting antsy. I've seen this before. Remember, tell only the good night guards when it's time to leave."

"Or what? Don't they have to let you go?"

He shook his head. "They say they…" He closed his mouth and looked away. "Forget it. Just don't go there."

Tom tried not to be angry. Being shower day, it would be busy by Rosemont standards. His eyes tracked Rich's tall shoulders when it was their turn to line up for showers, clean uniforms and blankets.

While dressing Tom noticed others shaking their heads at Rich. Called to form the line, he lost sight of Rich. Just as the door closed, he heard Winston say, "Now he's done it."

Tom found his seat, hearing murmurs ripple through the room. Some tried to crack jokes, but soon a suffocating silence hung in the air. Moments passed into hours with only a few quiet conversations. The shadows lengthened, and a chill crept back in.

The door burst open, hitting two in the knees. They recoiled, biting back any outcries.

The guard's eyes scanned the room. He pointed at Tom. "You, get up."

Tom rose. No one could stop him now. This was what he had wanted, but his heart began to beat more quickly. In the hall he saw others who were recent arrivals forming the duty line.

They marched to a large room across from the shower. The guard ordered Tom and two others to load the washing machines on the right-hand wall. The others followed the guard's instructions for making the meals at the small kitchen along the opposite wall.

"Step it up. We don't have all day." The head guard snarled. He shifted a rod in his hand.

Tom nodded, turned to the large canvas bags hung on wire frames and pulled out more uniforms. Some blankets didn't make it into the washing machines.

"Soap. Three pods each."

Tom stepped forward and added the soap when the other two residents didn't move.

"What's next?"

The guard shifted his head to the door and down the hall. Tom had never been past the last two rooms. The double doors opened to a garage-like area with three flatbed carts.

The guard gestured for the last inmate to take one cart back to the hall. "A cart each." He flicked a switch, and a garage door rolled up. "Walk, no dawdling."

"Where?"

"Follow the path to the yellow building."

Tom vaguely remembered the building and looked about to get his bearing. The other inmate nodded down the leftmost path. Tom shivered in the cold. The path was slightly uphill. Noticing his companion pushed his cart, Tom rotated his around and caught a glimpse of a full moon through the treetops—a beautiful winter moon, glistening in the frosty air. For a moment, the splendor of the winter woods filled his soul.

"Move it."

Tom quickened his pace, but his energy flagged quickly. They were drawing closer, and he could make out the faded yellow clapboards in the sun's dimming rays sinking behind them.

The guard surged forward and pulled open the double doors. They rolled the carts in, parking one in a narrow vestibule. Tom pushed his toward the inner double doors and waited while the other inmate pulled open the nearest door.

Seeing the cart would fit, he began to push it through.

"Wait!" The guard nodded to Tom. "Go in and ask how many."

Tom became aware of a stench seeping through the door. He could barely make out huddled figures in the dark interior. A stocky older man missing his left hand waited. "I'm Pastor Rick. Tell them we have five."

When Tom reported the number, the guard responded, "You, take three. He'll take the other two."

Tom stepped through with the cart, his eyes adjusting to the light. The rest of the building was a large room with all the windows boarded up except for two near the entrance. He saw three rows of pads, most with figures wrapped in blankets.

"I'm Tom Hutton." He would have asked some questions, but the pastor walked to five long bundles not far from the doors.

"I'll help you put three on your cart." He stood at the head end.

As Tom approached, he realized they were deceased inmates shrouded in rough canvas. His eyes roved the area. Only a few looked their way. He would have asked, but Pastor Rick shook his head. They lifted the bodies onto the cart.

Tom pulled his cart back into the foyer and watched the other cart emerge a short time later. The guard closed the doors and pointed along the path running downhill and around the edge of the tree line. "Hoof it."

The path degenerated into a packed snow-covered trail leading through a gap in the trees. Just past it he saw what looked like a hut of plastic tarps on the right and heard fans running. Floodlights illuminated the surrounding area and light shone through the heavy plastic.

The other inmate pushed the cart past the barrier held back by the guard and came to a sudden stop. Tom almost ran into him.

"Move," the guard yelled, bringing up his electric shock stick.

The inmate surged forward, and Tom followed.

"Go to the yellow markers. Unwrap them and throw them in."

Tom forced his feet to move, his eyes seeing, but his brain not comprehending the wide trench filled with bodies. He felt the large fan blowing, getting a whiff of a chemical smell he couldn't identify. Sometimes a scent of rotting flesh rose up, creating a strange, revolting taste in the back of his throat. Tom stepped to the first cart, and they carefully unrolled the body of the deceased inmate. The other inmate reached up to close the eyes, and they looked for a proper place to put him, but the guard yelled, "Throw them in, now. Move it."

Seeing the raised baton, they scrambled to place the bodies in the pit without throwing them. Out of the corner of his eye, Tom saw the third cart push through with four more. *Nine?* He couldn't think about any of this. As they lifted the last two, he turned to face the pit. Besides the faces he recognized, he knew Dr. Mitchell, Warren, and Doug by name. Scanning closer to the edge he saw Rich, eyes open, looking up, with a small black hole in his forehead.

The other worker grabbed his arm. "Time to go. We can't linger."

"It's Rich."

"I know."

The guards' yells broke through, and Tom walked to his cart, following the others back to their building. They picked up their bundles left along the hall.

Tom tried to angle himself to return to Room One, but the guard grabbed his arm and took him to Room Six. *They had tried to protect me.* One part of him wished he had been told, but part of him was grateful for the months of innocence.

He entered Six shortly before the food carts emerged from the kitchen. *Why hadn't I noticed before?* The stricken look on the one returning right before they lined up for soup and water. *Had I seen them signal the count with their fingers?*

Tom shook his head, his eyes adjusting to the harsh light from two ceiling bulbs illuminating those sitting underneath, casting shadows over the rest. Many figures wrapped in blankets hunched on their mats. He counted twelve—most of the rooms had over twenty. "Hi, I'm Tom."

No one rose, but they turned their heads to look at him. He wondered if silence would haunt their many hours.

"Well," a voice to the center right said, tapping a space just the right size. "Join us. So, you're the new worker for the room. How's Mitch?"

Tom tried to put a face to the name. "I think he's still with us." He paused, hearing the relief flow through the room. Instantly, he remembered Rich's still form and what the guard had said—*he had been released.*

"I'm Stan. Some here can't walk over to get the food. You're elected." He rose, along with some of the others.

Tom nodded. "Of course. Get to do the dishes too?" He added, "You're in luck. I'm experienced. Scrubbed pots and racks for three years in Hannibal. Do I get the job?"

Jokes and teasing jabs flew through the room, helping Tom relax a little. Cleaning up after supper kept him occupied. Not rushing through the dishwashing, he listened to the light chatter.

"You must be wondering about us. You're new?"

"Been here since late October." Tom's eyes surveyed the room. The truth could not be denied. "This is a death camp? No infirmary, no medical care." Pausing, he added, "I saw Rich there."

"Rich? He's in the pit?"

Tom nodded. "You knew him?"

"Was here quite a bit until recently."

He nodded. "So, this is where he disappeared. He was short, and Marcus has been gone for a while. They told him to wait…" He shook his head. "Why would he risk it?"

"There was a rumor word had gotten out, and they were now required to release those who had completed their sentences." The frail man wrapped his blanket closer. "Wishful thinking."

One by one they shared fond memories of their friend. Tom listened, the words evoking images of the one who had counseled him like an uncle. Each time, during a pause, Tom gathered his thoughts to share, until an inner storm threatened.

Eventually the comments died down, and Stan began to pray through his list—family, friends, church members, the guards, agents, lawyers and judges. One after another said their prayers, many nodding or voicing, "Amen." Tom, still too upset, shook his head when they said it was his turn.

A small wizened man patted his knee. "You saw a friend in the pit. We understand."

"Dr. Mitchell," Tom said, feeling tears run down his cheek. "You might not have known him. He taught at Mt. Zion Bible College. Went to the yellow house ten days ago." Tom cupped his head in the crook of his arm, balancing against his knee. Tom studied the faces he could see. "This room is different."

"We arrived at Rosemont, requiring daily medical treatments. The diabetics go directly to the yellow house. They don't last long, but the rest of us linger here until it's time."

"And if we survive to the end of our sentence?" Tom asked.

"Don't tell the day guards and only certain night guards."

"Marcus."

"Yes, Marcus is one; Lance's another."

"Marcus has been gone for ten days."

"Wife must have taken a turn for the worse."

"His wife is sick?" Tom asked.

"That's why he took this job. Had been a managing officer at a federal prison but felt working here would give him more time to care for his wife with cancer. They own a cabin not far from here."

"He smuggles out those who have completed their sentences. Remember, he's still a guard; you have to serve all your time."

"Rich had a lot on his mind. Had concerns about his wife and his daughters."

"He wanted to see his grandkids," a man in the far corner said. "We have it easier in that respect. We know we're going to die here, so we can focus on our task. We have been given the privilege, opportunity and time to engage in frontline spiritual warfare."

"'Praying at all times in the Spirit, with all prayer and supplication. To that end, keep alert with all perseverance, making supplication for all the saints.'[7] The capstone of our spiritual armor in Christ."

"Are you that one we have heard about? The one who memorized the Bible?"

"As much of it as I could."

"We pray for our families, our churches, the church of Christ in America and in the world; we pray for our nation, that God's will be done. Not for these bad times to pass, but that it would reap a harvest of souls for Christ."

Tom nodded. "Do you pray for our oppressors with as much fervor as for the salvation of our own? Do you pray for the collaborators, if they know Christ, that they will be restored?"

"We do," one replied without hesitation. "We are called to love our brothers that they might be reconciled and restored."

"Do you pray for the collaborators?" asked a robed figure on the edge of the group.

The voice stirred up memories. In the hush of the room, Tom said, "At North Platte I tried to tell them it's harder to accept the suffering of ones you love for the cause of Christ than your own." He turned to face the voice, still shrouded, unmoving. "But they didn't understand."

"What did they say?"

"That…" he paused, not yet certain of the speaker, "that he had sacrificed their families to save his."

The man turned and lowered his blanket.

"Pastor Timmens."

"How can you call me that after what you know about me?"

"I know that your mistake didn't negate the value of your earlier ministry. The fact you are here shows you found your way back." He walked over to sit next to him. "I told them they had to pray for you and your family."

"I lost my family."

"It's not over yet."

"It is for me. I have cancer." He looked at Tom.

Tom reached out and hugged him. "Then let's pray for God's peace and His will."

———— ∞ ————

They recited Scriptures; many sang. Tom drank in the fellowship of life. *"If the Spirit of him who raised Jesus from the dead dwells in you, he who raised Christ Jesus from the dead will also give life to your mortal bodies through his Spirit who dwells in you."*[8]

Many nodded. "It is only by the grace of God we live."

"Why do they do this?" Tom asked.

"Many believe our faith is more dangerous and destructive than violent criminal acts. The ones we disciple will reach others, multiplying the faithful. The growing numbers of followers of Christ in spite of their laws frightens them. They think they're doing a good deed, assuming evangelizing will soon be a capital crime."

"What is keeping them from putting all of us in the pit?"

"They're keeping up the charade."

"But their stats are already off. They're already getting away with it."

A strong voice spoke up. "Never forget that God is in control. He is allowing this. While we can't see what's He's doing, we know He is working His will. As long as we draw breath, we are to offer the sacrifice of praise with our lips, pray continuously and worship Him with spiritual songs."

Another said, "Only by faith and trust in God can we stand for Christ—even to the sacrifice of our families."

"The emptiness of being separated from God became my companion." Timmens' eyes coursed around the room. "I was raised in a Christian family and saved at a young age. My faith, for the most part, was immature, untested, with an arrogant belief that God would make everything work out." He looked at Tom. "I really thought and taught when you're saved, you don't go back. God would preserve you from falling. That's why I was convinced that your conviction proved you had sinned. It never occurred to me, despite all the Bible stories, that God would work through our suffering. But He had not forsaken me. He restored my fellowship when I repented."

Tom nodded. "I spent many days in solitary accepting that. In Hannibal some of them taunted me with the question, 'How could God be a good God if He treated me so badly?' He wiped his eyes. "I tried to answer back, but some days I said it when my heart didn't believe it."

A clear voice in the center began to sing "You are worthy, worthy of my all..."

Tom listened to the words of the song. He recalled images of his struggles, along with the realization he was still striving with his reality. "Who wrote that?"

"Andrew Brunson, a missionary jailed for his faith. God gave him the song when he was in a Turkish prison."[9] Others shared what they knew of the story.

"What a gift to us!" Tom looked away. *How could I ever doubt God would not be there for me?* Verses promising blessing through persecution rose up, but he was frozen, listening to others share their journeys. He held on to the knowledge that God would never fail him.

In time, the voices settled down to low whispers amongst small groups. Tom rose, stretched, and took his mat closer to the outer wall. Most inhabited a narrow band between the two inner walls. He set up close to, but not touching the outer wall, wrapped the blanket around him and lay down facing the high window. Feeling an inner exhaustion, he shut his eyes.

Tom's eyes flew open. He jumped up, stumbling to find his balance. When his eyes closed, he saw the unseeing eyes in the faces of the dead. Tom paced along the wall, trying to walk softly. He watched the bundles in the darkness, subtle heaving of the shoulders with each breath, a roll, a cough, the escape of sleep.

A current coursed through his being. Cells fired without thought. Verses, phrases of faith in God and hope in him, ran around in circles—headless, with no direction or feeling.

Periodically his body restarted the act of breathing. Looking without seeing, Tom fought against panic. *What if I can't sleep? How can I turn from my own thoughts, my own memories? Where can I escape from the eyes?*

Tom walked until he crumpled by the wall, finding the cold less painful. Eventually, he managed to fall exhausted on his mat as the pink of dawn began to touch the night's dark.

He had no idea how long he slept, but too soon many began to stir, take a drink, and welcome the day. *How can they be so calm?* Tom banished the thought. *How can I be so unsettled? Don't I believe?*

"Rough night?" a near neighbor asked.

"Why is it so hard? I know the truth."

"It takes time. Allow yourself to weep. We will weep with you."

Tear-free eyes looked unseeing. His inner tension continued unabated.

———⚬⚬⚬———

Tom survived the day by creating his own routine. He forced himself to count the days—batting down inner torments—working through the numbers until he had established days served and days remaining. Sighing, he kept his eyes open and picked up where he had left off in his verse review rotation just the day before.

"Tom, Tom…" Timmens placed a gentle hand on his knee. "Could you recite Psalm 71?"

"Of course," he tried to recall the Psalm, but the number 71 did not bring it up. Tom gathered himself, casting forward and back, until he recalled the first verse and the rest flowed. *I cannot survive if I forget the Word of God.*

Mitch followed with a prayer. Tom retreated into his memory, mumbling verses.

"What are you reciting?"

Tom lifted his head and raised his voice. *"From on high he sent fire; into my bones he made it descend; he spread a net for my feet."*[10] Tom completed the next few verses. "Lamentations." He waited for them to ask him to stop.

"Continue."

He recited verse after verse. *"But this I call to mind, and therefore I have hope: The steadfast love of the LORD never ceases, his mercies never come to an end; they are new every morning; great is your faithfulness."*[11] Many nodded. Mitch urged him to continue. Verse after verse spoke of hope in the midst of despair, a future in the midst of devastation and suffering. *"Restore us to yourself, O LORD, that we may be restored! Renew our days as of old—unless you have utterly rejected us, and you remain exceedingly angry with us."*[12]

"We must pray for our nation."

Tom listened, dry-eyed and empty.

Mid-afternoon before the guards came, Mitch and Stan began to talk to the ones who barely moved on their mats. One by one he heard them ask if they wanted to leave. Two nodded their heads, and they helped them move closer to the door. Tom moved the one who had passed in the night. He had been a part of this ritual in other rooms.

The guard came early and gestured him to come forward. "Get a cart," he ordered.

They allowed the inmates to help the two onto the cart, and a guard escorted Tom to the yellow house. They walked in with help. Tom noted the four bundles near the door.

"Why bother going back?" He looked down the path to the pit.

"Procedure. Bring back those ready to return." The guard added, seeing Tom's look. "Yes, some get better. Don't know how that's possible."

Tom hid a smile. "With God all things are possible. Our deaths are in His time. He is allowing you to do this to us, but He is still a good God."

The guard sneered and pointed to the door. Tom rotated the cart, opened the door and pulled it through. The small opportunity to share his faith lifted his soul.

CHAPTER 17

MARCUS RETURNED THE next week. He walked with Tom to the yellow house. "Sorry about Rich."

Tom stopped, and the two men looked at each other. What could he say? *Blame God—this was the man's destiny? Or that it was Rich's fault? After all, he had been warned to be patient.* If he had only waited a little longer, Marcus could have smuggled him out. Every day seeing the beloved of the Lord in the pit—those he had come to know and love—sucked the life out of his will to live. He heard himself saying, "We have a blessed hope, a certain inheritance that nothing can steal away." If only this hope was his destiny this day, and he turned once again from the sin of wishing it was over. Now he volunteered so recent arrivals would have the gift of ignorance. "They said your wife was sick?"

"She went into hospice." Marcus turned down the path. "The doctors thought she wouldn't make the night, but she's still alive." Marcus smiled. "Sharing her faith in Christ with all the staff. They're stunned she's so lucid."

"The ways of the Lord are so much higher than ours."

"Time to rotate you out of Six. New orders from the warden to balance out the rooms."

Tom spoke the names of the ones who had passed before he left Six. Dread rose up when Marcus opened Door Three, and he felt the Holy Spirit's inner warning. The door bolted shut behind him. Only eighteen looked at him and turned away without making room. Tom sat near an outer circle to soak up as much warmth as possible, still chilled from being outside.

Some whispered and looked in his direction. The rest looked through him as if he did not exist. Seeing the pit everyday robbed him of sleep; Three robbed him of fellowship. Tom withdrew to the wall.

He had hoped his night would be better, but a paralyzing numbness robbed him even of the horror of the eyes. Ash filled his stomach, overpowering hunger. The cold flavorless rice clumped in his mouth. He forced himself to eat ten bites and gave the rest to a large man sitting nearby. The man accepted it with thanks.

Three days later, Tom cried out in the night, pleading for the Lord to rescue him. Tom walked to the window, the dark staring back like a presence reaching for his throat. Wordlessly, he cried out again, praying for a glimpse of the moon.

A rush of joy, with dazzling light, carrying rays of hope and love enveloped him. Wallie, in gleaming robes, stood next to a figure beyond words or description—the risen Christ. He knew without words this was yet to come. Wallie would go before him—his fight complete and his battles done; they would be together in heaven. He longed to be faithful to the end, to stay the course. As in the box in Hannibal, he sensed that God had a job for him to do. He wondered how he would know. The assurance came with the promise of God's strength.

The vision left as suddenly as it came, but the peace remained. Seeing without sight, he picked up his blanket, wrapped it around his shoulders before lying down on his mat. Holding the presence of Christ in his soul, he closed his eyes and slept.

Some of the inner tension subsided, but the ashes in his stomach did not. Striving against the pull of death within him, he clung to God. He ate what he could and gave the rest away.

———※———

The head guard pulled Tom from the line after showering. "Get your things." He watched with dead eyes. "Not eating, huh? Bothered by the reality of your crimes? We're working for the future—a better world for our country."

Tom met his gaze, unflinching. The Spirit within him shut his mouth.

"Leroy, escort Hutton to the sick room. He doesn't deserve to be here."

A shock flowed through him. The man had purposefully placed him in Six and ordered Marcus to put him in Three.

"Yeah, this is the end. One day, this place will be empty because we will have rid ourselves of the likes of you."

He longed to boast God would win, but his mouth remained closed.

Tom curled up on his mat while the guard interrogated Pastor Rick about how many had died that day or were close to passing. He was a dead man walking.

Pastor Rick paused, sitting for a while by the door and the one dim light. He roused himself and walked the length of the room to Tom. "Why are you here, son?"

"I am dying."

"Why are you dying?"

"I feel dead inside."

"Tom, I need your help. Follow me." He walked to the end near the door and pointed to an empty spot near a low table with a water keg, buckets and cloths.

Tom followed and set up his mat and blanket.

Pastor Rick held out a small chocolate bar. "From my stash."

"Gifts from Marcus?" He let the sweetness melt in his mouth and the goodness soak into his soul. He turned to the soup pot that had just been delivered and felt a stirring of hunger.

Pastor Rick nodded to the twelve. "Help those who can sit up. I will fill the bowls."

He went, one by one, and helped them up. Together they helped them eat. "It's important that they at least drink the broth. It's the only warm food of the day."

"Why don't they pull workers to cook the rice in the morning?"

"And make some part of this less hard and cruel? We are in the enemy's camp."

Once they were done, they sat and poured soup into their bowls. Tom's fingers felt the heat. "It's still somewhat warm." His eyes noticed the pot sitting over a small hot plate.

"When we're done, rinse out the pot and fill it with water from the tap in the foyer." Rick's eyes returned to Tom. "When the water is warm, we'll help bathe the men who can't bathe themselves."

When Tom shared his time in the infirmary at North Platte and the hospital, Pastor Rick smiled. "I had been praying for help. Many can't handle this."

Tom looked about and rose to collect the empty bowls. He met Pastor's gaze and bowed his head, listening to the man's humble prayer.

One began a chorus, others joined in. The room grew still. Tom recited Psalm 139. Weak voices called for other verses.

Everyone curled up in their blankets. Tom soaked in the slight warmth from the heater and the peace of God in his soul.

The sounds of bumps, strangled cries broke through the fog of deep sleep. Tom rolled to his knees and was on his feet to see a man thrashing with a seizure. Tom balled up his blanket and rushed to put it under the man's head. Using the edge of the blanket, he pinned the arms after rolling him on his side in the safe position. Tom with the help of another held him close until the episode passed, and his body went still.

"Mack's not far now," Cecil said, releasing his hold on the man's legs. "He'll go back into his coma."

Tom rolled the man on his back, retrieving his blanket. "It's morning already?" For the first time he noticed the two bundles by the door. "Who helped him?" he asked Cecil. The man smiled at one near the door and returned to his mat.

After breakfast Tom tested the water. It was warm enough, and Pastor Rick stepped Tom through the washings with what little they had.

———∞∞∞———

The days turned into weeks, and a month ran by. The sun's angle began to lift and the days lengthened, but the bitter cold persisted. Mack and several others passed.

The head day guard burst in during a prayer time.

The guard's eyes roved the room, impatient for his eyes to adjust to the dim reaches of the interior. "You!" He pointed at Tom. "Get your stuff now."

Without a word he bundled his items in his blanket and rolled it up with the mat. They were gone in moments.

The guard put Tom in Room Four, and Tom assessed the grouping. *Something is off.*

"Yeah, they scrambled our groups. Trying to keep track with counts and recording inmates' deaths."

Tom reminded himself to breathe. The time with Pastor Rick had helped him regain his appetite. He could eat again. God had promised he would survive this. Glancing around the room, he saw Dale and moved close to him.

"Remember your Hebrew?" Seeing Tom's smile, they continued with the Psalms.

Tom's eyes counted fifteen in the room. "I thought they balanced out the rooms again."

"They have." Dale directed Tom's attention to Mitch. "Everyone left in Six is scattered across the units."

Tom nodded at Mitch, noticing the man's ragged cough and drawn face. He looked back at Dale who looked thinner than he had been.

"You're a scarecrow now. Thought you couldn't get any skinnier," Dale said, as if he read his mind.

"This is the fattest I've been in months." Tom tried to add levity to his voice, but his eyes scanned the seated forms—their hunched posture and scratchy voices if they spoke at all.

There seemed to be some order to the afternoon selections, and Tom was pulled every other day. They now had six working the three carts, piled two deep. More left than came to fill the spots, and Tom surveyed each room as the average number dropped from fifteen to twelve to ten.

Tom smiled when Marcus appeared at the door for volunteers. Stepping forward with Ian, they joined the others with the carts. There were almost enough to require two trips, but they made it up the short rise to the yellow house. It would be downhill from there.

Marcus, with Reggie, a trainee for the third shift, followed closely behind. At the edge, he said, "Proceed."

Tom nodded. That was their cue. The men worked quietly to place the bodies in the pit. Mel glanced at Tom and nodded.

The six stood in a circle facing the pit. Mel led with a short version of "Holy, Holy, Holy." One by one they joined in forming layers of harmony. With the last tone drifting away, Tom raised his hand. "'*Precious in the sight of the LORD is the death of his saints.*'[13] We commit our dear friends to the fellowship of the faithful. They have received their inheritance and the crown of life for they did not consider it too high a price to give up their lives as Christ gave His life, rising from the dead to conquer death."

Mel sang, "This I Believe" and gave the closing benediction.

"Thank you," Tom said to Marcus standing nearby. He noticed Marcus' drawn face. "How are you doing? Your wife passed last month?"

"Hanging in there."

"Something else?" He noticed Marcus sliding his phone into his pocket.

Marcus nodded. "I have cancer too—stage IV. It's not bad, not yet, but…" He welcomed the hugs of the brethren.

"Will you be leaving us?" Tom asked.

"I'll stay as long as I can. We had no children. You are family now."

CHAPTER 18

DEPUTY DIRECTOR WILL Masters glanced at his watch. The dog-and-pony show put on by the staff of Mount Vernon successfully ran down the clock. He entered the next session—cooperating residents presenting the justifications and rewards of compliance to a silent group in gray-striped uniforms.

The arguments were slim, the logic mostly missing—stick-and-carrot phrases more given to manipulation than to convince a reluctant audience prevailed. Standing by the back wall, he noticed all sat with their hands on their knees, eyes forward, barely breathing. The day officer walked about, slapping his thigh from time to time with a shock stick. Will couldn't wait to leave the oppressive room.

He had asked for a complete tour of the grounds. Sources had spoken of back buildings that did not adhere to federal standards, but the meeting droned on. Will strode out of the room, collected his briefcase and coat from the warden's aide and headed out the front door. He walked along the side of the white building to the back area. Two guards raced to catch up with him.

"Sir, we have more to show you in the main building."

"I want to see your back buildings."

"Just garages, maintenance—for old equipment, transfer vans."

The other officer answered his phone. "Director Masters, your ride to the airport is ready."

Will stopped. They took up positions in front of him, gesturing to the waiting taxi.

"Seems early."

"Forgot to mention traffic this time of day can be heavy, and it's a busy airport."

Will highly doubted both statements, but he would not cause a scene this time. Obviously, his suspicions about Sean were correct since only he knew about this visit.

Will found a seat near the boarding gate after quickly passing through screening and pulled out his laptop. Another email from Sean included more documents from Barrie. Kincaid was growing impatient, and Senator Matson's resistance group was the target.

He read the sense, running through the logical solutions, keeping his emotions at bay. He was now the Deputy Director, serving directly under Kincaid. Otis had taken his promotion hard, but Will worked to keep their relations amiable. It rankled that he still had to sign off on top-level documents for the Task Force prisons, but this overview provided justification for inspections. Not able to forget the video evidence Chris had shown him, he wondered how he could arrange a surprise trip to Rosemont.

In the video the former inmate described the Mount Vernon back buildings, but having failed to gain access to them, Will was no closer to confirming or denying the accusations. The charges against Rosemont were more serious. The *ping* of another message drew his attention away.

———— ✆✆✆ ————

Sean met Will at the airport and drove him directly to the Hill. Will reviewed the talking points.

The media storm on the Capitol steps tested Will's patience, but he soldiered on, answering reasonable questions and ignoring the rest. Revelations of the Task Force's involvement in Senator Matson's indictments reminded Will of warnings from Chris. Spouting his talking points, he assured the reporters the Task Force had merely supplied corroborating evidence. His aide tapped his watch and cleared a path to the next hearing.

Will squared his shoulders, mentally reviewed his briefing notes, but doubts dogged his steps. He stopped as soon as he found himself praying. *Why would God help me?* If what they said was true, he was on the wrong side.

A congressional intern led them to their seats. Will scanned the assembled committee. He was scheduled after the current witness. Senator Roxston's committee, still favorable to the Task Force, worked through their agenda supporting the proposed Bible. He was not sure how it had come to this, where the leak was or which side drove the early release of the upcoming version.

The *how* was immaterial at this point. The uproar even with a compliant news and social media had taken even Kincaid by surprise. However, their dogged persistence never wavered as if anticipating this would expose the opposition.

When his turn came, Will rose, catching a glimpse of Chris' golden hair in the second row of the balcony. A slight smile warmed his heart for an instant. Positioning himself in front of the mic, he resisted the urge to glance at his notes. The first interrogators would be Task Force enthusiasts.

Senator Walt headlined the opposition and met his gaze. He handed a stack of pages to the intern. "Deputy Director Masters, you have before you a list of citizens who entered the Task Force prison system and have not been heard from. Every day I receive reports of more Americans joining the ranks of the disappeared—a charge I never imagined could ever be made against our Republic. I request complete information on the location, status and health of each citizen. I remind you the Task Force is obligated to abide by federal incarceration standards."

Will gathered himself. "Senator, sending HCL offenders to federal prisons resulted in tragedy for some. Our goal was to develop Task Force facilities fashioned after the Bureau of Prison model. All wardens annually certify their facility's compliance with federal standards."

"Do you have direct knowledge of this compliance?"

"As Deputy Director, I no longer oversee the day-to-day operations, but properly filed freedom of information (FOIA) requests should provide the answers you seek."

The senator leaned forward. "We have filed multiple FOIAs to no avail. Many are considering censoring your Task Force, even requesting a special investigation." He sat back. "It should not be hard to provide the details, if you are indeed, in compliance."

Will spouted the usual response to FOIA requests. "I will instruct the FOIA Administrator to expedite all inquiries."

Senator Roxston gaveled the end of the senator's time, and Will eyed the next inquisitor, a middle-aged senator from Kentucky. She addressed him with all her Southern charm and asked, "Do you deny prisoners who have completed their sentences are shot and never heard from again?"

A shock ran through him. He knew that she had taken a great risk with the corruption trial of Senator Matson, the chief supporter of removing all regulations against the Bible, being all but a done deal. "As I said earlier to your esteemed colleague, Senator, I no longer have direct day-to-day oversight. Please direct your requests to the regional director of the particular facilities."

"Deputy Director Masters, as Senator Walt has stated, your agency has been neither cooperative nor forthcoming with any enquiries. The families of these people named in the list before you deserve answers."

Will poised himself to convey sympathy and empathy, but Senator Roxston ruled this line of questioning out of order. "Does the honorable Senator from Kentucky have a question pertaining to this hearing? If not, do you cede your time?"

Nodding in deference to the chairman, she launched her diatribe of the people's First Amendment rights to free expression of their religious beliefs. Ending with her assertions of the Bible's primacy in their faith, she asked, "Do you consider removing the Bible from the list of volumes being censured by the Task Force?"

"Senator, HR 756 gives us broad discretion, but the Task Force can be bound by specific laws passed by the House and ratified by the Senate that remove the Bible from any Task Force regulations." He found himself praying.

Near the end Chris signaled from the balcony to meet her in the halls. He almost texted back a more private place but reluctance to leave a trail on his phone stopped him. When he walked by, he whispered, "Back dining hall."

They took different routes, but he was pleased to see Chris farther up the cafeteria's service line. They met at their favorite table in a back corner.

"You verify Mt. Vernon and Rosemont?"

"My visit to Vernon was a bust, but I know who tipped them off."

"Well, take some personal days and visit Rosemont." Chris leaned closer. "I hope and pray these reports are exaggerations, but I fear they're not. Can you make a copy of the list they gave you before you forward it to your FOIA Administrator?" The hard edge of her voice made him look up. "Yes, Will, they're just as good at stonewalling these requests as any other agency with something to hide. Need to know who has been identified as missing."

"Chris, nothing has been substantiated."

She leaned forward, "In all our years with the agencies, have we ever heard anyone make up such stories? I haven't, and I don't think you have either. Take this seriously, Will. Due diligence requires no less of you." She extended her hand, the rest of her concerns unspoken. "We are not the enemy here."

"You know what these hearings are like. Being conciliatory doesn't get the job done."

"Make the case to prove us wrong."

"I haven't forgotten Asa. Have you?" Will asked.

"What kind of question is that? Of course not, and it proves my point. Not the one you think, making your prisons necessary, but of what many in the Task Force are capable of doing and the lines they're willing to cross to achieve their agenda." Chris shook her head. "Sorry, enough of work, all right?"

"You finishing up that degree?"

Chris nodded. "Working on sitting for the bar exams as soon as I'm done." She glanced around. "I need to skedaddle. Thanks for seeing me." She turned before she left. "And Will, you are in my prayers every day."

"Thanks," he said, her sincerity evident. He was pleased she still met with him. *In other lives, other times...* He shook his head, watching her walk out the door.

CHAPTER 19

They were still eating their rice the next day when he heard the guards calling out the first room.

Tom furrowed his brow and looked at his neighbor. "Sounds like three, at least, instead of the usual day guards. They were on edge yesterday." However, the shower time progressed as usual.

Most of the activity of the day happened at dawn and dusk. Always cold after the shower, the men huddled in the center of the room and slept. Tom realized they were sleeping almost sixteen hours a day. It no longer bothered him. Few would survive Rosemont. God had promised, but how would it happen?

They heard doors open and close, unfamiliar voices and the footfalls of leather shoes. Shouting to line up could be heard in the adjoining room. Many sat up with quizzical looks.

The door burst open. The warden stepped in and ordered them to form a line by the back wall. An officer entered with a notepad.

They began at the right end of the line. "Your name, city of arrest, and the length of your sentence."

The officer entered the information in his pad. "Found the file, seventy months left. Next."

Tom noticed the new guards facing them held rifles. He wet his lips. *Has the time come?*

One by one they worked down the line. "This one is short. Overstayed your welcome by a week." The officer nodded to the guard. "Stand by the door." They took the prisoner with them.

Tom and Dale had two months left. They exchanged glances and moved their mats closer together.

"Maybe they've discovered some are getting out alive." The rest was left unsaid.

They heard the culling of the rest of the rooms. No one spoke.

———— ⚬∞⚬ ————

Marcus pulled one from each room that afternoon. He nodded at the somber men. Tom volunteered.

Tom and Fred pushed the cart with four. Larry dragged the empty behind them. Marcus said nothing—not even his usual chatter about the weather or some news.

The guard stopped them at the inner door and faced the three.

Pastor Rick opened the door, tears streaming down his face. "I know they're safe, beyond reach, but…" He dissolved in tears. They encircled him with their love. After a while, he lifted his face. "Go on. They left only those who could stand and report."

At the pit Tom's eyes scanned for a place to set the four.

"Max'll be busy for the next few days." Marcus scanned the area. "Might have to move it again." Their eyes rested on the small skidder parked at the end not far from piles of dirt and bags of lime.

Marcus' eyes pooled and overflowed. None of them could say anything. The guard pulled out a handkerchief and wiped his face. "They fought the good fight. They finished the race, having kept their faith. Laid up for them is the crown of righteousness, the Lord, the righteous judge will give to them on that day."[14] He patted their shoulders. "My faith is stronger because of your witness through this terrible ordeal. May our country never forget what it cost."

Tom asked to stay with Pastor Rick.

Marcus nodded. "Stay with me, and we'll return with your kit."

On the walk back, Marcus said, "I'll still be able to get some of you out, but it will be fewer. We'll see how long they keep up the counts and track release dates."

Tom walked into the hospice room and placed his mat near Rick's.

"It's the shock. So sudden." Rick looked down the empty room. Four remained.

"How'd they take it?"

"Once they realized what was going on, they forced themselves to get up and answer the questions. The sickest lot yet." Rick shook his head. "Two who should have been able to survive just gave up and refused to stand."

Tom kept vigil with him as the night deepened.

Reggie pulled the door open and stared at the two inmates looking at him with hollow eyes and gaunt faces, their bony shoulders slumped. He stepped in and dropped to his knees. Reggie put a large lunch bag on the mat before them. He glanced quickly at the rest of the room. "I brought communion."

For the first time that day, Tom smiled and rose to his feet. He checked the remaining residents. They sat up and Rick brought his mat closer to them. Tom added his mat, and the six sat in silence.

"I had no idea today would be so dreadful, but a few days ago the Lord placed it on my heart to bring bread and juice for communion. The others in the main building are holding theirs right now. Would you allow me to join you?"

"Of course," Pastor Rick grasped Reggie's right hand. "Please open in prayer." The officer's prayer opened with desperate pleas to the Lord to rescind the laws and shut down Rosemont. He added prayers for the other facilities and those who had succumbed to Task Force threats. His voice choked. Reggie squeezed his eyes to stem the tide. "I don't know how much longer I can hold on."

"Officer Reginald Weeks, I will tell you what I told Officer Marcus Roth when he first came here—the work you do to help us, not torture us, not beat or abuse us, makes our time here bearable. To see so much death." His dry eyes scanned the faces of the others sitting on their mats. "Today you chose to live. You chose to live for Christ. You valued the life He gave you, not hastening the day. This takes great courage. Officer Weeks, you as well."

Tom's heart smote him naming the rebellion in his reluctance to eat, his pleas for this to end. *"All we like sheep have gone astray; we have— every one—to his own way; and the LORD has laid on him the iniquity of us all."*[15] Christ said, *'take heart; I have overcome the world.'* "[16]

"Oh, Lord," Tom prayed, "We can't see how You can work Your glory through this, but we don't have to. We believe. We stand on Your Word that You will build Your church and nothing can stop You—not even laws of men. We walk even though we cannot see the way." He looked at Pastor Rick.

"Son, you may lead the service."

Tom nodded and reciting from First Corinthians 11 spoke of Christ's example who gave His all in submission to the Father's will. They could do no more.

"It will be harder going forward. You must continue to pray for us. Marcus and I are ordered to pull the files for those whose release dates are three days away. The day staff will closely monitor video recordings." He stood to his feet.

Reggie gestured Tom to step out into the foyer. "There are few cameras here. Have any plans if you survive to your release date?"

"What I should have done the first time I was released—wander homeless, going from town to town preaching the gospel, encouraging the brethren, and warning them of the Task Force and Rosemont."

"Some take cover identities to start a new life."

Tom shook his head. "I determined long ago, even if by the laws of this country they make me a criminal, that does not force me to be one. May I never run away from God's call to be a pastor during this time."

Reggie pulled him forward into a hug. "We'll do what we can but no promises."

CHAPTER 20

THE MONTHS PASSED. Tom sat near Dale whenever he had the chance. They were three weeks away from their release dates but kept that news to themselves.

Friday came, and one of the day guards pulled the day's workers. The inmate returned after work and whispered the news to the one next to him. It filtered back to Tom and Dale. Marcus went to the hospital and was on his way to hospice. They mourned quietly.

By Monday Reggie took over the second shift and trained the new third-shift guard. His word to the residents—"Don't trust him!"

A few weeks later they called out Dale. Tom waited for his turn but it didn't come.

⸺✸⸺

Weeks later Reggie opened the door closely followed by a tall figure. Tom recognized Will Masters. He stood. "Agent Masters, what are you doing here?"

"Tom? Tom Hutton? I'm here to check on Rosemont."

"Yes, it's Tom." He looked at Reggie. "I need to see," he said.

Reggie nodded. "All right, if you think you can handle it."

Tom followed Reggie and the group of volunteers. He stepped through the assignments. The other guard stayed with the kitchen crew, and Reggie led the way to the carts. They only needed two with one guard for escort. Reggie explained the process while they watched the inmates bring out two from the rooms. They added one more from the yellow house.

Will asked questions, his face expressionless as he listened to the guard's calm answers.

Right before they entered the tarped area, Reggie stopped and explained the recent changes. "Prepare yourself." He pulled back the door flap. The inmates pushed the cart in, and Will followed.

Tom heard Masters suck in his breath. Tom's eyes roved the ditch, hoping against hope Dale was not there. His spirit crashed when he spied the reddish gold hair and freckled cheek.

Reggie said, "Tom, you know the drill."

Tom came to himself and helped position the bodies. He didn't care who was watching or how high up Masters was in the Task Force. He nodded at his fellow worker. The middle-aged man sang a haunting hymn of the cost of redemption and then began "He Is Worthy of My All." Tom joined in with the parts he knew before speaking final words for the slain. "You are now with the Savior, our deliverer, our God; you will never know tears, sorrow, want or misery again. Your witness and fellowship brightened our way." His voice shook. Feeling a friendly hand on his shoulder, he embraced him in a hug, sobbing.

Exiting the enclosure, Will surveyed the nearby gap in the fence, dilapidated outbuilding, and gaunt inmates. He looked at Reggie. "This is not what Rosemont was supposed to be. I had planned it to be a Level One camp where pastors could reflect and think about their choices. Not this…."

Tom looked at Reggie. "My friend Dale is there. We had the same release date."

"No, your release is in October."

Will said, "Tom served his first three months in a county jail before we could get him transferred." He took Reggie aside, and they talked quietly.

Little was said on the way back. Tom returned to his place and curled up in his blanket. No one forced him to eat. He dozed while light chatter flowed around him. *What will the guards do now?*

Reggie pulled the door open. "Tom, you get to take out the trash."

Tom rose mechanically.

"Take your stuff with you," Reggie ordered.

They loaded the cart, and Tom pushed it up the hill and over to the dumpsters. Reggie set Tom's items aside in the yellow house. "Tom, Deputy Director Masters ordered me to set you free."

As Reggie's words broke through, Tom followed him back to the yellow house. "Be ready. I'll come for you."

Pastor Rick hid Tom's items. "You might want the blanket. Wait near the back door."

Tom slid down near the door and wrapped the blanket around his shoulders. The dusk deepened to night. When the door creaked open, Tom rose and stepped into the darkness.

Reggie held his arm gently and walked him quickly down the path, staying in the shadow of over-branching trees. "This is out of sight of the cameras, and there are none by the back fence." They stepped past the pit, through the gap in the fence, down the path and to a waiting minivan. Reggie lifted the back hatch revealing a hidden area. "Get in the sleeping bag. I can't leave until my shift is over in a few hours." As Tom slid in, he added, "We'll be on our way soon."

Wordlessly, Tom extended his hand.

"It's okay. I wish we could have rescued more, but at least we could help you."

His eyes like wide pools, Tom nodded, his future still dark and uncertain. "You were a blessing to us. Don't ever forget that and be careful. Don't stay too long."

"If Masters can do what he said, I won't need to."

"He's one of the good guys; he interviewed me in Hannibal and said he'd fix things, but nothing changed." Tom shuddered when the door closed; he was still on the grounds.

Hours later Tom heard the van start and roll down the gravel path. It traveled for a while before it stopped. Waiting to hear the back door open, he started in surprise when Reggie returned and started the van. "Grabbing some supplies for the road. You still there?"

Tom called out, "Definitely."

———— ⤫ ————

Tom felt the van transition from winding, back roads to an interstate highway. The rumble lulled him to sleep despite himself. He lifted his head with a start when the van slowed, turned, and eventually bumped its way along a gravel drive.

He sat up and worked himself out of the blanket and sleeping bag, praying for what he did not know.

Reggie lifted the hatch and handed him a backpack. "In the barn."

Tom followed him to a nearby building and watched him enter a code on the keypad.

Reggie flicked a switch. Tom blinked in the light. "Go change in the RV. I need to take the prison uniform."

"Turn it in?"

"Destroy it."

Tom walked to the side and stepped in.

Reggie, right behind him, turned on the lights and stepped back down the two steps.

When Tom appeared with the uniform, Reggie said, "Marcus took video evidence of Rosemont. Twenty thumb drives with the video are in an inner pouch of your pack. God told us He would send one of you to get out the message. You are the one." He hugged Tom. "You can do this with God's help. You must. Not just for those back at the camps—Rosemont is not the only one—but for the nation." As Reggie turned to go, he added, "Don't go to homeless shelters or medical clinics. They passed a national ID law and are required even at shelters and clinics."

Tom nodded. In the blink of an eye Reggie was gone—the job God now had for him loomed as large as a mountain.

CHAPTER 21

WILL STARED AT the spreadsheet on his laptop and rubbed his eyes. The hour was late, and the East Coast was an hour ahead of them. Action items swirling in his mind, he saved the document and picked up his cellphone.

"Director Kincaid," he said, "hope it's not too late. This is Will calling about Rosemont."

"Rosemont? I thought you were on vacation. You're in Minnesota?"

"I am, sir." Will gathered his thoughts. "I needed to see what is really going on—conducted a surprise inspection…"

"Why would that be necessary? Didn't I tell you everything was under control?"

"I know sir, but I needed to see for myself to state with full assurance that the accusations had no merit." He cleared his throat. "I regret to inform you that the situation is far worse than I had imagined. The stories do not begin to describe the wanton cruelty and inhumanity at Rosemont." Before the director could reply, Will continued, "I request on-site management authority for this facility until I can bring it into compliance."

"Catch the first red-eye and come to headquarters."

"But sir, the situation is…"

"Not over an unsecured line. We'll discuss next steps at the office. Not a word— am I clear?"

"Understood."

"Text your travel plans. You flew?"

"Yes. I'll fly into D.C. and pick up my car."

"Come straight to the office, first thing. Did you call anyone else?"

"No, sir, only you."

Will sat back in the chair, devoid of energy. Fighting off a rising unease, he dialed his contact at United Airlines. The best the agent could do on short notice from Minneapolis was a flight arriving in the afternoon.

"Any earlier flights from ORD?" He glanced at his watch after confirming his reservation. He would drive to O'Hare, turn in the car and take a direct flight. It would be an all-night drive—he wouldn't be sleeping anyway.

———— ✸ ————

Will roused himself, stretching what little he could in the cramped middle seat without bothering those on either side of him. The plane taxied to the ramp. Sitting back, he visualized the green section in the economy lot. The shuttle bus would not take long.

Deep in his thoughts, Will didn't notice the cordoned-off area around his car before the officers spotted him. Sucking in his breath, he squared his shoulders.

A tall, well-muscled agent stepped under the tape and talked to the patrol officer guarding the perimeter. Will watched the officer move to the far side of the taped area. He knew what was coming, but set his face with a bland look, stepped forward, and moved to pull out his badge.

"Stop right there." The agent raised his weapon.

Will froze mid-stride, lifted his hands and dropped to his knees while the agent barked further commands. A black van pulled up, and they led him to the rear. Will turned his head in time to see a shorter officer advance with a black bag. The blood pounding in his temples, he fell into the darkened cargo hold.

They were in the Dulles parking lot just past morning rush hour. It should have taken maybe a half hour, not more than an hour to travel to headquarters, but the highway time seemed long. However, he knew it was impossible to tell. Will tried to keep his imagination from taking over. *This must be a case of mistaken identity.* Will ran through the questions he needed answered.

———— ∞∞∞ ————

Hours later, in a beige jumpsuit, his hands cuffed, Will surveyed the stack of Bibles, notes and study booklets piled to his right. These had been confiscated from his condo as well as his car. He glanced at the agent he did not recognize who would not answer any questions. The man was thoroughly efficient, obviously experienced and unbending in asking the same questions repeatedly.

"No, I am not a Christian. These materials are for background research to develop strategies." Will licked his lips, anticipating the next round of questions. "Yes, I have not directly headed up investigations, but all Task Force agents are required to be knowledgeable about the Bible."

The interrogator selected an old, black edition and turned to the inner cover. "This is the contraband unit signed out to you. Why didn't you turn in the rest upon your promotion?" Not giving him time to answer, he lifted two Hutton Bible packages. "Why were these not turned in for evidence?"

His mouth dry, he knew he could not state the truth. Will met his direct stare and said, "For demonstrations: media, training, interviews." He leaned forward, "During the Hannibal interview, Tom Hutton provided helpful Intel when presented with one." It seemed as if he were talking to an automaton who ignored his answers. He eventually refused to answer repeat queries.

———— ∞∞∞ ————

Will could not gauge how many days they kept him. Seeing the pit, looking at the starving prisoners, and going 24 hours with little sleep, along with the constant interrogations had pushed him into a surreal state. Eventually, his body won, and he slept despite the cold cell, hard shelf, and constant light.

Hunger fought with inner anxieties making food indigestible. Brackish, metallic water seemed to create more thirst after drinking. He sat against the wall on the floor and dropped his head in his hands, feeling a growing stubble. Will sat up, stroking his chin. *Three or four days,* he estimated.

Sometime later he was back in the room—he would not call it an interview room. He sat up with a start when Kincaid entered.

Kincaid set his leather briefcase on the floor, pulled his chair close to the table and looked directly at Will. A slight smile on his face, he leaned back. "At least you have the intelligence not to try excuses with me. Masters, this is your life if you continue down this road."

Will held the fixed gaze, unblinking.

Sighing, Kincaid spoke to his left. "Bring the service."

Food and coffee were brought.

"Here you go—an olive branch." Kincaid poured the coffee.

Will accepted the plate and began to eat. The food was decent, the coffee exceptional.

"We need you on board with our agenda. I know it might seem we're going beyond the law right now, but circumstances demand it. Eventually they'll add a death penalty for the incorrigible." Kincaid pulled out a Bible. "The slavish devotion to this book written by men has brainwashed thousands. Don't you see? It condones slavery. The church moved past that. It outlaws a woman's right to lead. The church grew again. And now, when they should know better, they can't see past their prejudices, thinking God would want them to continue this way. No," he swept the Bible aside, and it fell to the floor. "It stops now. Granted, we're not proud of how Rosemont has developed, but we're feeling our way. You saw Mt. Vernon—how we gave them every chance. If you want to keep your position, your grade, your generous salary, then you tell me right now that you are on board and consider Rosemont top secret. Believe me, other regions are working on enhanced solutions to this problem."

How do they think they can get away with this? The Task Force has stepped over the line. "I want out, but I'd keep quiet about what I saw."

"You really think that's a possibility now?" Kincaid pulled out a file and turned it so he could see his name on the tab. "This is your ticket to Leavenworth if you try to leave."

Will listened to Kincaid's brief description of the insider trading case they had developed against him. "My options?"

"In time. When you're ready." Kincaid looked through Will, rose, and exited the room.

He heard the director say, "Give him the treatment." A chill ran through him.

Will eyed the Bible on the floor and retrieved it. His hand slid over the soft leather cover, brought it up to catch a whiff of paper and ink. Gingerly, he opened the cover. He had seen the insignia on the spine, but he checked Romans 1 just the same. Will set his lips. If Kincaid had his way, this would be illegal soon.

CHAPTER 22

WILL SHUDDERED WITH the opening cell door. He no longer tried to guess the day or the time. The treatment was similar to what Tom had described in his Hannibal interview. Will tensed and rolled up on his side.

Two stepped through and pulled him to his feet. The chains clinked with each step. Will blinked in the harsh light and felt them secure him to a cold metal chair. He did not raise his head to watch them roll in a small table and chair.

The heavy door closed, but Will could still hear breathing. When someone cleared his throat, Will looked up into a blank face and dead eyes drilling into him.

"Do you believe in Jesus Christ?"

"Not as a Christian. I believe He existed, that He was crucified, that He rose from the dead, but I can't…" Will's eyes slid away. Silence filled the room.

"Let us begin." The inquisitor placed a Bible on the table. "Who authored the Bible?"

"God. God directed men to write it, but He is the true Author."

"Name the gospels," the voice droned on. Will answered as best he could. "Don't you know where the Sermon of the Mount is? What book?"

Will tilted his head. "Some do." Memories of Tom and others like him rose.

"How do they distinguish between believers and pretenders?"

"They…" He ran the question through his mind. "First, a true believer knows he is forgiven not by any works he has done." He nodded his head. "When an undercover bases his salvation on any work—Bible reading, memorization, church attendance, good deeds, it's over. They know."

"So, they don't have to be able to spout chapter and verse?"

"Well, significant gaps in knowledge can expose an agent, but he might still evade detection if he tells them he is a recent convert. At that point, they often will correct inaccuracies. However, if he is hostile, short-tempered, unforgiving, angry or violent, even if they think he is a believer, they will be suspicious and most likely withdraw."

"Why do you believe Christ exists?"

"I have seen the reality of God working in too many Christians. That book is like none other. It predicts the future."

"Many scholars would debate that."

"Many scholars deny the man even lived despite irrefutable historical evidence."

"So, what keeps you from going all the way?"

"How could I pledge my allegiance to a God who allows this to happen to His most faithful followers?" Will shook his head. Images of Rosemont returned—the singing, the compassion, the devotion.

Later, a pair of guards escorted him to an open shower room. After shaving his head and his growing beard, they hosed him down and stepped back for him to dress in a clean jumpsuit. Thinking he would at least be dry, he shuddered when they hosed him down before taking him to another cell.

Will shivered. Eventually everything dried, and he slept.

They brought him back to a room, removed the chains and shut the door. He sat on the far side of the table.

Sometime later Kincaid entered flanked by Barrie and Otis. Their faces broadcast their pleasure at his situation.

"Our *former* Deputy Director," Kincaid snidely commented as he glanced at Otis who smiled broadly. Barrie merely glared at his competition. They sat on the three chairs on the other side of the table.

"Now, you are probably wondering why you're still here and not in Rosemont. As you are well aware, my Task Force agents have many strengths. Successfully penetrating Christian organizations is not one of them." He paused, but Will did not respond. "You infiltrated Hawsley's organization."

"Yes, but Chris went in. I just staged the event so he'd take the bait."

"Well, unless you prefer to go directly to Rosemont, I'll be sending you to the Oklahoma Division for a deep-cover op."

"How long?"

"Regional Director Norton estimates six months or more. It's a multi-phased operation. You convince a group in Oklahoma you are on the run and desperate. Get them to send you to Texas to be smuggled out of the country." His laughter, short and deep, burst forth with Will's quizzical look. "That's right. The underground is smuggling top Bible scholars and leaders out of the country. I'd rather nip this at the source and what better way than through one of our own?" He leaned forward, "You can redeem yourself by delivering the marks."

"I'm not going back to the D.C. office." Will was not asking.

"Of course not. We have other offices that could use your skills." Kincaid lowered his tone and leaned forward. "I am giving you a chance to correct your past indiscretions and rejoin the cause." He added, "Will you do it?"

"What? Rejoin the cause or take the undercover op?"

"Let's begin with the case." He nodded at Otis who slid over glossies of the Oklahoma underground Christian groups.

Will scanned the pictures, trying not to think about their futures if he were successful. His eyes narrowed with the last picture of a Texas Ranger. He picked it up. "You can't be serious."

Kincaid nodded. Barrie asked, "What?"

"Our objective requires all Huttons be eliminated." Kincaid nodded at the photo, "That is Alex Hutton's son, Larry Hutton. Tom Hutton will be in the pit before the end of today."

"You sent a team up?"

"Why?"

"You trust the current staff?"

"Why not?"

"When do you plan on finishing off the rest of them?"

"As I said before, we are working on more efficient, humane facilities. Once everything is in place, we'll move them out."

"I'll do it. I'll take the cover, but I need a week to put my affairs in order."

"You have three days. They'll take you to your car."

His thoughts of walking out to his car evaporated when they clapped his hands behind him, put a bag over his head and bundled him into the back of a van.

They released him on a side street in Hagerstown. Will found his car, drove to a small restaurant and washed his hands. He longed for a shower to wash away the last week, but they had been in his condo. Lacking the courage to go home, he found a table, ordered a meal and searched for directions to the nearest public library. There Will printed out power of attorney (POA) forms and filled them out in his car. At a nearby bank, he had them notarized and set his sights on the D.C. beltway.

Taking his time, he wound his way through traffic to the law college at Georgetown U., found a parking ramp and stepped onto the sidewalk. It was suppertime, but he hoped Chris would still be in class. Grabbing an espresso from a sidewalk coffee bar, he strolled to a familiar building.

The day was cooling nicely. Will found a bench facing the building's entrance and waited. Many came and went. A smaller law library also occupied a floor in the large gray structure. Eventually, he watched her exit with three others.

Hesitant to approach in public, he followed until she separated from the group and headed to a large parking lot. Will whistled. Maybe she would remember.

She slowed imperceptibly. Will increased his pace without breaking into a run. He drew closer as she approached her car. This time he spoke her name.

"Will!" Chris looked about, unlocked the doors and gestured for him to get in. "What happened? Joe heard something about you but couldn't get any details." Her eyes mirrored her shock as she took in his bald head, gaunt face, and what looked like bruising on his neck and wrists.

Will pulled down his sleeve. "Rosemont." He swallowed, shook his head. "I can't believe I'm working for an agency that tortures and murders people. It's bad, Chris. Worse than I could have imagined." Will resisted the temptation to share about Tom's escape. He pulled out the POA forms and described his assignment. "Will you be my POA while I'm undercover?" He stopped and rubbed his eyes. "They found all my Bibles, study materials—everything."

"What shape is your place in?"

"Haven't had the heart to find out." He handed her the forms and handwritten instructions for his accounts, monthly bills and other items. "I'll rent a storage unit tomorrow and empty my place. Put it up for sale."

Chris set the papers down and reached for his hand. "I'm so sorry you had to go through this."

"I was a fool. Called Kincaid to let him know about the pit." He shook his head. "Knew I'd be walking into trouble but didn't have any other options. They arrested me at the airport." He described the treatment.

Chris nodded, remembering what Tom Hutton had told them. "What about those who had served their sentences?"

Will forced himself to look her in the eye. "They shot them." He described the pit with little emotion—the only way he could verbalize the betrayal. He grasped her hand tightly. "Your people have to pray he never gets away with this."

"Tell me where you're parked. I'll follow you to your place." She squeezed his hand. "You don't have to do this alone."

Chris drove to visitor parking and walked to the locked entrance to wait for Will.

He drove up to the underground garage door and flicked the remote. The door rolled up, just like any other day. He motored slowly to his spot. Sighing, he parked the car, cleaned out the side pockets, and retrieved his luggage from the trunk.

Chris waited at the entrance, and they walked together to the elevators, chatting lightly and smiling, just like any other couple. In the elevator, she stepped close and held his hand. "I've been praying for you all week."

Will nodded. "Like usual?"

"No, one night I woke up feeling compelled to pray for you and every day since."

Will nodded, heard, but didn't want to acknowledge God could care for him. They paused by the door, and he pulled out his keys. Gesturing her to stay behind him, he reached through the open door for the closest light switch. The entry-way bulb cast shadows into the open area. They both sighed, not seeing items strewn about or broken furniture.

The damage was subtle—slashed and poorly mended mattress; papers dumped in baskets; items thrown back into closets.

"You really are a minimalist." Chris surveyed the sparse furnishings in the one-bedroom condo. "Where do you eat?"

Will nodded in the direction of two tall chairs by the living room side of the kitchen counter. "Didn't entertain." He added, "Take a seat. I'll make tea."

He glanced at the rocker, love seat, small end table and entertainment center that completed the room. "Oh," he looked at the chest high bookcase to the left of the counter. "The rest of my books seem to be here."

"Your computer?"

"In the briefcase with my luggage."

Chris blew on her tea as she watched him check files on his phone and laptop perched on the counter. "Did you take pictures? Did they…?"

He nodded. "Gone. Cleaned out my Google backup too." Sitting back, he added, "Otis would have had no trouble opening that." He looked away, but it was past time to figure out who had done what. "The facility manager's also a realtor. She can handle the condo sale."

Chris glanced back to see the sun set over the Potomac with the lights of D. C. blinking on. "With this view and location, it should sell quickly." She reached for his hand. "You sure you're not coming back after the op?"

Will let the setting sun burn through his eyes. He glanced at Chris' profile. "There's no going back. I can't live in this city anymore. Kincaid thinks I'll be willing to transfer to another office, but…" He met her gaze. "It's time. Pray by the end of the operation he lets me go."

"I will. I can line up help for tomorrow's move."

Will nodded. They had assumed Kincaid's seemingly mercurial leadership style was haphazard, reactive. However, putting together overheard snippets, he was not so sure. One day he had walked in on Barrie and Otis talking about Phase Two, but they had concocted a flimsy story when asked for details. "Hate to admit I was the figurehead while he ran his teams in the background." Shaking his head to dispel the gloom, he rose and walked to the bedroom.

"Just a mattress? No bedframe?" Chris felt the suits in his closet. "Unless you want to pay for climate-controlled storage, these won't survive. I don't see much here. I have a spare closet in my apartment." She noticed the tiredness in his eyes. "You don't have to decide right now." She walked to the kitchen, opened the cupboards and shook her head.

"Disappointed I'm the typical bachelor?"

"No,. Chris leaned against the counter. "There's more to life than the agency." She longed to say more, but the Holy Spirit held her back. *In time when he's ready.* She prayed he would be someday.

"I'm beginning to accept that fact." Will headed to the closet near the door and pulled out three boxes. They filled two with his dishes and one with books.

Chris' phone rang. She headed into the bedroom and emerged a few minutes later. "It's arranged. Ready to go? I'll drive."

Will plugged in his phone to recharge and followed her out the door.

CHAPTER 23

THE SPLIT-LEVEL HOME nestled in an Annapolis neighborhood with narrow, winding roads. Some lots sported manicured flower beds, others overflowed with spreading clumps of hostas, daylilies, rangy shrubs and draped cottonwoods. Slight tints of green mold edged the dark wood railing leading up to a smudged off-white door. A tall, stout, gray-bearded man thrust the door open and embraced Chris in a bear hug. "Who do we have here?" He reached past to shake Will's hand.

"Will Masters." *No agent, no deputy director or other title.* Feeling naked, he stepped in close to the door. Two couches, various tables, lamps and chairs completed the wood-floored living area. The connected dining room had a large oval table, just off a small kitchen. Seven places were set. "We interrupting?"

"Not at all." The man headed to the top of a staircase and shouted down. "Supper." He looked at Chris and Will still by the door. "Pizza okay?" Disappearing into the kitchen, he followed a slender woman carrying a large bowl of salad. "Where do I put the plates?"

She deftly shifted two plates on the far end. "Mandy, bring up two chairs." The woman walked over to give Chris a quick peck on her cheek and smiled at Will. "We always have room for more."

Will walked to the chair the lady of the house pulled back for him. He glanced at Chris talking to the father in the shadows of a hall leading to the bedrooms. His attention was diverted when five teens bounded up the stairs. One stopped, glanced at his shaved head and giggled. The older son cracked a joke, and Will laughed while the sister reddened. He wished he could absorb their energy and enthusiasm.

"Will, let me show you downstairs," Chris said.

He followed her. A partially finished lower level wrapped around the center staircase.

Chris walked to a corner room and flicked on the light. "You can stay here for as long as you need it."

He surveyed the partially carpeted area. "What happened here?"

"In the middle of a remodel. This space had been a warren of small rooms." Chris paused. "Will, I didn't know they would be having company shortly. We could go somewhere."

His eyes narrowed, the light dawning. "No, just no names. I'm a friend, but this might help." Thoughts of Asa's upper room resurfaced. Shutting that down, he nodded to the stairs. "Let's not keep them waiting."

Chris nodded. "When do you have to report?"

"I'm to fly out Tuesday." He grasped the railing. "Was I blind? Was it always this bad?"

"No, or I wouldn't have brought you in. Kincaid could be a micromanager at times, but he gave me room to do my job."

"Or so we thought."

After supper Will joined the sons cleaning up the kitchen. He welcomed the refuge of family—the type of family he had once longed for years ago. The two teens teased the girls lounging on the couches, and they responded with witty comebacks. Conversations flowed easily. Mom hovered toward the end to ensure proper placement of dish and trash.

"Come on. Let's find a seat."

Will followed Chris down to the large room. Dad and the girls had set up three circles of chairs facing a makeshift podium. His pulse quickened, and his desire to hear rose up.

Chris pulled out a hidden box and handed him a Bible. He had to check. "Legal, for now."

The father approached. "News gone cold on when these will be illegal."

"The initiative seems to be on hold for now." Hefting the Bible, he met the man's gaze. "The storybook they want to replace this with—have you seen it?"

Chris said, "Our links no longer work. We were hoping they had canceled the version."

"They're waiting until it will be accepted," Will answered.

"What do you mean by that? What would change that this country's Christians would turn away from the Word of God?"

"They are eliminating the Christians who are willing to stand for God's Word." A shock ran through him when the father laughed.

"Then they have quite the task ahead of them." Hearing the doorbell, he excused himself.

"He's not afraid?" Will asked Chris.

"We have a mighty God."

"And the gates of hell will not be able to stop the true church of Christ?"

"Exactly," Chris led him to the back corner. "Let's go through some things to help you with your next assignment. Now, how well do you know the order of the books of the Bible?"

Will shook his head. "Not well enough, I assume," and proceeded to find out how much he did not know about this book or Chris' faith.

The words, the passages read and quoted, and the songs they sang recalled memories of Rosemont. He had witnessed a living faith standing against the darkness. One part of him longed to know more; the other part recoiled. *How can God forgive me for my involvement with the Task Force?*

Many went their way after the fellowship, but a good number stayed, and they moved to the back deck. Several of the teens gathered sticks. He followed the dad to the woodpile. In a short time, the group huddled around a bonfire, holding sticks topped with marshmallows.

Will sipped an iced tea, declined a stick, and found an open spot by the patriarch of the home. Before he knew it, he asked the question: "How could God allow this persecution?"

The eldest son answered, "It's not against flesh and blood that we strive, but the agents of Satan. It's a spiritual battle."

The father added, "Just think about history. Having a Christian country with religious freedom is rare, and from this vantage point, seems to be slipping away."

"But the hardships…"

"Have you never read the book of Job?"

"Job? No." His mind ran through the order of the books. "Old Testament? Just before the prophets?"

"Read it and realize how many of the arguments are still used today. If you are healthy and wealthy, God must be pleased with you. If you are going through tough times, you must be a sinner. God's ways are not our ways. He can work through our trials."

Will sat up. "Are you saying God planned this all along?" He listened to their answers, but their explanations still didn't make sense. He did know he would never be a part of sending anyone to the Task Force prisons. *How to accomplish that trick, I have no idea.*

Will awakened to the sounds of feet on the floor above. Amazed he had slept, he dressed and prepared to join the others. The aroma of pancakes and bacon drew him up the stairs.

"You woke him up?"

Will shook his head. "Needed to get up. Have to move out today and sell my apartment. Can I borrow a phone to call Chris?"

"She'll be here shortly." The mother nodded to the pile of pancakes and bacon in the center of the table. "Help yourself. Coffee's ready too."

"Thanks." He selected two each but went back for seconds. "These are great."

Dad, flipping another batch at the stove, said, "Secret family recipe and Mom makes homemade syrup. That's secret too."

"I need to get rid of my furniture. Not worth storing it. Would you consider taking it?"

"Sure, we can follow you and Chris."

"Let me check with Chris when she gets here."

"Here she is now."

Will walked out to see Chris pull up to the curb followed by Joe Lyle with his pickup. "The family will take my furniture. Looks like you can handle the short couch and chair. What about the mattress?"

"We'll make it fit."

Will took Joe aside. "Did she fill you in?" Seeing the nod, he added, "I'm in deep trouble, and I know they're watching me. I don't want anyone from this family at my condo. This is your chance to decline helping. I could rent…"

Joe tapped his shoulder. "Forget it. You're right about keeping them away from your place, but this is how we step up and trust God. I'll go in and let them know we'll be back soon."

"Joe—one thing. What's Phase Three? No one would tell me, but is that why they're delaying releasing the latest Bible edition?"

"You and I came onboard at the wrap-up of Phase One—the initial push to identify the groups most likely to push back against the new laws. Phase Two is ongoing."

"The pastors and church leaders." He stepped forward. "Their latest target is a group that has been smuggling out pastors."

Joe nodded. "Phase Three is a tightly guarded secret."

"I'll pass the word along if I learn more."

"Watch your back out there."

"Had any dealings with the Oklahoma office?"

"No, but Kincaid's been beefing it up to move investigations out there. It's headed by Norton from ATF. Had a short stint with DEA. Heard good things about his operational management, but he's as true a believer as any of them. You don't want to cross him."

"What he doesn't know won't hurt him."

"Like I said, watch your back, but realize even if you still do everything right, it might look like a disaster." Joe looked at him directly. "Remember, Jesus said, 'I have overcome the world.' Every believer slain by the Task Force is in heaven with Christ. Believe me—this group cannot begin to win against God."

He couldn't argue with that.

Will met with the manager before joining Chris and Joe to empty his apartment. Chris finished the cleaning before he could help.

The three lingered by the counter. "I'll stay tonight with the family, but Chris, can you take me back here tomorrow afternoon? I'll pick up my car and find a hotel. I don't want to endanger that family."

"How are you going to store it for six months?" Joe asked.

"That's a puzzle." He stared out the window. "Might as well make a clean break. Chris, I'll sign it over to you so you can sell it. Kincaid told me I'd be flying out." He picked up his phone to make sure it was off and set it down.

"Don't you want to see if he's contacted you?"

Will stared at them. "He can wait." The written rule with the FBI stated all agents were to have their cell phones available at all times. It had been his rule—until last week.

The hotel had a free shuttle to the airport. Chris dropped him off late Sunday afternoon. Will waited until he was in his room before turning on his phone. He had missed several phone calls and messages. Sighing, he called Otis first.

"You're in big trouble! Where have you been?"

"Getting my affairs in order."

"Glad to hear you understand the gravity of your situation. Kincaid's livid! Where is Hutton?"

"Tom Hutton?"

"Yes, Tom Hutton!"

"Well, didn't the guards at Rosemont…"

"Not on an unsecure line!"

"As I was about to say, his release date was months ago, so check the records." He waited for the response. Will visualized Reggie taking care of Hutton's records the same way all the other records had been disposed of—put through the cross-cut shredder during the system's automatic reboot cycle shortly before shift change. He could hear Otis trying to control his frustration.

"Why? Do you know his release date?"

"I followed his case; I kept an eye on a few." He also knew the judge who had sentenced Hutton to twelve months was completing his own sentence at a federal prison.

"Well, the timetable's been moved up. Thankfully, they need you ASAP at Oklahoma, so you miss out on the trip to Minnesota. You fly out tomorrow on the red eye. I'll text the travel arrangements."

"Do I need to touch base with Kincaid?"

"I will let him know you'll be on that flight. By the way, where have you been?"

"Enjoying my last bit of freedom." He ended the call and waited for the flight information to appear.

CHAPTER 24

TOM AWAKENED WITH a start, but lay still, clawing back the fear that haunted his days. *"You keep him in perfect peace whose mind is stayed on you, because he trusts in you."*[17] Wallace's light snoring punctuated the early morning quiet. *I trust You, Lord.* Tom willed himself to look to Jesus. He was worthy of trust.

Tom walked out the sliding glass door to breathe in the humid air of St. Louis. Any thoughts of the task before him set his blood pounding and his head spinning. He stood, feeling the flagstones beneath his feet. Doc Ryan's backyard, hemmed in with a tall fence and bordering trees, felt safe, but he knew he couldn't stay long.

Unbidden, his mind recalled the past few weeks—three days in the RV, five with a doting elderly church lady. The nightmares, the trouble sleeping and the nausea hadn't been unexpected. However, regular food had created unbelievable agony.

Doc Ryan's care worked, and his body was finally adjusting, but his inner terror persisted. A wall as tall as any penitentiary rose up in his mind when he thought about his traveling ministry. *There is no other way.* Hadn't Rosemont proved he couldn't live a normal life? He couldn't take a job, and if others helped him, he put them at risk. Even though he understood and believed God was faithful, the fear never really left.

Fighting back with all of his will, he reviewed 2 Corinthians—being weak so God could work through him, Philippians 4—the peace of God could be his if he kept his eyes on Christ.

Morning rays of the sun seeped through the bushes, burning his eyes. Birds sang and crickets chirped with the promise of heat and humidity. Grass tickled his toes as he drank in the beauty of daylilies, marigolds, and impatiens. He studied the orange daylilies, opening to the sun. *"Consider the lilies of the field, how they grow: they neither toil nor spin, yet I tell you even Solomon in all his glory was not arrayed like one of these."*[18]

Tom watched a small flock of sparrows flit from bush to bush. He bowed his head. *I surrender, Lord, to what You would have me to do.*

The joy of the Lord burst forth more completely than the sun's rays. He basked in the presence of the Lord, holding on for as long as possible. Without words, he knew; of course he knew God would provide the health, the companion, the meetings, open ears and hearts.

Fears of bringing the Task Force down upon those who helped him vanished with reminders that God would protect His own. Not one would be delivered to torture or imprisonment unless God allowed it. *I accept You sent me to Rosemont.*

Tom jumped, hearing the glass door slide open behind him. He turned instinctively. "Hi, Wallace. Up already? Hope I didn't wake you."

The tall black man stepped out to the stone patio.

"You're dressed. Going back to work? I really appreciate your taking care of me—holding my hand through the night terrors and helping me remember how to eat again."

"Wallie did the same for me when I walked out of the L." Wallace tilted his head, "But I didn't have the food issues." He surveyed Tom. "You're still too skinny."

"What's up?"

"Oh," Wallace began to turn, pausing at the door. "Boss called me in. I was thinking of putting in my two-week notice."

"Notice?"

Wallace furrowed his brow. "You really are dumb."

"What?" Tom cocked his head. "You'd go with me!"

"Thought you'd never ask. You want me to be your chauffeur?"

A broad smile crossed his face. Tom strode to his friend. "Not my chauffeur—my teammate. You'd give up the job God gave you to travel with me?"

Wallace shook his head, "Of course, I've known for a while."

"This is great news. I couldn't think of a better person."

Wallace laughed. "Boss let me rebuild my Impala, even fix some of the body work in the shop. I only had to pay for parts." He walked to the glass door. "Today's moving day."

"I remember." Tom saw the kitchen light turn on. "Patty's up."

"I figure you'll be here at least a few more weeks with the meetings they're setting up. Wait for me." Wallace waited for an answer.

Tom nodded. "Count on it. We'll be homeless—like the Lord."

"Foxes have holes and birds have nests."

"Yeah, like that. We'd have to be careful."

"I get it. I'm the former criminal, remember?"

Tom smiled. "That's why we'll make a great team. You heading to that coffee shop? I could grab a ride and walk back."

"Not quite ready to go. We'll meet up—maybe at Riser's?"

"Sure."

Tom walked around the side of the house and headed down the sidewalk. *A perfect day for walking.* He ran through his verses, the grip of fear muted and distant for the moment.

After getting his coffee, he found the man he had been talking to every morning for the past little while.

The body shop nestled in a small neighborhood not far from downtown. Wallace surveyed the two cars waiting their turn and the one ready to go. He headed to the back entrance and entered the code. Stepping in, he saw the boss's door open and the lights on. Breathing in, he squared his shoulders, praying how to tell the man he was quitting.

Sliding from fifty to sixty, the owner nodded when Wallace's figure appeared in the doorway. "Take a seat. Just the man I needed to see." He wet his lips. "You're probably wondering why I called you in."

"Well, thank you for the time off. I hate to do this, being you gave me a job, but…" Wallace rubbed his hand on his pants, "I have to give my notice. Something else came up that I have to do." He stopped. "Why you smiling?"

The boss shook his head. "Unbelievable. I was trying to figure out how to let you go. Truth is, my sister's kid just finished his classes, and he needs a job. Known about it for a while. Thought I could keep both of you, but then things slowed down." The boss pulled out an envelope. "Added a small bonus to the rest of your wages. Best I could do."

Wallace tried to keep his eyes from popping. "That's quite a gift, sir. God's timing is amazing."

"You earned it. You came from that Christian halfway house. What church do you go to now?"

Wallace paused, "Well, uh, there are lots of churches. You looking for one?"

"It helped you. How would I know which one to go to?"

"Compare what they say to what's in the Bible. Just check it out. Listen and watch. You want to find one that teaches the truth and is trying to help their people live it."

The boss nodded, casting his eyes out the window to look at the main street. "A few days ago, some fellas came around asking who you hang with."

"What kind?"

"Like parole officers. I thought you finished that."

"I did." Wallace smiled. "Don't need me today?"

"No." The man rose to shake his hand. "It's been a pleasure. Don't be a stranger."

"I won't."

Wallace cleared the building, making sure he was alone before he pulled out his cell phone.

———❧———

Patty was still sipping her coffee when Tom returned and sat down. "You ready?" she asked.

Tom nodded. *"Thanks" seems so inadequate.* "I'll miss you."

She nodded. "It's been great to see you again, but we all knew it had to be short. We'll never stop praying for you." She added, "Talk with Ryan?"

"When he came home last night."

Patty looked about the kitchen, her satchel ready for work. She rose and reached for her phone when it rang. She ended the call and tucked it away. "A car will be by in a few minutes. Let them in the garage. Stay out of sight." Gathering her bags, she hugged him one last time.

Shakespeare was right: Parting was sweet sorrow. Tom went through the motions of leaving and waited right inside the side door. He gasped when a short limo with darkened windows drove up.

The driver said nothing. Tom watched the neighborhood of stately homes and manicured gardens transition to small strip malls, restaurants and shops, before turning down a maze of streets with larger homes and wrought-iron fencing. The car slid into the first section of a three-car garage.

Riser walked down a short flight of stairs. "Home, sweet home," he greeted.

Without a chance to shower, Tom stood unshaven, his pack over his shoulder and holding a half-empty duffel.

"You look like something the cat dragged in." Riser tried to laugh.

"What happened?" Tom asked.

"Right, yeah, follow me. They're waiting for you."

Unsure who "they" were, he tried to keep a clear focus. Tom walked mechanically through Riser's kitchen and dining room past a living room with a vaulted ceiling to stairs going down. His pulse pounded as his mind screamed, *Trap!!* Settling his breath, he followed his host through a carpeted corridor to what looked like a mini cinema. "Hi, Jordan." Tom furrowed his brow. "Wallace?"

Jordan hugged him before Tom could set down his bags. "Wallace has news."

Tom's mouth went dry. He accepted a bottle of water and perched on the edge of the chair closest to the door.

"They know about you," Wallace said.

"Who? What do they know? They think I'm dead."

"Then why did my boss just ask me about the Christians I hang out with?" He explained what happened at the shop.

"Wallace, I think it's just the minders." Seeing everyone's puzzled looks, Jordan said, "I had to work with them at the church. They're more like social workers. Each one is assigned a district, and it's their job to make sure the churches are keeping to the regs. They have to generate leads every month for the agents to pursue. Meaning, they don't know about Tom, but they do know you were at the church's halfway house. Took them long enough to bother your boss."

"That must have been tough trying to minister under that microscope," Tom observed.

Jordan shook his head. "Best move ever leaving that place." He looked at them. "But we still have to be careful. Wallace, how soon can you and Tom hit the road?"

Wallace's eyes tracked back and forth. "Sell what I don't need, find someone to sublet my apartment. A week?"

"Send me to Wichita. We can meet up there." Tom was thankful they had been careful not to be seen together in public.

Jordan nodded. "Have a meeting here tonight and two more in the state. Will cancel the ones in Illinois."

"But your rehab. When's that happening?"

"Riser…" Tom met his gaze. "It's too risky to take me to the gym. Show me what I need to do, and I'll work on it myself."

"It's a plan, then?"

Wallace headed out. Riser gave Tom his first assignment in the small workout room down the hall. Jordan tagged along while Riser gave the house tour.

They nursed their sweet teas after Riser left for work. Tom's eyes softened. Jordan had shown up, been by his side, and listened to his tales of grief.

Jordan nodded. "Why did I waste those years with that church?"

"God does know what He's doing."

"Yeah, He does. Know how that group works. Anyway, what you preaching on tonight?" Jordan laughed, "Probably have it written and memorized by now."

Tom shook his head. "I tried. Really, but the Lord made it clear: I am to say what He wants me to say when He tells me. And He's not letting me write messages—not the way I used to." He studied Jordan's earnest face. "I have to minister moment by moment in God's grace. When He says stay, I stay; go, I go. Been over this with Wallace. Between the two of us, we might just be able to stay one step ahead of them."

"Lord willing."

"Exactly, Lord willing."

They talked of many things—ministry in Hannibal; Jordan shared lessons learned from working with a cooperating church. They talked of the spiritual growth of many and the collapse of others.

"It's like their Christian life grinds to a halt when they compromise. It's hard to describe."

Remembering Timmens, Tom shared his story. "It's not over till it's over." His voice lowered. "Do you think what I'm doing will have any effect?"

"On the believers, yes. How we get word out to the zombie majority, that's the question."

"That's not up to us, anyway. When the Holy Spirit works, it is beyond any agency of man. This thing I do know: this is what God wants me to do, and I just have to walk in it."

"Amen, brother, preach it!" Jordan sat up. "Hey, I just remembered. Tony's headed out to Wichita to work with the Lincolns. Setting up some flash VBS session." Looking at his calendar, he nodded. "Meeting here tonight, Tuesday one south of town, but Thursday's meet is more than halfway to K. C. Tony can drive you. Just keep on going."

Tom looked at Riser's exercise plan. "I have no excuse."

"Not one."

CHAPTER 25

THE PLANE LANDED at Will Rogers Airport at Oklahoma City shortly before noon. Will waited on the ramp for his carry-on and headed to the terminal, wondering who would meet him. Will found an empty bench and sat, watching the bustle of family pulling up to the curb and greeting their loved ones.

Regional Director Norton sent a text with a hotel address and reservation number. Will re-entered the terminal, ate lunch and stood in line for the courtesy airport shuttle—no reason to rush as check-in would not be until later in the afternoon.

Certain, directed, driven would have described him a few weeks ago, but not today—not since Rosemont. Working to keep his tumbling emotions in check, he tried to shut down the inconvenient truths he had learned.

Will texted his room number but told the director he couldn't access the room until three. He headed for the coffee service and sipped the strong brew, letting it slide down with all its hard, bitter flavors, not tempered by creamer or sweetener. Will slung his backpack onto his right shoulder, hefted his small duffel and headed for a winged-back chair near a short table. He settled in and almost without thinking pulled out the legal Bible he had picked up at the house of Chris' friend.

A sigh escaped him. The love, joy, peace and sense of purpose he had witnessed in that brief time with Chris' friends birthed a longing. For what, he did not know. He had witnessed an inner strength, even in the teens, that defied logic or understanding.

Remembering snide comments and jibes from Task Force members proved most seemed to view resistant Christians as deluded, brainwashed Neanderthals, poorly educated, unthinking flat-earth proponents. The intelligent answers to hard questions that weekend still astonished him.

He shook his head. *They can't be right, can they?* He opened the Bible and skimmed the chapter titles. At 2 Kings 6, he read the caption "Horses and Chariots of Fire." Intrigued, he read the story of Elisha's telling the king of the enemy's plans and the Syrian king's vain attempt to capture the prophet. *What had Joe said? "In some ways the spiritual world is more real than the physical."* His mind spinning, he closed the book.

It was moot. Yes, God existed. Yes, He was all-powerful, but he, Will, could not follow a God… He turned his head. *God, how can I forgive You for allowing Rosemont to exist?*

Shutting down that rabbit trail, Will began to read Proverbs 8, trying to ignore the truth that wisdom begins with God.

The two hours seemed to drag, but eventually, not receiving any texts from Norton, he walked up the stairs, along the hall and opened the door. The room had a king bed, a short couch, a standard desk and one chair. Will turned to his luggage and stopped. No laptop. Of course, his badge and service piece had been turned in. Securing the desk and chair would have been the high ground, but there was no need.

A light tapping sounded at the door.

"Did you check? Just going to let me in?" the man stated and walked past him.

"It depends." He paused. They had not given him his cover identity yet. "Director Norton?"

"Just call me Chuck," he said and sat at the desk.

"Make yourself at home," Will muttered. He sat on the couch since Chuck had secured the high ground.

"Will Masters, in the flesh."

"Yes." Will analyzed the graying hair, the slight paunch overflowing the beltline and round face. The direct gaze belied the director's friendly demeanor.

"Going to miss your airtime?"

"Sir?"

"Last year or so any meeting, any spokesperson, or any reporter either had clips of your statements or you were answering questions. Did you live at the Hill?"

"Some weeks it felt like it. And, no, I won't miss it."

"This op's not going to be one and done—not by a long shot. Once you make the contacts and uncover their networks, then you'll lead a team running down all the leads, prepping for the courts. Apprehending even four leaders can result in dozens of arrests. You can plan on being here for a year or so."

"Fine with me. I don't plan on going back East." He leaned forward and let his elbows take his weight on his knees. "Have the op specifics and cover ID?"

Chuck wet his lips. "You have to develop it."

"Great. No one at headquarters told me that." He hadn't set foot in the office since the day before he left for Rosemont. "It has to be back-stopped. Someone with access to the Task Force system needs to find a likely prospect." He nodded at his scruffy backpack and worn duffel. "And I left my laptop with my POA. It would be more of a liability with this cover."

"You're right." Chuck pulled his laptop from his soft briefcase and connected to the Internet through his hotspot, avoiding the hotel Wi-Fi. "Have at it." He glanced at Will's left arm, noting some bruising on the inside of his forearm. Only shadows remained on his wrists. He considered delaying sending him out but feared news would get out of an undercover agent.

They exchanged places. Will stroked his jaw, a day's stubble growing already. "My cover is on the run, you said, and is looking to hook up with a Christian group willing to help him hide. So, we need someone who's not from here—being I don't know this city, and we don't have time to overcome that—who is close enough to my description." He navigated to the open or recently closed cases. From there he selected target bios, scrolling through them.

"You do many undercover ops?"

"No, supervised Task Force investigations before I transferred to upper management. While with the FBI in the day, I helped coordinate multi-agency operations. My specialty was liaising between various divisions to develop team cohesion." He followed what looked like a good prospect but shook his head seeing the after-action report: "They caught him last week."

"They teach Bible classes at D. C.?"

"What?" Will asked while following another probable lead.

"I saw your interviews. How'd you learn all that?"

"When I came on-board, that was the directive—learn the Bible and understand it so you can better apprehend…" His hand paused over the enter key, trying not to anticipate another dead end. "Hmm, this might work." He navigated to the target's background.

Will smiled as he pulled up the most recent photo and turned the laptop to Norton. "Meet Warren Bells, construction worker from Pittsburgh and on the run after his Kentucky fellowship was taken down. I need an ID."

Norton shook his head. "Your cover is desperate and on the run with no ID. You need to convince them you have to be smuggled out of the country."

"What are the qualifications?"

"So far, we only know that Bible scholars, professors, top pastors and organizational leaders are showing up in other countries. Haven't a clue how this is happening or the organization behind it."

"Under their own names?"

"No, and their covers are good. Someone with skill, expertise, and money is helping them." He leaned forward. "Finding this organization should lead us to the mastermind behind the resistance. Need to button this up to lay the groundwork for the next phase."

Will turned his chair to face Norton. "What is holding up release of the next Bible edition?"

"Ensuring we have the proper environment for enforcement." Chuck nodded at the screen. "Need anything else?"

"Just a little more background and I'm good to go." Will broadened his search to social media. *What if Warren is in this region? Where would I flee?* He searched for the man's associates. Smiling, he was about to share with Chuck where the man might be hiding, but one look at the man's face dissuaded him. Warren had extensive family in New England and access to an old hunting cabin in northern Maine.

"Shut her down?" Seeing the nod, he closed the files, exited the programs and handed the laptop to Chuck. His mind continued to process the man's comment about proper operational environment. "You won't find the one leading resistant Christians this way."

"Why not? We expect results."

"I understand, but Jesus Christ is the true head of the church." Seeing Chuck's blank look, he explained, "He is both God and man. Right now, He is sitting at the right hand of the Father, leading His church on earth from heaven."

"What? Those fables?"

"Are real. Check it out. Multiple volumes have been written proving the historical reality of Christ, His death, and resurrection."

"Really? How does He do it? They mind meld or something?" He jeered as he waved his fingers by his head.

"Every true believer is indwelt by the Holy Spirit who is in direct contact with God the Father and God the Son. Nothing gets by them." Will leaned closer. "That is why so many of your undercovers were made; the Holy Spirit told them." He pulled out his Bible and opened it to Elisha's story. Seeing Chuck was not about to touch the book, he read aloud the story of the Syrian king who learned God was telling

Elisha the prophet to warn the king about Syrian raids. "It's not always 100 percent, but that's how some get through. So, I have to feel like a believer—not just spout the words."

"Okay, if all that is true…" Chuck leaned forward, "how are we arresting so many of them? If He is God and He cares, why have we gotten this far?" He waited for Will's reply with raised eyebrows.

"Because God is allowing it." Will sat back. "That really bites. Why are they still loyal to Him, singing that He is worthy of their ultimate sacrifice if He has delivered them up to destruction?"

"Well, if you're good, I'm out of here. You have my cell number. Text weekly updates."

"You have a mole?"

"We think so. How else would they sometimes be so hard to find? Anyway, this city's clean, but people from outlying areas come here to shop, so check the big-box stores. We welcome any Intel you uncover. Anyway, we'll set you up farther out if you don't make contact by Wednesday."

"Sure, my phone's been scrubbed, but it's still registered to me. If this group is as savvy as you say they are, I should use a prepaid phone. Do you have a better number for check-ins?"

Chuck nodded. He wrote down a number and handed it over. "Watch your back. I'll hold your phone for you."

Will handed it over. "You do know if these Christians discover who I really am, they will not kill me—probably won't harm me in any way. They'll neutralize me without doing harm. The Bible is true."

"In their world—not ours."

"They follow the command to love their enemies and do good to them. They will pray for me, help me. They are not the threat." Will rose. "Director Norton, think on this: we are the lawbreakers by killing them without cause. We are the problem if we make ourselves executioners. Men who had served their time were released…"

"They seem eager to get to heaven. We're just advancing the timetable. After all, everyone's going to die." Norton met his gaze. "Doesn't bother me one bit knowing we are preventing future illegal behavior. Think of it as similar to preventing the release of a known serial killer into the community. We gave them every chance and every opportunity; they chose resistance." Chuck patted Will's arm. "Cheer up! We're developing solutions. When you return, I'll show you the latest facilities with state-of-the-art, more humane methods."

Will did not voice his objections. The man smiled, nodded reassuringly as if he were a senior operative encouraging a young recruit. He wanted to like the man, assumed he was a good leader, but clearly, he had not heard. Certain of the virtue of their methods, he was blind to the carnage they had created.

The door closed. Will stood motionless for a while. He pulled back a drape and watched Norton walk across the parking lot and the next street to a nearby diner. An overwhelming tiredness overcame his curiosity. He lay down and slept deeply.

CHAPTER 26

WILL JERKED AWAKE with a start. The room was still bright, so it couldn't be that late. Hunger kicked in, but he showered before packing and leaving the room. Taking everything with him was a last-minute decision. If he did link up with a group, it wouldn't look good for him to retrieve his luggage from a nice hotel. Will took one last look and shut the door, wondering if Norton's team had been as effective as he had claimed.

The diner had a good selection of ribs, and he ate quickly. Will strolled the streets, letting the flow of traffic and pedestrian walkways direct him. He stopped at the first convenience shop to buy a prepaid phone and texted Norton.

The pedestrian traffic seemed thin given the perfect weather—not too hot with a slight breeze—however, this was Monday. Eventually, the walkway led to a warehouse district. Resting on the last park bench, he watched a pair of young women walk by and recognized a hymn they were singing. Once they passed, he noted their direction and headed across an open park to follow them.

They turned left and disappeared between two large warehouses. He sprinted, but the concrete drive between the buildings was empty apart from a few cars and a van by the time he rounded the buildings. The shutting of a heavy door echoed from the righthand building. Seeing no one in sight, he walked around the van and gingerly tried the nearest door. It did not yield; however, a small one farther down yielded to his push. Will gathered his breath and stepped in.

Before his eyes could adjust, he heard voices and quick steps approaching. A tall man with a military-like bearing drew close, his gaze direct. "What are you here for?"

"I…" Will tried to discern the words from the voices and sounds of boxes being pushed. "I wanted to talk to two women. They were singing a song I had heard before." He studied the man's face. "Do you know them?"

"Why are you here?"

"I am," he extended his hand and would have said his name, but the man interrupted him.

"Not necessary. You're not from around here?"

"That obvious? Listen, I was looking for," he wet his lips, and stepped closer to the door. "Need help, but…"

"Is He worthy of your all?"

"If by He, you mean Christ? Yes, I mean, I try, but they're on to me. Are you Christians?"

"Yes, follow me."

The man led him to a poorly lit large room with half the fluorescents burnt out. Shrink-wrapped pallets of boxes dotted an alcove under a walkway. People of all ages worked quickly to cut through many layers of plastic to free the boxes. Several talked amongst themselves, counting boxes, discussing how many trips it would take. He heard the tall man say, "We only get one shot. The team's set to roll out in an hour."

"We have another helper." The man stepped to the girls. "He heard you singing."

"We weren't singing. We were humming."

"Well, he made you."

"Sorry, we're on edge, okay?"

"Relax, remember next time." He glanced at Warren. "Want to help?"

Warren walked to an open box and knelt down, pulling out a wrapped package. "Hutton Bibles?" Bringing one close, he smelled the telltale aroma.

"Yes, this distribution center has been compromised. Have to move them out now."

"With the vehicles I saw outside?"

"You're right, we're under capacity. Have an alternate site for the overflow until another group can distribute them."

A man about his age with short, curly, sandy hair and hazel eyes approached. He reached past the larger packages to a smaller one, opening it quickly to reveal a slimline Bible with soft brown leather covers. "Here, take it. This is easier to hide when you're on the run." Seeing Warren's hesitation, he extended his hand. "You're on the run, right?"

Warren nodded, speechless.

"I'm Dan. What's your name?"

"Warren." He glanced at the military dude, but he was busy directing the loading of small carts to take to the vehicles.

"Help me then? You have a place to go tonight? Where did you come from?"

"Kentucky and no, not yet. This city let you sleep in the parks?"

"Some areas, but it's not a great idea." He gestured for Warren to follow him as he pushed a full cart to the door.

The lookout indicated the coast was clear, and they brought the boxes to a van. A driver jumped out and helped them load the boxes into the cargo area.

"Don't forget to leave room for me and Warren."

The man nodded without argument.

The group loaded more than half of the boxes. Three larger SUVs arrived. Lastly, an older man with a pickup oversaw the loading of the rest of the Bibles in his truck.

When others nodded for him to hop into the back of the cab, Warren jogged to the open door. He noticed Dan followed close behind him. The man nodded when he asked, "Change of plans?"

They drove to an office park across town. The driver began to back up to a lower service door. He turned his head to talk to the younger man in the front passenger seat. "Something's off." He threw the truck into gear.

"Getting that feeling again, Uncle?" the passenger said with a laugh.

"Don't knock it, buster." He looked at his passengers in the back bench. "Have more important cargo to worry about now. You that Dr. Dan we heard about?"

"Yes, but you can call me Dan." He glanced at Warren. "Old Testament languages doctorate—not a medical doctor."

Warren nodded, knowing better than to ask questions when they passed the interstate on-ramp and turned on to a dark two-lane county highway. He considered warning Dan to stay out of sight of the traffic cameras, but there seemed to be few of them. His respect for the group rose a notch.

They turned right onto another highway before turning onto a narrow back road. Warren felt the last of the sun's rays heat up the window on his left. Heading north the driver turned onto a dirt drive. The rough circular area bounded by a few trees sported a small, worn ranch, some small outbuildings and a large steel barn.

"Gomer," the driver said, "Open 'er up."

The passenger headed for the large double doors, swinging the left one to the side. He followed the truck in and closed the door.

"Home, sweet home," the driver said, glancing at them in the rearview mirror. "Not much, but close to Texas, if you get my drift."

Warren didn't, but he nodded just the same.

"We unloading, Uncle?"

"Let's check in." The driver turned and looked at Warren and Dan. "We'll get a bite to eat while I check the lay of the land. Name's Sam. I didn't get yours."

"Warren." He and Dan followed their hosts out a side door to the house. Crickets chirped in the heat. He thought he heard a coyote. The screen door squealed with complaints when Gomer thrust it open, and they filed into a small square kitchen.

"Take a seat," the driver invited and pulled out a worn chair near the wall. "Gomer's my nephew. Comes by to help sometimes." The nephew nodded, standing in front of the door. "You're not from around here, are ya?"

"Back east."

"Have a last name?"

"Bells. Used to live in Pittsburgh but been traveling around."

"Why?"

"Well, that Task Force is after me. Listen, Sam, don't want to cause trouble, but I need to find a quiet place to lay low. Thought Oklahoma City, being a religious town, would be a good place. Things heating up?"

"How'd you get here? To the city, I mean."

"Became a Christian when I was in Pittsburgh, but it's a bad time to convert. Things got hot, and I ended up in Louisville, but the Task Force was there too. They rounded us up." He kept the two men in view—Sam in front now leaning on the counter near a sink and Gomer to his left. Warren perched on the edge of a worn kitchen chair, ready for any sign they didn't believe his story.

"Wait…they nabbed you?"

"Yeah, took my ID and put me in a room. There was a distraction, and several of us scattered. I managed to retrieve my bags. Bought a small bike, but it died just outside of Oklahoma City. They said I could hook up with Christians here. Did something happen?"

"You could say that. Why should St. Peter let you through the pearly gates?"

"That's a verse?" A glance at Dr. Dan caught him trying to hide a leering smile. "Didn't Jesus say He is the door and the only way to God? He saved me—not the apostle Peter."

Sam reached under the sink and began to play with a sawed-off shotgun. Warren measured the distance between the door, Gomer and his chair. *I could make it if pushed.*

"We're in the foothills—nowhere to go." Sam stroked the weathered stock. "Rattlers, coyotes, and puma make it hard to travel around here. Old Betsey's been in the family for three generations now." He tipped the gun just past Warren's right shoulder. "Would you shoot a man to save your life?"

He looked between the three.

"Pa, you're scaring the guests again."

Sam leveled his gaze at Warren. His was no idle question.

"I've never shot a man. Don't intend to, don't want to, but if…" He looked between them. Praying, he heard himself say, "To protect the girls, like the ones I followed to the warehouse or ladies with kids, but if it's a choice between shooting one of those agents and sending him to hell or letting him shoot me, I guess I'd have to let him shoot me."

"Good answer." Sam smiled and put away the gun. He nodded at Gomer. "Show them. Dr. Dan, you see the Rosemont video? I don't know, but if I had a choice, I'd rather they shoot me dead than send me to that place."

"Rosemont." Gomer navigated to a video file and stepped back.

Warren leaned closer, his breath froze, seeing the tattered Rosemont sign and a few clips of the buildings. A guard he didn't recognize narrated the scenes, stepping through the rooms, the yellow house and the pit. The video documented the cruelty as well as the faith of the inmates as they sang and laid their brothers to rest. He noticed Dan's pale face.

"Unless you're willing to compromise, and many do, I hear they'll send you to a place like that."

"How is this happening in America?" Dan asked.

"Son, our country's been approaching these days one step at a time. Remember 2015 when those journalists uncovered abortion clinics selling baby body parts to research labs? Did anything change or did America just shrug its shoulders and go on with their day?"

"I don't think our people know about this." Warren's mind ran through the possibilities. *Is Tom Hutton spreading this video? How did it get out? Has Kincaid seen it?*

"Pa, why don't folks know about this?" Gomer asked.

"They shut down the reporters," Warren said. "You never see any news about the churches that have been shut down or the pastors jailed or their wives shot—something I will never forget seeing. Pastor Riles talked to me about God while I was putting a new roof on his house. God used him to help me know about Christ, and now the pastor's gone. Thought it was just some crazy local police, but then I found out about the Task Force. Hid out for a while in Kentucky, but they were there too."

"That's your problem, sticking with the big cities. They hit them first. Keep to the small towns. Here, the sheriff's not about to send any Christian to jail—unless they break the law and I'm talking about public safety laws—not those faith laws."

Warren turned when Gomer pulled out a pound of bacon and a dozen eggs. "Hungry?"

"I could eat."

"Gomer's a good egg chef. I cook the roasts. We eat simple around here."

"Sounds good."

They ate leisurely—as if the threat of imprisonment or death did not exist. Warren found himself relaxing and laughing at their jokes. They shared their stories and brought out a family Bible. Sam read from Romans 12. Dan nodded.

"We are called to love our enemies. Never forget, it's against the hosts of wickedness we battle, not flesh and blood." Seeing Warren's quizzical look, "You not learn that yet?"

"Didn't have time."

Sam and Gomer explained Ephesians 6. Reading from Isaiah to Ezekiel to Matthew and Revelation, Dan told the story of how Lucifer, God's most beautiful angel, became Satan.

"That's the long war against God?" Warren listened to Dan's answer, reciting verse after verse.

He heard Gomer go into another room to make a call. Gomer returned. "That's Sirl. Need to bring them to the farm so he can be on his way."

"They'll never find him here."

"Well, Sirl says things have changed."

They disappeared into the room and emerged moments later. The lines around Gomer's eyes were pinched tight. "Get ready to leave now."

Gomer hefted Dan's first backpack, swallowing a groan.

"My bookbag," Dan said. He retrieved his two other bags, and they followed Gomer.

Once in the barn, Warren headed for the truck, but Sam said, "No, you'll take the Ram."

He noticed the newer white, full-sized, four-wheel-drive pickup past Sam's. Gomer pulled down the tailgate on the older truck. Sam pulled back the tarp. Warren stepped past him and jumped into the bed. Box by box, they loaded the Hutton Bibles into Gomer's truck and snugged down the tarp.

The two said nothing. Their grave looks told the story.

Sam hugged Gomer tightly. "Keep the faith," he said, releasing his nephew.

CHAPTER 27

GOMER DROVE TO a two-story country house with a large garage and red barn. Several cars filled the circular drive, so he
parked on the grass near the barn. "Take your stuff. I'm just your taxi."

"Thanks." Warren collected his bags. Short steps led to a large
kitchen with a rectangular butcher-block table in the center. An aroma
of strong coffee saturated the room.

"I'm Sirl. Help yourself," a wiry man with dark hair said, nodding
to the coffeepot on the counter next to a rack of mugs. He stepped
past to talk to Gomer. The men talked, hugged, and Gomer stepped
through the door. Their new host tipped his head, touching the brim
of his dark brown Stetson.

"We drink it black around here," he said, glancing at Dan and Warren.

"So do I." Warren looked about, hefting his pack and duffel.

"Follow me," Sirl gestured for Warren to leave his bags near a wall
and led him around a corner to a small office. "Take a seat." He headed
out the door and returned with two mugs of coffee. "Sit a spell."

Warren sat down on a worn wooden chair by the door.

Sirl settled down on a worn reclining office chair. "Well," he leaned
forward, "we have a situation and hear you do too."

"You could say that."

"You escaped? How'd that happen?"

"Not sure who, but when a group overpowered the Task Force
agents, I ran."

"My Kentucky contacts were surprised you made it to the city. Thought you'd been shot."

"Must have seen the guy right behind me go down." Tempted to spin a story, he held back, uncertain of the details of the raid.

Sirl nodded. "Did you see the Rosemont video?"

"Sam showed me. It's what I'd heard, but hard to believe. Now I'm really glad I ran. Thought things would be better here."

"District Task Force headquarters are in OK City. The director's pretty effective." He leaned forward, "What do you think of the new laws?"

"Now that I believe in Jesus and understand the Bible is the Word of God, they're atrocious. Do they have a pit like Rosemont's near Oklahoma City?"

"No, their in-town office complex is standard for law enforcement—training, squad rooms, equipment. Their prisons are housed out a-ways from here." He shifted. "Even acquired a cremation chamber from a funeral home."

Warren sucked in his breath. "They don't cremate the pastors alive, do they? Use drugs?"

"Bullets are cheaper."

He looked aside. "Once they get rid of the resistant pastors, things will quiet down, right?"

"Not likely."

"Well, once a guy serves his time, he can go back, right?"

"They never stop watching him. Give them quotas."

"Quotas?"

"Successful graduates have to submit ten names a month to their community sponsors." The room fell silent. Sirl sighed. "I hear you met Daniel in the city. He's a biblical languages professor—not the kind an upstanding university would hire these days. Get my drift?" Seeing Warren's nod, he continued, "Need to keep him safe, but he's the academic type and wouldn't last a week on his own while he waits for a spot to open up."

"Spot?"

Sirl leaned forward. "They can only get a small number out of the country at a time. Have to be careful. Believe it. It's happening. We can't risk losing Bible scholars like Daniel."

"Agreed. What do you need?"

"A babysitter. He can read the Bible in Greek and Hebrew, has most of it memorized, but in the real world, he can be quite naive." Seeing Warren's nod, he continued, "Let me be clear. This could take months. You been out west before?"

"Never."

"Well, both of you will have your times of doing stupid things."

"Probably." Warren rubbed his left arm and covered his forearm with his hand.

"Rough you up?"

"Could say that."

Sirl stood and gestured to the kitchen. "We're close to the border with Texas. So far, they haven't been able to infiltrate the Rangers. May God continue to provide shelter."

Warren followed his host back to the kitchen. A small group sat at the table, listening to Dan.

Dan looked over. "We leave tomorrow?"

"Tonight."

"Tonight's op compromised?" Warren asked, regretting his choice of words the moment he said them. "I mean, did a team take out any of the others who had Bibles?"

"Almost. Too close this time."

"What do they do with the Bibles if they find them?" Warren asked.

"They burn them."

Warren said, "I thought they went to recycling centers."

Everyone looked at him and laughed. The woman he assumed was the wife said, "What do you think happened to the Bibles sent to most recycling centers?"

"They were sent to pulp-processing facilities?" Warren guessed.

"Wrong! For the most part, this country has not accepted these laws. Many were smuggled out and recycled to the community—for reuse!" She smiled.

Sirl interrupted, "Listen, they have to get on the road now." He looked at Dan, "Get your stuff." He looked at Warren, "You have a driver's license?"

"No, got away with my life intact, but without ID."

"I still have mine," Dan said. "I can drive but don't have a car."

"Follow us."

"Wait up," the wife said. She nodded at the teen. "Get the red backpack."

"Mom!"

"It's your old one from last year. Get over it." She reached for it when the teen returned and thrust it open. "Fill it with water bottles and food."

Sirl pulled out a box and began to sift through the items. He handed over breakfast bars, boxes of raisins, packs of beef jerky and some dark MREs."

"Honey, those military meals are ancient. I should have thrown them out."

"Not a problem, ma'am," Warren said, stuffing them in the pack. "Protein's the same to the body—no matter how bad the spicing." He winked and laughed, trying to lighten the mood.

Sirl closed it up and pushed it aside. The teen flopped a worn road atlas and Texas road map on the table. "You're heading for a ranch in Texas." He looked at his dad. "Take the back roads?"

Sirl traced the county roads from Oklahoma to Texas and switched to a detailed map of Northern Texas. "They'll get lost on the smaller roads." The host tapped a route. "This will do. You'll have no problems passing through the village of Miami. Once you're on North River Road, after the bend with Pats Creek Road, it's a little less than five miles to your turn off. If you cross Johns Creek, you've missed it. Take the first drive on your right. It's an old station with bunkhouse and barn. When they gather the cattle, do the branding and sorting, they set up there, but that only happens a few times a year, so you should have the place to yourself." He slid a small paper to Dan. "That's the combination for the door keypad."

They crossed the gravel drive to a large barn. An older blue Chevy pickup was right inside the large double doors. "Saddle up. Time to go." He pulled out two baseball caps. "Wear these hats." He removed his cowboy hat and pulled a cap low over his forehead. "Better to be safe. Miami's not big, but they do have a few cameras."

"No cowboy hats?" Warren laughed. "Just jokes." He put on a cap and pulled it low on his forehead. Looking at Dan, he said, "For those pesky traffic cameras."

"Best not to stop. She's full up. Shouldn't take you more than two and a half hours."

"Can't miss it?" Warren asked, grinning.

Sirl didn't crack a smile. "Pray the guys hunting you won't think to look on the open range."

Warren paused behind the truck next to Sirl. "Sam going to be okay?"

The man shrugged. "Pray for him. They must have snapped a picture of his tag at the office complex."

He hesitated to ask about Gomer's precious cargo. At least this group seemed to be one step ahead. Warren almost found himself praying. Shrugging off that inclination, he climbed into the truck.

Sirl strode to the barn door and pushed it open. "Safe travels," he said, tipping his hat as Dan drove by.

CHAPTER 28

THE NIGHT, DARK as silk, hovered close, just past the edges of the truck's headlights. The road ran straight with slight curves and rises. Warren felt more than saw trees here and there several feet from the road. He longed to see, having caught a glimpse of the vast plains on his drive to Sam's, but darkness shrouded the land.

Warren glanced at Dan, quiet, eyes front, both hands on the wheel. "We're on this road for a while." Not hearing a reply, he added, "Looking for 748 next."

"You're the navigator. I'm just driving." Dan tightened his grip.

"How long have you been on the run?"

"Too long." Getting a feel for the open road, he sat back, shifted, and rested his left arm on the door panel. "It's been a long time since I first heard of these laws. Didn't think much of it. Had just finished my last doctorate and was settling into a new seminary—new for me, anyway." He glanced at Warren. "Not a bad college, but it was small. Would have been good—lined up to teach Hebrew grammar, Old Testament theology, the Pentateuch…" His voice faded away. "Anyway, the Board was nervous, and they closed. I found one that looked like a good prospect. Worked for a while, but then they were forced to cooperate to stay open."

He tried not to shudder, remembering the meeting. "Called us in on a Saturday—never a good sign. The dean stood up and explained the law before trying to rationalize the justifications for all of us coming on board."

"Did the arguments sound valid?" Warren recalled what he had heard at Mount Vernon.

"Superficially, but it was essentially general phrases, couched with innocuous sentiments of acceptance, painting a picture of love for all carried on the winds of censorship. I tried to guess what my colleagues were thinking, but no one publicly denounced it. Thankfully, we weren't forced to make a decision that day."

"Here we go. The next route. Take a right." Warren squinted to try to distinguish between private dirt drives and their next county road. "This one." The road was a little narrower but just as straight as the previous highway.

Dan said nothing. Warren, deep in his thoughts, watched the sparse traffic of pickups, semis, and various vehicles hauling cattle trailers. Despite his circumstances, he felt his pulse quickening in anticipation. Fewer buildings and trees could be seen. Every so often, he spied the outlines of fencing—mostly wire, and some with what looked like branches between wooden posts.

He shifted feeling the truck slow a little. "Slower speed limits. Must be a town."

Warren shook his head to stay alert. "Miami," he said and pulled the cap lower on his head. Seeing Dan gripped the steering wheel with both hands, he pulled down the visor. "Can you still see?"

"Yes," Dan nervously wet his lips. "Good idea," he said, strictly observing the speed limit.

Warren eyed the quiet town. It was late—almost midnight. They breathed easier when through the village and back to highway speeds. They had to stay awake.

"Tell me about yourself."

Warren began his usual cover story.

"Sorry, I should have framed the question differently. How did you find Jesus Christ? Did it start with that first pastor who shared the gospel while you replaced his roof?"

"Well," he searched for a viable storyline, trying to keep it as close to the truth as possible. "Worked for a Pittsburgh contractor—framing, roofs, whatever jobs he had. Tried to run my own company, but it's harder than it sounds. Hard to admit I lacked the discipline. Well, I was in a low spot, feeling empty. Religion was never important in my family, and we had drifted apart. Dad's current wife hated my guts."

"Did you marry?"

"Naw, saw his problems. Figured it wasn't worth the hassle. Divorce is nasty." An idea formed. "That pastor had a loving wife. They maybe had a few mild disagreements but were never mean. She brought me iced tea. He checked on me to make sure I was okay. When I had to work late to finish up, she fixed a sandwich. And he just talked, like normal people—no fire and brimstone. Felt safe enough to start asking about our purpose in life."

"You just now on the run?"

"Oh, well, he lived out a-ways. Could tell his church was dealing with some issues. They were meeting in his barn but didn't say much about it. Didn't get an inkling of what they were up against until I began to attend some services. They always met on his property. Had Bibles." Warren shook his head, trying to recall the details of the hit in the Task Force database. "They arrested the pastor and his wife quietly. Everything looked fine. People showed up for service. I was late and had just pulled into the drive when one of them had a chance to text a warning. I backed out, stopped by an ATM to get cash and hit the road. I texted someone else I knew who believed, and they gave me the name of a congregation right outside of Louisville. They were more careful, but in time, they were hit too, and I wasn't so lucky."

He shook his head. "Took out the leadership. Shot some. Loaded us into the back of cargo vans with blackened windows. The pole barn they took us to had large chain-link fence cages. We sat for a while. That night a raid took out the two guards. I managed to grab my backpack and duffel—but couldn't find my ID."

"So, no more ATM withdrawals."

"That's long gone. Never a great one for savings."

"So, you read the Bible?"

"Some, but it's hard to understand. Things don't seem to add up at times. The pastor assured me it all agrees, but with so many authors from different backgrounds over hundreds of years. How is that possible?"

"God is the Author. Revelation from God grew over the centuries, but since it has a singular focus—revealing God's plan for the ages, it all agrees. Many of the truths are developed over time. In other words, key doctrines, hinted at in the earlier books, are more fully explained or elucidated in later ones. Many see the New Testament as the Old Testament revealed. What do you think is the one message of the Bible?"

"God loves us?"

"Who is the Bible about?"

"God finding man?"

Dan didn't say he was wrong, but he glanced over. "It is about the greatest rescue plan in the world—God reaching down to save sinners, but that is not its main purpose. It says in Revelation, *'For the testimony of Jesus is the spirit of prophecy.'*[19] The Bible is the record of God's creating man and delivering him from the bondage of sin for God's glory and honor." Dan asked, "What is man's purpose?"

He figured spouting the usual stock answer of finding Jesus or getting saved wouldn't be enough. It was more than that. It was before that. From a distant memory, he said, "To glorify God." Then he added, "To obey God and today that means obeying the commands of Christ, which is to…" He looked away and wiped his eye.

"Exactly. It's all about God and not us. Our little lives are so small and if we don't look far enough to God's bigger picture, we can get caught up in the chaos, the hardships…" Dan's voice faded. "I have to remind myself every day that He's still in control. He knows what He's doing." He glanced over. "I should be happy that He doesn't show us the future. I'd never get out of bed."

"You from a Christian family?"

"Yep. Some of my best friends in Bible college weren't so sheltered. At times I almost envied their stories—growing up in the world, overcoming difficulties and sin to find the Savior. I was saved when I was four—never doubted, well, mostly didn't. My faith was, for the most part, untested. It's been an education and not the kind I usually sign up for."

"What happened to your church?"

"My church? Oh, I'm not a pastor. Never wanted to be. Dealing with people's not my strong point."

"Really? Isn't that what it's all about?"

"My calling is to teach the pastors. Help them rightly divide the word of truth. Had a great uncle who was a professor. Thought that was my destiny until the laws took out the good seminaries." He stopped, not voicing how alien he felt in his own country.

"I've heard many say, 'When this blows over....' What do they think's going to stop it?"

"God. I know that sounds trite, but we are praying we'll get through this and things will be back to normal."

"Can we go back?"

"Probably not." Dan smiled. "But we are anticipating God is using this to transform the church." He glanced at Warren. "Many are praying for revival. This is how a holy God works through sufferings to create something new, something better."

"Have a family, a girlfriend?"

"No. Seems to make it easier, but lonelier, if that makes any sense."

Warren nodded. "I do." Unbidden memories rose up of Chris' warm embrace at the D.C. hotel just yesterday. His mind spinning, he studied the road. "Can't lose track, not out here. Here's our next turn."

Daniel nodded, the tires humming on the pavement. "So, back to what the Bible is all about—seeing God's plan for the ages, and He works long-term."

"Over centuries."

"Millennium. Start with Genesis."

"That pastor told me not to start with Genesis."

"That's what you tell a new believer—someone who found Christ last week or last month. But you already have a grasp of basic biblical concepts. In the gospels Christ came and offered the kingdom to the Jews, but they had to accept Him. They didn't, as we all know. The pivotal point is…" he paused.

"Isaiah 53, that's part of it, right?"

"Exactly. Christ came to die for the sins of all mankind from Adam to the last man—for all people for all time."

"So why aren't all men saved? Why do we have to ask for it?"

"God wants us to love Him of our own free will. He wants us to ask for the gift. A gift rejected is never received. Those who die saying no to God die in their sins and will experience the second death."

"Hell?"

"Yes."

"Even the good ones?"

"Romans 3 says, 'All have sinned and come short. There are none good; not one righteous; no one seeks after God;'[20] no one can earn his way to heaven."

"The pastor told me God didn't expect me to know it all up front. I just had to…" his voice caught, amazed at the things he just said. "I just have to trust." He wet his lips. "What am I looking for?"

"Read the Bible through quickly, beginning in Genesis to see the storyline of God's rescue plan for mankind. Sections can drag you down with genealogies or rituals. You can skim over those. Right in Genesis 3 God promised to bring a Savior to deliver mankind. Job trusted in a redeemer. Threads, hints, promises have been woven throughout the Old Testament."

Warren let Dan talk. He continued on, as if he were lecturing a class on the story of the greatest book in the world, amazed, enchanted and jealous that Dan could believe.

"Here's Route 70 coming up. We go right for five miles." He listened to Dan read the mileage. They became silent, drawing close to their hiding place.

"It feels desolate," Dan said. "I don't think I'll ever get used to this. I like routine—the same place for my books, my notes."

"Things will never be the same for me, but for you," Warren looked over. He found himself saying, "For you, if these laws eventually are overturned, you can teach again."

"What I pray for." Dan glanced at the odometer. "Four miles to go. Seminary was my hiding place. I could live in the passages of the great prophets—Isaiah, Jeremiah, Habakkuk. But I think I'm learning things I would have never discovered in the classroom."

Warren couldn't risk contemplating his future. *Not right now.* He almost said he would pray for each of them, but that would be another lie. He already had to tell too many. The truck slowed imperceptibly with the appearance of guardrails.

"Well, there is a sign. What do you know?"

Dan slowed the truck for the sharp turn. "Gravel."

"Our first dirt road."

They felt the vast emptiness. Dan tried to keep it up to 55 miles an hour, but pebbles hit the undercarriage, the rear wheels skidded in the soft spots, and he found himself easing up on the gas.

"It's okay. Drive where you're comfortable."

Dan stayed on North River as it curved to the left. "We're close."

They now rode in silence. Dan worked to stay on the road and avoid potholes. Just when they felt they were driving to the edge of the world, a fifth-wheel pickup drove by hauling a long trailer or a jeep zipped along the path barely wide enough for two. Each time Dan slowed down. They made their last turn.

"It's the first drive on our right."

The gravel drive led directly to a cluster of buildings: a bunkhouse, shed, and a small stable close to some corrals, a loading chute, and a large swinging gate. Rows of barbed-wire fencing stretched out into the darkness.

"Even though it's rarely used, we should be ready to go anytime," Warren said. He followed Dan to the main door in the center of the building's side. Painted logs, with mortar chinked between the logs, ran on either side. Dan pulled back the screen door, entered the combination and they stepped through.

The right half had six low beds with bedding neatly wrapped at the head of each one with a small kitchen area on the left next to a bathroom. A lower counter jutting out close to the door seemed to be the lone desk.

"Let's move in." He spun on his heels and retrieved his luggage.

Dan inspected the kitchen and small fridge. "Coffee, ketchup. No bread. We have some shopping to do."

Warren heard the comments as he entered with his bags and placed them on the closest bunk on the back wall. "Take the one by me or the next one." He didn't wait to see if Dan had heard or would listen. "I need the keys to park the truck."

"It's fine."

"It's in plain sight." He held out his hand. Dan did not reply but grudgingly dug out the keys with an irritated expression.

Warren stood in the shadows of the bunkhouse, surveying the floodlit area between the buildings. With no trees or bushes to obscure their truck from the road, he turned his attention to the wide sliding door of the stable. He walked over and pushed it aside. The aisle between the stalls appeared wide enough.

Warren backed the truck into the aisle with ease and carefully closed the door.

He worked at keeping his face straight, and his voice calm when he walked into the bunkhouse. "I said you can bunk by me or the one over, but don't bunk on the door side. I can't protect you if they reach you first."

Dan refused to look at him but moved his packs to the one next to Warren's and began to make the bed.

"Forget the bedding. Use the sleeping bags they gave us."

He set his bedding unopened on the floor. "Let's get this straight: even if they say we will be here a month, we don't move in, and keep everything packed, ready to go. If something happens and we need to move out, we need to be gone…" He snapped his fingers. "at a moment's notice." Warren's eyes took in the pile of books and laptop on the desk; mugs, tea bags and coffee canister on the counter; and maps on the bunk near the door. The guy had covered half the surfaces in the time it took him to hide the truck. "Pack your office and kitchen. Unpack what you need only when you need it and put it away when you're done."

Dan looked at him with bleary eyes, knitting his brows together. With a muscle jumping in his jaw, he replaced his items in his bags, pulled out his toothbrush and headed for the bathroom, slamming the door shut.

Warren sighed. After considering his options, he brushed his teeth at the sink and sat on his sleeping bag.

Dan emerged, avoiding eye contact and put his toiletries bag in his pack, muttering under his breath. "You get the light?" He looked over, suppressed rage in his eyes. "Pajamas?"

"If you're willing to run in them. It's up to you. Underwear works. I know it's hard."

"You think? Been moving from place to place for a year now. It's getting old."

"Did they say how long we might be here?"

"My next meeting is in two weeks."

"Meeting? I thought you were in hiding."

"I am, but different fellowships offer housing, shelter and I get a chance to teach, or preach, whatever they call it—minister the word." Dan glanced at his laptop and notebook poking out from the hastily stuffed backpack, missing an office where he could uncover the development of doctrines as the Lord provided clues through the ages. Each time he settled, it grew harder to focus, harder to pick up the thread and advance a line of inquiry.

He thought that was what God had called him to do. He thought that would be his life's work, and he couldn't accomplish it—not like this, not on the run.

Warren perceived Dan's despair and discouragement. The only thing he could think of saying was an awkward—*this is only temporary. Is that as naïve and baseless a wish as the seemingly futile prayers for this to be over?*

Dan slipped into the sleeping bag. Warren stepped across the room and turned out the main light and the one by the sink. The yard floodlight bathed the bunkhouse with a dim light.

"Leave the floods on?"

"Leave them on or it will look suspicious." *Probably very little traffic on this side dirt road, but that also means there were few roads.*

"Like when we backpack—pack out what you pack in."

"Yes," Warren slipped his feet into the bag, waiting for his body to cool down enough to sleep.

Dan stared at the ceiling without focusing. Warren's breathing settled into a soft rhythm. *How do I do this, Lord?* Dan almost gave into complaining that this was not what he had signed up for, but the decision to choose salvation included surrendering his life. His grandfather had laid out the exchange; he gave up his life that he might have eternal life with Christ. He recalled his grandfather saying, "Paul called himself the slave of Christ." His had always seemed an easy decision. While he knew this could be of God, his flesh revolted at the cost.

Show me how to live like this, Lord. He shut his eyes, willing himself to sleep. Praying through the Psalms of ascent, he didn't get to the second one before he found his refuge.

CHAPTER 29

WARREN ENTERED THE bunk house and glanced at Dan. Ten days in, and they hadn't killed each other yet—or walked out. Everything seemed to be a struggle for Dan, but he assumed it was the stress of being on the run. How else could he explain how unchristian-like the man could be?

Done with his morning run, exercises and perimeter sweep, he grabbed his Bible and papers—heading for the stable and a rough desk. Dan had claimed the only viable one in the bunkhouse.

It had taken a little while, but before he knew it, he had worked through the earlier books. Dan hadn't been exaggerating about God's plan. Despite the warnings he had noticed in the last chapters of Joshua, Warren was surprised to read of the depth of the Israelite's betrayal of the God who had set them free. They didn't last one generation past Joshua's before they turned against Him. The utter destruction of the binding chains of sin could not be denied.

His mind argued back and forth. *God was good; people were bad. Why did God allow this? But what of free will? What of the faithful?* Warren slipped the papers into the Bible with no notes for the day except many questions. It was almost time for Dan to make his second pot of coffee.

He left the stable door open and stretched in the sunshine, peering along the rolling plains, seeing few marks of mankind or their attempts at civilization. He hefted the Bible. Even the Israelites couldn't do it right. A distant sound tinged his ears. He looked over his left shoulder and saw in the distance the dust trail of three large vehicles, two towing long trailers.

Warren closed the stable door and ran to the bunkhouse. He shut off the lights. "Pack! Pack now!" Not waiting for Dan's usual resistance, he put the Bible in his pack and slung it over his shoulder. "Company's coming, and there's a lot of them. If we can get to the truck and head to the road while they're in the hollow, we can drive by, and they won't know we were here."

Dan poked his nose out the door. Warren swallowed his groan when he heard Dan say, "Too late. They already turned our way."

"Pack! Let's hope they're driving past and not headed here." It would be impossible to hide if they came to this station. "If they do come, we politely make our exit."

The lead truck skidded to a halt in front of the bunkhouse, and a young man wearing leg chaps with spurs on his pointed boots exited the vehicle and walked into the bunkhouse. He froze when he caught sight of Dan packing his bags.

"Hello," Warren said calmly. "Fellow said we could bunk here, but we…" About to take a step, he gathered himself when the cowboy drew a 9mm Glock.

"Now," he held up one hand, palm forward, "Our friend gave us…"

The kid backed up, opened the door and yelled, "Squatters!"

In the instant he looked over his shoulder toward the yard, Warren, not far from the counter and the kid's blind side, closed the distance, simultaneously thrust out his knee to buckle the left leg and gained control of the man's right arm. With a twist, he forced the kid to drop the gun. "Get it!" Warren glanced at Dan. "Pick up the gun and hand it to me."

Old habits die hard, but he resisted the urge to flip the man onto his chest and secure his arms behind him. Instead, he pushed him down on the closest bunk. Once he had the gun, he held the kid firmly with his other hand.

About to point out the evidence they had an invite, he did the only thing he could do when the crew began to assemble. He yanked the kid to his feet. "No need to worry." He flicked his eyes to Dan. "Get in the truck. Now!"

Carefully, he pushed the kid in front of him and out into the yard. The crew of five stepped back. "Just let us pass, and we'll be on our way." Warren watched four of them look at a well-weathered man in his mid-forties.

"Let him by. If he wanted to make trouble, it would have been done already."

Warren nodded, pushed the kid toward the group, dropped the pistol's magazine and ejected the chambered round. "Maybe you're a little too trigger happy to keep one in the chamber." He collected his bags from Dan, and they strode to the truck. One of the ranch hands had pulled back the stable door.

Warren paused by the senior cowboy and handed him the gun and magazine. "We had the key code. Sorry for the inconvenience. We'll be on our way." He resisted a smile when the man nodded in understanding.

Dan drove out, his eyes wide as saucers. They turned onto North River and headed south on 70 to Pampa, the nearest town. "I think I get it." His hand began to shake.

"Pull over."

"But…"

"They're not going to check my ID out here. You can drive when your nerves settle down. You did good."

"He pulled a gun on us!"

"He's a fool. Bet that other guy's the real cow boss." He looked at Dan. "Dig out your phone and let your contact know we need another place but use code words. They give you code words?"

Dan's hands shook so badly he couldn't enter the password for his cell phone. He nearly tossed the phone in the air when it rang. "No," he breathed a little easier when he recognized the number. "Hello? Yes,

we're on 70 heading to Pampa." He paused, "Uh-huh, heading south."
Dan nodded. "Sure, we can do that."

"Well?"

"Turn around. We go north on 70. He gave directions for the big
house. That's what they call it." He shook his head. "How did he know?"

"I imagine our friend called him." *That was too close.* Thankfully,
the cowboys did not look like former law enforcement, especially not
the twenty-something.

Almost two hours later, Dan pointed to the ranch sign. "3-B Ranch.
That's it."

The paved drive curved and crossed a small dry gulch. In the distance he saw an irrigated lawn with four buildings. A large wood stable
with corral and fencing sat on the right. The barns and fences did not
have the look of new construction like those on the left. On a rise overlooking the area rose a sprawling mini-mansion with high windows
and a circular drive in front.

Warren parked on the far end closest to the road. Dan led the way
to the front door. A young man in Western casual wear opened the
door. "Dr. Smith and…?"

"Warren Bells," Will said, swallowing the hesitation. He had almost
given his real name. Surprised at his reluctance to lie, he surveyed the
great room with two-story-high vaulted ceilings. Banks of windows
overlooked the rolling plains and escarpments. It took a moment for
him to notice the tall, broad-shouldered man with a turquoise lariat
and alligator cowboy boots. The just-as-tall trim man standing to his
left studied him.

The owner and his security. Warren detected the stance of Secret
Service or former FBI. Before he could stop him, Dan approached the
ranch owner with an outstretched hand. Warren relaxed a little when
the man walked forward to greet him.

"Dr. Smith, sorry for the inconvenience. The ranch manager called
a midsummer gather for extra vaccinations." He surveyed the pair.

"Welcome to my ranch—my hideaway from the world out in the panhandle. I'm Merle Washington and my assistant, Cal Larson."

Warren stood close to Dan's right side, just opposite the bodyguard or head of security.

"Well, we made it here." Dan glanced at Warren and resisted the urge to complain about the incident. "You can call me Dan."

Merle gestured to the doorman. "Sam will show you to the guest house."

Before Warren could follow Dan, Cal pointed to a door on the left. "After you."

Warren tipped his head, but he kept up his vigilance with the man behind him. The expansive wood paneled office with large mahogany desk and built-in bookcases overlooked a plunging escarpment and plains reaching out to the horizon. Forcing himself to ignore the view, he stood in the center of the room.

Merle looked at him for a while before speaking. "Ethan can be excitable."

Warren wondered how the young man was related to Merle—a nephew, perhaps?

"I hear you're a construction worker. How did you disarm him? He's actually a superb marksman."

"He drew first. Didn't ask questions. He failed to notice the lack of forced entry." Warren stopped, regretting his choice of words.

"You in the military?" Cal asked.

Warren nodded. "Did my time in the Army, Military Police." He hadn't been in the military but his uncle had, and he hoped he was familiar enough to allay suspicion. "One tour was enough to convince me to go back to construction. Not as unpredictable."

Merle glanced at Cal, who shrugged his shoulders.

"Well, Warren, it seems we were lucky this time. Ethan needed a summer internship." Merle didn't add any further details.

Warren nodded.

"What's your specialty?"

"Jack of all trades, and master of none. Whatever job I can find." He almost caught himself praying he wouldn't be asked for a demonstration of his skills.

"Well, Cal can take you to the guest house."

Warren resisted the urge to jockey for position and let the security expert take up the position right behind his right shoulder. Cal tested him by approaching and drawing back, but he acted as if he were unaware of the maneuvers behind him. When he pulled the door open to the small building, their eyes met. "Thanks," he said, trying to lighten the atmosphere. The guy was not convinced.

"Take care," he said with a Southeastern accent.

Dan smiled. "Took long enough. What's up?"

"Had more questions about our little incident." He bit back his irritation at Dan's items already strewn across the small living area. "Which is mine?"

"You can take that one." Dan nodded to the bed farthest from the desk but closest to the bathroom. "We head out for a meeting in a few days. Dine with Merle tonight before he leaves." He headed to the kitchen. "We have a fully stocked kitchen." Dan turned. "Do you cook?"

Warren grimaced.

"I guess we'll both learn together. Grab a light lunch and get settled." Dan walked to the desk and turned on his laptop already assembled with all the accessories.

Warren set his duffel on the suitcase caddy, placed his pack by the nightstand, and pulled out his Bible. Beyond the kitchen area and the detailed mahogany desk facing a bank of windows, a love seat and two padded dark leather chairs trimmed in dark wood formed a semi-circle facing the view. Dan was already into his latest Bible investigation. Warren found iced tea in the fridge and made a sandwich. He sat in the farthest padded chair. The Bible opened to Judges, and Warren recalled his questions interrupted by the incident.

"Have a question?" Dan asked.

"I do, but it might be more than one." He smoothed out the pages, glancing again at the descriptions of failures throughout the book. "On second thought, I'll write them down for you. Today's probably not the best day."

"You in Judges?" Seeing the nod, he added, "It's a mess. You'd think they would have done better, but they had the law without the Holy Spirit to help keep it. Check out Jeremiah 31:31-34 and let me know what you think."

Warren was tired, irritated, and concerned. He caught Dan studying him while he turned to Jeremiah without referencing the table of contents. "31?"

"31:31-34. It's the new covenant that Christ referred to at His last supper in the gospels."

He read and re-read the five verses. It was English. He could make some sense of it, but not really. Warren ate his sandwich and drank the tea. *What had Chris said? That the Holy Spirit helps believers understand this book? Hopeless.*

Warren walked out of the guesthouse and followed a path that led to the edge of the rise. Even in the browns of summer's dryness he marveled at the shades that curved and bent with the land. Tall grasses blown over created a soft carpet. The constant wind rustling the standing grasses blended with the crickets. Warren drank in the vast sky reaching beyond the horizon, the rolling hills giving way to taller mounds in the distance. Space stretched out before him.

Warren turned his head when he heard leather soles slapping the walk. Cal was not a quiet stalker.

"Perimeter's on a security system." He nodded to the notices on the posts at the edge of the lawn.

"Active now?"

"Depends. Come on, I'll show you the stables and indoor arena. By the way, the regular cowboys put up with Ethan."

Warren looked about the circular front drive, graveled lot in front of the stable. Cameras were ever-present. "They recording?"

"Mostly." He headed across the drive.

Warren kept pace. "That Glock usual cowboy issue?"

"Rarely, and Glocks would be their last choice." Cal shook his head. "They prefer rifles for shooting snakes or other vermin."

The barn and accompanying buildings, worn and weathered, stood against the sky. The large barn door appeared to be permanently open, with straggly weeds crowding the slide rails. Warren peered into the darker interior of the stable's center aisle. He could make out horses tied on either side and detected two figures moving around them.

"The horse wrangler's responsible for keeping a good herd for handling livestock. Most of the horses are in the back corrals, but the boss also keeps some of his own show horses here along with those needing special attention."

"Does he train them too?"

Cal shrugged. "Just the ranch mounts. Supposedly the show trainer's responsible for Mr. Washington's stock, but he spends most of his time on the road. Boss's daughter is doing the rodeo circuit right now."

"Rodeo?"

"Yeah, she's a top barrel racer. That doesn't happen without investments in the right horses and trainer."

Warren followed Cal past the first horse.

"Hey, Giles, I'd like you to meet Warren. He and Dan will be at the guest house for a while," Cal said. The short, bowlegged cowboy with graying hair and scruffy face barely looked at Warren.

Being pro-active, Warren stepped past Cal and extended his hand. "Warren Bells, nice to meet you. Can you show me what you have going here?"

"Giles MacGregor." He quietly surveyed the younger man and returned the firm handshake. "From back East? We tip our hats more than shake hands on the Panhandle."

"Thanks. I'll keep that in mind." He glanced at Cal. "Mind if I hang around here for a while? I think I can find my way back home."

"Sure." Cal tipped his head at Giles and left.

"It's cooler here than outside—air conditioned?"

"No, good barn design." Giles explained. The bay standing near him turned his head to muzzle the wrangler. He gently stroked the head. "This one is young and green broke. That big one needs to re-learn his manners." He whistled and the farmhand looked his way. "Len, show him how to tack Tiny."

Warren followed Len to a large room with rows upon rows of saddles and pegs with bridles, halters and long lines. They returned with the gear. Giles kept up a running monologue as he tacked the bay. Warren watched the stablehand mirror the trainer's movements.

"Now out West we don't walk our horses. We ride them. Follow us to the arena."

Warren closed the gate to the nearby steel building and walked behind the short wall in front of a set of bleachers and open area. He watched them put the horses through their paces.

Eventually they brought the two horses to a stop, and the men talked quietly. The stablehand looked at him, and Giles smiled for the first time. "You ever ride?"

"No."

"Let's give it a try. Len'll help."

Warren walked up to Tiny—a tall, light-brown horse with a scruffy mane and tattered tail. He lifted his hand to pet him.

"Careful, he likes to nip."

"Thanks for the warning." Warren grasped the side of the bridle to hold him, and he carefully ran his hand along the horse's face as he said, "There, boy, just making friends." He looked at Len. "How do I get on?"

"Not from that side. Always mount on the horse's left side."

He put his foot into the stirrup, grasped the saddle horn and pulled himself up, swinging his leg over.

"Whoa," Len said pulling back on the reins. "You need to grab the reins to keep him from walking away on you."

"Okay," Warren settled himself in the saddle, found the other stirrup and felt the power of the horse beneath him. Following Giles' instructions, the two horses walked around the arena then transitioned to an easy trot. He grasped the horn tightly until he found his balance and let his weight settle.

"Feel heavy in the seat, as if glued to the saddle and relax."

Warren tried to smile, but felt it looked more like a grimace. "This is great. Can we go faster?"

"Sure," It seemed as if the other horse burst into a run. Warren nearly fell back when Tiny did the same, but he hung on, feeling for the rhythm of the canter. Over and over they transitioned through the gaits—walk, trot, and canter.

Warren felt that things were going very well until Giles parked his bay in the center and told him to ride the perimeter. Tiny repeatedly turned to the center, and Warren pulled on the reins to tack him back to the fence.

Giles and Len laughed. Warren smiled, laughed, and forced Tiny to walk close to the perimeter. He managed to get him to trot but couldn't force him to go faster.

"That's enough. Don't want him to learn bad habits. Len, put him through his paces."

Warren watched them work the horses running circles, turning on a dime, breaking into a run, stopping, turning. He listened as Giles described the importance of each movement for cutting calves from the cows and other ranch chores.

Eventually Warren headed back to the guest house, thinking Dan would be wondering where he was. He found Dan, staring fixedly at his laptop.

Dan glanced at him when he walked in. "Clean up," he said. "Almost time to go over for supper."

After Warren emerged from the bathroom, showered and dressed, he looked at Dan to see he was still focused on his studies. Not feeling like reading, he grabbed a soda from the fridge and sat looking out onto the plains. Later, when he was ready, he would ask to go on a trail ride.

Sam tapped on the door. Dan shut down his computer, and they headed for the main house. He led them through the double doors on the right. What looked like cherry collapsible walls separated the dining area on the left from the kitchen.

A dark oak table stretched across the room with a glass chandelier hung over the center. Warren tried not to stare out the bank of windows facing the table. Sunlight began to tip into the room.

"Should I close the shades?"

"Not yet," Warren found himself saying. He came to himself and looked at the five places set at the end of the table. Stepping back, he gestured for Dan to take the far seat closest to the wall. He stood by the next one.

"Suit yourself. But about this time, it can flood the room. Close them when you're ready. Mr. Washington will be here shortly."

They settled in the slightly padded wood chairs. The dark wood high-back had scrolling that matched the elegant table pedestal and routed table edging. Warren studied the plains.

"Hey, you in there?" Dan asked. "Your Judges questions?"

"Here? Well," he tried to sort through the morass within. "Why didn't it work? They said they wanted to follow God. He told them how to do it, but they failed."

"How many people do you know can keep rules perfectly or even want to try?"

"Good point," he said, recalling his problems trying to run the investigations unit. "Most look for ways to circumvent the rules." He added with a laugh. "And those who do try are often mocked, ridiculed or despised."

"Exactly—proof we are all sinners."

"So, religion doesn't work?" He looked over. "How many Christians really live like God matters in their lives?"

"Good point." Dan stared at him thoughtfully. "As you have already experienced, salvation, while great in the beginning, does not remove our troubles. It adds another dimension—learning how to live godly. It's a lifelong struggle to learn how to slay the sinful flesh."

"If Christians are saved, why is sin still a problem?"

Dan furrowed his brow, running through how to answer. Hearing the door open, he turned.

They both stood when Merle and Cal entered the dining room followed by an older man in a trim, dark-blue suit.

"Glad to see you. Please sit down." Merle walked to the head of the table and nodded to Sam who closed the blinds. "Finding your accommodations adequate?"

"Superb," Dan said. "I'm Dan Smith," he said to the newcomer.

"Bertrand Louden."

"Dr. Louden! This is an honor."

"I'm Warren Bells, Dan's traveling companion. Dr. Louden, what is your specialty?"

"Usually, ancient languages, specifically biblical variants, along with a side interest in the histories of the first church leaders."

"Actually, Dr. Louden is the foremost American expert on the first century patriarchs of the faith—Clement, Ignatius, Polycarp, besides the apostles, as well as Origen and other variant teachers," Dan explained.

"Dr. Smith, your thesis on the structure of the millennial sacrifices from Ezekiel was interesting. Have you followed up on the question of purpose and implications hinted at in your latest monograph?"

"Well, I…" he paused.

"Perhaps H.R. 756 suspended such study?" Warren postulated.

"756?" they asked.

"The laws that spawned the Task Force and the reason Dr. Smith is hiding in your guesthouse and not expostulating the ramifications of obscure matters of the Hebrew writings." Warren swallowed, noting the look of disdain on Louden's face.

"This man is not slated for the program, is he?"

"Not at this time," Merle smiled.

"Didn't mean to step on toes. I'm definitely not a Bible scholar, but I understand the need for those who can study the Bible at that level."

"Our first course," Merle said, casting a glance at Warren.

He listened to Louden and Dan discuss the finer points of the Levitical sacrifices and tried not to smile at Cal's equal unease with the topic of discussion. Merle jumped in from time to time with a question or apt comment. The man knew his Bible.

"Well," Merle said, as they finished their steaks smothered with buttered mushrooms, "perhaps we could retire to the study."

Cal led the way across the great room. Warren held back, letting the scholars exit first. He stood by Cal at the study door. "Cal, I think I'll check the grounds."

"I'll join you."

Warren nodded. They walked along the buildings, and stood on the high point, the study windows visible. "This area pretty safe?"

"So far. Texas has been more resistant than the coastal states."

"Or Oklahoma."

"That's a problem. As you can see, we are networking across the country."

"In compartmented cells, I hope."

"As much as we can." He turned to Warren. "Heard chatter about attempts to infiltrate the Texas Rangers. You know anything?"

"Not specifically, although some individuals are going to be targets, but Rich in Kentucky talked about a Phase Three. You know anything about that?"

"First time I heard about phases. We always thought this would be shut down fairly quickly. But, for many, it's as if nothing has changed—even though everything has changed." Cal looked at him closely. "When Dan moves on, we'll do what we can to help you find a place to settle."

"Much appreciated. The constant moving is really getting to him. It would be good if he could stay here."

"Our plan." Cal wet his lips. "Do you want to get an ID?"

Warren considered his responses. Reason dictated he should say yes to discover their sources, but he remembered a comment Tom Hutton said. Copying it, he said, "Is it right, do you think? Using false ID has always been illegal. So, we break other laws because some laws make our faith illegal?" He repressed his smile at seeing Cal's surprised and pleased response.

"Exactly. How can we, in good conscience, stand for God and be lawbreakers? Of course, we can't follow laws that go against God's higher law, but Jesus did say to render to Caesar what is Caesar's and to God what is God's. We share our faith. We live our faith, but as those who do right. And in the end, no matter what, God Himself will justify us before the world. Don't give up. You're on the right track."

"They good?"

"Yeah, I'll take first watch," Cal said with a smile.

"I'll check on Giles then head to bed. How long can they go on about that stuff?"

"Quite a while, but then they wouldn't last long talking about construction, would they?"

"Probably not."

So, have I convinced Cal I am legit?

CHAPTER 30

WARREN ENTERED THE barn, found the bag of carrots and headed for Tiny's stall. Seeing it empty, he walked out the back to the narrow track running alongside several small corrals. Tiny was in the third one, playfully nuzzling bunches of dried hay and throwing them in the air.

"Hey, Tiny. Don't like the grub? Know how that feels." He clicked, called the horse's name and extended his hand with the carrot. Remembering Giles' instruction, he held out the treat. Tiny took it, his powerful jaws crushing it in seconds. "That's it. All I have." He reached over and petted the broad neck. "You're beautiful."

"Downright worst confirmation on a horse, but he's a top range mount," Giles said. "Don't know a thing about horses?"

"That about says it, but he looks fine to me."

"I'd pick him any day. Not afraid and knows what to do when he hears a rattler. If a cowboy has a problem with him, it'd be his fault—not Tiny's."

"Why is he here?"

"Bad rider. Didn't see it until he'd learned some mighty bad habits. If I can't get him back to the good cow horse he used to be, he's out to pasture." Giles watched Warren pet the horse. "He likes you."

"Not to the glue factory?"

"Naw. We turn them out." He reached over and patted the tall horse's shoulder. "Has his years on him, that he does. Maybe it's time."

"Think he'd like that? Looks like he'd get bored."

"What gave you that idea?"

"He looks bored already."

"You're right. That's his problem. He's one of the smart ones, and a working horse has plenty to think about."

"When can I go on a trail ride?"

"In a little bit. Won't be long." He studied the horse. Tiny lifted his head, snorted and neighed. "He misses the range, as do I sometimes." Giles looked past the corrals to a neat, white clapboard house. "Come on. You can meet the missus and have some pie. You like pie?"

"Of course. What kind?"

"Depends on what's good at the store or what can she decided to open. It can be a surprise, sometimes." He glanced at Warren who fell into step with him. "Be good and say it's great, even if it's a little different."

"I'm not fussy." The house had flower boxes by the small windows bordering the door.

"Hard to keep flowers when it's so hot. I try to remember to water, but she's the gardener—or used to be."

"Is she sick?"

"In a way. One thing and another. She was my rodeo gal. Top barrel racer in the county, and we had dreams." He pulled open the screen door. "Dreams change, but being with the one you love never grows old. We have each other." He cast a glance at the barn. "It's enough for us—for me, anyway."

"Guess that's what it's all about."

He followed him through the side door to a small entryway. "Leave your shoes here. Keeps the house clean."

The small square kitchen with an aluminum-framed table sparkled with scents of lemon-scented Pine-Sol. "Hello, Mother," Giles said to a slender figure with sun-bleached hair wearing jeans and house slippers.

She lifted her head, put down her reading glances and inspected him. "Who's the guest?"

"Warren, staying in the guest house for a time. Tiny likes him."

A broad smile emerged. "Well, if Tiny likes him, he must be okay."

Warren tipped his head. "Good day, ma'am."

"Oh, quite formal. You can call me Alexa. Where you from?"

"Originally, Pittsburgh, but this area looks pretty good." He cast a glance at Giles, "If I can talk him into letting me go on a trail ride, I might be inclined to stay a while."

Giles snorted. "Well, let's see you make a horse do your bidding in the corral first."

"Green?" she asked with a laugh.

"Emerald, through and through," Warren said, joining in the laughter. "But everyone starts from ground zero."

"I don't know." Giles shook his head, "Alex was riding before she was born."

Not wanting to be contrary, he kept his peace.

"Due to circumstances on the ranch, my momma helped cut the calves from the cows on the ranch's orneriest cowpony week before I was born, and that wasn't the first time. I figure I had an unfair advantage."

"I'll accept that." Warren recalled the agents from families with generations of law enforcement experience. Some took to it as if it were in their genes. He had worked at overcoming his family deficits.

"Promised him some pie, Momma."

"Strawberry rhubarb acceptable?" She rose and pulled down some plates.

"Sounds great. Two bachelors who don't cook are at the guest house."

"Playing my violin for you," she laughed, cutting generous portions from a freshly baked pie as she told the story of Grandma's rhubarb patch.

"Bring back a year's worth when up at the mesa ranch house." Seeing Warren's quizzical look, he explained, "The ranch's original homestead in the day. We live up there for part of the year." Alexa shook her head at him. "Anyway, the family sold out years ago. Washington's the third owner. Not near as bad as the last one. He lets the ranch manager call the shots, mostly." Giles worked his lip. "Any who…" He pulled his pie closer. "You ready or too full after eating at the big house?"

"Gourmet cooking does not come with generous portions. And I have never turned down home-cooked pie." His fork bore down on the crust, and it flaked into several layers. He smiled at Alexa. "Prize-winning crust too."

"Thank you kindly. So, you one of those Christians who've been traipsing through here?"

"Yes." He looked at Giles and Alexa, wanting to ask, but feared inviting questions he might not know the answers to.

"Maybe you can tell me why your God took my babies." Alexa's warmth vanished, and a chill tightened her gaze.

Warren tried not to choke on his bite of pie. "Well…" His mind began casting about for what to say. Stalling for time, he said, "Can you tell me what happened?"

"Lexi!" Giles said, placing a hand on hers.

"No, that's all right. With everything going on, the last thing we need is not to be honest with each other. I found the Lord—rather He found me—a little over a year ago. I don't know that much yet, but Dr. Dan might have some answers."

"Well, I haven't met a Bible doc or preacher who has ever been able to come up with anything close to sense and reason."

Giles retrieved the tissue box. "Okay, tell the story."

She shared their hopes and struggles—bad years, missed opportunities, hard times and then she detailed her two miscarriages and her baby lost to SIDS.

Warren shook his head, thinking through any thread, any hope he could offer. "I think from what I've heard that babies go straight to heaven."

"Well, that's helpful, mister."

"If you have asked Jesus to save you and you know Him, you will see your children in heaven."

"And we haven't?"

"I wouldn't know."

"Reverend said there's no such verse in the Bible anyway."

He rose, "Wait a sec. I believe there is. Maybe not one that says all babies go to heaven, but verses that show it is highly likely." Not waiting for any rebuttals, he left the little clapboard house.

Dan was back in the guest house, staring at his computer.

"Hi, Dan. Hey, where in the Bible is that story about David and the death of his infant son?" He paused, "Dan, I have a couple who want answers about the babies they lost."

Not even looking his way, he scrolled to another reference. "2 Samuel 12:23." Dan looked at him for the first time. "Many scholars will deny this verse is valid. There are no verses, even in the Torah, stipulating the idea of an age of accountability whereby those who die before they come to understanding go to heaven. But God is fair and just. Knowing that Christ died for all, I cannot believe He would send those to eternal death who died too young to accept Jesus." He returned to his document. "Good luck."

"Maybe," Warren gestured to the door. "Maybe, you could come with me. What if you could encourage them where others failed?"

"Look, you've made the connection. Let me know how it goes."

Warren grabbed his Bible, stunned.

"Maybe after the meeting. Okay?"

This feels so wrong! Lacking the words to combat Dan's reasoning, he reached for the door.

"I will pray for you."

Warren narrowed his eyes and held back his rebuke. The night was dark; distant sounds of thunder rolled from the distance. *They're waiting. I have to show up.* Warren paused, seeing the mass of dark clouds visible in the last of the sun's rays. *God, why me?* With a backward glance at the guest house, he walked quickly to the little house behind the corrals.

"Thanks for waiting." He put the Bible on the table. Seeing Alexa's unease, he brought it close to the table edge and opened to 2 Samuel. "There are no verses that clearly state babies go straight to heaven, but there is a story that shows this is true." He describes King David's distress concerning his infant son's sickness and how he prayed and fasted until the baby died. He read the verses describing David's change when he heard the baby had died and his assurance that he would see him in heaven.

They stared at him. Afraid of the silence, Warren tried to guess what a true Christian would say. "God is just, but He is also loving and kind…"

"Loving?" Alexa glared at him. "Kind? Really? I'm glad someone has found the Savior gracious and merciful." She slammed her hand on the table, pushed her chair back against the wall, leaned forward and stood.

Warren noticed her slurred speech. Her left foot caught on a chair leg, and she lurched over, catching herself on the nearby countertop. Giles rose, but she lifted a hand, turned to lean against the cabinets and said, "Where was He when my grandfather called me the spawn of Satan?" She nodded her head. "Yeah, where was He when he took my baby sister, or my dad, or drove my best friend away? Where was He when He…"

She pitched forward, her eyes rolling back in her head, her limbs twitching.

Giles caught her and wrapped his arms around her. Warren ran to the small sitting room and grabbed the nearest afghan. He placed it on the floor and helped Giles position his wife.

Through clenched teeth, Giles said, "The cancer treatment killed her worse than the cancer would have."

His phone was off and in the guest house. "How do I dial 9-1-1?"

"They sent her home. No more treatments. She has her good days and her bad days."

"I'm so sorry. I didn't mean…"

"No, you were right. Needed to get this out. She's been showing signs all day she was going to have another spell. Right on time. Only the second one this week. I never dabbled with church or religion, but her family was right hard by the book—down the line. Her grandfather preached through the towns of the Panhandle—sawdust trail all the way. Her dad toed the line and ruled his family with an iron fist. Good folk, they said. Upstanding citizens, but we knew it was not for the likes of us. Anyway, I had a chance to train up a young mare, and she was the best barrel racer, but I needed a top rider and the likes of me didn't know any. So, at the county fair I saw Lexa riding an old cow horse and watched her make him dance. Came in third cause no matter how good you are, if you don't have the money, placing's the best you're going to get.

"She trained faster than the horse, and it's usually the other way 'round. We burnt up the circuit that year. But she had to sneak out cause her family considered that kind of showing of the Devil, and those who worked the rodeo were the 'spawn of Satan'—the very words for their own flesh and blood."

Giles shifted his hold as she began to settle into his arms. "We eloped the next day, and she never looked back. The owner lets us stay here as it's closer to hospitals but having these Christians come through…"

"Acts like a trigger." Warren sat back on his heals. "I'm sorry to hear that." He studied her still form. "May I help you get her up?"

Giles nodded and slid her into Warren's arms. He rose and followed the man to the back bedroom and watched him tuck her in. Warren fetched a glass of water when she began to wake up. He returned to see Giles stroking her hair and kissing her hand.

No one loved me like that. For an instant, he wished that was not true.

"For what it's worth, there will always be those who say they speak for God, but get it wrong." He described Hawsley and his following. "Jesus had the harshest words for those who misrepresented God. He told them they needed to love. I have seen believers in Jesus, crushed and hurting, distraught at the death of those close to them turn and forgive the ones who murdered their loved ones. Many forgave them as they shared the love of God."

"I saw the Rosemont video," Giles said. "It's for real?"

"Yes." He stood in the doorway. "Do you need anything?"

"No," Giles said, not taking his eyes off Lexi.

"All right. I'll check on you in the morning. Thanks for the pie."

Dan had seemingly turned on every light in the guest house. Warren held back the words he had for him.

"How did it go?" Dan asked, not looking up from the laptop.

"You missed out," Warren said, trying to hold back his anger. "I thought you were called to love."

"Well, I have to get this right. In two days, we go to that meeting, and I have to be good enough."

"So, your hopes are on this group. They send you out? You escape all this?"

"That or I continue running from place to place, reaching small groups at a time." Dan sat back, rubbed his eyes, shook his head and turned back to his work.

"How does it work, exactly? They have to give you a false identity with documents and a backstory, maybe even alter your appearance slightly so you can exit the country. Then in a foreign country, every person you meet, every relationship you develop will be a lie. You will have to lie about your name, your family, your background. How exactly will that work? Do you think it will be easy? Jesus will just say, 'Yeah, not a problem, live a lie because I allowed this law to ruin your life'?"

Dan cocked his head and glared at him. "Of course, I know it's not going to be easy. Don't you think I haven't wrestled with this? There are no easy options, no perfect solutions."

His eyes pinched, he looked away. "That's why I've been doing this for over a year, but I can't make a difference in the future if I'm dead."

"Isn't that God's call?"

He slapped the table. "I think this is what God wants me to do. Sorry if it disturbs your image of how a Bible professor should be. We're all struggling. All of us are having a hard time. Now, if you don't mind, I have work to do."

Before he could stop himself, Warren said, "You might be a teacher, but you are no pastor." Thinking of the couple yards away in a small house and their need to see God's love, he shook his head, grabbed his sleeping bag and headed out the door.

Warren awakened, hearing Giles whistling. He threw back the edge of the sleeping bag and stretched. The loose hay had been surprisingly comfortable. He stretched and stood in the small area of piled bales and metal grain bins.

Giles looked at him. "Your roommate kicked you out?"

"He's all nervous about this meeting."

"He should be. I hear them talk. Don't have enough spots for everybody, so they have to weed them out somehow. Bad days, my friend when your own country turns on you." He stretched his back.

"How's Alexa doing?"

"Fine. Up bright and early. Fresh pot of coffee." He stepped back and looked down the aisle. "You hear anyone coming in?"

"No, but…" He followed Giles down the aisle.

The man stopped at the four large box stalls and peered through the doors. He swore loudly. "That kid's gone." He looked at Warren. "Stable hand has shirked his job again. Needed those stalls cleaned yesterday, and he's still not done it." He pulled out his phone and checked the messages. "And he's taking the day off, 'cause he asked the ranch manager behind my back. Now they're both in hot water with me."

"Show me how it's done. Don't have anything else to do, and Dan doesn't want company."

"Fine, but coffee first. Let's go."

——— ❦ ———

They provided a new suit for Dan. Warren pulled out his best shirt and pair of jeans and ran them through the washer. Cal laid out the schedule and had their blue truck parked by the front door. They would drive to a remote cabin. From there, they would go to an undisclosed location where Dan would present his work and ministry.

They drove in silence. "Ready?" he asked him.

"I hope so," Dan replied, his eyes trained on the road.

Everyone expressed anxiety differently—Warren knew that. He tried not to judge the man, but he could not stop comparing him to Tom or Asa or the others he had met. *Are they saving the right ones?*

The meeting was unlike any Warren had attended so far—though admittedly he had only been to a few. In a back room at a dealership after hours, following a brief introduction by a familiar-looking man, Dan walked to the slim podium. He placed his notes on the pedestal and began to lecture about the ramifications of the unique qualities of Ezekiel's millennial temple sacrifices and postulate how they related to the reign of the King of Glory in Jerusalem. Warren could not ignore the fact that the man was brilliant, easy to listen to, with clear and direct language. If he introduced a new or unfamiliar term, he briefly defined it. The pacing was good, the delivery superb, making the subject interesting.

After it was over, the men in the front rows thanked him and exited the room—the host leading the way. Merle rose and walked back to the rows where Cal, himself and a few others sat. "Well, Larry, what do you think?" Warren finally recognized Larry Hutton. "Is he as good as advertised?"

"Yes, and most likely, he would be a top prospect." Larry glanced around the room before continuing. "but we're under pressure right now. Had to wait on moving the last three out. We can't bring in too many until we're ready to process them for emigration."

"The Oklahoma City office?" Warren suggested.

Larry nodded, turning his way. "Larry."

"Warren."

The man stared at him for a little longer than expected. Uncertain of what that meant, Warren tried to maintain a calm, relaxed demeanor.

"Hear you are friends with Giles now."

He couldn't hold back his smile. "A nice couple. He's teaching me how to ride. Maybe I'll graduate to a trail ride when we get back."

"That brings up a point, Larry," Merle interrupted. "My daughter is due back for a two-week break with the trainer in a few days. I was hoping to have moved them on by then."

"Not likely."

"What about the mesa ranch house?" The others looked at him. "Giles talked about leaving for the mesa complex. Could we tag along?" Warren noticed Dan approach; his face drained of emotion with an almost shell-shocked look. Warren shook his hand. "Good job. Even I could follow it…sort of." Laughing lightly, he was happy to hear others join in. "Listen," he said to Merle, "Giles and Alexa are good people. She's a great cook and makes awesome pies. We could help them. Dan could answer their questions that I can't. Do it for the Lord?"

"I don't know. She's quite sick," Merle said.

Warren added, "Giles could use help with that too. She had a spell when I was visiting. I think we can be a blessing."

"I'll take it under consideration."

Warren tried not to reveal his disappointment. Merle didn't look too excited about the idea. His other reason for wanting to hang with

Giles was that the man seemed willing to take him along for shopping trips or auctions. Those were his best opportunities to activate his cell phone and text Norton not near the ranch.

Dan glared at him.

"I'm sure he'll find the best possible situation for you, Dan." Warren tried to reassure him, but he still looked fragile.

Back at Merle's main house, Dan moped. He had qualified for the program but would have to wait. Cal stated Merle and Larry were considering several options—of course, without specifics.

While they waited, he introduced Dan to Giles and Alexa. Thankfully, Dan was a gentleman, and within a day, they were eating pie together. Dan even volunteered to do their laundry; the guest house had the latest washing machine. "Hey, that is one thing my mom taught me how to do."

"You mean those are the lessons you paid attention to."

"Guilty as charged."

Before Alexa could object, Giles emerged from the bedroom with two stuffed pillowcases. "Here we sort the barn dirty from house dirty."

"Got it."

Eventually, Cal announced the plans. Dan drove the blue truck following Giles' massive black-as-night Ford dually with four wheels in the back, hauling a trailer long enough to transport several horses and the gear. Their truck held supplies, food, bedding and more gear.

As they travelled north, the roads became narrower and the traffic nonexistent. Warren's mind wandered to the transformation of Giles and Alexa. She seemed to have reconnected with her faith. Giles was studying the Bible with Dan, and he watched it, like an outsider. His heart felt torn within him—that they could believe when he could not.

CHAPTER 31

TOM WALKED THE bicycle to the head of a city bike trail. September in Jackson, Tennessee, was almost perfect—slightly cooler days, lower humidity, less rain. They had been two and a half months on the road, and Wallace was ready to find a place to settle.

He held the bike, swung his leg over, and began to pedal, his thoughts on the choices before him. Their travels had taken them from Iowa to Kansas and Arkansas, through Illinois and Indiana, and many of the southeast coastal states. Never staying long in one place, God led them. Most days, they both agreed. Usually, Tom deferred to Wallace's judgment when it was time to leave an area.

Jackson, Tennessee, had caught Wallace's eye. A small congregation formed from the collapse of three churches had captured Tom's heart as well. He longed for God to release them to help the Jackson fellowship.

The head elder lived in a small ranch close to Muse Park. That night he had essentially asked Tom to help them rebuild the church with a vision that fit the community's needs—one that stood for the truth with love in action. How his heart yearned to say yes. He had wanted to, but Tom shook his head, pausing for a chance to pass a couple pushing a baby carriage after another biker sped by.

Praying as he pedaled, trying to remember to remain vigilant, he paused for a drink of water from his bottle and wiped his brow. It felt good to think he could fit somewhere. His heart thrilled watching Wallace interact with the fellowship, how they accepted him, encouraged him and taught him. A few older members were former Sunday school teachers with an excellent understanding of the Bible—perfect for Wallace to increase his Bible knowledge.

Hearing the lobbing of balls from the tennis courts, Tom crossed the road and biked to the side of the nearby parking area. He paused in the shade of a large tree and watched two older men play a leisurely game. Out of the corner of his eye, he noticed a third throw a towel over his shoulder, pick up his bag and wave to his friends, turning in Tom's direction.

They looked at each other for a second. In that instant Tom recognized Rosemont's head guard. As the man shouted, blocked by the tall fencing, Tom pulled the bike to the road and swung his leg over. In moments he was putting as much distance as possible between them.

His mind reeling, Tom realized he was headed away from the house. Trying to see a way to double back without being tracked, he pedaled down another side road and around a bend. The road looked familiar, and he decided to pick a different destination.

After two wrong turns he saw Chester's small green house with a shed not far from the gravel drive. He found the hidden shed key and pulled the bike inside. Seeing no one about, he tapped on the back door, tried the knob and stepped in.

"Sorry," Tom said, trying to catch his breath. "I didn't mean to interrupt, but can I hide here a while?"

The large black policeman, still in uniform, rose. "What's up Tom?"

"The Rosemont head guard just saw me in the park. I have to get out of this city right now."

Chester gestured down the short hall to the bedrooms. "Okay, go, first door on your left." The man followed Tom in, pleased the shades were drawn in their spare room and makeshift office.

Tom stood, praying the man would understand the necessity for quick action. "Can you help me? I didn't want to lead them to Ron's place."

"Tonight, when it's dark."

"I don't think I can wait that long." He stepped forward, but the man raised his hand, thinking of the possibilities. "Just a minute." Chester pulled out his phone, "Yeah, Son, need you to make a trip. Come home so we can set it up." He paused to listen. "That can wait. We'll cover the gas, don't worry."

About to give Tom the details, he stopped him. "The less I know the better. Just get me out of the city. If this is of the Lord, He will provide a way of escape."

"If not?"

"He's still God, and I'm still guaranteed a place in heaven—according to Daniel 3."

Chester nodded.

"He does need a viable reason for the trip."

"That's why I'm sending him. He has an old two-door pickup. How do we hide you?"

"Put me in a tub or a large toolbox."

"Won't be comfortable."

"I don't need comfortable. I need to be gone." Tom added, "Let Wallace know what happened. Let's hope they don't discover who's been helping me."

"Done. Need anything?"

"Some water. I'll wait here."

Chester's son arrived with the truck. After outfitting a large plastic tub, the two men put it in the back of the truck bed. Tom felt every bump, his heart pounding, He prayed he was doing right. They had discussed this possibility, along with all the others they could imagine.

Waiting for the truck to settle out to highway speeds, Tom eventually realized the young man was driving back roads. One part of him knew this was the right choice, but the sharp corners and quick stops were playing havoc with his stomach. He braced himself and focused on the light coming in through ragged ventilation holes. Tom tried to distract himself with his prayer list, which brought up waves of grief and sorrow. He reverted to reviewing the Psalms.

The truck came to a halt on a gravel drive, but no one came to retrieve him. Tom forced himself to stay still, despite shooting pains in his hips, knees and shoulders. Hearing distant voices, Tom felt the truck move forward slowly and heard a large door roll back.

Tom shut his eyes when light streamed in with the lifting of the lid from the box.

"You still alive in there?"

"Yes," Tom lifted up a hand, trying to grasp the side, but it bent toward him. He felt a hand, and he grasped the strong arm that lifted him to his feet. Blinking as he stood in the back of the rusty pickup, he surveyed a large tobacco barn and noticed Marvin standing with his gap-toothed smile.

"Well, well, the preacher's come to visit."

"Yeah, seems like we only show up when we need something." Tom smiled back.

"Can't keep you here."

Tom nodded.

"But I have a need for parts." He rubbed his head, the hair close cropped. "Ready for another drive or want to set a spell?"

Tom lifted his foot to step out of the box and almost fell, the world swirling about. The young man steadied him, and Tom made it down to the solid floor in time to vomit. "Sorry." He looked about for cleaning rags.

"Well, Son, not surprising the way you drive." Marvin thrust a roll of paper towels to Tom after handing several to the driver. "Wipe it off. And I'll get that load of potatoes your family wanted."

Marvin placed a large bag of potatoes in the box, and the two lifted it up. Chester's son pulled out a backpack from the cab and handed it to Tom. "Mom packed this for you." He nodded at Tom. "Sorry you have to leave. We'll miss you."

Tom nodded, trying to clear his throat. "Tell your family, everyone, it's been an honor to have known you." He found himself engulfed in a hug. "Pray for me—that I can keep on going."

"Ready?" Marvin pushed back the door, and they watched the truck back out and head down the gravel drive. "Now, let's get you in the house."

Tom looked about the large open area with partially assembled tractors, disking decks, old toolboxes and piles of wood and iron lengths. "Maybe I should stay here."

"Fiddle-dee-dee, knowing God can make seeing eyes blind, the last thing we need to do is worry the neighbors with shenanigans. You need some of Ma's chicken salad, her fresh brewed sweet iced tea and set a spell by the air conditioner. You definitely look mighty peaked. From those Northern states?"

"Ohio." He stepped out into the blazing sun. He could barely wait to feel a cool breeze on his shoulders and drink the tea—a habit he had grown to enjoy while in Jackson.

No one was about. Tall trees and shrubs shielded the neighbor's house from view. The curtains were drawn, and Belle greeted them with a smile and tall glasses of iced tea.

Marvin turned on the conditioning unit. "Tea and chicken salad. We have a traveler needing refreshing. I'll let you know when we're ready to go." Before he reached the door, the scanner squawked with a missing person bulletin for Tom Hutton.

"That's imaginative." Tom shuddered listening to the brief description of himself and the bicycle. Tom finished the iced tea, thanked Belle and stood. "Can we go?"

Marvin led him to an older sedan near the house and insisted he sit up front. "We're going by back country. You'll have an easier time if you sit like any normal passenger." He handed Tom a large bag and cold mug of iced tea. "Belle, being robbed of the chance to show you proper hospitality, sent us with treasures for the journey."

"That was fast."

Marvin smiled, turning his attention to the back-country road.

Tom found it easier to keep his stomach settled watching the road rise and fall over gentle hills, along with the sharp curves and varying speed limits.

"To avoid larger towns and highways, we'll be taking the scenic route."

Tom nodded, glad the old car's air conditioning worked. They were traveling during the hottest part of the day.

"Thought you'd stick around."

"I wanted to. Was praying about it this morning while I rode through the park. I have God's answer—one I didn't want to hear, but He knows what He's doing." Repeating the mantra in his head, he wished his heart would catch up. They usually didn't stay so long in one place. "Jackson's special." He glanced at Marvin. "It would have been an honor to minister to your group, but..." He looked away. "Take good care of Wallace."

"It's safe for him to stay?"

Tom nodded, "As long as they don't connect me to him or your group. I didn't ride in his car in the city; we worked at not travelling together in town. Why I couldn't go back to the house. With all my heart, I wanted to settle down." He watched the road bend and curve before him like a ribbon. His life felt like an unsettled never-ending journey. Resisting the desire to be a part of a local fellowship, he focused on Christ, his cornerstone, his fixed point, the only sure foundation. The living Word echoed the assurances of God's good plans and a future.

"Tell me about yourselves. Were you and Belle raised in Christian families?" Tom sat back and listened to the stories of farming and raising children, seeing God's providence in their lives and their church. Then he shared his story of leaving home to go to Bible college and his time in prisons. "Wichita was good too, but I had to leave. Didn't want to bring the Task Force to them. God will provide another driver if I'm to go on." He glanced over. "Do you think getting the word out about Rosemont is going to make a difference?"

"Probably not. It's like we have no voice, no power. Maybe if the last election had gone a different way. Any who, God is greater than all that. If our nation doesn't care, we're already done for."

"No act of man, no law, no bars, no walls can stop the Spirit of God from working in the hearts of men."

"I tell you what is going to make a difference—if they follow through with the new Bibles."

"What new Bibles?"

"Almost here, Northern Mississippi." Marvin smacked his lips. "They think they can outlaw the whole thing and give us a storybook instead. That'll be the day we rise up. That will be."

They were silent for a while. "So, this is what Mississippi looks like. No bayous, moss in the trees?"

"That's farther south, closer to the Gulf. Not much different from home, except a tad hotter. Can't say they get more storms and tornadoes. That's through all of this." He glanced at Tom and noticed his furrowed brow and slumped shoulders. "We'll help Wallace. He's been a blessing already, and we're growing attached to him."

"Here it is," he turned the car into a mostly vacant dirt-gravel area in front of an off-white metal building, butting up against fencing covered with various shades of plastic obscuring what lay behind. The sign read *Mulligan's Parts and Motorcycle.* "New sign. Son took over the business when he got back. Quite an upgrade."

Tom stepped out of the vehicle and looked about. The parking lot was empty apart from two salvage vehicles sitting by what appeared to be the gate through an enclosure.

"Tow truck's out. I told him we'd be by." Marvin walked to the double glass doors and pulled. "Locked." He tapped on the door before pulling out his cell phone. Before he could select a number, a tall figure pulled the door open. "We got here as soon as we could. You ready to deal?"

"Sure, old man."

The voice sounded familiar. Tom followed Marvin in and stared.

"Tom?" he said.

"Todd!" Tom stepped forward to shake his hand, but the tall man wrapped him in a hug.

He shook his head at Marvin. "Said you'd be by with a package, but this's even better."

"You know each other?"

"Sure do. Met up in Hannibal." Still beaming, he nodded at Tom, "God used him to help me see the light."

"Don't forget your letters from home, now."

"But he helped me see it was for real." He looked at the two. "What's up, Tom?"

"They found me."

"I saw the Rosemont video. Posting it online helped spread it. I think the whole country knows."

"The true followers of Christ, you mean." Marvin stepped to the counter. "That part ready?" He placed an envelope of cash on the counter. "I'd best be going. Belle's expecting me home 'fore midnight."

"Al just pulled and refurbished it this morning. Thought you'd come by with Belle for the weekend."

Marvin glanced at Tom. "It was timely. Good reason to drive 'most two hours for a tractor part, but no one can beat your parts."

"Glad to hear." Todd disappeared in the aisles of floor-to-ceiling metal shelving housing all types of parts.

"Best salvage place in the area, and Todd's additions have added to it." Marvin nodded at the half dozen motorcycles on display at the far end of the storefront.

Tom noticed the short coffee bar on the opposite side. "That real espresso?"

"That it is." Todd said, returning with the part. "Had enough of bad coffee. Have to beat the competition. We take our coffee seriously in this town." Todd handed over the part for inspection, wrote out an invoice and counted the cash. "Mom will miss seeing Belle. Drop by when you get a chance."

"We will." Marvin hefted the part. "Thanks, will be seeing y'all."

Tom watched him drive away. He stepped aside for Todd to lock the door. "So, looks like you're stuck with me now."

"Just wait till Shirley meets you in person."

"Oh, you've been talking about me?" He turned and surveyed the small retail area. "Quite the business."

Todd showed off his motorcycles, small parts area, and other odds and ends. "Well, they will be wondering what happened to us. Supper's waiting. You hungry?"

"Yeah, maybe."

Todd's eyes narrowed. "We have a lot of catching up to do."

"It's wonderful to see you, Todd. Wish…" he took one last look through the glass doors before they both turned to the back of the building and walked down the darkened aisles of new and used parts of all descriptions.

A large work area opened up. Cars, motorcycles, and tractors on lifts or partly assembled, surrounded by large bins, shelves and tall toolboxes, occupied most of the garage. "You have built quite the enterprise here."

Todd nodded. "Took over after Dad passed. Keep it in the family. It pays the bills and provides connections to the community. I added some new parts, the motorcycle sales and service." He grinned and added, "My son Saul wants to start fixing small engines—lawn mowers, weed trimmers." He placed a hand on Tom's shoulder. "All this creates doors for the ministry right here in Boonville, and you are the Bible teacher I have been praying for. Imagine that."

"Absolutely." They walked through the building, and Todd cracked the door open to reveal the salvage yard. "How is Wallie doing?" Tom asked.

"Good, he's doing just fine. Misses you, of course, but Bruce visits him when he gets a chance."

"Bruce is out?"

"Come on. I have so much to show you, and the family will be glad to meet you."

Tom shouldered his pack and followed Todd to a large metallic green Chevy Silverado. "Fancy. Who lives in the house nearby?"

"Mom."

"How did Bruce get out? He was practically a lifer."

"One of those truth projects found the real killer, and the prosecutors actually did their job and reversed his conviction. Happened so fast, he didn't know what to do. You know, many who are in for a long time lose touch with people on the outside." Todd turned from the country road to a small subdivision across from cornfields. "Stayed with us for a while, but he found a good job as a foreman with this wealthy guy who owns ranches northwest of here." Todd smiled broadly.

"What? You're holding back."

"Don't be hasty."

CHAPTER 32

WARREN GLANCED AT Giles when he pulled into the large, crowded lot at the auction yards. "How many horses you hoping to buy?" His few months at mesa had greatly broadened his riding ability and knowledge of horses, but he still had far to go.

Giles slowed the truck, checking for the best place to park with the long trailer. "Three, maybe four if the lot's good."

When Giles selected a parking spot, Warren slipped out of the truck and positioned himself to help direct the trailer—not that the man needed help. He was as good backing up the long trailer as he was thinking like a horse. What had Alexa called him—*a horse whisperer?*

Dan had also settled in well at mesa, regularly answering their questions and teaching from the Bible. Warren found himself pulling back, almost shutting one ear to the lessons, but he could not avoid hearing. He still recoiled at the thought of faith and belief.

The auction yard on Amarillo's northern edge teemed with people milling about. Giles surveyed the scene. He stepped out of the truck and handed the list to Warren. "What we need from the stores. Alexa's used to us men shopping for her."

Warren nodded and helped him unhitch the trailer. "How much time do I have?"

"Four hours or so. I like to arrive early to check the stock."

"I'll head out later."

"When the bidding starts. It always takes time to pay and load up."

Warren followed Giles while he chatted with the various sellers, wandering from place to place.

After returning to a few working pens to view the prospects, Giles collected his number and headed to the seats.

Warren said, "Might as well head out. I'll meet you at the trailer."

Warren parked the truck minus the trailer at Walmart, pulled out his cell phone and waited for it to power up. Giles traveled far and wide to train or purchase supplies as well as horses, giving Warren chances to check in far away from the ranch. Norton had not complained about the infrequent check-ins and had never responded or initiated contact.

Zoning out, he was surprised to hear the phone chirp with incoming messages. Warren entered the password and opened the most recent text from Norton. Seeing the frantic messages about not responding, he scrolled to the first one and sucked in his breath. It read, "Return to base immediately. Tom Hutton is at large!" The others were sterner warnings, threatening to find him if he didn't report.

A dread rose up in his chest, along with a sweet longing formed by images of the four of them laughing together and enjoying each other's company at the mesa ranch. He couldn't simply leave without saying something to Giles, but he couldn't break his cover.

Striving back and forth within himself, he reviewed the list and stepped out of the truck. Holding the phone in his hand, he reasoned through the risks of texting from Amarillo. Remembering they already knew that Larry Hutton was stationed there and lived near the city, it shouldn't raise any red flags.

Warren texted a quick reply that he was working on his extraction and would be there by tomorrow. But first, he had obligations to fulfill.

Warren had discussed this possibility with Dan—that a Task Force agent might spot him, and he would have to leave quickly without notice. He paused. Giles knew about the Task Force, had seen the video and should accept that explanation.

Warren walked past a gaggle of teen girls, still pondering what he would actually say to Giles. Recalling the layout of the stores he knew back home, Warren paused by the shoes. This store seemed scrambled. Backtracking to find the dry goods first and food last, he started again at one end, working his way through the mammoth store. It took a few hours, but he was finally on his way.

As he backed up and hitched the trailer, he heard the auctioneer calling. Warren headed to the stands. Eventually, he saw Giles standing on the far side talking with another cowboy. They looked well matched with graying hair, worn hats and bowed legs.

"There he is." Giles greeted him warmly. "Proof our cowboys could do better if they wanted to. Two of the horses I've fixed my eye on are replacements for ones the boys broke."

"Careless or ignorant?"

Shaking his head, he nodded at Warren. "Meet Ed. Now this young man is from the East, and he already knows more than some who've been on the job for years."

"More slim pickings for cowboys today, it seems."

Warren listened to them bemoan the state of the ranches, the herds, their mounts and the nation, all wrapped in a stream of consciousness between the two. He tapped his foot, his mouth pasty dry, fearing he would say too little, too much, or the wrong thing.

Eventually, Giles turned his attention to the latest offering and headed to stand close to the small corral.

"He's got a great eye. You're lucky to work with him," Ed said.

Warren nodded.

"Planning on staying?"

"I'd like to, but things can come up." He glanced at Ed. "You buying?"

"Selling."

———— ∞ ————

The horses were loaded before Warren had a chance to talk with Giles. He ran through the short version, but it still didn't feel right.

"Giles, I think the Task Force is on to me." Conjuring up lies to cover the truth, he waited for Giles' reaction.

The man stared at him thoughtfully. "They spot you?"

"At Walmart. Didn't think I'd see agents from Kentucky in Texas."

"What you going to do?"

The sharp edge of his voice sent a jolt through Will. The man knew or he thought he did! Remembering it was common to assume a cover had been blown, he steadied himself. "Get out of Dodge and as far away from the ranch as possible."

Even if the man could practically train a horse to stand on his head, he was still a civilian. Hadn't he said they had to be honest with each other? *Will my betrayal rob this man of his blossoming faith?*

Giles seemed deep in his own thoughts as well.

"Yeah, well, see you around." Warren opened the second door to retrieve his bag.

"You running out just like that? What you going to do now?"

"Guess I'll walk to a truck stop and hitch a ride heading west."

Giles chewed his lip. "Hop in." He put the truck in gear. "I have a better idea." Giles drove to a rundown repair shop on the outskirts of Amarillo. "Follow me." He walked to the house on the property and banged on the door.

"Yo, Cash, you in there?"

An older man thrust the door open. "Not seen you in ages. Hauling horses again for the ranch? Thought you swore off that operation."

"Finally has a decent boss, and the cowboys these days don't appreciate the craft. Someone's got to keep things in line."

"Not like it used to be. What you need?"

"A bike," he nodded at Will. "He needs to take a quick trip, and I don't have time to get back and get him on the road. What do you have?"

They walked around the largest barn to rows of decrepit vehicles of every description. He stopped by a smaller motorcycle with a torn seat.

"She run?"

"Yep, not pretty, but she'll get you from here to there."

"Sold." Giles pulled out the cash after they haggled over the price. "Fill her up with gas too."

Despite the grumbles, Cash told Warren to walk it to an old gas pump. "Have at it."

Warren filled the bike and retrieved his backpack from the truck. "I don't know what…"

Giles cut him short. "I should be thanking you and Dan for helping Alexa reconnect with God and getting me on the straight and narrow."

Warren nodded, ignoring his guilt, swung on the pack, straddled the bike and took off. He waited until he was miles away from the garage before he stopped to search for directions to Oklahoma City. Reconsidering his options, he stood under the shade of a tree and started to type in the address for the Amarillo DPS location that housed the Texas Rangers' office. He tucked away his phone when a dusty pickup parked right behind him. Taking advantage of the opportunity, he waved and approached the driver. "Hi, lost my bearings trying to get to the DMV."

The driver nodded and told him how to find the law enforcement complex on Canyon Drive.

Nodding his thanks, Will began to make his way through the city streets, drawing closer to the city center. He parked the bike by a residential area right behind the complex and went to find the staff parking lot. Taking a sip from a bottle of water, he realized the man might not be in the office today.

Okay, God, for Larry—not me. He needs to know. Will wiped his brow and watched the sun slowly approach the horizon. Fearing he would have to try the man's house, he leaned forward, seeing a tall man with broad shoulders and a white Stetson walk around the building.

Will began to walk and increased his pace. "Officer Hutton. Texas Ranger Hutton," he said, hoping the man heard him. Eventually, he slowed his gait and turned to Will.

"Need to talk with you," he looked about, seeing multiple cameras. "In private," he nodded to a spot hidden by a roof overhang. Blurting it out, he said, "I need to warn you Tom Hutton is out of Rosemont and on the run. He's just been spotted by the Task Force. Someone's got to keep him safe. Would that program work for him?"

"Aren't you that guy with Dr. Smith?"

Will nodded. *It's time. I have to say it, have been wanting to for a long time.* "Oklahoma sent me in undercover, but I will not turn in anyone to the Task Force. Rosemont was supposed to be a Level One facility—not a death camp. The Task Force is out of control, and someone has to stop it. They're after you too. Watch your back." He stepped back to disappear again.

Larry said, "Wait, who are you?"

"Will Masters and don't search for that name on any network that can be traced. I'm going back to Oklahoma City. I won't tell them who I have been with or what I know. I want out of the Task Force."

"So you were the one we heard about."

"Move Dan ASAP and try to scrub all evidence he was with Giles or at Washington's."

"Understood. You believe?"

He wanted to nod, wanted to be able to say it, but he shook his head. "Not with what I've seen. I'm on your side—but not your God's. Sorry about your family." Will walked away, not looking back. *The man has been warned. That's the best I can do.*

CHAPTER 33

WILL MADE IT to the edge of Oklahoma City, ditched the bike, and hitchhiked the rest of the way. He would have stayed at a motel, but having no ID, he texted Norton that he was in town.

The director picked him up and drove to his house in a newer subdivision. Tom surveyed the sand-colored bricks and fancy stonework. "Beautiful house."

"You'll find many things are affordable out here." He led Will through the open garage door and into the kitchen. "Hungry?"

"Sure."

Norton pulled out leftovers from the fridge and heated them up. "Wife's in Dallas with her sisters."

"Children?"

"Out of the house and on their own." He sat across from Will at the table in front of a sliding glass door. "Have family?"

Will shook his head.

Norton leaned back, "So, you're one of those."

"Yep, FBI was my life."

"Was? Think of us as the extension of the service, only with a focused mandate." He waited for Will to finish the steak. "Hook up with the underground?"

"Not really. Only Christians I met were the tame ones, so to speak. There are a lot of churches in Amarillo." He wondered when Norton would mention Hutton.

"How'd you get out there?"

"Tried to hitchhike but decided better to get a ride from a trucker." Seeing Norton nod, he let him fill in the details. "Hutton's a busy ranger. Often out of town for weeks at a time." He shook his head. "Couldn't tie him to anything illegal—not that I could see." Amazingly, the director almost looked happy.

Norton sat back, swirling his sweet tea before sipping it. "You worked closely with Kincaid. It seems he can get sidetracked, tunnel-vision, even lose the big picture. His distraction with the Huttons can get us off track." He leaned forward. "Why I was willing to let an outsider take a shot at it and not divert my best talent from the real objective."

Will tried to nod as if he were right in step, but a chill ran through him. The director seemed to think he did have agents who could have penetrated Hutton's group. "From your vantage point, sir, what is the real objective?"

"Well, if Congress had the guts to take this threat seriously, we could eliminate most of the opposition."

"By killing resistant pastors and church leaders," his voice thin.

"Absolutely. It makes no sense to get this far only to engage in an endless catch-and-release program."

"Not much different than the war on drugs." Will shook his head. "But witnessing is not a capital crime. Legally, you need to release every inmate who has completed his sentence."

The director smiled. "But, unlike the hapless DEA, we have a dispensation from Washington. Kincaid told me himself." Norton added, "I don't want to name names, but they gave him the go-ahead for Rosemont. I've been tasked with creating next-generation facilities."

This admission answered many of Will's questions about Kincaid's frequent trips to the White House. "So, if I understand you correctly, the administration fully supports and will defend these actions."

"Those necessary to meet our objectives, and that is where Kincaid is off base in focusing on the Huttons. Don't let him know I said that."

"It's safe with me. I don't plan on working with him again. I don't think he'd take me back." He half-smiled.

The director laughed. "Exactly. We finish mopping up resistant church leaders, but we also need to eliminate the resistance in law enforcement."

Will nodded, "Phase Three. Aren't you almost ready? Isn't that why he wants that Texas Ranger?"

"It's too soon. I'm glad you didn't find a connection, and you can survive Kincaid's thinking you're a lost cause. Like I said, Hutton's a distraction for now."

"Why recall me at this point?"

"Discovering Tom Hutton is alive provided the justification to pull you out." He explained what had happened in Jackson. "They can't pinpoint when or how he escaped." The director leaned forward with a smile on his lips. "Seems the guards were so afraid of being caught, they shredded the documents for deceased inmates and only kept a week's worth of video. There is no paper trail and no video documenting the time of his escape, so they have nothing to go on."

"Any guards suspected?"

"That guard, Marcus, died of cancer before we could take him down."

"Marcus?" Will knew he had to pretend he had not seen the video.

"A night guard, the one we think helped them escape, made a video of the camp. I hear it's gone viral with the underground church. Kincaid has his top IT people trying to crack the source of the cloud uploads. We take one down, and it pops up somewhere else. But give it time. Eventually, we'll get them." Norton lifted his brows, "Kincaid wanted me to ask you about Tom Hutton, but I don't think it's an issue."

Relieved the man didn't think he had been involved, he smiled. *They probably assume it happened months earlier.*

"So, I see no reason you can't join us here. I'm very impressed with your credentials and accomplishments in investigations and administration. You're a good spokesperson as well. We could use your capabilities, and you'll rise to the top, just like in D.C., but without having to appear on the Hill."

"What's your plan?"

"Give you the tour tomorrow."

"I need to see everything."

"You will and then we can discuss where you'd like to be." He sat back. "Think of it as your next step in bringing our country forward."

Different words—same ideas. Maybe the crematory looked more humane than the pit, but the toll was the same. "Of course, look forward to it," he heard himself say.

Declining a beer, he expressed his exhaustion and followed his host to a second-floor guest room with a private bath. Will sat on the edge of the bed, spent, empty, beyond feeling. *I want out. Make it happen.*

Do they know they're risking a civil war? If they fully outlaw the Bible without also outlawing guns, this country will erupt. When are You going to stop this?

—————— ᗰᗷᗬ ——————

After a filling steak and eggs breakfast, Will rode to headquarters with the director. In clean clothes, his ID back, he should have felt relieved, but the tension mounted with each new unit he toured. The faces were, for the most part, fresh and eager. He assumed conflicted agents had already made their exit as Chris and Joe had.

Will tried to hide his compassion and empathy for inmates sitting through lectures on how to report the uncooperative. Thankfully, they didn't make him sit through the lectures for those still undecided. Spartan dorm tents out in the heat warehoused men with hollowed cheeks and bowed posture. However, at times he caught the glint in their eyes of solid opposition. How did the Bible state it in Ephesians 6? *Stand therefore, hold your ground.* He knew they would and where that would take them. *Did they know?*

His heart almost broke when the lieutenant had him accompany a small group being shown the last building with the cremation chamber to watch an execution. Will worked at keeping his face immobile, tear-free.

"Stand fast," he whispered as he lingered next to the line when the guard was distracted.

"With the power of Christ, we will."

How he wanted to arrange an escape, how he longed to step in and make it right, but that would accomplish nothing. Somehow, he would do something, but he had to be wise and do it outside of the Task Force.

After a congenial meal at a restaurant with the division's executive staff, Norton and Will returned to the director's large office. The man grew quiet and looked at Will sharply. "Have you seen enough to make a decision?"

Will nodded. "What you are doing violates every oath, every principle of law enforcement." Left unsaid were memories of former operations that had cost their blood and treasure only to see criminals walk free after short prison sentences. Norton should have known better. "I want out."

Norton kept his face neutral. "Fine, we'll put through a transfer to the FBI as an entry-level field agent. There's an opening at an experimental resident agency in Gillette, Wyoming."

"Well, it's not Fargo," Will said, cracking a smile.

"That is the least of your worries."

Will took in the hard tone and direct gaze of the formerly congenial director. "Transmit the contact, and I'll be on my way."

"I'll put you up in the hotel, and you can arrange your transportation from there."

Norton printed out the details, and they walked to Norton's heavy-duty pickup. One thing Will did know—he wanted to live out west and own a pickup. Shaking his head, he said nothing during the short drive to the hotel where he had stayed a few months earlier.

CHAPTER 34

WILL SET UP the GPS directions in his new off-road, limited edition, jet-black Silverado pickup and pulled out of the Oklahoma dealership on his way to Hannibal, Missouri. Butch Connors was fine with his arriving that evening. Chris would meet him there the next day.

Legal, with ID, not having to hide, cruising down the interstates, Will tried to shake off the past two months. Being done with the Task Force and back with the FBI felt great.

Tuning into a station, he let the country music fill the cab as the miles flew by.

Will reviewed the past 24 hours in his mind—returning to the same hotel a few months later and working with Chris. She suggested they meet halfway in Hannibal at Butch Connors' retirement home. He had been surprised to hear Connors was a Christian.

But then considering he had had direct contact with Tom Hutton, it seemed almost inevitable. Musing over the threat of Christians like Tom, he could see Norton's point of view. However, he could never agree with the solution. People like Tom would never push or force their beliefs on anyone. They gave more than they took or would receive. The country's problems would not be solved by eliminating them.

The dimming light of the last rays of the sun cast warm shadows along a porch with rocking chairs and a swinging double. Will tapped on the front door and greeted the older woman with gray-streaked hair who pulled the door open. "Will Masters. Is Butch in?"

"Of course, we've been waiting for you. Care for some sweet tea? I'm Jenny Connors. It's good to meet you."

"You as well! Tea would be fine, thank you." His eyes surveyed the modest ranch with cherry cabinets, granite countertops and a dining nook set in front of a sliding glass door. Will walked up to see the backyard. "Is that a stable?" he asked about the barn-like structure with white fencing.

"It was, but it now holds our lawn equipment along with Butch's four-wheeler and other toys." She brought a tumbler, and Will quickly drank half. "I'll fix a meal."

"As long as it's not too much trouble."

Jennie asked from the kitchen, "Did you drive directly from Oklahoma City?"

"I did." He turned to see Butch heading up the carpeted steps. He didn't realize it had been so long since meeting at the prison. Biting back the urge to say Butch was getting old, he just smiled.

"You look happy. What's the occasion?"

"Finally, free of the Task Force! Chris told me that you believe in Christ."

Butch walked to the kitchen and grasped his wife's hand. "Christ saved our marriage. Been together forty years now. Around the time we reconnected at Hannibal, things were getting shaky at home." He gestured to the table and accepted a cold soda from Jenny. "You see the light, yet?"

"I know it's real. I've seen the lives of remarkable Christians, but…" He traced the pattern on the cloth placemat and looked up. "Not yet," he said lamely, chickening out on exposing his soul. "The last time we met, no one would have ever mistaken you for a Christian."

Butch shared the breakthrough when Tom forgave him. "It shook me to my core. Because of Tom's mercy, I saw my hard heart, the anger, the lack of forgiveness. Over that week God showed me how I was destroying my marriage."

Jenny brought a plate and sat by Butch. "A month later he told me we were going to go to church. I nearly filed divorce papers right then—back then church left a dirty taste in my mouth, but he found a good one. I didn't know they existed. The people were kind. And then he said we needed to go to counseling." She held his hand. "He's the romantic one. I can be quite distant."

"That's the nice way of saying it."

She shot him a look and laughed lightly. "Well, one thing and another…he went first, and I waited."

"She waited six months."

"Had to know it was real."

"Almost lost hope, but then the Lord reminded me that she had not had the opportunity to see the changes in Wallie, Bruce, and many others. Wallie went in and preached to the guys in 24-hour lockdown, and some came out. Not all of them became Christians, but they were able to take their place in general population."

"Have you seen the video on Rosemont?"

"No."

Will nodded toward the laptop sitting on the counter. "May I?" He navigated to the video and watched their faces.

"That's happening here in the States?"

Will nodded, "And the Task Force supports this. Remember when I contacted you about federal prison regulations after we received approval to set up our own prisons? The official reason focused on pastors who were killed in prison, but what you saw in Hannibal happened in every prison we sent them."

They both nodded. "The power of the pastors' witness could not be refuted. I used to feel the same way." Butch added, "That securities fraud case they brought against Warden Foster—that was the Task Force?"

"Yes, and he's not the only one—judges, legislators, and anyone else who showed resistance. Kincaid showed me my case if I didn't go along."

"How did you get out?"

"Not sure, but I've been bumped down to field agent. That's fine by me. Going to Wyoming. That makes it even better." He winked at Butch. "Did you see my new ride? Bought myself a new off-road, full package Silverado."

"Aww, that's too bad. I hear Wyoming is Ford country."

"Well, guess I will continue to be outstanding."

"Standing out as an Easterner is more like it!"

"Of course. So long as I get to catch the bad guys, I'll be just fine."

"That you will." They discussed old times. Butch and Jennie made some attempts to share their faith, but Will sidestepped the comments, focusing on the present and things of this world. He wasn't ready to share—not yet and not in front of Jennie.

After breakfast Butch showed Will his barn of treasures. "You're holding something back," Butch expressed.

Will nodded. "I don't think Jennie needs to hear this. I should have waited and showed the video to you."

"No, she needs to be aware of the stakes, but what this means. I couldn't stop thinking about it."

Will relayed what Norton had told him.

"This is chilling," Butch said, "From ATF and you with FBI, we've all had those cases where the criminals are back on the streets and doing it again. It's dangerous to have the luxury of eliminating career criminals. Doesn't Kincaid know this?"

"He's former Marine."

"Yeah, but Norton's not." Butch shook his head. "I guess, without God, I might think it a viable option, but we have separation of powers for this very reason. I nearly killed Tom with that attitude, and he could have reported me and deep-sixed my career. But he forgave me. I was mad he had hooked up with another jailed black pastor, and they were breaking the color barrier first in the yard and then on Sunday. Made us nervous. I thought I'd teach him a lesson, but God won that fight. Glad He did." He looked at Will. "Okay, so I know you believe God exists."

"Yes."

"You've seen how He has preserved his people."

With tightened lips, Will disagreed. "I've seen how He's led His people to the slaughter and done nothing. Why should I bow to a God who does that?"

Butch met his hard look. "Well, everyone in the end will bow their knee to Him. Even the ones on their way to the lake of fire forever." He wanted to press the point, move into the gospel, but the Holy Spirit held him back.

"I know. I had to learn the Bible to sound like a Christian to infiltrate. I got the ball rolling to help a couple get back with God. I saw the changes in them, but I couldn't follow." He shook his head. "Those men at Oklahoma City have a crematorium. They brought in the ones who would not yield, executed a pastor in front of them and burned his body. And they stood. Not one of them accepted the offer to cooperate. They stood, just as it says in Ephesians. Why would God do that to His own?"

Butch shook his head. Nothing came to mind, no answer appeared. "I don't know what to say."

"You don't have to say anything, Butch. You can pray for me, and I probably couldn't stop you if I asked."

"Do you want me to pray for you?"

"Yes, it's like…" He shook his head, unable to verbalize his thoughts.

"Got it."

⬤

They walked the property. Will stared at the little stream running through the back lot. "But there are no horses."

"Not our thing. The barn's great, and the fences are pretty."

"Jenny has beautiful flower beds."

"And gardens. Her retirement hobby." They turned, hearing her call. "And that would be lunch. Chris should be here soon."

Will smiled when he noticed Chris through the kitchen window. "She's here already. She believes."

"I know. Hey, wasn't that other pastor from St. Louis?"

Will stopped. "Butch, try to forget that fact if you can and don't tell me anything more about any Christians you know."

"Sure."

"But how's that chaplain? The officer Tom mentioned?"

"He died. Had a bad heart condition."

"Natural causes?"

"Definitely."

"Do you keep in touch with the warden?"

"Foster, yes. Write, for now. He'll be out soon."

"I was sorry to hear about his conviction. Heard he was a good warden. His replacement good?"

"Why do you think I took an early retirement package? Anyway, I think they're waiting for us."

After lunch it took minutes to transfer Will's boxes to his truck. He asked Butch if they could store his two suits. "Don't think I'll need them for a while."

"And if you do, gives you a good excuse to visit," Jennie said with a smile. "You're welcome any time."

Back in the house, Will looked at their hosts. "I'll show her the property."

He walked close by Chris' side, resisting the urge to hold her hand. He accepted her with her newfound faith, but did she still care for him? Facing uncertain days, he sidestepped any discussions of a personal nature and told her everything he knew of Norton's Oklahoma operation and the Texas Christian underground.

When she began to share some details she knew, Will stopped at the edge of the stream and reached for her hand. "Don't say, not yet. They said they've let me go, but let's give it time. For now, assume they're still tracking me."

"Of course," Chris stared at him, concern and empathy in her clear brown eyes.

He almost told her he loved her, but the weight of uncertainty and fears held him back. "It's so good to know you have my back. And I would never want to do anything to put you in jeopardy."

"Will, you can trust God."

"Really? Not so sure, seeing what He does to His own."

"Will, after all you've given up for the FBI, after all the stakeouts, and after this deep cover op, you still don't understand God is more worthy of our devotion and sacrifice than any government, agency or organization of man?"

He froze. "Do you know that song about He is worthy?"

"I do."

Turning away to watch a small flock of birds work their way through the bushes and day-lilies lining the path, he said, "I'm glad for you." He left unsaid his awareness that he was unmoored, floating rudderless, driven by wind and wave, helpless to do anything but hang on. To what, he did not know.

Chris placed a gentle hand on his arm. "I understand. There is something else I have to give you."

They made their way to her guestroom near the basement sliding glass door under the deck. Will waited in the sitting room when she emerged with a wooden box.

"Please sit," Chris patted the love seat and placed the box on the coffee table. "It's a treasure box." She paused and pulled out a tissue. "Fran gave it to me after Asa's death." She met his gaze. "Knowing he was dead because he worked with us, she forgave us and said he would have wanted us to have it."

Chris revealed the hidden drawer. "In your darkest moments, He will not turn away when you call." She pushed the drawer back in and handed it to him. "I give it to you."

Will could only nod his head, setting the box on his lap. *What had they said in the last building? That they had to gag the prisoners before they shot them to keep them from saying they forgave their executioners? Had he heard it whispered among the watchers that day?* In the night, in his dreams, the words haunted him. "Thank you," he said with lowered head.

"Let's get it tucked away, shall we?"

That night they laughed and told stories. Chris had more from her law classes. Will shared about learning how to ride with Giles. He found himself saying he never wanted to go back.

"We hear Wyoming is a great place to visit."

Eventually, they began to share their stories of faith. His chest tightened, but Will didn't have the heart to shut it down. Finding Christ or Christ finding them had left its mark. From the outside looking in, he understood intellectually.

Jennifer went to refill the iced tea, and Chris followed her to the kitchen.

"Taking a while. Getting lost?" Butch laughed and shook his head. "This retirement home has a few more square feet, but it's a better layout for a couple. Jennie's never had such a big kitchen."

Chris carried the tumblers of iced tea and Jennie had a plate of cookies. She pulled out a paperback under the plate.

"Will, check out this book. It might answer some of your questions, or at least help you to sift through the roadblocks. It helped me." She smiled toward Butch. "He had me read it."

Choking back a mocking laugh at the title, *The Story of Reality,*[21] he worked to find the right words.

"Hear him out, pal," Butch said. "It's in plain English. Read it for yourself and decide on your own. But you need to see the big picture, and I know you don't have time to hang around and spend hours in Bible study with my pastor. It looks at the Bible's main focus and answers your questions head-on about the goodness of God in the face of evil."

"By Gregory Koukl? Never heard of him."

"Neither had I, but it's a great read."

"How long may I borrow it?"

"Keep it," Jenny said.

"My wife collects good books and hands them out to everyone. I believe this one went out to the kids, sisters, brothers and cousins last Christmas."

"Three years ago, Honey."

"Looks interesting," Chris examined the back cover and table of contents and handed it back to Will.

"I'll get you a copy too." Jenny emerged with another. She settled in her winged-back chair next to a small table piled with papers, a journal and a Bible. "Coming to faith is a process, Will. I know it was with me." She beamed at Butch. "He gave me time to get there. Answered a lot of questions. We scoured the Internet for answers."

"Some were pretty bad. Check the verses as well as the passage. The Bible is the standard by which we judge truth. John 17:17."

"I remember—from the Lord's prayer to the Father the night before the crucifixion."

"I can see why you were able to pass as a Christian," Butch said. He walked to his desk at the end of the sitting room and pulled out several thumb drives. Handing them to Will and Chris, "Audio of Officer Curtis, Jordan, and Tom's sermons recorded at Hannibal. I think you'll find them helpful."

Will pocketed them, uncertain if he would ever listen, but he knew the man meant well.

CHAPTER 35

THE DRIVE TO Gillette took 14 hours. Chris' trip back to Maryland would only be two hours shorter. They both left before six in the morning.

Will dropped the thumb drives in the cupholder, set out on the interstate, scanning for anything decent to listen to. Talk radio was all commercials. The music stations failed to hit the sweet spot. After his second cup of coffee and working at not falling asleep on a monotonous interstate, he grabbed a thumb drive and pushed it into the USB port. Of course, it would be one of Tom's sermons.

The first one hit hard on Christians dividing and attacking one another. "Yeah, name it and claim the reality," he muttered. Pausing the play, he recalled what Butch had said. Officer Curtis had put Christian inmates in key positions, and he assigned guards hostile to Christianity to oversee Sunday events, forcing them to hear the gospel. Maybe the Task Force was onto something. They had to purge Christians from the ranks as well as from the churches.

Tempted to pull to the side, ask Norton's forgiveness and hand over all the Christians subverting the law, he recalled the images of the Rosemont pit, Oklahoma's last building, the sound of the pistol ejecting a round, the explosive cacophony as the guard's hand jerked slightly with the recoil. The strains of "He Is Worthy" rose up.

The traffic increased as he neared another city full of citizens on their way in the morning hours, focusing his attention. Hundreds of miles rolled by, and the urge to call Norton faded away.

A little after eight in the evening, past the sun's setting, Will rolled into the small parking lot of the U-shaped Bison Range Motel, less than a mile from the FBI office. He put the truck in park and surveyed the long, narrow, one-story buildings circling cracked, gray pavement.

Once settled in, he walked past the law enforcement complex, crossed the street and looked at a weathered residence turned into a federal office building. A small notice taped to the inside of a front window was the only indication this was no longer a home.

The front door was locked. No lights were on. Having no idea if the posted agent was diligent or a slacker, he felt the oncoming malaise of uncertainty. Occupying a corner lot, it seemed to have a good-sized garage with two wide doors. Walking along the side road, he studied the back half of the rundown building jutting into the yard.

He paused under the shadow of the trees near the road. What had Butch said? That the reasons we acknowledged to explain the choices we made were often smokescreens covering up deeper issues. Butch shared how he had had to admit his pride and arrogance—traits that worked well at ATF but not at home.

Will's pride welled up as he recalled the federal buildings in Philadelphia or D.C. But memories of the Task Force's Maryland complex also recalled the tension of living with secrets, betrayals and the revulsion of Task Force methods. To halt despair, Will recalled past cases, working with other federal agents in remote locations. If he could once again be part of a team, with a mission he could embrace to pursue criminals, deliver justice, and stop evil, it wouldn't matter what the office looked like.

Resisting the call of neon signs on his walk back, he stopped by a convenience store for groceries and headed for his new home. He had until tomorrow to apply for weekly rates.

Something within him drove him to retrieve Asa's treasure box.

For the first time, he opened the hidden drawer and pulled out the slim Bible—complete, unabridged, and illegal. But what man declared wrong did not make it wrong in God's eyes. Where was that verse—woe to those who call evil good and good evil? Not knowing where to look, he opened the cover and a slip of paper with a list of verses fell out.

Will sighed, running his hands over the note written in Chris' neat script. He looked up each one, seeing her notes in the margins. The storm within him threatened to blow. He closed the Bible but held it in his hands. Opening the Bible, he read Psalm 23 over and over again.

———⚬⚬⚬———

The next morning, showered and dressed in his usual office suit, he left early. Briefcase in hand with laptop and phone, Will found a place to park and tried the door—locked. He walked to a small downtown shopping area, purchased coffee and breakfast. Heading back to the building he found it was still locked. The contact phone number went straight to voice mail.

Waiting in sight of the main door, he approached the first person to appear and followed her in. The young receptionist pointed at the chairs along the wall.

"When does Special Agent Esterly report?" He glanced at the clock, already past eight.

She wrinkled her nose. "Well, this is a shared facility, and they don't usually provide their schedules. When a case comes in, it can change things." Nodding at the sign over the chairs. "Do you have an appointment?"

"How do I make one?"

"Call him. Have his number?" She disappeared down a short hall and started the coffee pot. "Help yourself when it's done."

Will left a voice mail. "Special Agent Masters reporting at the office. When can we meet?"

"He responds better to texts."

"Thanks for the tip."

"Sometimes finishes up paperwork at home."

"I imagine some of the cases can be a long drive from Gillette."

"Most of them."

Seeing no response to his text, he set down his briefcase. "Mind if I wait?"

"Not at all."

He noticed the agency shields and insignia on the front wall. "DEA, ATF, ICE, they have offices here?"

"Not official satellite offices yet. It's a trial program. Agent Esterly has been here two years. When the program expanded, they bought the building and moved in last year." She took her position behind the desk.

Will pulled out the book from Jennifer and settled in.

Special Agent Esterly arrived an hour later. Will rose to greet him, but the man breezed past and headed for the back-corner door at the end of the hall.

Will waited a bit to give him time to settle. "Do you need to let him know I'm here, Stephanie?"

"I don't think so," she smiled. "Good luck."

Will strode to the open door and tapped on the molding. "Special Agent Esterly, I'm Special Agent Will Masters reporting."

The close-cropped, sandy-haired agent looked at Will for a moment. "Which agency are you with? Where's your badge?" His eyes flicked over Will's frame. "Planning on going to court?"

"Court? No, and I turned in my badge at my last posting. I'm the transfer for your vacancy. They didn't tell you I was coming?"

"I'm still interviewing. Have some likely prospects in mind. Where are you transferring from?"

"HCL Task Force, D.C. Office, though I just finished a deep-cover op through the Oklahoma City Office with Director Norton."

The muscles jumped along Agent Esterly's jaw. "*You* sent the text?"

"Most likely."

"Well," Scot Esterly sat forward and leaned his arms on his weathered wooden desk, "Agent Masters, I have a report to file, open cases to follow, and I wasn't planning on conducting any interviews in the near-term until I narrow down my list."

"I'm staying at the Bison Range Motel. How long shall I tell them I will be in town?"

"Go home and I'll call you—if you make the short list." He swiveled to his desk computer and turned it on.

Will nodded and walked out. Back in his motel room, he started calling his old FBI contacts. It took a while for him to connect; eight years had passed since he had worked at the D.C. office. The news was not encouraging—either Kincaid or Norton had had his file flagged. There were openings, but most were in large metro areas along the coasts. However, a Texas resident agency held promise. By lunchtime Will had applied to three openings with the FBI.

Tempted to ask Connors to pray for him, he instinctively tamped down that idea. He didn't deserve God's help. Will's hand froze over his laptop keyboard. That was probably it—*Why should God forgive me? After all, wasn't I responsible for Rosemont?* While he knew he was not directly responsible, he had been a part of the Task Force. That was probably enough in God's books.

Will walked the attractive downtown district and decided he might as well drive back to Hannibal and work on his problem from there. He should have checked out and headed for Butch's, but starting fresh in the morning wouldn't be a bad idea.

Exhaustion took over and he found himself napping after lunch. Will rolled on his side when his phone chirped. "Yes?" he said, lying on his back.

"Agent Masters, you still in town?"

"Yes, sir." He sat up.

"Come back to the office." Scot Esterly ended the call before Will could reply.

Will returned and sat on a worn chair in front of Esterly's desk. The man went through the usual questions, listening to Will describe his years with the FBI and the Task Force. The man's stare was cold, his jaw rigid and shoulders tense.

"Seems we have a situation. My SAC says I *have* to hire you. That director, what did he tell you?"

"My transfer had gone through."

"Well, maybe in somebody's mind, but not in our system."

"Your SAC will have to clear it up on his end, most likely. Dubois, the Special Agent in Charge, for the Denver Office? Would you like me to give him a call?"

Agent Esterly blanched. "No, I can handle it." He rocked slightly in his office chair. "You would be reporting to me. I'd be sending you out on stakeouts; you'll have plenty of paperwork to complete after hours. We're an experimental office reporting to the Casper Resident Agency. It's an inter-agency initiative to handle backlogged cases. Usually DEA, ATF, highway patrol, or Campbell County Deputies are listed as lead, and they get the credit. You clear on this? You will not be advancing your career from this office."

"Sounds fine with me. I like liaising between agencies. Makes for better variety of cases." Will smiled. "I put in my years in the advancement track, and it took me to the Task Force and too many hearings. Agent Esterly, this is exactly what I'm looking for." Trying to lessen the tension, he added, "Let's see it as probationary. After two years I can apply for a transfer if this is not a good fit." He sat back. "I'm looking forward to getting back to real investigations."

"You're done with the Task Force?"

"Completely." He looked at the wall maps of Wyoming, Gillette, Campbell County and nearby counties, next to a white board of open cases and incidents. "Can you show me your open cases?"

The agent stood and walked to the map. He extended his hand, "Special Agent Scot Esterly." Pausing briefly, he outlined seven open cases, two with county deputies, two with DEA, one with ATF and two just FBI for the present.

Will suppressed a smile as he heard about cases ranging from drug and prostitution rings, human trafficking, and organized thefts of mining equipment. "No cattle rustling?"

Scot tried to hide his grimace. "Only if it crosses state lines. Not usually on our radar, but we might have to assist the sheriff's deputy or state patrol officer. Most rustling is someone taking one or two cows in a remote area. Hardly any prosecutions made with those. The rancher's lucky if he becomes aware of a theft within the month it happens." Esterly chewed his lip. "Masters, you can officially decline the posting and walk. This is still a free country. I am obligated to take you as a special agent, but you do not have to accept."

He allowed himself to smile. "Special Agent Esterly, I would be honored to work with you. And, like I said, if after two years it doesn't work, just let me know, and I'll pursue other positions. Good?"

"Fine."

"Now, can you recommend apartments near here?"

"Gillette's still booming with the energy industry, so nice places are pretty pricey."

"Just need a place to sleep—not much more."

"No family?"

"Single."

Scot pulled up a directory and wrote down the contact for a real estate agent. "She should be able to help you." He handed the card to Will, meeting his gaze. "So, what happened with the Task Force?"

"Let's say they decided to go in a direction I didn't feel comfortable going. After trying to work from the inside, I finally realized they weren't going to change."

Scot nodded. "Take your time. Check in tomorrow. I'll try to have your badge and service piece ready." He glanced at the space to the right of the maps. "We'll be sharing an office. It might take longer to requisition a desk."

Will spent the rest of the day opening a bank account, connecting with the real estate agent and perusing local furniture stores while he waited for the early evening showing of the first apartment.

Will met the agent at the street-side visitor's section for a sprawling complex on the edge of town. White clapboard buildings with chipped molding, little to no landscaping, and older cars parked near the units didn't look encouraging. He exited his truck when the agent pulled up in her gray Chevy Trax. Hearing her tell him to follow her, he put his truck in gear and wound through the complex to the back section. The open plains could be seen between the final two buildings with fresh paint and unfinished landscaping.

After exchanging greetings, Sue nodded at the low building opposite the three-story apartments. "You can rent a garage unit." She looked at Will's leather shoes, new jeans and pressed shirt. "You from out of state?"

"You could say that."

"Well, we can get an inch of snow or half a foot, or sleet, hail or rain. This is the plains; things can change in a minute." She looked at his truck, "New? Then a garage would be a good idea."

"I'll definitely consider it."

There were no elevators, but each floor of the long building had its own mini-laundry area with washing machine and dryer. The long hall faced the inner court. The one-bedroom apartment near the stairs at the end of the building was as small as his condo, without the wood trim and granite countertops.

Will surveyed the compact space, his eyes fixated on the rolling plains through the large living room window. He barely heard her descriptions of the kitchen appliances, small full bath and narrow bedroom with a folding ladder for a fire escape.

"I'll take it," he said standing near the kitchen.

"There are two others available in your price range."

He rotated to look out the window. "I think this will be just fine."

Friday, the next day, Will parked in the back lot behind the office building and walked to the main door at eight. The administrative assistant was already there.

"Hello, Miss Stephanie, you early today?"

She smiled. "Yes, siree. I'm leaving early to drive to my grandmother's this afternoon."

Will nodded, glancing down the hall. "Is Special Agent Esterly in already?"

"Yes."

Will walked to the door and tapped on the molding. Various boxes and other items had been moved away from the large windows on the facing wall and lined up along the wall to the right of the door.

"I'll have the maps closest to the windows moved. We can put your desk by the wall."

"Is it on order, Special Agent Esterly?"

His new boss cast him a withering look. "Not yet. You can call me Scot if I can call you Will."

"Fine with me." Will pulled up his saved selection from Office Depot and hit the buy button. "Just bought a desk. It'll be ready for pick-up in an hour." He looked around at the three standing file cabinets along the end wall. "Have a small two or three-drawer somewhere?"

"Let's check the storage area."

Scot led the way across the street to the complex, entered through open bay doors and headed to a side area with industrial shelves of large boxes of towels and other supplies. The end was crammed with discarded office paraphernalia. Will snagged a beige colored two-drawer filing cabinet and a basic office chair.

"I can order a real chair."

"This will do." He lifted the cabinet and Scot took the chair.

"You still at the Bison?"

"Yep, couldn't order my furniture until I had a place. Might pick it up tonight if it's ready."

"You can stay with us until you're ready to move in. Alice was horrified to hear you stayed in a motel."

Will glanced over. Scot was not joking. "That would be nice. I can check out when I go fetch the desk." They were back at the house. "Have enough to keep me busy?"

Scot smiled. "We're still the bureau. We have procedures for everything. Fill out the paperwork and log into the system. When you're back with your desk and settled, you'll have the training videos and programs to wade through."

"Better than having to develop them on your own." As frustrating as bureau regulations could be, they also provided guidelines and structure. *It feels good to be back.*

Scot didn't say a word when Will returned later that morning with a standing desk.

Scot and Alice were gracious hosts. Scot grilled steaks on a protected gas grill on their deck. "Getting a little chilly, but no snow, at least not yet."

"I heard it can come anytime. Does it stay around long?"

"Not usually this time of year. Wyoming weather is rarely boring. It can go either way in September."

The next morning after home-cooked biscuits and gravy with all the trimmings, Scot and Will settled in the lower-level sitting room, coffee cups in hand.

"Will, you've been at field offices during most of your time with the bureau?"

"Yes, Philadelphia and then Washington D.C., but I've worked with resident agency offices."

"Our resident agency in Casper has a staff of 17. I've been here two years by myself. Now the grant for this office has a few years left on it to prove the case for a permanent office."

"What precipitated opening one here?"

"Too many field agents were regularly working cases here starting with the energy boom, and it hasn't slowed. Feels like this is the fastest growing part of the state. You're not just going to do field work, but you will also have to fill the shoes of analysts and assistants." Scot leaned forward, "This was requested by the governor, so we need to make it work."

"You and Alice from here?"

"No, used to be near Casper, but the family ranch is southwest of here. My son runs it. He didn't get the itch."

"Did you have any previous connections to Gillette?"

Scot smiled. "I pulled the short straw." He shook his head. "It's worked out better than expected. Alice likes the area. It helped this happened shortly after our daughter married—she was the last one at home. It's a good place to settle." He leaned forward. "We're spread out in this state and city, county and state enforcement need on-site access to what the bureau has to offer."

"We have the best databases."

"We have a lot of work to do getting them caught up with this area's data and stats. You'll find yourself spending a lot of time running searches for them."

"They have a good handle on what we need to get results?" Seeing Scot shake his head, he smiled. "Sounds like fun—create ways to educate."

Will went to the guest room and pulled out a pad. Together they charted the next few months.

Scot's phone rang, and he exited the room while he answered.

Will surveyed the charts and lists. *This will keep me occupied.* He raised his head when his boss returned.

"Got a case."

"Should I ride along?"

"Not this time. It's a follow-up. I'll arrange proper introductions Monday."

"I'll head out to the office to run through the training programs. You don't have dedicated remote access?"

"Not yet. I can do limited searches in the field, but mostly rely on running them in the office."

"Well, I'll be in the office if you need anything." Will was glad to hit the ground running. He picked up his phone to answer a call from the furniture store. He should be in his new apartment by the evening.

CHAPTER 36

TOM HAD A sermon topic in mind, but he prayed again, waiting for Todd's son to fetch him. Nearly a month had passed, and something within him resisted the urge to call Boonville, Mississippi, home. He would take every day with Todd, his family and the folks of the small village as a gift from God—one to hold on to lightly and release. If only he could walk away with joy and not sorrow.

Bruce stepped into the back room—as large as life as he had been in Hannibal when he ran the unit in which Tom lived—and when they had reconnected just a week ago.

"You again!" he exclaimed, but he hugged the man, now a brother in the Lord.

"You're up."

Nodding, he prayed again. It had taken a few weeks to learn to rest in the Lord for all things during this time of wandering—ministering, preaching, listening, sharing, or witnessing as the Lord led. He slept where he was, whether in a nice house, a back shed, a basement or the back seat of Wallace's Impala. He ate what was set before him, and sometimes that was harder than anything else.

That morning, Tom shared what had been on his heart—of total trust, faith, reliance on God no matter what. Obey the authorities in all things except for those laws against God's orders to share the faith and speak His words to a country desperately in need of hearing the gospel.

Continuing on that God's Word is truth, Tom did not perceive the commotion until Todd approached him.

"Thank you," Todd nodded at the people crowded into the small apartment. "I need a minute with our speaker." Nearly pushing Tom to the back room. He whispered quietly, "Go, and don't give me trouble."

Tom picked up his bags.

"You packed already?"

"The Lord told me something was up yesterday, but I didn't want to believe it." He would have said more, but Todd directed him to a back staircase. They emerged from the building.

Todd peered about and nodded at a white four-door truck at the exit end of the parking lot. "Get in the back and stay out of sight."

Tom said quickly, "Todd, it's been…"

"Get before I drag you. Yes, He told me too." For a moment in time, they stared in each other's eyes, just like in the yard before the hit.

"Meet you on the other side, for eternity," Tom said and disappeared in the darkness, hugging the shadows. As the truck was under floodlights, Tom slipped in the back door on the side closest to the next vehicle.

He crouched down and waited, thinking of the day, only a week ago when Bruce had walked into Todd's kitchen. He had blanched with a fear learned from past experiences with the man in Hannibal. Large with pockmarked face and hair tied back at the nape of his neck, the man had walked to him and enveloped him in a tight bear hug.

"I have wanted to tell you how thankful I am that you had the courage to tell me about God and His love."

Once released, Tom had stood back, in shock. "You're saved?"

"Don't look so surprised." Todd laughed.

Bruce didn't know how many times he had looked at Tom in anger. It felt as if he had wanted to rip him from limb to limb. Tom knew part of it was his fault. He often pushed, sharing verses or aspects of the faith—trying not to take pleasure in Bruce's distress. The last time he had seen him, Bruce had blamed him for the gang war because of Todd's conversion.

The meeting with Bruce had been too short. Bruce brought the pictures of his wife and daughter, and their house beside a barn during the little time they had. Finally believing, he felt the joy of knowing a man he greatly respected would be a good friend in heaven someday. But now he was going with him, and Tom's nerves jumped again.

The front door opened. "You there, little buddy?"

"Yep. What happened?"

"Caught a guy posting your sermon online. He confessed this was the third time. You should have seen Todd."

"Maybe he's clueless."

"Or an informant. Either way, you're with me." Tom braced for the turns and sudden stops of the truck. "When we hit the open roads, you can sit up."

"I never really had a chance to hear your testimony. Wallie preached to you?"

"Every day, but you had a big part of it." Bruce paused to navigate the evening crowd in the center of town.

Eventually, Tom heard him say, "You can sit up." Relieved to stretch out of the crouch, he twisted into the seat, wrapped his hoodie about him, and buckled in. Their eyes met in the rearview mirror. "You know I prayed for you."

"Now I have the chance to tell you. Yes, Wallie led me to the Lord, but your witness drove me there. You know why you made me so angry?" Bruce laughed. "You kept on bursting my fine plans to build my own stairway to heaven—saving Wallie, running the kitchen. You remember that massive headache."

Tom laughed. "You spent half the time yelling and threatening, but your kitchen put out better food than the prison camp did."

"Taking care of Wallie was all part of my trying to do enough good things to overcome all the evil I'd been a part of. And you burst that bubble not just with your preaching but by how you lived. I saw how they treated you, and you refused to get even. I wondered how long you'd last, but God preserved you. Did Todd tell you how many times they tried to take you out and things just happened that stopped it? At first, I thought it was coincidence, but eventually, I couldn't ignore that the great Creator God had your back."

"So, what now?"

"You hear of the program?"

"No."

"My boss is getting pastors like you out of the country."

"Wouldn't that be running away from God's plan for me? He called me to be a pastor in this country just as the persecution started. Why would I sin by running away?"

"Because maybe this is God's way to keep you alive until it's over." He looked at Tom through the mirror. "The church is going to need pastors like you to rebuild and get it right this time."

Tom tried to hide his smile and swallowed his laugh.

"You doubt we can do better, but there were times in the past reformers set the church a-right. That's what it needs now."

"I'll pray about it. I really will, but…" His voice faded away. Tom sat back, staring into the darkness. "It was great to be with Todd."

"He's going to make a great pastor."

"He already is. My time with him was filling in the blanks of what he had already learned and taught himself. Smart guy."

Tom sat back, remembering the warm welcome from Sam's family. How he longed to share, but it was not time to open up.

"It was good I didn't meet you a few years earlier."

"Wouldn't have survived? Too much of a know-it-all?"

"Quoting chapter and verse. That didn't go over very well."

"Rick and Bob let me know about that one. I needed to hear that."

The miles rolled by while they reminisced about their days in Hannibal. Tom sat back as he watched the signs fly by on the interstate. He didn't ask where they were going. This was his next step—his heart still swirling that he was with Bruce.

"Wallie okay?"

Bruce kept his eyes on the road and cleared his throat. "Was fine a few months ago, but he's not feeling that great. I told him to go to the infirmary. Can you pray that he will? Some things they can't fix if they wait too long."

Wallie was still alive, so he had a little more time. "I will. You can't tell him about me. If they knew how close we were, I don't think they'd leave him alone. We discussed it that last day, that we'd..." his voice catching, "see each other in heaven." Not ready to share his vision, he added, "I'll pray he recovers. Still teaching reading?"

"Don't think he'll ever give that up, but having a hard time with the current officer running the programs. Mark keeps him in line, though."

"Did Mark ever?"

"Naw, he's smart. I don't get how he's missed it. He worked with you every day for a few years."

"You do know, Bruce, the fact that any of us believe is a gift of God? He performed miracles to get past our hard hearts. He placed within us the desire for more—for true love, for Him. I was twelve."

"I was thirty-nine." Bruce noted the signs for Joplin, Missouri. Knowing the route well, he drove to the two-story restored country farmhouse a little north of the city.

Bruce pulled into the driveway and tapped his horn. A garage door opened, and he drove into a large three-car garage and parked. Turning to look at Tom, he said, "This is the home of a retired Bible professor; we can stay here tonight. It's very important you answer his questions and be polite."

Tom laughed. "Aren't I always?"

"Hannibal polite is not the same."

"Don't forget, I've been out for a while." Tom looked around the garage. "Listen, considering everything, it's best if I don't know his name and don't know where I am, okay?"

"Of course." He followed Bruce to a short set of stairs that led to a dimly lit dining-kitchen area. A tall gentleman in his mid-seventies greeted Bruce and led them around a corner and down a narrow flight of stairs.

They settled in with bottles of water, and the professor began to ask him questions about his faith. "Which Bible college did you graduate from?"

"Mt. Zion, but they closed the college before I could finish. I completed three years."

The man looked at Bruce, sighed, and began to grill Tom on doctrine. Answering most questions easily, Tom cited chapter and verse.

Their host looked at Bruce. "You weren't exaggerating about the depth of his Bible knowledge." Returning to Tom, he asked for his ministry experience since prison.

Beginning to fluster, Tom spouted his work with the teens, helping the Lincolns and then his traveling ministry.

When they were alone, Tom asked Bruce, "What was that questioning all about?"

"Look, we need to get you into the program."

"I haven't had a chance to pray about it."

"Well, you can always turn them down, but you have to at least get your foot in the door. What if this is God's will for you? Hasn't He surprised you before with the direction He sent you?"

"Okay." Tom shut his mouth when the host arrived with three sandwiches.

"A light snack. Tell me, Tom, what has been the most amazing work you have seen God do?"

"That's easy—that He let me see Walllie's transformation." He nodded at Bruce. "You were there. You saw it. It actually happened when I was in the hole."

Bruce smiled and shared the story, describing how completely the Lord had rescued Wallie.

"That's an incredible story."

"God can work anywhere. He can't be stopped." Tom shared the wonder of God's saving grace in action.

The next morning, they rose early and headed for Livermore, Colorado.

Tom sat in the back and snoozed, letting the miles fly by. He tried to pray about the opportunity to flee his troubles, but his heart wasn't in it. *How can it be God's will? I don't have the heart to disappoint Bruce, though.* He'd go along. If it was God's will, they'd take him; if not, they wouldn't.

It was great to meet Bruce's family. He stayed with them for a few days and didn't want to leave, but the day came for him to go before the committee.

The modern dark wood structure sat on the open plains surrounded by trees and landscaped grounds. The polished wood, hanging chandeliers and flowing drapes set Tom's teeth on edge. Bruce had said the benefactor was a wealthy man. They walked to a room with floor-to-ceiling windows overlooking the foothills with the mountains in the distance. Comfortable chairs in a semicircle faced a glowing gas fireplace.

Tom accepted the cup of coffee and held it awkwardly in his hands. Four were already in the room. Bruce passed out the copies of the professor's assessment. Tom worked at not squirming in his seat while they read the report.

The members talked amongst themselves. "You ready?" Who wants to go first?" "Is this complete?" The last one shrugged. Eventually, they faced him and introduced themselves—all doctors of theology, Bible languages, or ministry.

Tom worked at quieting his nerves.

Dr. Dan Smith started the session. "Tom, when did you complete your undergraduate degree?"

"My Bible college closed. I only had a chance to finish three years before my arrest."

"But you have been out for how many years? You didn't pursue your studies then?"

His mouth dry, the sweat forming on his palms, Tom resisted looking at Bruce. "I was out for two years before Rosemont." His face paled. "I escaped this summer." How could he describe what it had been like: the shame of being a felon, the difficulty of obtaining employment, the constant fear he would lead the Task Force to his friends, or his terror at being arrested and possibly tortured.

"Escaped? Are there warrants out for you?"

"I'm sure they'll come up with some excuse. After all, I openly preach in the streets, in the malls, in the coffeeshops—anywhere I can find someone to share the good news that Jesus Christ is the only way to heaven. If an evangelist is not breaking these laws, then he is not preaching Christ. But I served my time. Have you seen the Rosemont video? Do you not understand that every inmate who survives to his release date is taken to the pit, shot, and thrown into it?" He looked directly at each one, seeing them look away. "It was by God's providence that the guard was able to sneak me out three weeks *after* my release date."

An awkward silence filled the air. The four muttered amongst themselves. The redness crept up Tom's neck. He had experienced this before. Bracing himself for what was to come, he held his breath.

Dr. Smith said, "Mr. Hutton, I'm sorry, but you're not qualified for this program. We are only accepting those with a minimum of a master's degree. While we applaud your ministry, perhaps we can reconsider in the future…"

Tom rose, set the coffee cup on a nearby table. "Thank you for your time and consideration," he said and fled the room. It felt like the review board all over again.

Bruce said nothing when he followed Tom out to the open deck.

"What were you thinking? Didn't you know?"

"But I thought your ministry experience could supersede the academic requirements. Sure, the guys they rescue might be able to read the Bible backward and forward in Greek and Hebrew, but they can't hold a candle to you in the ministry of the Word. You are a pastor, a shepherd for average, common, everyday people. I would like to see them handle Hannibal as well as you did. I would like to see them extend forgiveness to their persecutors." Bruce paused, "I'm sorry, if I had had any idea, I never would have pushed for it."

"Well, at least I have the Lord's answer." Tom leaned against the railing. "What now? I can't stay with you." Feeling the chill in the air and the darkening sky, Tom said, "I need a place to shelter through the winter."

Bruce pulled out his phone as if to call, but he put it back in his pocket. "Let's make a meal in the kitchen, and I'll see what I can do."

"Will they be there?" Seeing the nod, Tom said, "I think I'd rather go hungry."

"Fine."

Tom followed Bruce to the truck, and they drove the winding roads up into the foothills. Bruce stopped at a convenience store and returned with some food. Tom hardly cared what it was.

"The professor considered you a good candidate. I could go back and…"

"Just stop, Bruce."

He nodded and said no more. After an hour of winding roads, he pulled the truck up to a log cabin on the right across from a small barn and two corrals. Bruce looked back at Tom. "Mack and Elsie Diggins. They keep the way station. Sometimes they leave horses for him to work. Elsie had a stroke earlier in the year, and Mack's struggling to keep up. He doesn't want to retire. This has been their home for a long time. If you could help, they might be able to hang on for a while longer. You know anything about horses or cleaning a barn?"

"No, but I can learn." Tom smiled. He liked the look of the place already. "I can wash dishes. Not great at cooking though."

"I don't think they do fancy meals." Bruce grabbed Tom's bags and headed to the door with cross-hatched windows. He tapped lightly on the glass and pushed the door open.

Tom followed, surveying the brown wood paneling glowing in amber lights. A warmth emanated from a potbelly wood stove near a sitting area. A short counter with cabinets ran along the right wall A woman rocked, her gray hair swept up into a bun, with an afghan across her lap.

"Hi, Elsie. Is Mack in?"

"At the barn, checking out the latest arrivals. I'll let him know you're here." She pulled up her phone. "Are you going to introduce me?" Elsie asked. With a twinkle in her eyes, she added, "The manners these days."

"Sure! Elsie Diggins, this is Tom Hutton. I wanted to go over this with both of you."

"Tom, are you one of the guests?"

"Guests?" He glanced at Bruce, shook his head. "No, I didn't make the cut."

Elsie furrowed her brow. Before she could question Tom further, a spry man wearing a wool-lined jacket, jeans and worn boots opened the door.

"Hi, Mack." Bruce extended his hand for a shake. "Meet my friend, Tom Hutton."

"Hutton? Not…"

"Not Alex Hutton—his nephew," Tom said.

"Can we chat a moment?" Bruce pulled a chair from the table by the kitchen area. Tom followed. They faced the couple sitting in their padded chairs by the stove. Bruce explained Tom's situation, giving a brief history. "Can he stay with you until spring? He'd help with chores, here and in the barn."

A silence settled over the cabin. Mack rubbed his chin.

"Mack!" Elsie said, "What's there to think? It's okay by the boss or his man wouldn't be here." She smiled. "I'm not throwing away a chance to help a pastor during these terrible times."

"What do you say, young man?" Mack asked, studying Tom.

"That it would be a blessing." His eyes rose to the stairs leading to a balcony and small area over what he assumed was the bedroom below. "I'm willing to help with anything." He smiled. "I washed dishes for Bruce in Hannibal. Can't be worse than that."

"Sure." Mack rose and set the kettle on the stove. "Of course, have to stay for a cup of tea…or coffee?"

"I'll try the tea." He watched Elsie pull her walker around and join Mack.

Bruce walked over, accepted a cup from Elsie and poured a cup from the coffee pot on the woodstove.

"It'll be old."

"Mmm, good!" Bruce smiled.

"Still better than Hannibal coffee?" Tom joked. Once their hosts were seated, and he had wrapped his fingers around the warm mug of tea, he asked, "And what is your story?"

Each taking turns, they shared their lives with the Lord, each other and at the ranch.

───────⌘───────

The room grew silent when Bruce's phone rang. He walked to the door to answer the call.

"You can take your bags up to the loft—our guest room, so to speak." Mack studied the two backpacks. "That's it?"

"Yep." Tom headed for the rough wood steps.

"Tom, Mack, Elsie, team meeting at the ranch house. You good?"

"Yes, sirree. Don't worry about a thing, young man."

Bruce smiled, seeing Tom's answering nod.

Tom looked at Mack. "You call everyone *young*?"

"When you get to be my age, most everyone I see's young. All in the perspective."

Driving back to the ranch house, Bruce parked, noticing only a few other vehicles nearby. He swiped to his calendar. As he had remembered, the usual monthly supervisors' meeting was a week away. Stilling his nerves, he headed for the side door.

Zackary Taylor, oil magnate, ranch owner, and chairman of the committee spiriting Christian scholars out of the country, gestured for Bruce to enter the inner office. Cherry wood paneled, banked with windows, the sprawling inner sanctum rarely hosted others besides Zackary's ranch manager, chef, or the facility manager.

"Shut the door," Zack said, striding to his large wood desk carved from a Sequoia. He sat down, tapping his forefingers together.

Bruce settled in a short-backed leather chair; his eyes focused on the bookcases running behind the desk. Once in place, he met his employer's gaze.

"I had an interesting talk with Wilson." Zack leaned forward. "I give you broad latitude since I respect your opinion, but you should have run this by me."

"Professor Larkin vetted Tom. Said he was a good candidate. Did you read his report?"

"I saw it. What were you thinking? Now the program's been revealed to someone who can expose us."

"Tom will keep our confidence. Besides, he'll stay with the Digginses for the winter."

"He will? The last thing Mack needs is someone else to care for."

"Just the opposite—Tom will help them greatly."

"You sure of that, Bruce?"

"Absolutely."

Bruce watched Zack open and close his left fist, a sure tell that he was on edge. "Is there a meeting?"

"Yes, there are developments on the range and with the program.

Range bosses will be in shortly, and Edward has security news. Seems the feds have updated their facial recognition protocols."

"Do we have the latest surveillance list from our Task Force contact?"

"Another problem is prioritizing who we have to add to the list."

Bruce nodded. "It's more like triage."

Zack nodded. "And then there are those who won't leave, no matter what." He stared at Bruce. "For example, the brilliant, but stubborn Professor Larkin."

"He's in his seventies and feels the effort should be spent on younger men."

"He knows the program, and he's seen Hutton." Zack's lips formed a thin line.

"Oh."

"Didn't think of that, did you? Hutton's on their radar now with the Rosemont video. You did remember he's in that video?"

Bruce smiled, absorbing his boss's grim assessment and scolding for keeping him on the ranch.

"What do you want? Have me cut him loose? Have him hitchhiking? Or I drive hundreds of miles to get rid of him? Or hide him here in a cabin, miles away from any town? He will not wander off. He will not say anything about our program. He has evaded capture for months now."

"He's on their watch list. A video of him preaching in a park was used to issue warrants for his arrest." Zack leaned forward. "Do I have to spell it out for you?"

"No. I know what's at stake. We all do. The right to practice our faith is under attack. We all agreed it was worth it to rescue those who could shape the future of our churches. What are we doing here? Rescuing the professors but not the pastors? Tom lives the Word of God. He cares about people and knows how to share his faith and help them. I thought that was worth saving too."

"Don't do it again."

Bruce nodded. "Not a problem. Pastors like Tom are not easy to find. I've seen enough pastors and churches to understand finding a true pastor is rare."

"Anyway, they're here. Everything's set up in the conference room."

CHAPTER 37

WILL SURVEYED THE two semis parked among the row of vehicles at the truck stop. Their drivers were still lingering over their dinners. Resisting the urge to ask Esterly if highway patrol had arrived, he nodded assurances to the DEA agents in their vehicles. The wind buffeted the car, the heater barely keeping up with the sub-zero cold. With no blizzards forecast, weather probably wasn't the reason for patrol's absence. There could be any number of reasons why their backup was delayed.

Will's pulse quickened when the two drivers left the restaurant and headed to the trucks. Breathing in relief, he watched them walk to the end of the row and swing up into the high cabs.

Scot radioed, "Our guys are coming out. Go without backup?"

"Go," the other agents said.

The assigned lead for this takedown, Will, gave the command: "Execute!" He considered six seasoned agents could handle two truckers. Unless they could fire up their rigs in record order and were willing to drive over the agents' pickups, they would not escape today.

County and city crime scene specialists went through the cargo parked in a maintenance garage while the agents interviewed the drivers in the office area. Scot took Will aside when the technicians failed to find the fentanyl. "Plenty of meth and weed—but not what we'd been expecting."

Will talked to the DEA agents, and they headed for the truck cabs. "They'll find it. Don't worry," he told Scot. "And if they don't, I'll give it a try. These guys are smugglers. It's not going to be in plain sight."

"Think they were a decoy for the real shipment? Way to smoke out our CI?"

"Maybe. Just because we haven't found it doesn't mean it's not there." Will headed toward the garage area.

"The K-9 unit won't risk their dog on this."

"Not to worry." He walked to the truck cab, climbed in and helped a DEA agent remove the seats. Scot and Will began to take the seats apart. Small bags of fentanyl powder were stowed in the bottom of the seat cushions. "Guys, check for heroin bricks under the mattress shelf."

"Found them." The DEA agents emerged with ten. Will smiled.

Assembling the evidence and statements, the sheriff's office transported the drivers to county lockup. Will accompanied the other agents to their office where they held a late-night strategy session.

Early in the morning, Will gathered the notes and left them on his desk.

"You can make the filings tomorrow," Scot said.

"I'll just process the transfer request to the US Marshals." He confirmed with Esterly, "To Casper?"

"Cheyenne, since the DEA wants to run this case. We have enough to do here." Scot asked, "You coming to the ranch for Christmas?"

"Plan on it—unless an urgent case gets in the way."

"There are advantages to not being local police or highway patrol."

"Unless there's a high-profile murder, kidnapping or missing person." Will smiled, remembering riding horses Scot trucked in to find a missing child.

"There's always that."

"Well, I've got this." He watched his boss put on his coat and head for the door. Their friendship was solid; he respected the agent's professionalism, and most of all his morality. He seemed to be able to maintain the spirit of the law as well as the letter.

Waiting for his sign-on to the Marshall service network, he set the drivers' information by the keyboard. Will had no doubt that Scot was a Christian—even suspected the couple ran a Bible study in their dining room, but he chose not to see. Many of the city, county and state officers with whom he worked were either Christians or supportive of the faith, feeling as if they were beyond the Task Force's reach. Will would not do anything to change that.

During off times or waiting for hamburgers to grill, he asked his questions. Their answers drove more. Faith in Christ seemed just out of reach. Most of his objections had been cleared away with logical, sound reasoning along with biblical proofs, but an inner resistance remained in Will.

The intake screen opened, and Will stepped through the process. Finishing a short time later, he wished holidays didn't collide with winter weather in this part of the nation. If she weren't hundreds of miles away, he would have invited Chris to join them, but then again, why would he? Brain fog threatened to take over. Will exited the programs, shut down his computer and headed to his empty apartment.

By Saturday afternoon Will had checked the name when his phone rang. Saving his work in the database, he said, "Aren't you at work like any self-respecting, underpaid civil servant?" Will smiled hearing Chris' laughter.

"Still at the office?"

Staring out the window, he smiled, "You know me too well. Am I talking to the newest member of the D.C. bar?"

"Absolutely, Maryland is next and will probably tackle Virginia after the new year."

"Consider Pennsylvania?"

"Not unless I have to."

"Going to join the dark side?"

"Meaning, will I work for a law firm? Well…" Chris rotated in her chair between the kitchen and living room. Taking a breath, she said, "I accepted a promotion."

"With the Secret Service?"

"Yes, I wouldn't consider working for anyone else at this point. The Task Force has roped the FBI into helping with their investigations."

"More than providing information?" He knew her reference and was glad she was being careful.

"Yes. Anything like that out your way?"

"We assist local, state and the usual alphabet soup agencies. You would be surprised what travels our interstates."

"Not at all."

"The agent for the Gillette office is great to work with—career, but with a good life-work balance. Actually, I think the whole state's more laid back."

"I hear you."

"He's invited me to their family ranch in central Wyoming for Christmas. You could join us—if it would work out for you. I know that's a hard time of year to travel."

"I'd love to, but I've been tasked with revamping training, agent assessment and internal investigations." She leaned forward, "I have a chance to help shape the Secret Service. It has a great history, an essential mandate, and with a little work, could be the best place for agent development and retention."

He remembered those days, feeling like he could make a difference. "Go for it." Will almost added he would pray she'd find success, but he couldn't—not yet.

They chatted about little things. Will set down the phone and stared at the screen. *The work never stops. There's always more to do.* Seeing the day darken, he shut down his system and headed to his favorite restaurant.

---⚬⚬⚬---

The winter came in hard in early November and stayed. On the way to the Esterly ranch the Saturday before Christmas, Will watched small clouds of powdered snow snake behind the Esterlys' tires and slither to disappear in low snow piles along the side. He sat back, now comfortable driving his truck in Wyoming's winter weather.

Shifting, he stared at the metallic sky—not blue, not white, but an indistinct color as unsatisfying as his life. Will shook his head and repositioned. He assumed getting back to investigations would right the world again, but a wordless void continued to dog his nights. Busy days and working late forced its retreat to the shadows, but never extinguished it.

Will recalled the family pictures Alice Esterly had shown him the last weekend he had been in their house. Of all their children, Michael and his wife Cheryl had spurned the siren song of city life and had taken up the challenge of running the family ranch—they were the fifth generation. He remembered Alice's descriptions of Cheryl's first years. "Once she adjusted to the quiet and the changing weather, you'd never know she'd been raised in Denver."

They had three children. He recalled the picture and the Esterlys' stories—Lee, a typical fourteen year old, and two younger daughters, ten and five. Mandy, the middle child, was solid while Rachel, the youngest, was a tornado. Almost laughing recalling Alice's stories of the girls, he hoped this visit turned out to be a good idea. If not, he would be five days with strangers in a remote area.

The roads grew narrower then turned to gravel. Some spots appeared frozen dirt—paths worked hard by trucks, cattle trailers, and tractors. The two-story ranch house, visible in the distance, looked strangely alone and isolated, with a large barn a distance away. Checking the gauges, noting a half tank, Will focused on the drive.

Trees graced the yard, a pretty circular path wound around bare bushes and flower beds. The white house reached back from the road with a porch running down the side. Encased in the winter's cold, empty flower urns, a frame for a swinging seat and an antique milk box matched his mood.

Will shifted his bag to pull open the screen door for Alice carrying a tray of pies and cookies. He returned Scot's smile. "Another load?"

"We'll help her with her boxes then we can store your gear."

One part of Will hoped there would be a call to whisk him away. He had insisted he would take emergency calls during the week. Hovering by the door, he followed Scot and Alice into the long, narrow kitchen, bright with yellow sunflower photos and other floral art throughout the busy room. Will waited for the greetings to die down between son, grandkids and the Esterlys. And there was more family—Scot's other son and his daughter, a few cousins, and a friendly aunt.

A short energetic woman with a tiny frame extended her hand, "I'm Cheryl. So nice to meet you. Drive good?"

Before Will could answer, Cheryl ran through everyone's name. From the pictures on Scot's desk, he recognized their children: Lee, Mandy and a petite Rachel, who proudly held up one hand and said, "I'm five."

"That's great. You're that big!" Will watched her siblings shake their heads and roll their eyes. "Don't knock it," Will teased back. "Being five is better than being four, isn't it, Rachel? Are you in school now?" He listened to her tales until her father, Michael, sent her to help set the table.

Michael tipped his head in Will's direction. "This way to your room." He entered a long hall and turned right, passed through a door to the garage and up a set of stairs at the far end. He pushed the door open slightly. When it swung freely, he smiled. "They moved the boxes after all."

Will followed him into a somewhat heated storage area with wooden shelves and hooks. Some sections had a semblance of order, others were obscured by piled boxes and bins.

"Both doors lock." Michael dug into his pocket, "Here is the key. Works all three locks."

"Three?"

"Door to the garage, to the guest room and to the second-floor hall." Michael pushed the inner door open. "You can set your bag here. Will this work for your gear?"

"Should be fine."

"Thanks for taking on-call. Dad usually gets it every Christmas."

Will furrowed his brow. "He lacked seniority?"

"He usually volunteered when he was in Casper. Since they lived close to town, he liked to give some of the other agents a chance to go home."

That fact didn't surprise Will. "Probably won't get any calls."

"Yes, but if a blizzard blows through, they'll call you in." He laughed. "And Dad will most likely be right behind you."

"Ahh, so that's why he had me pack double."

"They'll be calling us for dinner soon. Let's get your gear in."

"Much obliged." Will followed him down to the garage and out a side door near the house. "Should I move my truck?"

"You can back it in near the stairs." Michael shook his head. "But they didn't move that mess."

"I think we can handle it." Will looked at the tubs labeled "Christmas."

Will backed the truck in, and they finished unloading just as they heard the dinner call for the midday meal.

The kitchen was buzzing, and the long, draped table in the dining room, set for fifteen, sported a line of casseroles and hot dishes down its center. Whisking back and forth, Cheryl directed the operation. In moments, everyone was seated. "Dad, would you say the blessing?"

Scot nodded and spoke to God as if they were well acquainted.

Spare and to the point, choruses of "Amen" followed, and Cheryl made certain Will had a chance to fill his plate. Talk flowed about the afternoon's activities. It was a Saturday, and Rachel had to be frequently admonished to eat and quit interrupting.

Eventually, Will realized they were discussing a baptism service to be held in the nearby barn. He glanced at Scot, who with a smile, said, "Heated tub, of course!"

Eventually, he asked, "Who is the lucky person?" Will tried not to blanch when the room grew silent.

"I am," Rachel called out. "I asked Jesus into my heart this summer, and Dad said if I could be a good Christian, I could be baptized."

"Well," Michael said, "We wanted to confirm she had made the decision herself and was growing in Christ."

"My cousin, Pastor Hanson, will officiate," Cheryl said and her cousin, sitting at the head of the table, nodded at Will.

Returning the nod, he held back his questions. Rachel, with strawberry-blond hair, curling around her temples and a dusting of freckles across her nose appeared as innocent and average as any other five-year old. His attention returned to the discussion of heating the water. Eventually, they decided to hold it later that day just before supper.

"Snowmobiling?" Lee asked his father.

"Sure." Many were in agreement, and Will followed the flow of mostly men and teens to an overhang beside the barn sheltering four full-sized models. Of course, they had put on three or more layers of outer clothing, along with boots, mitts and face masks.

Pastor Hanson and Cheryl stayed to finish preparations for the baptism.

Michael led the snowmobiling group. He stepped to his son Lee. "You can drive for the Easterner," he said with a smile and a wink at his dad.

Will, about to protest that he had completed his snowmobile training, held it in when Scot shook his head. Instead, he stepped aside, watched Lee put every ounce into starting the machine and swung his leg over to sit behind him on the long seat.

Lee hung back. Positioning his helmet, Will stared into the gray-whiteness of a nearly invisible horizon. Thick clouds, brightened slightly by the hidden sun, were barely distinguishable from the white-purple haze of snow as far as the eye could see. The rolling hills obscured ravines and gullies until they drew close and turned away to continue on past sight of any building.

Will breathed in the crisp air tinged with exhaust and the roar of engines. Stopping by a stream encased in snow and ice, the group paused for the leaders to huddle. Will dismounted, removed his helmet and drank in the stillness.

"Deciding which trail to take," Lee explained.

Will nodded. He stepped forward, finding parts drifted over with deep unpacked snow. "Need to stick with the trail?"

"Sometimes," Lee shrugged, then said, "depends on how much fun they'll let us have," with a mischievous gleam in his eye.

Will glanced at Lee, wondering what the teen had planned. He noticed the rest return to their sleds and start the engines. "We don't want to be left behind."

"Maybe, maybe not." Lee took his time. "If they go where I think they're going, I know a shortcut where we can beat them."

Before Will could lodge his concerns, Lee started the engine, and they followed the group.

He stayed about one length from the third, but slowed his pace when Scot led the group to run along a creek bed. Lee allowed the distance to increase, losing sight of the snowmobile in front of them. Eventually, between two sharp turns, Lee surged up a dip in the banks and on to an open plateau. The ghost of a path rejoined the creek past a large "S" curve.

At first, the plateau had few drifts, and they sailed along. Will tightened his grip when their plateau seemed to disappear into space. A steep culvert lay before them. Lee leaned forward, rolling his hands around to open up the engine. They accelerated into the first dip. Slightly airborne, Lee maintained the throttle, and they landed with forward momentum pulling them down into the culvert.

Impressed that Lee had avoided a sudden stop on landing, Will leaned with the young driver as they followed the curving descent of the culvert wall.

A wall of snow, hidden in the shadows, first slowed, then sent them tumbling down the escarpment. Will jumped clear seconds before the machine slid down to settle in two feet of soft packed snow.

Thankfully, the snowmobile hadn't flipped, but had fallen on its side, the hood encased in snow. Will scrambled over and checked Lee. His left leg was pinned under the machine. Together they worked the snow, while Will righted it.

Lee scrambled out and laughed. "That was awesome."

Will nodded, laughed and said, "*Awesome* will be riding her out of here." He slapped Lee's back to dislodge the snow. "Need to clear anything?"

"Naw, I'm good." He looked about. "Forgot about that weird storm last week."

"Came from the east? Probably why your dad didn't go this way."

"Well, this isn't his usual route."

Checking out the extent of the drifts, they found a wind-cleared path to the other side. Huffing from the exertion of packing snow down, Will said, "We'll have to walk it over."

Lee nodded and let Will walk alongside the snowmobile to work it out of the drifts. Once mostly clear of the soft pack, Will set a knee on the seat and gingerly drove it over and onto the plateau. "Completed my snowmobile training a while ago. Been on a few ops on these things. Getting stuck is often not a question of *if*, but *when*."

"Yeah, well, Dad thinks only people born here know how to handle these things."

"You're the designated driver."

Lee smiled, found his place, adjusted the throttle and the machine surged forward.

Will could see the group far up ahead. They wouldn't beat them, but he figured they had had more excitement than the rest. They drew close to the group shortly before the next stop.

Michael walked over. "How was your little detour?"

"What?" Lee asked, putting on an innocent, "I-don't-know-what-you're-talking-about" look.

Will winked at Michael. "Hey, it was memorable. We're here." Everyone laughed.

Michael looked between the two, shook his head and headed for his snowmobile. "By the way," he said to the group, "Aunt Sara promised her homemade hot chocolate."

"I made cookies," Mandy said. She glared at Lee before sitting behind her dad.

"You in trouble?" Will asked.

"Not this time, but probably won't get the keys again for a while. But it was worth it."

Hesitant to agree, he settled in, and Lee stayed the proper distance behind the cousin's machine.

Once indoors, armed with hot cocoa and cookies, Lee followed Will to a seat in the living room. "Tell me why FBI's better than highway patrol. Seems you all spend too much time in the office."

"Let's take it over there," Will walked to a pair of chairs on the side of the room. He launched into the thrill of catching the bad guys with the nation's most extensive databases. Plying him with story after story, he recalled investigations that rescued hostages, shut down human traffickers and drug cartels, along with aiding state and local investigations. "Let me talk to your grandfather to see if you can join us for the spring youth encounter. You'll get to see it."

"I thought that was local fire and police."

"I added an agency segment, with a focus on the FBI. You'll get to see DEA and ATF in action too." Will paused when half the group began to make their way to the barn.

Taking advantage of the lull, Will asked Lee, "Why does your sister need to be saved? She's just five."

"Dude, we're all sinners."

"Right, but she's that bad of a sinner at five?"

"The Bible says everyone's a sinner, and no one wants to do the right thing. From the day they pop out and hit, scream, or carry on, they're just doing what they are." He studied Will closely. "You don't believe? Hope you were warned it's church all day Sunday, Christmas Eve—besides what they've got planned for us tonight."

"Your grandpa told me. Don't knock having a family to celebrate with. My mom is on her third marriage, and my sister's a drug user." He dropped the subject when Cheryl and Pastor Hanson, along with several others, headed for the barn.

"Can I check out your gear?"

"Sure." They headed for the upstairs room. In the storage area, Will pulled out his duffel with vests, trauma and first-aid kits, rope coils, spare holsters, magazines, ties and webbing and other odds and ends.

"You always carry this much?"

"Packed double, just in case we both have to go." He helped Lee try on the vest. "FBI regs require an agent be always ready to go, even off-duty. We keep our phones with us at all times."

Lee nodded. "Can I see the weapons?"

"I assume you had basic firearm training."

"In Wyoming? Of course."

Will opened up the hard cases for the rifle and shotgun. "What's keeping you from getting baptized tonight?"

"Like it's going to make a difference. I've seen enough people at church to know some are great; the rest are just like everybody else."

Nodding, Will said, "I've witnessed Christians do amazing acts of grace and mercy, but I've also seen others who seem to be missing something."

"The worst is when your own family judges you. Never can be good enough."

"You have to separate that out from your inner guilt. The Holy Spirit convicts us of sin."

"Like He's real?"

Will retrieved the shotgun and placed it in its cut-out. "Yes, I have seen that the spiritual world is real."

"Not someone imagining something more?" Lee said, mockingly.

Facing the teen, he said, "It's not just wishful thinking. God's spiritual kingdom is as real as this physical world. Think of it like another dimension. I've seen too many instances where only the hand of God could have warned a target of a coming takedown. Operations that should have been easy were beset with strange accidents and setbacks. One team found all their assault vehicles had flat tires."

"Come on, maybe someone slipped in and slashed the tires."

"They weren't slashed. The staging area was locked down, with razor wire topping twelve-foot high chain-link fencing. We checked the security videos. Even scrubbed the hard drives for deletions. Didn't find anything. God exists, and He is working."

"And you don't believe?"

"I'm still working through it."

They heard the call for the baptism. Will secured the locks, and they exited through the garage, running across the driveway to the barn.

Soft music played in the background. Lights flooded the nearby equipment bay. Will felt warmth from radiant heaters. A large oval galvanized tub, probably a watering trough, sat in the center. Rachel stood, beaming and shuffling her feet. She glanced at Pastor Hanson.

Seeing everyone present, he said, "We are gathered here today to witness the declaration that Rachel Esterly has accepted Christ as her Savior." He bent down, "Miss Rachel, please share your testimony."

Rachel looked shyly at the crowd standing around her and rubbed her foot sideways.

Cheryl stepped closer and said quietly, "It's okay, honey. Just tell them what you told me."

Nodding, her curls dancing, she began softly.

"Look up and say it so everyone can hear, sweetie."

"Jesus showed me I was a sinner." Her eyes snapped, but she regained her train of thought. "And I knew that…" She began to sniffle, "if I died, I'd go to the bad place. I talked to Mommy, and she helped me pray." A smile formed. "I told God I was bad and asked Him to make me better, and He did."

Will heard Lee groan and say, "Another one brainwashed."

Pastor Hanson said, "We have heard Rachel's testimony of saving faith in Christ."

Seeing the nods, Cheryl lifted her daughter into the tub, helped her place her hands on her chest and slid a handkerchief in her palms.

The pastor leaned over, placed a hand on her back, grasped the hands and brought them to her nose to cover it, and began to lower her into the water. "Buried therefore with Him by baptism into death, in order that…" Her form, suspended under the water, was lifted out. *"just as Christ was raised from the dead by the glory of the Father, we too might walk in newness of life."*[22]

He bent down to hug her, oblivious to the dripping water, "Rachel, as you have believed in your heart and confessed with your lips your faith in the Lord Jesus Christ before many, may you walk in the Spirit."

The pastor stepped aside. Rachel beamed. Spontaneously, beginning with Scot, they sang "In Christ Alone." They continued with other songs of God's grace and mercy and love.

The hint of faith and the love of God whispered past Will. If only he could catch it. Both of them stood motionless, barely breathing. Tempted to repeat that it was real, Will started to open his mouth, but something stopped him. Words would only ruin the moment.

Supper followed—a casual affair of hearty chili, thick slices of buttered bread, with a decorated cake and ice cream.

———— ✦ ————

Will found himself sitting close to Scot and Alice. Knowing he was FBI, some of the cousins asked for stories, and they both plied their best. He had none to share from the Task Force and was thankful no one asked.

Eventually, he excused himself and headed to bed. The weather did not look that great, and he found himself hoping there would be no emergencies.

The night was dark—darker than a mine miles deep. He turned, feeling his way, but he knew in his soul the pursuer grew close, almost upon him. Running, he tripped. Staggering, he faltered. A force stopped him, and he could not move. The knowledge that a bottomless pit lay before him traveled past him like a shadow. "Don't let me go!" he said wordlessly.

Will sat up gasping for breath, not speaking what his mind tried to say—*save me!* He rose and walked quietly to the bathroom for a drink of water. *You will be alone at the judgment*, he heard inside his head. His breath caught in his throat.

Choosing not to pray, he tried to settle back into sleep, hoping against hope the nightmare would not return. *I will be alone on judgment day*. The thought clung. Casting about in his mind for what it might mean, he hesitated to try to find it and refused to ask Scot that morning.

———— ✦ ————

The church was decked in Christmas finery with green boughs, red bows, draped strings of lights, three Christmas trees and aromas of hot cocoa and donuts. The little country church burst with hugs and laughter.

Will and Lee sat together through the combined Sunday school class with a cute Christmas program. The Christmas hymns recalled days gone by for Will. He joined the singing, and Lee eventually sang as well.

Pastor Hanson's message focused mainly on the Christmas story of the Son of God entering life to save us, but it didn't end there. Toward the end of the message as he appeared to be working to a conclusion, he began to recite from Revelation 20:11-15.

Will plucked a Bible from the hymn holder and followed along, his heart pounding. The judgment, at the end of the ages, brought doom for all not recorded in the Lamb's Book of Life. Will listened, almost dispassionately as it was too much to take in, too much to grasp, too much to believe.

If only I had driven my truck, I could have excused myself… But he had ridden with the Esterlys. Thankfully, everyone was too busy greeting one another to accost him.

Will stood by the coatrack, knowing they would eventually return to the ranch. Lee stood beside him. He wanted to say something, but again, his mouth refused to open. The dream, the words in the morning service merged and joined with images of the great white throne judgment, but he was not ready.

They ate leftovers for dinner, and Will excused himself for a nap. Just as he fell into sleep, his phone rang. He was being called in.

He went downstairs to let Scot know. "It looks like they just need one of us to aid in the investigation. I have everything I need."

Scot helped him load his truck, and he was on his way. Will's mind swirling, he pulled over to the side of the road and put his hands on his thighs to steady them. *If I died today, I know where I would go.* Hadn't God shown him in the dream? Hadn't God warned him? A part of him knew there would be fewer calls if he continued to resist.

Dropping his head in his hands, he called out, "Lord, help me. Save me. Deliver me, for…" The tears streaming down his face, he cried, "May You be my God and may I be your people." He breathed deeply and wiped his face. *Can it be that simple? Is it too good to be true? No, it's true.* "Help my unbelief," he said, and the assurance arose unbidden.

Willing his hands to be still, he breathed, checked his mirrors, and continued on his way. But now he knew—if he died today, he would be in heaven with God…with Chris.

———∞∞∞———

One other agent had responded, and they processed the evidence collected. Declining an offer to stay over, he chose to drive back.

He let himself in through the storage area. Everyone seemed to be asleep. Hearing a tap on the bedroom door, he beckoned Scot in and described the case.

"Do you want anything?"

"Just some sleep." Will added, "Rachel's baptism touched me. I hadn't realized what Romans 3 meant." Seeing Scot's nod, he continued, "I asked Jesus to save me. Finally. Why did I wait so long?"

Scot laughed. "I'm happy for you. What is important is that you did accept Him. My dad was practically a preacher; he knew his Bible that well. But I didn't surrender until my first year in college. I think they thought if I found the light, God would tell me to go back to the ranch."

Scot smiled, "You should have seen their reactions when I told them God wanted me to join the state highway patrol."

"You started there?"

"Most guys out here don't make it to the FBI. They promote hotshots like you who use it for a springboard to better postings, and we end up training over and over again. Why I was death on you in the beginning. It's been nice having someone who knows what he's doing."

"You as well. Good to see an agent who's invested in the community. That makes a difference." He looked about. "You know, eventually the Task Force will make their way here. Unless the laws are overturned, and that doesn't look likely, your churches had better hide their illegal Bibles."

Scot rubbed his short-cropped hair. "Take those Bibles with missing verses?"

"Or pull them altogether." Will drew close. "They said they let me go, but it was too easy. It's been at the back of my mind for a while that they sent me here because they suspect many in this state are believers."

"Or they know we have a right to practice our faith."

"I could be under surveillance and when they're ready, they'll swoop in. I can justify our spending time together, but I can't know who the other Christians are." Stepping back, he could see Scot understood. "Will you tell Alice? Warn the pastor?"

"Yes, I'll convey the warnings. Hard to believe it's true."

The next day, Christmas Eve, Will went to the small-town market with Cheryl and Mandie. "Where are the Christmas cards?" Will asked.

"Going to write a letter? A little late?"

"I need to write a very dear friend, Christine."

Cheryl said, "I have lots of Christmas cards. Bought double last year and only sent half out. We have plenty you can choose from to send to your lady friend."

"Much obliged."

CHAPTER 38

TOM SETTLED THE afghan around Elsie's lap and made sure her mug of water with a straw was close at hand.

"I'd like to hear the Psalms, young man," Elsie said, her voice thin and reedy.

"Any one in particular?" Seeing the shake of her head, Tom began with 118 and on to 119. Dishes sat in the sink, the floor needed more than sweeping, and chores waited in the barn, but he sat and recited the verses with an even tempo, watching a peace settle over her.

Mack returned, gritting past the pain of his left hip and sat in the easy chair next to the rocker.

Tom finished the stanza. "I'll finish the barn chores. When do you want me to do the turn outs?"

"Put the second batch out this afternoon. Should be good today. You not heading to the Black Forest?"

"If I get time."

"Make time. This can sit a while." Mack leaned back.

"Lunch is on the stove." Tom rose and reached for his coat.

"I want to go to church this Sunday." Seeing their expressions, she added, "It's Easter. I feel better."

Mack patted his wife's knee. "Listen, you've just recovered from pneumonia."

"And the doctor said I could go out."

Tom tried to let him know it sounded like a good idea, but Mack only had eyes for his fragile wife. Tom settled his coat around his shoulders and stepped through the door. Elsie had continued to have small strokes, and over the last month, she had progressed from a cold to the flu to pneumonia. Last week they thought she wouldn't make it, but she appeared to have rallied.

Tom cleaned out the stalls on the north side, added hay and retrieved the first group enjoying the sunshine and sprigs of grass greening in a week of rain and warmth. Putting out the second group, he completed the barn chores before returning to the cabin.

Mack dozed lightly in his chair.

Tom, not wanting to wake him, backed out of the cabin, saddled a large bay and headed for the Black Forest Shop and local cafe.

It had become a ritual; he told stories to the children in the play corner stocked with books, puzzles and games, or struck up conversations with those sipping coffee or tea. Every week Christians gathered in the store for singing, teaching and fellowship. It was a loose arrangement with three preachers taking turns, teaching or preaching depending upon their style. In the back country of Colorado, far from cities, he felt at home.

Upon his return Tom saw Mack reaching for a heavy saddle. He walked over, took it down, and followed Mack to the roan tied in the center aisle. "This youngster's going to get his training today? You want me to ride?"

"Naw." Mack patted the tall horse's shoulder. "Just tack him up."

"Elsie needs to go, you know." Tom would have pressed it, but he focused on the final grooming and bent to clean out the hooves. The young gelding didn't like his right rear being messed with. Securing the leg with his knees, cooing reassurances, he ran the pick around the frog of the hoof, releasing a small wedged pebble.

Mack sighed. "I know."

Tom stood. "God will keep her here until the time." He paused.

Nodding, Mack said, "I know. I'd like to hold her—hold her and never let go, but..." He looked over with tired eyes. "You get to preach?"

"I'll take the sunrise service."

"Then, that's the one we'll go to." Their eyes met. "You have any word from the Lord about when you're moving on?"

"Nothing." Tom smiled. "I wouldn't mind staying, as long as it works."

"You stay as long as you like." Mack moved to the side, accepted the reins from Tom, grasped some mane in his hand and swung up.

Easter was early that year, but the day dawned with a warm sun poised to burst forth from the foothills. Tom looked at the small crowd assembled past the lean-to and hitching rails behind the Black Forest. "Let us pray," Tom said, waiting for the young man on his right to start the prayers.

One by one they prayed for family, friends, and the nation—that from the ashes of grief and sorrow, a new faith would arise. They walked to the shop after Tom's prayer. He stood in front of three dozen chairs, all filled. Nodding at the song leader, he listened to the blending of voices raised in joy and praise for He is risen!

He had wanted to preach on the marvelous gift, to recite resurrection passages, but the Spirit drove him to speak of the "greater things" believers would do in Christ's name until the whole world heard. Christ came to serve the Father; Christ calls His disciples and sends them out.

Ending with the joys of a heavenly inheritance, certain and waiting, they would, one day be together in the presence of God and the angels. This time of parting was only for a season. Tom hadn't wanted to end on such a note, but heads nodded. And they sang Easter hymns as Cal strummed his guitar.

Bruce organized the kitchen crew. Tom helped set up the tables. Elsie talked to those who stopped by to greet her. Mack tried to help, but Tom said, "Keep her company. We have more than enough hands."

Tom headed back to the kitchen to see if the bacon, eggs and biscuits were ready.

"Tom," Bruce called. "When did Mack's hip get so bad?"

"More than a month now."

Bruce looked past the serving counter. "She's not well."

Tom nodded.

"Does Mack know?"

"A part of him, maybe."

They watched Mack not taking his eyes off his wife as she hugged another youngster. "I think she knows. She insisted on coming today." Tom could see the shadows thickening around her eyes. "Probably need to head home soon. She's not eating that much. I'll fix them some plates."

"Do that."

Two weeks later, an hour past midnight, Mack sat up, feeling Elsie's body shake. Turning on the light, he saw her head pulled back, her eyes closed, her hands spasming in the air. "Tom! Tom!" he yelled. Oblivious to the pain in his leg, he rolled out of bed and around to his wife's side.

Tom appeared.

"Call 9-1-1."

He headed for the phone and called, but the ambulance would take a long time to come. "Do you want to take her directly to the hospital? We could meet them." Tom froze when he realized Elsie lay still.

Mack felt for a pulse.

"CPR?"

He shook his head. "She has a do-not-resuscitate order. Her body would never survive it. That's what the doctor said."

Tom relayed the message to the ambulance service and sat with Mack. The sheriff came before the medical examiner. Mack called his children and her brother.

Early that morning Bruce dropped by. Tom listened to them talk, feeling his world dissolve. Mack's upbeat smile and squared shoulders were gone. He sat, deflated and small, his eyes unfocused. Tom brought coffee, rode to the Black Forest and returned with his favorite pastries, but Mack merely nodded and said little.

They drank coffee and ate the strudels, listening to the sighs.

Mack said, "It's time. That new station ready for the last four?"

Bruce nodded.

"What? But I thought," Tom began.

Mack patted Tom's knee. "This was *her* home, *her* range. I held out for her. Would have broken her heart not to die in sight of her beloved Colorado Rockies. I'm from a migrant family; we worked the ranches traipsing up and down from Montana to Texas. Momma settled me, that she did." His eyes grew distant.

A trailer came for the horses. Tom helped Bruce bring a load of boxes for Mack.

"Where will you go?" Bruce asked.

Staring out the kitchen window, Mack replied, "Billings, my son has a room ready." He looked at Bruce and Tom. "Probably get a place of my own before end of summer. Billings will work, and I have…" His hands hid his face while his shoulders shook.

Tom laid a gentle hand on his shoulder. Nothing needed to be said. When Mack wiped his eyes and formed a meager smile, Tom asked, "Would you like me to help you pack?"

Mack nodded.

Bruce moved to the door and gestured for Tom to follow him outside. "Once family gets here, I'll find a place for you."

Tom leaned against the cabin. "Nothing from the Lord. No sense of where I'm to go."

"We're praying. Let's see what God does."

He tried to smile, put on a brave face, but Bruce wrapped him in a hug. "He's not abandoned you yet, and He's not going to now."

"I know. I should be grateful I had such a wonderful time here. It hurts to move on."

"We have been blessed having you here. We'll miss you."

Several cars followed the hearse to the family plot. The fellowship assembled around the graveside. Mack nodded at Tom.

He read Elsie's life story. Tom added the blessings and faith he had seen in her. Looking at the group—most he knew along with the family he had just met—and said, "This is your turn to share a memory, a story, or a thought."

Summarizing the woman's life of faith, he talked of the heavenly joys she was experiencing. Tom's gaze settled on Mack. "Parting is for a moment, but eternity will be forever; a certain hope undergirds our griefs with joy."

After the simple graveside ceremony, they drove to a nearby restaurant. Tom hung back with Bruce and his family.

A man walked up to Bruce and greeted the family. They seemed to know each other well. Tom had seen him attend some meetings or stop by the Black Forest.

The man turned to him and extended his hand. "Zackary Taylor—Tom, right?"

Tom nodded, suspecting who this was, but afraid to ask.

Zack said to Bruce, "You and Tom drop by this afternoon."

Tom looked at Bruce. When they were by themselves, he asked, "Is that your boss?" Tom watched the man work his way out of the restaurant after talking with Mack. "What do you think he wants?"

"Haven't a clue—not today anyway." He looked at Tom. "Your stuff is still at my house."

"And it will probably stay there—for a while anyway." His chest tightened, his heart skipped a beat, but pastoral habits took over and Tom began to visit.

⸻⸙⸺

That afternoon Tom and Bruce said nothing on the drive to ranch headquarters. His pulse quickened seeing the building.

"He will lead you, Tom." Bruce smiled and hugged him.

They walked up the steps and through the side door. Bruce led him to Taylor's office and knocked on the door. He pushed the door open and directed Tom to the chair in front of Zack's desk.

Tom headed to the seat, feeling it with his hands, not taking his eyes off Taylor.

"Well, Tom, I've been impressed with your ministry and haven't had a chance to thank you for helping the Digginses stay as long as they could. Circumstances now dictate other options. I heard your sunrise service was excellent. Many appreciated your message today." He paused, "Do you have plans?"

"Plans?" Tom's mouth went dry. He glanced at Bruce. "No, I'm waiting on the Lord but haven't received any direction yet."

"We have an opening." Zack paused, seeing Tom's face turn pale. "I know the board didn't find you technically qualified, but I can override that." He leaned forward, "Our latest prospect couldn't travel due to illness. You'd be a perfect fit. We already have a professor in the same city. You could support one another. So," Zack smiled, anticipating relief, acceptance, and gratitude from Tom.

"But…" Tom said and looked at Bruce. "Didn't you tell him?"

"What?"

"God already answered. He said no through the board. How can this be God's will?"

"You're turning it down?" Zack asked incredulously.

Bruce said, "Let's give Tom time to pray about it." He looked at his friend. "Tom, what if you haven't received further guidance from the Lord because this is what you're supposed to do?"

Tom remembered that look—one he had seen countless times in

the kitchen or their unit. Bruce would have his way no matter what, but not this time. He rose about to decline the offer with sufficient thanks not to totally offend this man, but Bruce rose at the same time.

"Give him time to pray about it," he said to his boss. "How long does he have?"

"Twenty-four hours."

"Tom, don't run away. This is not the time to hide. You heard him. By tomorrow this time, you return with an answer. You can be early, but don't be late, and..." he lowered his voice, "don't be afraid to let us help you. The church of Christ will need you when this is over."

Looking between the two of them, feeling trapped, Tom opened his mouth and shut it; nothing coming out.

"Tom..." Bruce laid a gentle hand on his shoulder. "You are not alone. I know transitions are hard, but God will be with you even through this. And just as Elsie is in a better place, maybe God has something so much better for you that you can't even imagine. You could finish your degree, learn to read the Bible in Hebrew, get those courses that you missed. Promise me you will honestly pray about this."

"I will." Tom looked about before he fled the room. He headed over the hill, across the road and along the trails he had traversed on horseback. His mind swirling, he barely recognized where he was until he stood on a hilltop, the station visible in the distance. Finding a warm spot on sun-heated rocks, he sat, wept and tried to pray, but his heart fought, holding on to what was.

Before daylight gave way to dusk, Tom walked to the station and slipped in the side door of the barn. The stalls were empty, but hay and some blankets remained. After peeking out to see the cars and trucks parked by the cabin, he retreated to an inner stall and curled up.

He dozed only to start awake, turn, and roll—over and over again. The fight continued, until at the deepening of the night, right before the dawning, he surrendered. "Lord, do You ask this of me? Is this Your will or my weakness? Did You not put me in this country at this time for a reason? Was it to run away? Make Your will clear, and I will do it. What are You sending me to do?"

His mind turned to the hopelessness that lurked never far away. Remembering Bruce say it was to keep him safe until it was over—but what would it take to shut down the Task Force? Tom sat up, hardly believing the answer he thought he had received.

He stood, stepped out of the barn to see the light of a new day creep across the road. Tom set his face. Even if they would not understand, he would complete the task.

He arrived at the ranch house a few hours after dawn. A groundskeeper let him in and offered some coffee. Tom drank it, for the first time aware that bits of hay was clinging to his trousers, his hair was matted, and his hands were dirty. He sat on a chair along the entrance hall.

Tom rose when Bruce walked in. "Okay, I'll do it."

"That's it?" Seeing Tom shake his head, Bruce hefted the duffel. "Here are your things. Where do you want to leave anything that could be traced to you?"

Tom knew what he meant—his notes, the doctrine and verse memory pages. "Keep them or give them away. I use a different name to get through the checkpoints until I'm in-country?"

"You will live under that name." When Tom's eyes opened wide and he stepped back, Bruce said, "It's the only way. It'll all get sorted out later." Tom's back remained rigid. "You're going to have to let us cut your hair."

The spell broken; Tom laughed. "Well, I assume your barber's better than the ones in Hannibal." Drawing closer, he said, "Remember, Bruce, everything I do will be what God told me to do. Don't forget that."

"But you're going, right?" He smiled for the first time. "When's the last time you ate?"

"At the funeral dinner. I'm okay."

"Tom," Bruce lowered his voice, "You can't do that. You have to eat. Choose life."

His head shot up and he asked, "How is Wallie anyway?"

Bruce shook his head. "Stage 4 pancreatic cancer. They've moved him to hospice."

He wanted to share but was afraid if he talked about his vision of Wallie, he would tell the rest and Bruce couldn't know.

CHAPTER 39

Tom hung back in his seat, watching the other passengers walk down the aisle to disembark. He rose, pulled down his carry-on and followed the last one. The corridor led to an open area with a line of small booths for immigrations and customs. Tom hefted his pack and pulled his rolling carry-on to keep up as the line snaked around portable web barriers. Sweat formed on his upper lip.

Near the end of the flight from Iceland, Tom had pulled out his hidden identification and made sure the thumb drive was in his pocket. He looked at the faded copy of his birth certificate, expired driver's license and social security card thanks to Reggie, the Rosemont guard.

A mid-morning sun warmed his neck through large plate glass windows. He rubbed his eyes, still bleary from spending a night in the Reykjavik Airport, and shuffled forward.

The agent gestured for him to approach the high counter. "Traveling from the United States?" Tom nodded. "Reason for travel?"

Tom pushed his fake travel documents under the window and cleared his throat, the blood pounding in his neck. "I want to apply for asylum—refugee status."

The agent looked at him closely, pursed his brow, the corner of his mouth curling up. "Say again?"

"I am Tom Hutton." He presented what ID he had. "I'm requesting asylum as my life is in danger." He paused, waiting for the man's laughter to ease. "I fear for my life because of religious persecution."

"You're not this person here?" the officer held up the passport.

"No. That ID was necessary so I could leave the country."

"Are you saying you are under threat of arrest?"

"Most likely."

"What offense?"

"Preaching the gospel of the kingdom, that Jesus Christ is the only way to heaven."

"Seriously? That's a crime now?"

"It is in the States."

The agent noticed the rest of the passengers had cleared customs. He piled Tom's documents together. "Go with that security guard."

The guard led him down a side hall and swung a door open. "Step in. Set your luggage on this table and step back." A customs agent and another officer entered. Two searched his bags while the customs agent patted him down.

He sat at a small table, his back against the wall. Tom dodged questions about his travel documents. The officers left the room, having found nothing illegal in his luggage splayed out on the long table. A short time later another officer took his fingerprints with a small pad. An immigration officer continued with his questions.

Tom answered as best he could with an even voice. In the middle of explaining his incarcerations, an officer stepped in and handed a notebook to the immigration officer.

They both looked at Tom. "Your country has an arrest warrant for you. Care to explain?"

"Does it detail the charges?"

"I'm asking the questions here."

"Well, most likely the charges have to do with preaching the gospel of Jesus Christ."

They both laughed. "Is that right? You think we're going to believe that?" The customs officer was about to say more, but the immigration officer shook his head.

"Find any contraband in his luggage?"

"No, sir."

"Was it scanned?"

"Yes, everything looks good."

"Write up that he traveled with forged documents and that he's requesting asylum." Holding back his laughter, he shook his head.

"IPO matter now?" Seeing the nod, he directed Tom's luggage be reassembled.

Tom found himself in a holding area with a small toilet/sink area. They even fed the growing group of detainees. He gathered from the conversations swirling around him, they would be transferred to Cloverhill Prison. His stomach knotting, he shoved it down and set his face, trying to remember that God did know what He was doing.

A van holding five detainees slipped along a highway, bounded by tall trees and high barriers. Tops of warehouses were visible here and there. Tom noticed a vehicle with "Motorway Van" lettering parked on the shoulder and reminded himself that he was in a different country. He listened to the talk around him, trying to identify the new vocabulary—with the accent; it was sometimes hard to make out the words.

"What's the IPO?" he asked the one sitting next to him.

The man smiled sideways and laughed. "International Protection Office, what you want with them?"

"They deal with refugees?"

The man nodded, describing exactly what he thought of the system that let in the world's unwanted and paid them to sit around. "And Direct Provision—we should be taking care of our own." Many joined in with their opinions on granting asylum. "So," he asked Tom, "from the US of A? What got you a ride to the gaol?"

Tom swallowed. Before he could frame the best answer, the van passed the last apartment building and drove through gates bounded by razor-wire topped fencing.

Separated after a brief intake, Tom surveyed the blank walls in a small room, wondering who'd walk in next. Two IPO officers entered, and one introduced himself, speaking quickly and indistinctly with a thick accent. Tom couldn't make out any of their names. The questioning went round and round. Tom answered only those about himself. None admitted or even acknowledged if they had watched his video evidence.

Instead, they thrust a pad across the table. "Write out your story, including your earlier arrests and what you were charged with."

Eventually they led him to a simple single cell. He drank from the sink and lay down. Sleep came quickly despite his inner tension.

They came for him mid-morning.

The first IPO officer said, "You cannot be granted asylum if you broke any laws coming here. Let us help you. Tell us who provided the student VISA and passport."

Tom shook his head. "Not doing it. I accepted the help. What did you think of my evidence?"

The lines crinkled around his eyes, but he held back a laugh. "Pretty sophisticated group you're with. What's the play?"

"Play?"

"End game? Expose Direct Provision?"

"Let the world know my country's killing their pastors. It's really happening."

"Let's start again—with the truth this time."

Tom slid his gaze away, focusing on stains on the battered table and reviewed Psalm 119 in his mind, trying to shut out the noise.

He had to admit, they were treating him better than the Task Force. He had received regular meals and bathroom breaks. Assuming it was the afternoon already, he yielded to heavy eyelids and rested his head on the table. He jerked up, clearing his eyes when the door burst open, and a new officer in a gray suit entered the room after the IPO officers.

The new officer asked, "How many others from your group have entered the country?"

About to deny it was his group, he swallowed and answered, "I did not enquire, nor did I want to know about anyone else in the program." He clipped the sentence, seeing the light shine in the questioner's eyes. "I have nothing further to say."

"Why risk it? You could have sailed through customs to university. Why?"

"Jesus said to render to Caesar what is Caesar's and to God what is God's. When my country that I love passed HR 756, they made Christians into criminals. I have always tried to keep the laws of man that do not encroach on God's territory. I only took the ID to leave my country; it would not have been possible if I had tried to travel under my own name. That is why I surrendered them to the first authority."

"You changed airlines in Iceland."

"Yes, but I never passed through their customs. It never occurred to me to apply for asylum there. I passed through customs at Dublin."

"Your silence will not protect your organization, Mr. Hutton. Documents always tell a tale. So, help us so we can help you."

Tom heard it, the subtle difference in tone and inflection. The officer did not sound like the other two—maybe a British intelligence officer? "Be aware that anything you relay about this matter to the United States will be transmitted to the Task Force. They will use any and every means to shut this down."

"Is the video a forgery?"

"The video documents a great crime."

"Then why the media silence? Why are the churches still open in America?" His accent changed again to British with an Eastern seaboard tinge.

"It goes up to the President. They are pressuring judges, all levels of government, as well as the media. Did you read my statement? A reporter tried to write about my arrests when I was in county lockup in Wichita, Kansas. He was killed in an automobile accident the following week. It might seem circumstantial, but looking at the big picture reveals the pattern. Churches can function in the public square only by cooperating with the Task Force. They are required to report their neighbors and members. The government dictates what constitutes a legal Bible; they torture and murder behind closed doors. That is why I took this risk—that if I told the world, my people would know what is really happening. Hundreds have disappeared at the hands of my country. And if Ireland did grant me asylum as a refugee; if I could prove religious persecution is occurring right now on US soil, then maybe the citizens of my country would rise up, search out the truth and take action against what is going on in secret."

The IPO officer on his right said, "The United States is considered a safe country of origin."

"That would have been true ten years ago."

The officer furrowed his brow and raised his voice slightly. "Even without the forgery charges, your claim would still be denied without evidence supporting the video, including affidavits from witnesses."

Feelings of doom and hopelessness washed over him. He resisted questioning why God sent him on a seemingly hopeless errand. "Asking others to testify will bring them and their families to the attention of the Task Force."

"You will be deported."

Tom nodded, "That's the agreement. I apply for asylum and if you issue a deportation order, I will abide by it. Do not mistake my breaking of laws that go against God's higher laws to mean that I am a law-breaker."

"You broke our laws by entering using forged documents."

Tom shrugged his shoulders. "There was no other way to flee my country."

"We tried to corroborate your story. Mt Zion Bible College doesn't exist."

"It shut down years ago when the laws came into force. They must have taken down their website. Search for my uncle, Alex Hutton. He used to be part owner of Hutton Family Furniture Stores. He became a pastor in Kentucky. When they assaulted his farm, they killed his wife and sent him to Leavenworth. Contact the prison; they should provide information on his incarceration. He died in prison at the age of 59."

The officers rose and left the room. Tom couldn't keep from jumping slightly when the door slammed shut. *God has a way; I just have to find it.* Running through the possibilities, Tom hatched a plan.

Hours later he went through intake, similar to district detention and was escorted to the committals area for arrivals and orientation. The two-tiered block was clean with light-yellow walls and single occupancy cells. Residents milled about the commons area.

He settled into his cell, having received paper and a pen, but not a Bible. They said the chaplain would be by later.

Tom hovered by his solid door, assessing the groups. Selecting the tamest-looking bunch, he walked over to join them.

As polite as any group trying to jockey for good placement in a facility, they nodded back and continued on with their conversations. Tom listened to the unfamiliar words and accents, drinking in the ebb and flow of their speech.

After supper, a guard called him out of his cell. Tom noticed an older priest in black robes just behind the officer. "The chaplain?"

"Fr. John," the priest said and gestured to a nearby table.

"Tom Hutton." He looked at the Bible the priest slid to him. "Thanks. I'd like to sign up for Bible studies. How do I do that?"

The white-haired, slim priest smiled. "Of course, tell me about yourself."

Tom didn't hold back. The man with steady hazel eyes listened without comment. "If I'm here long enough, I'd like to volunteer to lead Bible studies, but I need to figure out the lay of the land."

Fr. John nodded. Asking Tom about his volunteer activities, he smiled broadly when he heard Tom talk about telling stories to the children.

CHAPTER 40

"**H**AVE A GOOD Easter, Dad?" Michael asked as he passed the bowl to Will. "I heard you were baptized."

Will noticed Lee's shocked look. Michael and Lee were visiting for the Campbell County Spring Law Enforcement Camp. Praying for an opportunity to talk with the teen, he scooped out a generous portion of mashed potatoes and handed the bowl to Lee.

"We enjoyed a quiet Easter—despite the surprise blizzard."

"Didn't make it down to us," Lee said. "Grandpa, you running the evening sessions?"

"No." He nodded at Will. "My sidekick's running the show tonight. But be ready for tomorrow. We'll put you through the drills. So, don't make it too late."

Michael nodded, but Lee shot a questioning look at Will and smiled, seeing a reassuring nod. They were going to squeeze in a little rock climbing in town that night.

Will left for the county training center to finalize the setup. Michael and Lee would arrive with the rest of the attendees. Tables lined the foyer, and Will joked lightly with the officers waiting for people to arrive.

It had surprised him that he had been selected to emcee the evening. He kept the presenters moving through the various segments, finishing up with the bureau and how it tied everything together. Ignoring the buzzing of his cell, he wrapped up the session and stepped aside to check the message.

Reading the text, Will looked up. The Denver Deputy Special Agent in Charge, Otis, and Sean, whom Will assumed now worked for Otis, and two other agents filled the back doorway. He approached the group and followed them out to the foyer. Scot stood with arms crossed and a grim look, but they didn't have a chance to talk.

Sean said, "Hi, Will," with a dismissive look and handed an envelope to his former boss. "Warrants to search your premises."

Will shifted, scanned the group, saw Scot's nod and unfolded the order. He breathed a little deeper, seeing it was only for his personal effects and not any of his work areas.

"Agents are executing a search of your apartment as we speak," Sean said, stepping to Otis' side. "Now, for the office."

"No," Scot approached, glancing at the Deputy SAC, "The warrant does not cover any bureau areas. As his superior, I guarantee Special Agent Masters has no personal items in the office, his desk, or his bureau computer. We will conduct the interview in Room 3B."

The Denver deputy expressed his agreement.

Chris had visited for Easter and had brought both him and Scot up to date on the Task Force's misuse of bureau data access. His chest quickened, hoping he had put his Bible away last night. If not, he would be arrested and outside of any chance of Esterly's help. Will felt the agents surround him.

Otis tried to run the interview, but Scot laid down the ground rules. Sean started the voice recorder, opening the session as Will would have.

Otis smiled, cleared his throat, and after a quick statement concerning Special Agent Esterly's obstruction not granting office access said, "Two days ago Tom Hutton applied for asylum at the Dublin Airport."

Will saw the hardened looks from the other two agents and realized they worked for Norton. He slid his eyes away to gauge Otis' next move. If they had proof that he was responsible for Tom's release from Rosemont, he would have been arrested already.

An agent from Oklahoma began the interrogation, reading transcripts of Will's debrief after his undercover assignment. "Do you remember seeing a Dr. Dan Smith?" Before Will could reply, the agent continued. "A man resembling Dr. Smith has been spotted at Trinity College in Dublin, Ireland." He leaned forward. "When Hutton requested asylum, he presented not only his own identification but forged documents for a cover identity. Remember the group you were tasked to uncover—the one that you had failed to penetrate?" The agent leveled a direct gaze. "This would be a good time to come clean. Lying to federal agents is a crime. I ask you again, do you have any knowledge of the group protecting Hutton? The level of sophistication of the documents reveal a well-funded, highly placed organization. Hutton flew out of the Denver Airport."

That fact accounted for the Deputy SAC's cowed look. Thankfully, they did not bring up Dan again, and he avoided responding to the question. "Airport surveillance never flagged him?"

Otis sputtered, "Biometrics are still being worked out."

"They probably altered his appearance enough to make a reading inconclusive."

Otis, sitting closest to Will, leaned forward and lowered his voice. "I believe you had contact with that group."

He forced his shoulders to relax, leaned back slightly, and with a sympathetic look said, "I'm sorry you feel that way. Heard rumors that they were only sending out Bible professors. I wouldn't have thought Hutton qualified. He never completed his undergraduate degree."

Otis, the spit flying from his mouth, snapped, "Not a college graduate?"

"No, his Bible college closed the summer the law took effect. It's in Hutton's interview from Hannibal—the one Agent Worden and I conducted. I don't think he's had a chance to finish that last year, considering your continued interest in him." Will tried not to smile. "If he was at Rosemont as you say he was, perhaps the fault lies with the decision to execute prisoners not charged with a capital crime. After viewing the Rosemont video, wouldn't you say that rises to the level of religious persecution? Severe enough for a country like Ireland to grant asylum?"

He hoped the Denver deputy would take the warnings to heart. Seeing the opportunity, he added, "Is the crematorium still working at the Oklahoma Center? I personally watched the execution of prisoners and their remains cremated in the last building at the Oklahoma Task Force prison complex." Now bureau executives could not deny they had not heard about this.

"We are here to investigate you, Masters." Otis collected himself.

"As the program was described to me, you can understand how I was not able to infiltrate, considering my cover was that of a recent convert with no formal education."

Scot tapped the table with his finger. Will glanced his way. The man was ready to shut this down. "Do you have any further questions for my agent?" Scot asked.

Otis nodded. Sean opened up a file and began to work through the questions.

Will knew how this worked. Ask many questions, often seemingly minor, but in random order, circling back to elicit inconsistencies, half-truths or lies. They had covered his movements in Texas. It had been a while since Will had even thought about his time there, but keeping his emotions at bay, he recalled the mnemonic he used to obscure his time at Washington's ranch. Each trip with Giles, he found a local business or ranch where he could have worked under the table. He knew they would be looking for mistakes. With calm, measured answers, he described his time going from town to town north and west of Amarillo working odd jobs.

Eventually, the Deputy SAC grew impatient. "Do you have any further line of inquiry?"

Otis shook his head.

"Did your team find anything in Masters' apartment?"

Again, Otis shook his head.

"Then, this interview is over."

After the Task Force agents left, the Deputy SAC asked, "What was that about?"

"Kincaid has an obsession with the Huttons. He sent Tom's uncle to Leavenworth. Pursued Tom relentlessly—the reason for my interview with him at Hannibal arose from two agents who tried to torture Tom in front of prison officers."

The Deputy SAC shook his head. "Have they requested access to FBI data?"

"Not yet."

"Forward any Task Force requests directly to me. Word is they push the boundaries and have no respect for classification protocols."

Scot nodded. "Good to know." They walked to the door. "We have a guest room."

"I'm set up at the inn. The remodel really improved the facility."

"Well, touch base if you need anything."

The foyer was empty apart from Will and Scot. "You want company?" He looked at Will.

"No," Will gestured to the door. After they were in the middle of an empty parking lot, he said softly, "I fear Wyoming's in their sights."

"Understood. See you tomorrow?"

"Absolutely. Hey, Scot, I promised Lee I'd take him to the rock-climbing park in the mall tonight. If we can't work anything out this weekend, I'll find a way later in the summer."

CHAPTER 41

THE NEXT DAY out of their cells during their free time, Tom visited with those who seemed eager to have someone with whom to talk. He continued to write while locked in, praying for an opportunity to advance his plan. Many had been moved out by lunchtime, and a new set transferred in through the afternoon.

Tom hung out at the table closest to the guards, wondering if he should retreat to his cell, but an inmate who resembled Todd approached with a questioning nod.

"Sure thing," Tom nodded at the opposite bench. "You're still here? I'm Tom, just in case you didn't catch my name yesterday."

"Seamus. Yeah, I heard. Buddy-buddy with Fr. John?"

"Brought a Bible. Said he could get me into some Bible studies. He's a good listener."

"God and me's not on speaking terms right now."

"He is near and will not turn away any who call on Him."

"You sure of that? Don't know what I've done."

"He definitely knows, and it's already been paid for by Christ on the cross. Ask and He will save you."

Seamus almost turned to go, but he sighed, watching a group of youngsters getting rowdy over a card game. He glanced back at Tom. "They'll get us all in trouble."

Tom nodded. "So, what do you want to talk about?"

He told his tale. Tom listened, not judging, praying for a bridge to connect.

When they called for lights out, Tom said, "See you around, Seamus. I'll be praying for you."

Just after they locked the doors, an officer came for him and led him to an interview room. Tom sat, his hands in his lap. Two new officers walked through followed by one he assumed was an intelligence officer from earlier sessions.

They started their questioning, trying to learn how many others had infiltrated their country. Tom said nothing, reviewing the book of Ezekiel in his mind. He sat up when an officer brought in his latest writings.

"Memoirs," he said with a smile. "Don't want to forget."

Disappointed that Tom had provided no clues in his letters, they resumed the questioning, focusing on his travel documents. "How did you get to Denver?" "How did you evade detection?" "Who financed your trip?" "How did you qualify for a student's visa?"

Long after they left, an officer put him in a holding cell. The next morning, he was handed his items, including his Bible.

To his surprise, they escorted him to an afternoon Bible study with Fr. John. An officer stood by the door. Tom listened to the priest work through the description of love in action from 1 Corinthians 13.

An inmate sitting across from him scoffed. "Yeah, like we can live this in here."

"You can. I did. What is impossible with man is possible with God. All who have asked Jesus to save them have the Holy Spirit. If they choose to listen to the Holy Spirit, He will help them be kind, considerate."

"Hogwash!"

"You don't show respect? You don't act polite to earn a place in an open prison?"

"Don't call that love! Call it looking out for number one."

"So, acting kind and considerate is possible in prison. Isn't it better to be doing it for the Lord's sake?"

"See them take it and run with it? What do you do with that?"

"Pray for them but being loving doesn't mean you do it with your eyes closed. God calls us to be wise as serpents, but innocent as doves." Seeing the opening, Tom shared God's gift of Christ and salvation, weaving in verses. When he touched on the work of faith alone, Fr. John redirected the study, finishing with love is greater than all.

The officer nodded and left the room. Fr. John gave the reading assignment for the next study. "Tom, just a minute." When the room emptied, the chaplain said, "You willing to lead Bible studies even when you're at Direct Provision?"

"Of course, it would be an honor." Tom tried not to get too excited about leaving Cloverhill.

The room was small with one long table and six chairs. He rose with Fr. John and stepped forward to follow him out, but an officer entered. "He stays."

He recognized the three as two from IPO and the intelligence analyst. They interrogated him on the 756 laws. Tom answered as completely as he could. However, he could not provide an exact location for Rosemont having been transported in closed vans. "I heard it was an abandoned Boy Scout camp just north of Minneapolis."

They kept him in committals for two more days before transferring him to remands—holding for those awaiting trials. Many hid their nervous tension with morose silence or bawdy jokes. Tom signed up for library visits and investigated the newspapers and periodicals.

Useless to try to hide that he was an American, he kept to himself, watching and waiting. He was able to follow more of what they were saying. He should be starting a Bible study, or at least attempting it, but he didn't feel ready.

The next afternoon during free time, he sat near a middle-aged man with curly black hair and a lined face. "Tom," he said. The man could talk for himself if he wanted to.

"Clint." He nodded toward Tom's cell. "You have a Bible. Believe it?"

"Yes, do you believe?" Tom looked at the Bible on the bench beside him.

"Yeah, for all the good it did me," he said with little light in his eyes.

"Give it up."

"What?"

"Yeah, sorry—what happened?"

"I tried to follow God, and I still ended up in here." When Tom waited, he said, "Years ago did something really bad and stupid. Found God, finished my apprenticeship and finally landed a decent job, but then a rat turned me in. Thought God would make things work out."

"You tried to follow God, put Him first in your life?" Seeing Clint nod, Tom asked, "Does your wife believe?"

"She does, but she has three little ones to care for and what are we going to do?"

"He's really putting you to the test, Clint, but we know He is faithful, and He will provide." Tom opened to 1 Corinthians 10:13 and read it. "God always provides a way of escape, His way, in His time." Casting about for verses to encourage Clint, Tom paused and said, "Clint, are you glad you repented of your sins and could have peace with God? Would you be willing to share this with others who also need to hear and know that God can make a difference in their lives? Jesus didn't save us to hide us. He saved us to spread the Word, and you can do this in here. Walls can't keep God out." Tom added, "God the Father, God the Son and God the Holy Spirit are in here with you. We are ambassadors for Christ. Let us never fail to complete the works He has for us." He handed the Bible to Clint. "Read Ephesians 2:8-10, especially 10."

It took a while for Clint to find Ephesians. He read the verses with a monotone. Tom unpacked the verses, focusing on the works God had planned for them before the beginning of time—works they could accomplish only by abiding in Christ and letting God work through them.

Tom said, "I have to confess, I've been complaining to God about why I'm here. Maybe He sent me here to help you."

"He'd do that?"

"Absolutely. Do you have a Bible?" Seeing the nod, he said, "Get it and meet me here. There's more I'd like to show you."

Tom smiled for the first time that day. *Okay, Lord, I get it. In Your time and Your way, it will happen.* Praying he'd not waste his time, he smiled when Clint returned.

CHAPTER 42

THREE DAYS LATER Tom sat in a bench in a large cargo van. At the third stop, the driver looked back and called out Tom's name. He made his way to the side door and worked his way out. They piled his luggage by the building. What looked like a security guard came out. "This is the reception centre at Cary House."

Tom looked at the u-shaped complex of square buildings composed of red and gray bricks punctuated in places with steel siding.

"Grab your bags and follow me." They walked through the double doors, down a wide hall, took a left and paused by an open door. The plaque on the door read 'Director Catherine Walsh.' "Go in."

Tom stepped in. Three file cabinets occupied the narrow space behind the desk. Files overflowing the in-basket, pen holders, a tea cup and office miscellaneous surrounded an oval in front of a square monitor. His eye rested on a small framed cross-stitch.

"Come now, let us reason together, says the LORD: Isaiah 1:18," Tom read, reciting the verse encircled by flowing vines with purple and white flowers. He met the manager's gaze, "though your sins are like scarlet, they shall be as white as snow; though they are red like crimson, they shall become like wool. That's the rest of the verse. Miss Catherine, are you a Christian?"

"I am." She did not rise. "Please sit. Are you Tom Hutton?"

Tom extended his hand, "The very one, pleased to make your acquaintance, Miss Catherine." He sat, gazing into her green eyes flecked with gold.

She glanced back at Tom's file in the computer. "Mr. Hutton…" She looked back as she addressed him. "You're from the United States, which is considered to be a safe country of origin. No one has been admitted to the program from your country. The fact you are here does not indicate you will be granted asylum."

"I understand." He reached into his bag and pulled out a slip of paper. "Here is the link to my video evidence. Perhaps, if you watched it, you'd understand?"

"I've seen it," she said, her lips tight. "While I sympathize with your situation, it will be up to the tribunal to determine the legitimacy of your claim." She paused, as if she had more to say and changed her mind. "Well, Mr. Hutton, you have been granted temporary residence at this centre. You will reside in the single men's dormitory—the third floor of this building. This is not a prison, but please let us know where you are so we can inform you of your Substantive Interview and other appointments."

"When will that be?"

Catherine sighed and sat back in her chair. "There's a backlog, you see. They are trying to get through as many as possible, but…" She looked away. "Officially, it should be within six months, but it might be two years or more." She pulled out a pamphlet and ran through the health centre, weekly stipend, jobs board, and a map of the complex.

"Miss Walsh, is it true the rejection rate is 95 percent?"

"It is." She rose stiffly. "Byrne will take you to your pod and give you a tour." Catherine picked up her cell phone. "He'll meet you in the hallway."

Tom rose. "Thank you."

Tom slung his backpack over his shoulder, lifted the suitcase to extend the handle and waited by the long wall next to Catherine's door. He heard her talking on her cell, discussing where to house him. "All right, if you think that's our only option. Keep an eye out for Isler, though."

He just had to get through this—take the next step and complete the plan. A slim, fortyish man with close-cropped curly hair and dark eyes approached. "Tom Hutton?"

"That's me. Byrne?" Tom extended his hand. The man smiled in return.

"I'll take you to your pod, and we can walk the centre." He nodded down the hall.

Tom followed him to an elevator. They exited on the third floor.

"Laundry's to the left, pay per load." Byrne led Tom out the short hall and turned left. "This is the short section. You'll be sharing a pod with Isler."

Each pod was bounded by three-quarter walls painted a soft yellow. He saw two single beds with tall lockers, short bureaus, and a simple desk. The first was neat and orderly, the one next to it a disordered mess. "No inspections?"

"Here? Keep your mess in your space and get along with your podmate." Byrne continued on to the back right corner pod. "Here's Isler's pod. He's from Ethiopia.

Tom peeked in and saw a man wrapped in a light blanket sitting on his bed. He paused at the open doorway for a moment, then tapped lightly on the upright. "Hello, Isler. I'm Tom. May I come in?"

The man nodded without turning away from the wall.

"I will leave you to your prayers." Tom left his bags near the empty bed and rejoined Byrne in the hall.

They walked back to the short hall. Tom asked, "What's the short story on Isler?"

"He came from a good-sized Christian village. After his community was pillaged, the survivors arrived at the refugee camps as cholera was sweeping through. That, along with food convoys being attacked by militants, decimated what remained of the village. As far as we know, five made it Europe. He's the only one in Ireland."

"He been here long?"

"A year and a half."

"Having problems giving a statement?"

Byrne nodded. "We understand how hard it is to relive it for the tribunal. His case is remanded until he's ready."

"We'll do just fine."

They walked back to the elevators after getting a look at the laundry room with washers, dryers and a short counter area.

"Ironing board and iron." Byrne opened a locked cabinet and handed Tom a set of sheets. "Exchange for clean ones every Monday before supper."

Tom set the sheets on his bed, and they walked through the other end of the wing—various curtains hung across some openings. The sounds of music and aromas of spicy foods filled the air at the end near the stairs. "I see you gave me the quiet end."

Byrne nodded and continued with the tour, walking down to the first floor by the gym. "Where we hold many of the children's activities and large gatherings. Some groups use the space for theatre or readings. Most are at school or upstairs with their mothers."

Following with few questions, Tom thanked Byrne for the tour. "When can I volunteer to help with the children's programs?"

Byrne tapped his shoulder, "When Miss Catherine has a chance to evaluate you. You can always apply for a job."

"I'll think about it." Tom watched Byrne walk down the hall and into an office. Knowing he had a short period of time before lunch, Tom headed for the computer area near the dining hall.

After lunch Tom walked out a side door, turned left to the street closest to the River Liffey and began walking. Not having found a local office for *The Guardian* reporter, the *Irish Times* would have to do. He fingered his handwritten story in his pocket—what the officers had looked at yet had returned to him. He thanked God for that small blessing.

Approaching the street, he found the building. Tom began with the news desk. The reporter he requested was not in, but he eventually obtained an interview with an editor. A young woman led him to a corner office. The plaque read Colin Dougherty.

"Mr. Dougherty, he might have a story," she said and stepped aside.

"Mr. Dougherty, Tom Hutton."

"What is it about?"

"The asylum process and Direct Provision. May I?"

"Take a seat," he waved to a pair of mended padded chairs surrounded by boxes.

Tom pulled out his statement. "I am from the US and have applied for asylum. My country is killing its pastors and Bible scholars." He put his papers on the desk in front of the editor. "Please read that and watch my video evidence. If you are interested in the story, I will answer your questions." He sat back, trying not to stare at the man with a receding hairline and broad paunch.

Colin picked up the papers, looked at them quickly before smoothing them out. The room grew quiet. Tom tried to breathe, finding himself holding his breath.

"Why?"

"Why what?"

"Why try to get this published—assuming this is for real?"

"Please look at the video evidence. I checked the link earlier today." Tom watched Colin turn to his computer and open the video. He tried to shut out what he heard, wishing the man had used headphones, but he was already asking a lot of this newspaper.

Colin looked at him. "You the Tom in the video?" Seeing the nod, he asked, "Why haven't we heard of this?"

"The Task Force is a joint agency operation with the full backing of the President. When I was in county lockup in Wichita, a reporter interviewed me. He was killed in a traffic accident two weeks later. Look it up—Cecil Rhodes of *The Wichita Press*."

The editor ran the search, furrowed his brow, looked back at Tom. "But there are churches in the States."

"The Task Force is starting out in larger cities and prominent regions, but they are continually expanding their enforcement areas. A church with open doors today will have signed onto the initiatives, be reporting every donor and informing the Task Force of those not adhering to the regulations. When your country deports me, and they will since this is the only evidence I have, Task Force agents will torture and kill me."

He rubbed his chin. "I'll have my reporter check this out and get back to you. What's your mobile?"

"Mobile? I walked here."

"I mean your phone number?"

"Oh, cell phone? I don't have one. Too easy to track me. I haven't had one in years. I can get away a few hours in the afternoon. If you can provide the address for a coffee shop where I could talk to your reporter, I will be there each afternoon from 1:30 to 3:30."

"They don't know you're here?"

"No. My own people didn't believe me either—until the Task Force came and arrested them. Please, I don't know how long I will have until they send me back to Cloverhill."

"Why were you at Cloverhill?"

"To escape my country, I had to use fake documents."

"I see. We don't like refugees who start off breaking the rules."

"I get that, but there was no other way to tell the world what is going on. I had hoped, if I could be granted asylum, my people would know what has been happening in secret. Telling someone Christ is the only way to heaven is not a capital crime, but they are killing us just the same."

Colin rotated to his computer, ran a quick search and printed out directions. "This should be in walking distance from Cary House." His lips pulled back in a tight smile. "What do you think of our Direct Provision?"

"It is a very generous program. Very nice facilities. Cloverhill Prison seems to be well run."

"Do you now? Interesting." He held the papers in his hand. "You do understand we will be checking this out. If we decline…"

"Don't contact me at the centre. If I don't meet anyone in three days, I'll try another paper—if I haven't been sent back."

"Did they tell when they'd do this?"

"They never tell prisoners anything. But they seemed to want to deport me quickly. There are the document charges."

"There is that. Too bad you told them."

Tom cocked his head. "I could do no less. Just because my country made me a criminal by outlawing my faith, I don't have to let that turn me into a criminal."

"You are in some eyes."

Tom nodded. "Tyranny begins with the criminalization and suppression of religious expression. It is the first freedom to fall." He rose. "Thank you for your time."

Tom went to the street, surveyed the terrain, walked to the coffee shop around the block, and headed back to Cary House.

Back at the centre he stepped past Catherine's closed door. He continued to the dining hall, passing a little shop on his way. The guards had returned his money; he could buy a lock, but he hated to spend it—not knowing what was to come.

The kitchen staff was setting up the cafeteria line. Tom recognized Isler sitting at a back table. He poured two cups of tea and sat across from him, his back closer to the wall. *How can the man feel comfortable with his back unguarded?*

"How do you like your tea?"

Isler accepted the cup and shrugged his shoulders. His lips formed a meager smile and sipped the tea.

Tom sipped his, trying to ignore his inner tension. He tried reviewing the Psalms, but found more help with the gospel of John. They sat in silence as people began to filter in. Tom followed Isler to the end of the line for supper and back to their table. No one asked him where he had gone. He should have felt relieved, but uncertainty threatened his joy.

Tom watched Catherine breeze in through the door closest to the kitchen. She greeted the servers, stopped to speak with some of the residents, and walked back into the kitchen. Tom heard the distant sounds of children's laughter. Perhaps the afternoon kids' activities had finished. Shoving down desires to fit in, he found himself tracking her steps through the kitchen—occasionally able to glimpse her broad smile as her auburn red hair flowed around her shoulders. In time, she exited the kitchen and began to greet the diners, table by table. Theirs was last.

"Hello, Isler," she said.

"Please join us for a few moments, Miss Walsh. May I fetch a cup of tea?"

"Coffee, cream and sugar."

She was sitting not far from Isler. Returning to his seat, he asked, "Did you have a good day, ma'am?"

"You can call me Miss Walsh, Mr. Hutton."

"You may call me Tom."

"Are you settling in?"

"Very well, thank you." Tom paused, wanting to share, but there seemed to be a wall between them.

She finished the coffee and rose. "Thank you. Evening staff can answer any questions, and Isler has been here a while."

"Of course. Good evening." Tom watched her leave, trying not to think she could hardly wait to put distance between them. Of course, if she did know what he was up to, she might have reason to send him back. He had no idea. The only thing he could do was to put one foot in front of the other and take the next step.

—⚬❀⚬—

Tom hid his valuables, unpacked enough for the next day and pulled out his Bible and papers. Regretting not buying a notebook at the shop, he determined to do that the next day. Seeing Isler looking at him, he said, "Would you like me to read? What is your favorite book?"

"Jeremiah."

Tom started with chapter 31 and the new covenant.

"The blood of the new covenant, Jesus talked of this on His last night." Isler talked about the last supper. "A good portion. I also like the beginning."

"Jeremiah's call." Tom recited the first part of the chapter. *"Before I formed you in the womb I knew you, and before you were born I consecrated you; I appointed you a prophet to the nations."*[23]

"He is the weeping prophet, but he saw beyond his time."

Tom listened to Isler reminisce—the times his people worshipped, drinking in the words of the prophets, seeing God and His heaven in the midst of their lives. He gathered breath. "So, the sorrows have reached your land?"

Tom nodded. It felt good to share with one who understood.

The next day it seemed to take forever for lunchtime to arrive. He arrived early at the coffee shop with his new notebook and Bible. Finding a table in the back with a view of the narrow shop, he tried to focus on his Bible. People came, one after another. A few wandered to the back. A group of women laughed over their drinks and pastries—half tea, the other, various types of coffee—cold brewed, latte or regular.

A young woman with dark hair bobbed close to her ears walked back, eying the patrons.

Tom at first discounted her until she approached. "Tom Hutton?"

"Yes," he said, rising, pulling out a chair for her to sit. "Are you from *The Times*?"

"I am."

"May I see your card?" He read her business card—International Desk. "But I thought I'd be talking to someone from the news desk?" He handed it back.

"You can keep it. That way you can call if need be." She sat back, eying him closely. "The editors gathered you're really wanting a story of the persecution you have suffered in the States—not one about Direct Provision?"

"That sounds right. What did you think of my story and the video?"

"It won't be enough."

"I know that. Why I need this published. Mr. Dougherty said someone would verify the facts. Were they able to confirm? I mean, I told him my Bible college closed down when the laws came into effect, and they're not on the Internet."

"For those who know where to look, there's always something to find. Well, let's get started."

"You'll publish it?"

"We'll publish something. Exactly what we write is up to us."

Tom nodded and answered her questions—thorough, chronological and detailed.

Thinking the Admin area would be as quiet as the day before, he opened the first set of doors. Daylight shrouded the figures, but images, shapes, moving to the door became distinct once he stepped inside.

Catherine Walsh, along with two burly security guards, stood looking at him.

Catherine asked, "Tom, what have you done?" Taking in his set jaw, his wide eyes and tense shoulders, she nodded at the guards. The group headed to the elevators and exited on the second floor. The guards marched him to a room and told him to sit on the far side of the table. Catherine sat across from him. The guards crossed their arms.

"You went to the papers."

"I did."

"What did you tell them about us?"

Tom surveyed the group and cocked his head. "That Cary House is a fine facility; Direct Provision is a very generous program, and you have nice prisons."

"We have nice prisons?" They laughed.

"In comparison to a concentration camp."

"That puts it into perspective."

Tom looked away. He tucked his shaking hands in his lap.

"Tom," Catherine said. "What's the matter?"

He glanced past her, his eyes taking in the two guards by the door, the others staring at him. Swallowing he said, "Will you by sending me back?" He thought he had accepted that the Task Force would kill him, but the specter of deportation loomed.

Catherine looked at the staff. "Everything's fine. Please return to your normal duties." She turned to Tom.

"Tom," she said gently. "I owe you an apology. Some months ago, a reporter posing as a refugee wrote a terrible story about another facility. Being you were from the States, I just assumed the worst of you. No, we won't be sending you back. However, the IPO might want to talk with you."

"Thank you. Then we have a lot of work to do. My time might be short here." Tom laid out his plans for Cloverhill. "I need to follow up with Clint and Seamus in Cloverhill. How do I receive permission to visit prisoners, conduct Bible studies?" Tom outlined his ideas for Bible studies at Cary House with Catherine. "Oh, Isler knows his Bible. He might be able to lead the advanced class when I'm gone."

"Isler's talking?"

"Yes, is that unusual?"

"This is great news. He ready to make a statement?"

"I wouldn't know. Let me find a good time to ask."

"I have to report this to your IPO officer. While we can't publicize your story, there are no rules on the books that forbid you from telling your story. However, you can't talk about anyone here."

"Of course. I would never violate their privacy. Miss Walsh, may I help with the children?"

"Definitely. The afternoon program is done for today, but starting tomorrow you are welcome to attend and observe. Fr. John is the Cloverhill chaplain. Contact him for ministering in the prison."

Tom met with the reporter the next afternoon. She brought a photographer.

"We'll do a Saturday feature," she said and launched into her follow-up questions.

He arrived back at Cary House in time to watch Catherine dismiss the children. Mothers in various types of dress—some traditional, others modern—gathered their children like hens with outstretched wings. They exited through the far doors to the family quarters.

"You were gone a long time."

"She brought a photographer. They're planning to do a feature. Is that good?"

Catherine smiled. "Means they took your story seriously." She looked about, ensuring the staff was resetting the gym for evening activities. "Let's talk in my office."

"Tomorrow for the children's activities?"

"Is Saturday. Maybe Monday."

They stopped by the kitchen for tea. Tom relaxed as they exchanged glances and laughed.

"Do you find our tea different?"

"Never drank it much. Coffee usually, but it never hurts to expand my horizons. What do you think of it?"

Catherine smiled, with a lift of her eyebrows and open face, shook her head. "I should bring some of the better blends. Not quite part of a facility budget."

"It's better than I had expected, actually. If this is the cheap tea, I look forward to better ones."

They settled in her office, and Tom shut the door.

"Your officer's not happy with you. Be ready for a visit."

CHAPTER 43

Tom's first Saturday at Cary House dawned early. He woke before five. Dressing quietly, he headed down to the kitchen to make a cup of coffee and read his Bible until he became sleepy enough to return to bed.

He smiled at the cook turning on the kitchen lights and rose to help her clear the trash.

"You'd think taking out the day's trash would happen on the day." She smiled and told him where the dumpster was.

He never did make it back to bed. The cook was a charming storyteller, and he soaked in the culture and language of Dublin; her thick brogue now mostly understandable. "And watch if you don't sound like us in a month."

"That would be great."

Catherine found him after breakfast. "The IPO is sending a ride to pick you up within the hour." She added, "Take everything with you."

A shiver ran up his spine. He nodded and headed up the stairs.

Isler asked, "You leaving already?"

"They're calling me in." Tom hugged his roommate. "It's been an honor knowing you. If I don't see you sooner, I'll meet you on the other side."

"Across the river."

Tom settled in the chair, rubbed his hands together and pulled them into his lap. It looked like any other interrogation room. The door opened, and five officers entered.

"Tom Hutton," a tall man said and sat down. "I'm your IPO officer, Miles Stanley."

His eyes scanned the other four whom he recognized from previous interrogations.

"Your country is requesting your extradition as a wanted terrorist."

"Would you consider terrorist activities to include being in possession of a Bible and reciting verses such as John 14:6, where Jesus states He is the way, the truth, the life and the only path to God?" Noting their blank faces, he said, "They have defined violators of 756 as hate-crime terrorists on the basis of certain religious phrases that are now deemed inflammatory."

"What did you do?"

Again, he described his path through federal prisons and the Task Force facilities.

"You expect us to believe that the government of the United States considers Bibles and religious phrases acts of terror?"

"Read the law as it has been added to over the years and as it has been executed by the Task Force. This is happening with the approval of the President and his administration."

"How do you know this? What proof do you have?"

"The Rosemont video."

"Proves only one instance at one place."

"You shared it with the government?"

"Yes, and they stated they would pursue those responsible. The crimes you are charged with only carry prison time—not death."

Tom groaned. "I was given twelve months and ended up at a death camp. Any who are not willing to cooperate and turn in other Christians are sent to these death camps where they will not survive, either by starvation, disease or execution. That is why I risked applying for asylum."

An intelligence officer opened up his laptop. "Do you recognize anyone?"

Tom shuddered, seeing Dublin landmarks in the backgrounds. He swiped past two. "No." The blood chilled in his veins at the third. "That's Trainer. He's one of the ones who tortured me." The man looked a little older, drawn somehow but he would never forget that face. "When was this taken?"

"We're asking the questions. What exactly did he do that you considered torture?"

"It may not rise to the level of torture according to your determination, but it felt like it to me." He described his three weeks in a flat monotone, trying not to relive it. Their bland faces revealed nothing. "That treatment violated US federal guidelines. The Investigations Manager and a Task Force agent told me they would look into it and deal with the agents. However, as you can see, nothing's been done."

"Or your accusations were not credible."

"That's one way to look at it."

"We have good reports on you from Clorverhill and Cary House but are concerned that other terrorists might be here. You said there was a program. Who leads it? Who funds it? Where is it located? How many have been sent to Ireland and the UK?"

"Made it my business not to know."

Miles set his face. "You're not helping yourself."

"Please remember that information you give them will be used to destroy another family and send more people to their death camps." Not looking away, he said, "Look at the ones who we can identify in the Rosemont pit. Dr. Mitchell was my Bible professor at Mt. Zion Bible College. Dale was a father of three, a pastor and a Hebrew scholar. He taught me the alphabet and Psalm 119 in Hebrew." Tom listed off the others he knew until one of the officers cut him off.

"You know what they told you. Of course, no one condones Rosemont, but it's up to your government to correct it. It's up to us to deport criminals."

"You will be denied asylum and extradited to the United States," Officer Stanley stated.

"There will be others. I might be the first to apply for asylum, but I won't be the last."

They tried to pursue other lines of questioning, but Tom refused to respond.

Beyond tears, hunger or thirst, he curled up on the slab in a holding cell.

CHAPTER 44

CATHERINE TRIED TO learn of Tom's fate, but Officer Stanley did not return her calls. She contacted everyone she knew, but it was Saturday. She would have to wait out the weekend.

Sunday morning, she finally read yesterday's issue of *The Irish Times* and hoping against hope, searched for Tom's article. Grasping the paper in her hand, she held back a cry of both joy and sorrow, seeing the photo of Tom looking off into the distance—resolute, certain, slightly sad, but determined. The prose wove a haunting story of faith's endurance through darkness. She prayed with all her heart for God's rescue.

While Sunday was her official day off, she still checked in after church to make sure everything was functioning properly. Turning the key to her office, she swung the door open. Her mobile rang. It was Nancy from the IPO office, a close friend and inside source.

"Catherine, are you sitting down?"

She walked to the nearest chair. "I am now."

"They've withdrawn his claim and will be extraditing him to the States."

"Has his solicitor been informed? Did they send him back to Cloverhill?"

"To an undisclosed location. I could not gain access to that part of his file. I have the formal withdrawal, and they started the deportation order. Army intelligence has taken over the process."

Catherine sighed, holding back her emotions. "Thank you. Is there anything I can do?"

She heard Nancy click through screens, with the standard *beep* or *chirp* depending upon success or access denied. "When his file first came across my desk, I felt this would be likely."

"Did you see his story in the *Times*?"

"No, I'll check it out. Haven't subscribed for ages."

"I'll send a scan. Are you at the office? On a Sunday?" She tried to joke, as they usually did, but her voice fell, flat and heavy.

"And you're not?"

"Guilty as charged." She didn't have the energy to make a rebuttal.

Nancy, hearing the sorrow in her friend's voice, said, "We can pray. I'll spread the word. At this point it's all we can do."

"This one is real, Nancy, as hard to believe as it sounds. I'll send over an image"

Catherine sat back, lethargic and weepy. But she forced herself to head for the scanner, shaking her head. The point of creating the IPO had been to shelter these victims from the heartless ravages of politics, or so she had assumed. Sighing, knowing the force of politics, she scanned the news story and emailed it to Nancy.

Catherine tried not to give in to a rising anger. Whatever action needed to be taken would have to come from the solicitors.

She navigated to Tom's file, smiled seeing they had not yet pulled his Temporary Residence Certificate and his withdrawal was still listed as pending. Printing Tom's documents and his file summary, she made copies and called the solicitor listed for his case. Of course, no one answered. She left a voice mail and sent a text and an email.

As her usual custom, Catherine roamed the facility, chatting with residents sipping tea, teasing playfully with small groups of children in the gym. On her way back she saw Isler with his customary cup of tea, made a cup for herself and headed in his direction.

"Hello," she said, looking to see if he wanted to talk.

He looked past her, as many did—a cultural habit from a distant land. "Is my friend doing well?"

Catherine pulled up a chair and sat, feeling the warm mug in her hands. "I don't think so. They will deport him."

"They will kill him."

"I know that." She wiped her eyes with a tissue and tucked it away.

"Miss Catherine, God will never lose him. Whether he goes or stays, his God will be with him, and we will meet again—on the other side."

Catherine nodded, marveling again at the world they inhabited, so different from her own. While they dwelt in the same city, their futures were so uncertain, so bleak. *How do they get through each day?* "I have told everyone I can so they can pray."

Isler smiled, thin lips straight across, but his eyes shone with life. "Now we will see what God will do."

"Thank you. I'll try not to forget who really is in control."

They sat for moments uncounted, sipping their tea. She imagined they were both praying in their own ways in their own native tongues, and their prayers, carried by the Holy Spirit, ascended to heaven's throne of grace.

After a light meal at home, Catherine overcame her reluctance to move and drove to Trinity College for the Sunday evening fellowship. The week before she had told Ron, an American helping establish the Hebrew Centre, that another American would be with her. Wondering what she should say, she entered the large open room with rows of padded chairs.

Ron found her first with his usual greeting. "Hello, Catherine. It's good to see you." But his manner changed. "You came alone. Where is your new friend?"

Catherine, searching for an answer, turned when Dr. Chaim Wohlberg, Director of the Hebrew Centre, approached with Tom's article.

"This American, Tom Hutton, he's at Cary House? Can we meet?"

Catherine looked away in time to see Ron pale. She could no longer hold back the tears. "They arrested him yesterday and will be sending him back. They have withdrawn his application. I communicated this to his solicitor but haven't heard anything."

The tall, burly man said, "Do you know they released the Rosemont video?" Seeing Catherine and Ron were speechless, Chaim added, "It's gone viral."

"Did it break through the US firewall?"

"Why do you ask this, my friend?"

"Why do you think I chose to come here to help with your centre and not work with one in the States? The Task Force has silenced any opposition. Reporters, congressmen, wardens, and anyone who gets in their way is eliminated or framed and sent to prison. Open churches are monitored, registered and collaborating. Everything Tom says is true. The video is true," Ron affirmed.

"The threat he faces when he is returned home is real?"

"Yes," Ron declared.

Catherine said, "I didn't believe him at first, but after watching him at Cary House, I believe now."

"Fear not. Our God is great. Ron, convey my regards to David, but I know who would be willing to defend this refugee." Chaim nodded goodbye and left.

Catherine watched him leave. "He can do that?"

"Absolutely."

Ron sat by her side. She forced herself to sing and listen to the message—prayers for Tom never left her mind. As the preacher drew to a close, she pulled out a copy of Tom's article. "Diane O'Leary," she whispered. Once people began to stir, she searched for the reporter's mobile number and left a message. *Maybe they'd want to do a follow-up.* Immigration's reaction to the story was news as well.

Solicitor Helen Boyle of Murphy, Walsh and O'Brien settled in the plastic chair in a small room at Mountjoy Prison. She had not met the man before, but had read his application, news story, and reviewed the information Miss Walsh and Dr. Wohlberg had sent. Hearing steps outside the door, she rose to greet her new client, but he kept his head down and slid into a chair, shriveled and drawn, barely breathing. She did not speak until the guards stepped out. "Mr. Tom Hutton, I'm Solicitor Helen Boyle and here to represent you." She slid a two-page document toward him. "If you will accept transferring your case to our firm, we can begin discussing filing an appeal on your behalf."

"My assigned solicitor?" Tom lifted his head a little. The woman was middle-aged but confident, relaxed and assured.

"Willingly agrees to the transfer as your situation has become complicated."

"Impossible would be more accurate." Tom met her gaze for the first time. "Have you heard recordings of my interrogations by the IPO and intelligence officers?"

"No."

"I thought it was a done deal. They told me they had denied my request, and I would be returned to my country."

"They found a reason to withdraw your application."

Tom guessed, "For lack of cooperation by not providing requested information?"

"Something like that."

"May I see it?" He read the document she produced from her briefcase, his hand shaking as he read. "They don't believe me. Even my own people don't know what their government is doing in secret." He slid it back. "The remedy?"

She had prepared a draft of the appeal. "This buys us time."

"Doesn't proof they will kill me provide sufficient cause to stay this action?"

"Ahh, but the United States claims those killed at Rosemont died of natural causes or were shot attacking guards and trying to escape.

We have to prove you would be irreparably harmed if sent back to your country. They have provided transcripts of the laws, statutes and regulations. None of them are capital crimes."

Tom sat back, deflated. He tucked his shaking hand in his lap.

"Apart from obtaining communications ordering staff to execute you, if we could find similar offenders were executed while in custody, or if we could show persecution of a group that you belong to, that would be sufficient to restore your Temporary Resident Certificate and put you back on the path for consideration."

"When you watch the Rosemont video, there is a man in the pit, Mitch, who was shot when he told them he was a week past his release date. In fact, the guards called 'releasing prisoners' meant taking them to the pit and shooting them. He reported his release date in the morning. That afternoon I was selected to take the dead to the pit, and he was there with a bullet hole in his forehead."

"Do you have his full name?" She watched Tom shake his head. "Does the video clearly show him?"

"I'm not sure." He looked back. "It will take a miracle."

"Filing your appeal gives us time to find and develop the evidence. It is there, isn't it, Mr. Hutton?"

"If you can wrest it out of a government bent on hiding it and suppressing any who would expose them."

"Somewhere we will find that chink—that proof your situation not only warrants, but demands, acceptance of your asylum claim."

Tom reached for the appeal and read it, asking clarifying questions. He set it down and signed both documents. "Ms. Boyle, decades ago, in the last century, a civilized country began to kill off segments of its population—aged, sick, and unwanted ethnic groups. They did it in the shadows, and many who lived near the death chambers didn't know. Because other countries were not aware of the atrocities, they sent refugees back to that country—to the death chambers. The sorrow and regret stayed with us for a long time. We thought we would never forget and would not repeat that mistake. I tell you, Ms. Boyle, it is happening in my country—the country that I love. I do this not for my own sake but to tell the world so that my people will also know what is happening behind walls and locked doors. I will pray for God to give you wisdom and guidance in seeking the proofs."

Helen thanked him, slid the documents into her case and rose.

Tom rose and extended his hand. "Thank you, I have accepted the fact that the Task Force will kill me. I hope it won't be in vain."

Solicitor Boyle shook his hand. She left the room determined to prove his claim.

⚬⚬⚬

Later that night, Catherine looked at her phone as an unknown number rang through. "Hello?"

"Miss Walsh with Direct Provision? I'm Sean Dempsey with *The Irish Times*. We need to know where to send the information we've been receiving concerning Tom Hutton."

"Oh," she fumbled for the new solicitor's contact information. "Did you get the message they arrested him and are trying to send him back?"

"No, did you contact Ms. O'Leary?"

"I left a message with the contact mobile I found on your site."

"I'll text over her direct mobile number. Call her immediately."

Will it be enough? After leaving a message for O'Leary, she tried Nancy's mobile and listened to it ring three times. Just before she ended the call, her friend picked up.

"Do you know where Tom is?"

"In solitary at Mountjoy Prison."

CHAPTER 45

NOT QUITE FINISHED with his first cup of coffee, Norton looked up when his office door burst open and Leo, his assistant, rushed in. "This better be good."

Leo set the day's copy of the *Wall Street Journal* on the desk. "Below the fold."

Norton sucked in his breath. "How did this happen?"

"At the bottom of the second page," Leo waited for Norton to open the paper and pointed. "*The Irish Times* broke the story a few days ago. *The Guardian* picked it up and it's online with the BBC and AP. There's also a link to the Rosemont video—the one we tried to quarantine."

"Call everyone in."

Norton turned to his monitor. With a sigh, he accessed their internal network. Thirty-eight were in Building 2, waiting for processing. His last report from his Rosemont contact had reported forty-seven at that location. Oklahoma had absorbed the inmates from the third camp when it was decommissioned. However, with this latest crisis he'd have to advance the timetable.

Within an hour Norton's five top executives filed in. Leo sat near the door, available for any last-minute requests. Norton waved to Leo to show them the news article and outline the story's global extent.

"Wicker and George, see to the dismantling of the cremation chamber and find an out-of-the-way storage solution. Mack and Roan, get started on transforming Building 2 into a Level 1, similar to Building 1 for a holding capacity of 90."

Mack said, "If we copy 1's pod format, the best we can do is 56."

"Dormitory style will be fine, but they'll need similar facilities—kitchen, dining area, and laundry. They can utilize Building 1's infirmary, but give them the same diet, commissary, visiting, phone and mail privileges."

Wicker raised his hand. "Director, what about the boxes in 3?" Seeing a puzzled look, he added, "The ashes, sir?"

"Right." He thought a moment. "Scatter them amongst regular trash and make sure it's sent to the landfill." Norton surveyed the group. "This is top priority. Any issues clearing your schedules, inform Leo, and we'll deal with it. This does not leave this room, and it is not to be discussed except through secure channels. Leo will handle all media requests."

"The FOIA's?"

"Send to Leo." Norton surveyed his group. "Questions? All right, weekly updates here if I don't ask before the next scheduled meeting."

Deputy Director George filed out last. He shut the door and hovered by Norton's desk. They exchanged glances. "You hear anything from Kincaid?"

Norton shook his head.

George lowered his voice. "He has to shut down Rosemont."

"I know that. We all know that, but we can't tell him that. I'll let you know if I'm called to D.C. You know what to do. And get rid of the ashes. Whose bright idea was it to save them?"

"Sir, we thought the remains would be claimed, once they could be released."

Norton shook his head. "Fine mess we're in now." He nodded at a chair. "Our bugs pick up anything on Masters?"

"He's definitely crossed over. Goes to church sometimes, reads a Bible every day."

Norton wasn't surprised to hear this. He knew the man had double-crossed them. "Any leads on the organization or Larry Hutton?"

"Not really. It would help if we had a cyber division to parse out the network."

"Appears to be well funded by a group of wealthy sympathizers. Hutton's probably just a low-level grunt." Norton met George's gaze. "Forget Hutton, have enough to roll up Masters?"

"Yes, my local informant has recordings of outlawed HCL statements. He's gained the man's trust." He waited. Norton shifted in his chair, his eyes heavy, deep lines crossing his forehead. "Sir, do we bring him in?"

Sighing, he shook his head. "I assume surveillance has not uncovered any substantial leads to the underground?"

"They're careful, and they're law enforcement. They know how we work and how to stay off the grid. The Northern Plains states have fewer cameras; we have fewer informants."

"Let's keep Masters in play," he leaned forward. "But we reel him in if we get any hint Kincaid's going for him." He noticed George's puzzled look. "He's one of the ones the man will never let go of."

Norton watched George exit and close the door behind him. He sat back, his eyes resting on last year's family reunion photo. For them, for the future of the country, but without quick action, Kincaid's brutal tactics would undermine everything. He scanned incoming emails and deleted the nonsense ones. More than likely they'd purge law enforcement of sympathetic elements once they were past this.

He didn't hear from Kincaid until two days later. Norton stopped by George's office with his flight details on his way to Washington. He hated taking the time but didn't want to discuss any of this over the phone—not even on secure lines.

The man sent a long limo to pick him up at the airport. Norton rankled inside, worked at bottling up his distaste and focused on the scenery. It was a pretty time of year with the trees still budding—before the oppressive humidity turned the heat into a wall that sucked the life out of a person.

Kincaid wanted to meet in his elegant penthouse-type office—over the top, like everything else with mahogany desk and bookcases, gold-tinted curtains and a wall of service awards, military photos, and signed portraits of the last three presidents.

"Let's talk in a secure room." Norton narrowed his eyes, watching Kincaid's eyes track back and forth, his breathing quick and shallow. He hazarded a guess the man's blood pressure was elevated along with his cortisol levels. *The iceberg is cracking.*

"Of course, setup." Kincaid momentarily glared at Norton before looking away to reach for his phone. His hand hovered over buttons for the phone lines, furrowing his brow. The third finger punched the second line. When the speaker sounded, he lifted the handset. "Sean, get everyone in."

Norton smiled. "Lovely spring. Turning hot already."

"Imagine Oklahoma's almost up to summer's heat by now."

"For the most part. Weather can shift from Gulf heat or Canada cold. Variety." He continued the small talk, hoping to settle the director and help him focus.

Eventually, they headed down the hall to a recessed door. An agent collected their cell phones and placed them in a sealed locker. Norton breathed a little easier. First, he'd let Kincaid lead, but if he didn't show up, he would have to take charge. He glanced at his watch, hoping he'd have time to meet with Senator Roxston by the end of the day. Kincaid didn't need to know.

No agendas, no memos, no directives—just five tired men with worry lines above their eyes. Norton nodded at Sean, Barrie and Otis. Thankfully, he knew everyone in the room, hopefully well enough.

"We have a situation." Kincaid exhaled as if breathing took effort. Fire burned behind his eyes as he scanned the room. Speaking to Sean sitting next to him, he said, "Get Cooper in here."

After the assistant left, Kincaid turned his gaze on Norton who met and matched it. Breathing again, he asked, "Masters involved at all? What's he up to?"

Norton smiled and replied evenly, "Busy running searches and assisting the locals. He's keeping his nose clean—doing grunt analyst and field office work."

"Don't have to worry about him then. Any movement on that area's intelligence? Leads, chatter that something's up?"

Norton shook his head, glad the man hadn't pressed for the latest numbers on Hutton Bible seizures. That used to be the first stat he asked for. Frankly, they had probably seized most of them by now. "Numbers for Level 3 inmates is down. I think we burned through the bulk of the resisters. The majority sign off on the program." He didn't need to tell Kincaid he had backed off on the monthly reporting requirements. "Some are opening churches again."

"Registered?"

"Yes, that's the requirement. While they can technically have a dedicated church building without non-profit status, there are ways to make that difficult. Essentially, if you are starting a church, you must have an IRS 501(c)(3) determination." Things looked normal, from a street level point of view. Norton looked at Otis. "Timetable for the next Bible edition?"

"Was on track for this summer, but…" He flicked a glance at Kincaid who nodded for him to continue. "We're still getting pushback from Congress."

"Well, it can always be instituted later."

Kincaid tried to smile. "That's probably what's going to happen."

Norton wondered why they were waiting for an agent. The name sounded familiar, but he couldn't remember the man's status.

Sean entered with a middle-aged agent who pulled out a chair with a shaking hand.

Kincaid came to life. He sat up, pulled back his shoulders, and directed his full attention at the agent with dark circles under his eyes. "You need to explain how the Hutton situation got so out of hand. I thought you had in-theater assets."

"Well, sir, we do, and they said it usually takes a year or more before the tribunal hears his case. Word was they didn't buy his story and didn't consider the video credible. With no affidavits but his own, it seemed likely his claim would be rejected, and he'd be deported."

Kincaid's fist hit the table. "How did this happen?"

"We never expected him to go public and talk to a reporter."

"And why was that? Wouldn't that be the first thing you'd think he would do?"

"No, most try not to publicize their claims for fear of retaliation from their countries. They put him in jail because of it."

"And you can't get an assassin in the jail?"

Norton said, "Let's think this through."

Kincaid directed his glare at the Oklahoma director. "What is there to think about?"

"Run the scenario. For every action, there is a reaction. To get an assassin in a prison, we'd have to work with corrupt guards or inmates, who are notorious for not keeping secrets. At this point, will Hutton's death help or hurt? What's your assessment, Barrie?"

Seeing Kincaid's nod, Barrie said, "We're going to kill him anyway, so if we can wait it out, his claim will be denied, and we get him here."

"Except the families have already contacted the newspaper with the names of executed inmates," Sean said. "Well, he might win asylum if he can prove his life is in danger if he's sent back. They don't believe in capital punishment."

"What is our greatest liability, right now, apart from Hutton?" Norton asked.

"Rosemont," Kincaid said, his voice quiet and deflated.

"Exactly. My crematorium is being dismantled, and we are upgrading Building 2. We can take Rosemont's population within the month."

He looked at Barrie. "Can we hold off any on-site inspections? Can the President delay appointment of a special council?"

Barrie shifted, looking at Kincaid who seemed frozen. "Well," his eyes flicked back to Norton. "The Chief of Staff is furious. Thankfully, it's not an election year, but the optics are bad. The Task Force was one of his initiatives." He didn't voice the hour-long meeting he had sat through with Kincaid at an off-site location.

Norton knew it would be petty to bring up the fact they had been led to believe the President had endorsed Rosemont. "Remember, the initial reaction to the video is disbelief. Let's help reinforce that opinion. How many are we talking about?"

"I'd have to get the numbers together."

"Remember, we do not have to account for any who died while with in federal custody." He described the cover-up it would take, scanning the room to see if any looked like they could pull it off. Smiling slightly, seeing the glimmers of hope in Barrie and Otis, he nodded at Kincaid. "It will take work, but it's doable. But Rosemont must close."

Kincaid nodded. "Make it so."

Norton breathed a little easier, hearing Barrie develop next steps. He helped him hand out assignments. Wondering if he should press home the other repercussions for assassinating Hutton on foreign soil, he decided they had been forced to contemplate enough reality that day. He'd bring it up later, or a more capable, less prone to ultimate-solution director could be found for the Task Force.

Norton called a cab and headed to his hotel. Roxston's aide picked him up at the scheduled time. Heading away from the city center, the quiet Lexus floated through traffic. Norton watched people go about their lives. *How many know? How many care? How many want justice or just had a taste for blood?* He tried to clear his mind—fear and anxiety would only cloud his thinking.

They stopped at a long mall of shops and drove around to a restaurant in the back—Watsall & Henry, the sign read. The maître de nodded at the aide and led them to a small room in the back. Roxston was already seated with a glass of red wine. He never drank red wine before a meal. "Iced tea, sweet," he ordered as he sat down.

"Long day?" the senator swirled the wine in the glass and sipped. He leaned forward and let out a string of expletives. "What were you thinking? Who's responsible for Rosemont?"

Norton kept his face neutral, but it was past time for games. "Kincaid." He waited again for the tirade to stop. "Yes, Rosemont is real. What did you think the FOIA requests and hearings were about?" Norton remembered Masters' words: "You have violated every oath."

Roxston sputtered. "Well, what are you going to do about it?"

Norton allowed a small smile to emerge. "I just left his office. We have a plan in the works, apologize for the lack of communication." He paused before adding, "Help them to understand the Rosemont video is not credible."

"Is it valid? Is that what happened?"

"Yes." *The man needed to know.* "But only those who proved they were incorrigible and would never be turned." He didn't seem ready for the line, 'It was for the good of the nation.' "

"Deal with it. I don't want to know how you do it, but deal with it. Get back to the original vision."

The waiter arrived with their meals. Norton looked at the steak, mashed potato with sour cream, and buttered baby carrots. Their original vision had brought them here. He paused, knowing they had exceeded the letter of the law.

"Of course. Our educational outreaches, literature distribution, and growing percentage of participating centers of worship highlight the best of the Task Force."

"One bad apple can ruin the whole bushel." Roxston looked at him directly. "Someone will have to pay for this."

Norton nodded. He asked about the senator's ailing wife and congratulated him for his daughter's promotion to Assistant District Attorney. The man joked about his standard poodle and granddaughter's frisky pony. Norton wove tales of the West. "You should visit sometime. We have warm falls. I could recommend a resort—the plains are beautiful."

The aide drove him back to his hotel, and he checked his flights, setting his alarm for the morning red eye back home.

Norton was about to change when a knock sounded on his door. He saw Barrie through the keyhole and opened it. Kincaid followed right behind him.

"How did the meeting go with our mutual friend?" Kincaid leaned closer, his voice low, "Did you tell him we have things under control?"

Norton swallowed. "I told him we'd handle it." He nodded, "We just need to get past this and back to the letter of the legislation."

Kincaid's eyes tightened. "Which they left deliberately vague so we would have the latitude to do what needs to be done. The vision of ridding the country of hate crimes for the good of all was *our* vision and *our* mission. We might have run ahead a little too quickly, but we will soldier on. Well," his eyes surveyed the room. "I see you continue to spend frugally. That's good. Keep your eye on Masters. We're going to need him some day."

"Have a good night, Director," Norton said at the end of their little exchange. The hairs still tingled up his neck. Kincaid's extensive network of informants and operatives made his blood chill. He hadn't shared any of that with the senator. *Should I have? But then, would Kincaid have heard about it somehow?*

CHAPTER 46

TOM SHIFTED IN his cell, the din from his end of the range often obscured any warning of meal deliveries or an officer asking questions through the slot in his door. He ignored the regular peering in to his metal coffin by the guards to certify he still breathed.

Tom opened his Bible and added a checkmark—14 days—two weeks in solitary, almost a week in this section. He instinctively shrank back when they pulled his door open.

"Hutton," a hard voice called.

Surrounded by guards, they walked down the hall. Eventually, he realized they were releasing him when he was handed his street clothes, and they returned his luggage.

"Sir, where are they taking me?"

"You're being released. Call your family."

"But I'm a refugee."

"What did your IPO officer tell you?"

"Nothing." It had been at least eight days since his last interrogation. "I was staying at Cary House. When does the van run?"

"It's Saturday." The guard turned to the intake counter. "Have the Cary House number?" He punched in the number in his mobile and tapped his foot on the floor. After a short conversation, he said to Tom, "Wait outside. They'll send someone to pick you up—when they can make the arrangement."

Tom headed for the door, down the walk and leaned against the wrought-iron fencing bordering the walkway. He felt exposed. Dread rose up, and he fought to focus on praising God and not his circumstances. Tom reminded himself—*even if they kill me, God will find a way to tell the world. Of course, He can. He is God.*

At times bustling crowds walked past, talking on their mobiles or with each other. Tom scanned the groups, focusing on solitary figures. His pulse pounded when a glimpse out of the corner of his eye sent his pulse racing. Quieting his breaths, he refocused on the joy of the Lord. *Your will be done, Lord. In me let Your will be done.* He repeated it over and over, waiting, feeling, seeking that inner peace that could only come from the Creator Himself.

A car pulled up. Tom, taken aback when the driver emerged from the right side of the car, found himself smiling. "Catherine!"

"Tom! I came as quickly as I could." She reached for his suitcase and opened the back door in her small Honda.

He swung his duffel around and placed it on the seat. They settled in the car, and Catherine headed to the main streets, navigating narrow brick roadways, pedestrians and tall buses.

Tom held his breath, almost dizzy with the onslaught of sound, sight and movement.

"How was Mountjoy? Any joy there?" Catherine glanced at his profile. She hadn't known him that long—only five days or so until his arrest. In a brief moment between paying attention to traffic, Catherine took in his hollow eyes and distant look when he turned to her voice.

Two turns later he replied, "Only what joy God sends in the darkness." Tom tried to focus on the buildings, the green trees, blooming flowers and cloud painted sky visible here and there. To speak brought him back, and he didn't want to remember the darkness of the last cell block.

Catherine nodded in understanding. They could talk at the residence. Forcing herself not to give into the urge to arrive as quickly as possible, she slowed the car for each turn and did not jackrabbit with the turn of the traffic lights.

Pauli, her favorite security guard, was waiting and met them in front of the door. He collected Tom's bags.

Tom's heart skipped when she drove away and then recovered, seeing her park in her spot. He followed Pauli to the short hall leading to the elevator and stopped. The dark, narrow space reached out a hand to clutch his throat. He was back in his cell—in a half-light worse than the dark, hearing cries of despair.

Catherine stepped through the entranceway and reached for his arm. "Pauli, take his bags up. Let Isler know he's back. Come, Tom…" She smiled to reassure him. "I have news."

Tom nodded and followed her to the last set of doors. He saw a small suite with table, chairs, kitchenette, and sitting area.

"Wait here," Catherine pointed to a chair. She returned with a file. Tom, still standing turned to her. She spread out newspaper clippings on the table. "The world knows. Tom! They've seen the video. You can't believe the pressure the office is under, the outcry they received when your arrest and deportation was reported. Tom, we've won. Well," she paused, reaching out to grasp his hand, "you've won."

"My application?"

"Accepted, your residence reinstated, the deportation order vacated. You are back in the program. Now this puts you at the end of the line…"

Tom stepped closer and reached for her hand, "This is great news." He stepped aside, almost pacing. "There is so much to do. I need to work with Fr. John to get back into Clorverhill."

"You want to go back to prison?"

"As a volunteer chaplain. I have to find His lost ones, like Seamus, and see what we can do to help Clint and his family." He ran his hand through his hair. "And I have to get back into Mountjoy to help the ones in the dark places. And the children here, and the Bible studies— seeker's classes for those interested in learning about Jesus and the way of salvation as well as advanced classes for those like Isler."

Catherine thought a moment. "But there's more."

"What more can there be but taking advantage of every opportunity God gives us during this brief time we are here?"

She longed to jump right in, work with him side-by-side, but she had to tell him the rest. "Tom, I support you in this. I do, but it's not over yet. They will need your help." Catherine pushed the articles aside to make way for the summaries Solicitor Boyle had prepared.

Isler walked in and headed for Tom. He wrapped him in a hug. "Our God has delivered you. Returned you to us. Tell me, how was it?" He grasped Tom's hand in his.

"The darkness of the lost is so great. They cry out in the night, cursing and swearing." His eyes wide and empty, as if wet with dew. "But the terror of torture and death made it worse. It was a long two weeks. I don't know how I could have made it without the prayers, your prayers, and those of many others." Tom smiled at both of them. "But I have completed what God sent me here to do—to tell the world."

"Never forget—our Jesus is greater than the Wicked One," Isler said.

She reached for Tom's hand. "Things are moving very quickly. There is so much to tell you…" Catherine turned her head when she heard the main doors open and close. "That might be your visitors."

"Visitors?" Tom saw Pauli at the door followed by a couple. It took a moment to recognize them. "Mom, Dad, what are you doing here?"

Stella Hutton, as tall as her husband, reached Tom first and hugged him close. "Do you forgive us?"

"Of course!" Tom reached for his father's hand. "That Task Force… I couldn't bring them back to you. Please forgive me for going home. If I had known…"

"Son, I would not trade those months we had with you—not for anything."

Stella looked at Catherine. "Is he up to date?"

"Not quite. We were just getting started." Catherine tucked away the articles and drew out the documents.

Stella set her briefcase on a chair, perused them, placing them in order. She added others from her files.

Tom, near his father, watched, remembering something. "Mom? She's the reason you finally expanded?"

Charles smiled. "Meet the vice-president and chief corporate attorney for Hutton Family Furniture Stores. After we found the Lord, she earned her law degree and stepped up. It helped us deal with losing you." He gripped Tom's shoulder. "We've been here a week. Once the news broke through, they couldn't stop it."

"How'd…"

"The Lord found us. Mom starting reading her Bible after you left, but it came together when we were with Larry and his family for Uncle Al's funeral."

Stella rose. "When we learned you were in Dublin, we felt the Lord saying it was time."

A tear rolled down his dad's cheek. "I prayed for you every day." He added, "They're here; at least one of the Task Force agents has been in Dublin."

"I read the report. The solicitors gained access to your interviews," Stella said, tight-lipped.

"Interrogations?" Tom stared at the piles, fearing what he would be forced to relive. He met her gaze, "So you know? The Task Force agents are here?"

She nodded and gestured him to sit.

"Tom," Catherine added, "Affidavits and corroborating statements are pouring in. Your mother has been helping sort through them. They need your input."

"You see, dear, they have to separate valid evidence from malicious attempts to discredit your claim."

"Solicitors? But Ms. Boyle is pro-bono, and she must have limited staff."

"I put the firm on retainer, dear."

"Ahh, of course you did."

Tom sat at last. He glanced at the three earnest faces. *I am not alone. Could there be hope?*

"Since the news reached the States, affidavits, video and audio evidence as well as photos have been submitted." Stella produced lists. "We have the names of hundreds who have entered the Task Force prisons, never to be heard from again; dozens of journalists and editors either killed or victims of fatal accidents; and the unjust imprisonment of those who resisted the enforcement of these laws." She nodded. "This helps your claim, but it's still not a sure win. We have to overcome the hurdle that the United States is considered a safe country of origin and that you, personally, are at risk of torture or death."

Stella pulled out a phone. "This is yours. We have acquired a flat near the law office where I can stay while I'm here, and you can use it anytime."

"I need to get back soon, Son," Charles said. "We have a little time this weekend. It has been such a gift to see you today."

"You can stay at the flat if it's too late or not safe for you to return here." Catherine nodded. "So, the rest…"

"If it's of God, He will show me how to find the time." He looked at the three. "I'm in, of course. This is not just about me. This is for all these…" He held his hand over the documents. "I speak for them."

Charles said, "Catherine has graciously agreed to give us a tour of Trinity College. After supper, we can visit the Hebrew Centre and meet Dr. Wohlberg."

In answer to Tom's quizzical look, Charles said, "Chaim appealed to Solicitor Boyle to take your case. He's been so helpful and gracious."

Tom resisted the urge to curl up and hibernate. Allowing the joy to blossom, he said. "I need to get ready." He looked at his parents, almost giddy from the joy of their reunion, "If you haven't met Isler, you should."

Tom was thankful Catherine knew the city and how to get about. It still felt odd to see her at the wheel on the right side of the car. He watched Catherine and his mother chat easily while she drove. He glanced at his father, feeling a warmth he had never experienced from him before. *Not only are they here, but we are one in the Lord, part of the family of God.*

Once parked, they wound their way through the old square and center monument. The large, open green area sparkled in the midday sun. Catherine pointed out the buildings of Trinity College, and they headed to the library with bookshelves reaching up to dizzying heights.

Tom watched the great variety of people, all ages. "Are these all students?"

"And tourists," Catherine added with a smile. "Like you." She stepped aside to discuss something with Stella.

"Dad, do you still travel?"

"More than I'd like with the nine locations."

"I mean going on cruises, visiting strange lands?"

"We're more settled, content." Charles Hutton smiled wistfully. "Christ makes a difference. And to have you back."

Tom turned to face his father. "This life is short. Someday, we will all be together—never to be apart." A part of him wanted to speak of what he feared, but the warnings were so vague and uncertain. Soon with the Lord could be months or years away. The decision to say no more was made when Catherine and Stella joined them.

"Shall we? Are you hungry?" Stella asked her son.

"I might be." He added, "Of course, I could eat. Lead the way, Catherine."

Just the beginning of the dinner hour, the restaurant was quiet. Tom asked Catherine, "So what is your favorite here?"

Catherine told of what she liked and why, weaving family stories in with delightful tidbits of where not to order certain items.

Tom looked away, too enchanted by her green eyes, expressive face and flowing hair that shone when caught by the sun's lowering rays.

———⚬⚬⚬———

After supper they made their way to the Arts Building, a modern affair with tall glass sides and a slanted glass extension. Catherine led them to a lower level that opened into a wide hall with a glass-walled library and short hall extending along it. A long wall on the right read "The Hebrew Centre" surrounded by bas relief menorahs and Hebrew inscriptions. A pictorial history beginning with the formation of Israel to the diaspora and back to the land counted the centuries along the wall.

A tall man with full beard and piercing dark eyes approached. "Miss Catherine and the Huttons, greetings." He extended a hand to Tom, "So, Tom, we meet at last. So great is our God."

Tom shook his hand. "Thank you," was all he could say.

"It was our pleasure." He nodded at a figure approaching from the left wing. "Our Activity Director we have borrowed from your land, Ron Eggers. He is enhancing our outreach and educational resources."

Ron greeted the Huttons, smiled broadly at Catherine and rested his gaze on Tom. Trying to act as if they had never met, he extended his hand, "A pleasure."

Tom responded in kind. He tried to focus on Chaim Wohlberg as he walked them through the library, small video room, meeting and conference rooms. "A large work that reaches across national boundaries, in a small space." He nodded to Ron, "I will leave the rest of the tour to our American director."

Ron led them back to the video room and started a quick presentation of their programs. He gestured for Tom to step back into the library.

"What were you thinking?" He added, "And don't tell me God told you to do this. How did you get into the program?"

Tom relayed few details. "But it was God's plan, and it worked."

"Really?"

"Yes, the world knows. The rest is up to our country. We will see if they agree or will rise up to put an end to the persecution."

"People will die because of what you've done."

"They're already dying. Ron, I'm not afraid to pay the price so you can go home and be a part of rebuilding the church of Christ in America." He paused, hearing the presentation was still going. "How can I obtain a Hebrew interlinear and lexicon? To learn what I can while I'm here."

Ron nodded. "I'll find some for you by Sunday evening fellowship. You can attend?"

"Yes. Oh, Ron, could you help with advanced Bible studies at Cary House?" Seeing his quizzical look, he added, "We can talk more about that when I have a better idea of who might attend. I know of at least one refugee at Cary who is ready and willing to learn. I'm sure we can find others. While we are here, let us make good use of the time. You might be the one God sends to help prepare Christians for raising up congregations in their countries. Would you at least pray about it?"

"Of course."

CHAPTER 47

HARD TO BELIEVE it had been two months and the older children were at school during the day. Tom watched a few toddlers playing nearby while the woman asked her question again. Tom's afternoon Seekers' Class at Cary House attracted mostly the women, but some men not working day jobs often listened in.

Praying for wisdom, he tried to explain a believer's relationship with God—that God was a loving Father living within a believer. But the distance between languages and cultures could not be closed. If only Isler were here, but he was in the advanced study class led by Ron on the second floor.

A young man hovering along the outer circle, said quietly, "As a mother cares for her children…" he nodded at the little one on her lap, "so God who made the world, lives in our souls." He beat his breast, saying some words in his native tongue, but her brow furrowed.

"No! We are dirty inside. Not worthy."

"Aww," Tom thought he perceived the issue, "Christ makes us clean. Remember Isaiah 6, when he confessed the dirt of sin and the angel brought the coal from the altar to cleanse his soul? God cleans us up inside. We cannot. Christ conquered all our sin and sets us free."

The young man described his own journey to the light.

The sounds of a bus ramping back up to gear, feet running through the corridor to the gym, laughter and the high voices of children floated in. Tom hated to end now, but soon the gym would burst with young ones flocking to their mothers and their answering calls. "Let us pray." He ended asking for God's Holy Spirit to open eyes, for Christ to cleanse hearts and for the Father to save all who call upon Him.

Tom took notice of the young man who had answered so wisely. He had not seen him before.

Mahdi jumped on Tom before he could rise from sitting on the floor. The energetic seven year old, now Tom's frequent companion, tried to pin him to the floor, but Tom rolled out of the hold, rose, lifting the slim boy. "Your mother needs her greeting, little one."

He set Mahdi down and watched him run to his mother, stopping just short of upsetting his little sister. The little boy missing a right hand had become dear to him in such a short time.

Tom made his way to the newcomer. "I'm Tom. You're new here."

"Barak, just arrived. Good class."

"Great answers. Thanks for the help. We have an advanced Bible study."

Barak shuffled his feet. Tom understood not to push. "What country are you from?"

"Ethiopia."

"My roommate is from Ethiopia. His name is Isler."

It seemed as if Barak's face fell, but Tom was still learning how to read their expressions. "Where is he?"

"Should be here soon. We start the afternoon children's programs shortly." Tom looked toward the front hallway entrance. "Let's meet them. He's in the advanced class." Again, seeing a solemn look on the young man's face, he led him to the hall.

Others would set up the chairs and blankets for those wanting to sit on the floor. Catherine and her helpers would bring out the props, song sheets and instruments. He had time to make introductions.

Isler stepped through the doorway. His recognition of Barak was instantaneous. The young man ran and wrapped his arms around Isler, almost dancing in place. While Tom could not understand a word they said, he could hear the resounding joy of loved ones reunited.

Catherine stepped to his side. "This is the hardest part of running a residence."

Tom looked at her. "Hard? Isn't he new?"

"No, he's not a resident." She laid a gentle hand on his arm. "Last week an immigration officer from London contacted me. Barak has come to take Isler back to London with him. He recognized Isler in a photo in the paper. It turns out there's quite a substantial group in London." She nodded her head. "I am so happy for him, but we'll miss him." She wiped her eye. "Anyway, that's our job—to help them find a life here, or wherever God leads them."

"Yes."

Ron joined them. "You care to tell me what that's about?"

"You're losing your star pupil."

"I'd call him my assistant." They watched the joyous reunion. He looked at Tom. "I too wish to be back home, at peace, with family." He smiled when Tom met his gaze. "Well, to the work, as some say." He helped order the two rows of chairs in perfect semi-circles and instructed the helpers in laying the blankets in rows.

"He's very detail-oriented."

Tom almost quipped that was a requirement for a top Hebrew scholar but held it back in time.

"I'm up, and you're to attend to your following." With a light laugh, Catherine headed for the pile of illustrated song sheets.

Tom greeted the children now heading for him after depositing their school treasures with their mothers. As usual, Mahdi stayed close to his side. Tom sat on the last row of blankets, near the end. Glancing back, he wondered if Isler would join them. Calling for order, the children settled down as Catherine began the song in her clear voice, on-key and at the perfect tempo. Tom marveled at her rich voice. They sang a few before all rose for the action songs. By that time Barak sat near Isler on the last row of chairs.

Tom prayed again for the story. He had his idea, but God sometimes changed things at the last minute. Noticing the songs Catherine picked, a story idea took shape.

Rising from his place on the blanket, he began to ask leading questions. They laughed at the answers, some on target and others funny or silly. By the time he stood at the front and bowed his head for prayer, they were waiting for the story.

Ron sat on the chairs, helping the children sit as still as possible. He walked up to Tom after the dismissal. "You make a good team." His eyes rested on Catherine. "You're a lucky man, Mr. Hutton." Lifting his brow, he laughed and added, "I mean that in the spiritual way—God has blessed you."

"He has. When I considered coming here, it felt like the end. I had no idea it would be just the beginning."

"You never know what God's going to do next."

Tom nodded, their eyes on Barak and Isler. They both smiled when the Ethiopians approached them.

Impatient to put his plan into motion, Tom talked to several as the groups disbursed. Isler left to give Barak a tour. Ron headed to catch the bus. With another glance at the clock, he helped Catherine make sure all the supplies were properly stored. "You ready?"

"For our date?" she laughed, her eyes twinkling. "And you can't tell me where we're going?"

"You'll know soon enough."

"If you'd let me drive?"

Tom smiled. "How is it a date if..." He tried not to redden. "my date has to drive?" He drank in the green flecks in her eyes. "So, do you need to freshen up?" Her laughter trilled. "Well, I do," he said nodding his head. Tom walked briskly up the hall and stepped outside. The threatened rain had not developed. The streets were dry, the air as fresh as possible in a city, and wispy clouds spread across the sky.

Scrubbed and changed, Tom tapped on her office door, watching her read the latest emails. "Still at work?"

She rested her head on her hand. "No, just waiting for my date to get around to being ready."

"Up for a stroll?"

By the second block, they were holding hands. They walked leisurely past tall brick warehouses, apartment complexes with playgrounds, and rows of friendly looking homes. They talked of little things—like how the cook resisted *foreign* food. Catherine complained she would never finish the counterpoint cross-stitch her grandmother had given her for Christmas, and the usual light teasing.

His mother had asked her to help convince him to acquire a suit, but Tom shook his head. "And look like a solicitor and not a refugee needing help? I don't want to remind them my family is rich—even if I am not."

"You're waiting for your inheritance."

"I am rich, Catherine." He looked at her, but the words melted away. *At the right place. At the right time.*

"You're really not going to tell me where we're going?"

"I have it mapped out."

"I'm sure you have. You don't do anything without figuring it out ahead of time. Like your mother, you know. Very detailed-oriented." She smiled at his look.

"Yeah, yeah. If I get us lost, then I will have to rely on my damsel for the rescue. Deal?"

"Deal."

"Just enjoy the stroll and your beautiful city." They headed along, as if going to Trinity College, but he turned toward the gardens and an inn he had in mind. The hour was early, so they would have no problems getting seated.

"Flanahan's & O'Leary's? You checked the dress code?"

"Business casual."

"That's the minimum."

"It still gets us in the door." He grasped the outer door handle and held it open, gesturing for her to go in. "Table for two," he said to the maître de. For the past few weeks Tom had probed for the type of restaurant she liked, insisting she dream big and not be concerned about the cost in euros. By the third try, he had narrowed down the possibilities.

"What do you want?" Catherine said, her eyes still popping at the prices on the right.

"It's covered. This is your day. Choose a starter." He tapped the edge of her menu. "And ignore the cost."

They navigated the menu. Tom ordered. They sipped their water, and Catherine drank her tea and sighed.

"Good tea?"

She smiled and sat back, meeting his gaze. Tom reached along the right side to hold her left hand. *Why should I delay?* Suddenly flustered, he discarded every opening line he had envisioned saying.

"Tom, just tell me what's on your heart."

Taking a deep breath, he nodded. "I love you. Catherine, despite everything and what it took to be here, it was worth it to meet you. I love you."

Tears formed in her eyes. She set down her teacup. "I love you too." Wiping her eyes, she laughed lightly. "The first day we met, I was attracted, but I was so afraid you were a fraud. But now I have seen your love for God—how you are not afraid to follow Him, how the children adore you, how you love the Word of God and your drive to share it, how you care for others."

Nodding, Tom had to share. "I love your rich, sweet voice; your constant care for those at the centre, and those you don't know but pray for." He held her hand gently. He had to hold some back for later. "I think, together, we can serve the Lord—wherever He leads." *Can I ask this of her?*

"I would. No matter where. I'd leave my mum and pop. Because if we go with God, nothing can stop us." She shook her head. "Ma was a little chill to you when you met her."

"I noticed. Is there anything I can do?"

She shook her head. "She knows." Catherine's voice lowered, "If you are able to go back home, you will, won't you?"

"Most likely, though one can never say where the Lord could call us next." He grew silent and sat back. They had talked of children and childrearing. They knew each other's views on church and faith and marriage. They had one more matter to settle, but that would have to wait until the gardens.

Their love assured and out in the open, they shared more deeply of their faith in God. Taking their time through the meal, the sun was beginning to lower in the sky.

Tom walked her to St. Stephen's Gardens and the place he had picked out. Having to go a little past his preferred spot, he asked her to take a seat on a bench, and he dropped to one knee. "Over the years I accepted the fact that I would follow God alone. Never did I imagine that in Dublin I would meet my true love—a soul mate who would walk with me. I never imagined I would meet someone like you—someone who fits with me as if we were made for each other. Catherine Walsh, will you marry me?"

"Yes," she said even before his words drifted away in the light breeze. Reaching for him, inviting him to sit beside her, she added, "Soon? Before…"

Cupping her hands in his, he said, "Catherine, I've prayed and thought about this. When I win asylum and am given residency, then we can wed. Wouldn't it look suspicious? Wouldn't it bring risk to your job? No, I feel God saying yes, but wait."

She nodded. "You're right…about the job too." She looked at him. "But what if they…" She couldn't voice her thoughts.

"If…if the unmentionable happens, know that God will be with you even in that."

"And you?"

"I know God will take me home. I will be home in heaven." Unspoken was the vision. Not mentioned was the nagging certainty that haunted his waking moments and lingered while trying to find sleep.

Lord, let this be. If not, may Your will be done.

END NOTES

U NLESS OTHERWISE INDICATED, all Scripture quotations are taken from the Holy Bible, the English Standard Version®, copyright © 2001 by Crossway, a publishing ministry of Good News Publishers. Used by permission. All rights reserved.

1 Matthew 5:11-12.
2 Romans 1:16, paraphrase.
3 John 14:6.
4 Hebrews 11:38.
5 Hebrews 11:10 paraphrase; 11:16 quoted.
6 Psalm 19:14, paraphrase.
7 Ephesians 6:18.
8 Romans 8:1.1
9 Andrew Brunson with Craig Borlase, *God's Hostage: A True Story of Persecution, Imprisonment, and Perseverance* (Grand Rapids: Baker Books, 2019), 249.
10 Lamentations 1:13.
11 Lamentations 3:21-23.
12 Lamentations 5:21-22.
13 Psalm 116:15.
14 2 Timothy 4:7-8, paraphrase.
15 Isaiah 53:6.
16 John 16:33.
17 Isaiah 26:3.

[18] Matthew 6:28-29.

[19] Revelation 19:10.

[20] Romans 3:10-12, 23, paraphrase.

[21] Gregory Koukl, *The Story of Reality: How the World Began, How It Ends, and Everything Important That Happens in Between* (Grand Rapids: Zondervan, 2017).

[22] Romans 6:4.

[23] Jeremiah 1:5.

Made in the USA
Middletown, DE
13 June 2021

42034737R00189